Maya

by

Dane Alexander

First Edition

Jo-Ann Langseth, Editor
Bob Spear, Editing and Interior Design
Angela Farley Cover Design

ISBN Number 0-9679619-0-4
Library of Congress ISSN Number 1533-8728X

Printed in the U.S.A.

10 9 8 7 6 5 4 3 2 1

Truth is a strange medicine:
Often bitter
and hard to swallow,
it must first dissolve the ego
before it can heal the heart.

THE SECRET

Remember that dream, the one so vivid and compelling it begged the question, "Is this the true reality, and my daily life just an illusion? Or—?" But, as often happens, you were snatched from sleep, awakened before receiving the answer. In that instant and to your amazement, a door slowly opened before your eyes. Trembling with trepidation, you held your breath, stepped through, and…became born.

Flashing forward—having traveled life's twisting path, you find yourself emerging from the shadows. The pre-dawn darkness leaves no hint the season is well into late fall. Alone, cautiously, you descend the sloping, grassy bank to a clump of willows at the marsh's edge. Your eyes strain to scan the water, a broad, mirror-flat expanse sliding under the rising mist, glowing faintly from the breaking morning rays. A foreboding tingles your senses. Sadly, it goes unnoticed by most who reach this far. They place their trust in the lulling silence, ignoring occasional cries of an unseen loon. In nearby reeds, an iridescent-winged dragonfly clutches a floating twig while being watched by a frog, transfixed in the moment. Frost-covered leaves make a crunching sound as you walk toward the raft. Here, Destiny waits to ferry you across. Somewhere beyond lies a spiritual dawning…in this, the new millennium.

Gliding through the clouded veil you hear a distant cry: "Blessed be ye born of this time, for ye cannot help but weigh heavily in the balance of things yet to pass. Assume not that thy slightest thought or smallest act has little value. In truth, *those who seem the least are empowered to tip the scales of tomorrow.*

"But know this, Pilgrim: be nonjudgmental as ye journey here, for all is not as it seems. It is far, far greater. As Shakespeare wrote, "There are more things in Heaven and Earth, Horatio, than are dreamt of in your philosophy."

And which of you has not asked, "What lies ahead, beyond my vision? What is the future?" Unfortunately, your only map has been copied from religions that paint tomorrow in apocalyptic hues. In full agreement, science, too, notes that we are being immersed in many sorrows: tectonic plate shifts, tsunamis, droughts spanning entire regions, famines, global warming, a rapidly advancing Ice Age, extinction of critically needed animal and plant species, human overpopulation, pandemics, cataclysmic earthquakes, increasing volcanic activity, and an approaching collision with a mega-asteroid. At the same time, military powers anticipate deaths from biochemical attacks, nuclear weapons in the hands of zealots plotting to wipe out all nonbelievers, the formal starting of World War III, and other miseries so great that, if any of the foregoing are left unchecked, they will surely push mankind to the brink of annihilation. And as if these were not enough, as the climax to this epoch, it has been further prophesied that the handful who survive will bear witness to the ultimate struggle—between the titanic forces of good and evil.

"Like a thief in the night," such events do indeed seem to be stealthily nearing, each unfolding while most of humanity sleeps. As one of the few who can read these signs, you silently watch and wait, standing half-hidden in a cloud of gathering gloom.

That was, until this very moment. For there exists a spiritual key—a law so powerful it shatters dogma, gives insight, and *helps you and those you love* to safely traverse the future. Therefore, observe carefully, and MAYA will give up its secret.

So rejoice! This is a story of forgotten ancient power—your Divine birthright. It tells not only how to change your future, *but that of the planet as well.*

Blessed Spiritual Being, the hour is nigh. Come, spread your wings; soar once again. Greater happiness than you can imagine awaits, for these are not "The End Times. "They are "The Beginning!"

CHAPTER I

CARPE DITUS

Looking like a dangling spider, Rigden King, III, swung helplessly three hundred feet over a sheer Grand Canyon cliff. His eyes were riveted downward—nothing but a three-quarter mile void beneath his feet, ending with cascading escarpments flowing into jagged rocks at the Colorado's edge. His mind was in lockdown, overridden by a suffocating, clamp-like tension; breathing all but stopped. This further constricted his throat, stifling even the smallest scream. Elsewhere, a jackhammer pounding heart pushed to its outside limit as his face drained of blood.

Viewed from afar, though, the desert panorama appeared quite calm. The explorer was but an insignificant, almost invisible speck against this ancient monolithic wall, one of reddish browns and grays, accented by the green of a lone juniper wedged in a narrow crack. Scattered randomly across this rocky face, clinging dots of sagebrush added still more points of visual variation. From the east, the sun was making its daily run along this path as it had billions of times since Earth began. Spanning the mile-wide canyon, shadows came and went with shifting light. Purples, yellows, sienna, all blended together on this micro-section of the cosmic palette. And as if floating in this picture of tranquility, here hung Rig, frozen, rigid with terror.

Compounding his angst, the mountain-climbing harness straps rode up—biting, and constricting. Uncomfortable as underwear that forms a wedgie, it forced him to squirm as he futilely tried to alter a minor part of his predicament.

The combination of both situations shaped a facial expression that was hard to interpret. Not known for frequent smiling, King's slender frame was crowned by a face with chiseled features—one that usually exhibited a Calvin Klein model's annoyed look. Such an appearance, while thought handsome by some, had only a small percentage of the opposite sex elevating him to the "gorgeous" category. However, like the chameleon moods of a politician, Rigden King, III, could artificially turn on and off radiant charm, much as one does a light switch. But because he'd spent most of his existence trying to force square pegs into life's round holes, these bleached-white teeth remained mostly in the dark.

Swaying back and forth, forgetting to inhale, the sobered climber at last understood how much of a suicidal gamble this 1,480-foot lowering would be. To reach the cave, a descent of nearly a third of a mile, he was at the mercy of a single, skinny thread. But this distance was only half his problem. Past the ledge, the raging river below was another two thousand feet... nearly straight down.

Being strapped in a professional climbing harness offered little solace. Moreover, the backpack tethered to the chair rubbed against his calves, yet another distracting annoyance. With attention primarily forced elsewhere, his hands maintained their choking, white-knuckled grip on the lifeline.

Even to most experienced mountaineers, such a rappel would be a scary undertaking. For this neophyte rock climber, a thirty-eight-year-old stockbroker from Phoenix, the odds for death seemed almost certain, calculated now as a nearly vertical time-line on his longevity graph.

With the beginning of the long descent, fear shifted the rappeler's concept of time. As if entering an alternate reality, everything took on an eerie, dreamlike quality. The mind ceased its linear dynamic. There was no thought of tomorrow or even of the next minute. Attention was riveted, fixed only to this one atom in the tapestry of infinity. He ignored rivulets of sweat from the sweltering 114-degree, August afternoon, and the annoying fly landing on his nose. Nothing broke his concentration.

To worsen matters, the whipping force of even the slightest breeze had become a serious problem. Unfortunately, that factor hadn't been calculated, but there was much this weekend warrior failed to anticipate—like the yo-yo effect.

Slammed by a gust of wind, Rig's kneecap cracked against the canyon wall. Overcome with nausea, he lurched forward, letting go of breakfast. The thick, liquid mass momentarily seemed to float, then drift, first elongating, finally taking several twisting shapes before disappearing into nothingness. Instantly, this emptying process left him feeling slightly better.

Above, near the clouds, two eagles circled. At least, he hoped they were eagles and not buzzards. The thought came: *I must look like a roasted duck, suspended in some Chinese grocer's window.* Followed by: *Wait your turn, guys...wait your turn.*

To him, nothing else in life at this moment mattered except the fortune, and to survive this asinine stunt. If he found what he hoped for, even being slightly crippled could be worth the risk. Thinking aloud he said, "Just to go on breathing would be good...well, rich and breathing."

"Did you say something?" asked a gentle voice over the headset.

"Nooo!"

His reply was hard to get out. Still woozy, the stomach again sloshed and churned. Forcefully re-swallowing chunky bits that were trying to exit, King barely kept the cork on a repeat performance.

"Thought I heard something," said his companion, perched safely near the truck on top of the rim at the cliff's edge.

"Just don't let me down so fast," he barked.

A soft reply, masking a light chuckle, flew back with equal speed: "Sorry...Scared yet?"

"Of course I'm scared." His answer came through clenched teeth. "I'm not stupid, ya know."

"I should have gone," the female insisted. "I'm the experienced climber."

"Look, we already covered that. *Me first, then you. Got it?"*

"Have you ever faced the fact," she jested, although her tone carried a serious note, "that you're a wee bit of a chauvinist?"

"Quiet! I've got to concentrate."

Exasperated, they ceased to communicate. Like the rope, this period of silence also stretched. Looking around, Rig's eyes and other senses lied, telling him he was stationary, while the cliff appeared to move upward. He knew this was an optical illusion. As he twisted and turned, scenes of the canyon came and went from his view. The visual confusion laminated yet another layer to the Phoenician's feeling of helplessness.

A shrill voice in the back of his mind screamed, *You frickin' idiot! Why on Earth did you put your life into the hands of some chick you just met?* A second later, a calmer sense spoke. *That's true; she's probably a risky choice with the winch. After all, it does control whether I live or die.* Sighing, it added, *Oh, well, what's done is done.*

No shit, Sherlock! About time you figured that out, the suspicious half of his ego butted in with more whining. *For all you know, she could lose concentration or have a sneezing fit and we'll go into a free-fall. It'll be just like one of those bungee jumpers we've seen on TV when the line snapped. The* timorous aspect put further comments on a very brief hold...*except at this height, there'd be more time to scream before slamming into the rocks.*

Shut up! retorted the mature part of his mind. *I had no choice; she blackmailed me! Stupid witch was going to reveal the location on the Internet if I didn't allow her to come. Besides, if any treasure's found, this way I won't have to share; what's-her-name's only along to explore caves for that Washington, D.C., foundation of hers, and for research on that hokey screenplay she's working on.* King's mind blathered nonstop as his body continued its treacherous descent.

Life-or-death situations such as these tended to sober a man, cleansing his thinking as if standing in a shower of cold reality. As the moments passed, Rig's hopes and plans were quickly going down the drain.

Weighing the improbability of success, coupled with the incredible risk, the explorer was coming to a conclusion: a more reliable partner such as John, his childhood friend and coworker, should have been pressed into service. *Why'd I cave in to Johnny's whining? I mean, he's always canceling our plans at the last moment, bleating like a lovesick ram about needing to go out with some bimbo du jour he's just found. Would have been better if I'd told him to tie a knot in it and shanghaied the bastard. He owes me…big-time.*

For the treasure hunter, there was one more omitted calculation. This part of the canyon wall was not a perfect vertical drop. Down 293 feet from the rim jutted a small, knife-blade ledge. Having already gone past it, that outcropping was now 600 feet over his head.

Unbeknownst to him, the most immediate danger was not the fraying rope, made thinner by its dragging back and forth over the jagged edge. The rhythmic popping of threads, while hazardous was the lesser of a yet more critical life-threatening situation: the upper part of the cord had slipped into a crack, dislodging a football-sized rock.

With uncanny precision, he and the cannon-ball object were vectoring toward a collision course. Gravity dictated the missile speed would reach 125 miles an hour—just three more pendulum swings of the rope and the plummeting stone would make sickening contact with the fragile skull below.

Continuing to stare downward, Rig was oblivious to either crisis. Keeping the mind distracted, he chattered to himself, something people often do when alone and afraid. In a half-whisper, He quoted the famous Woody Allen comment on mortality. "I'm not afraid to die; I just don't want to be there when it happens."

A rain of pebbles caught his attention. As eyes looked up, a vision of death headed straight for his face. The truth of the moment was inescapable. In the split second it took for the brain to recognize the situation, every muscle tensed, again to the point of spasm. Realizing all was lost, he surrendered—knowing that in a short period, the rock would make its contact. As if hovering outside his dangling body, the weekend warrior coldly analyzed the events. The sequence was simple: First, the impact would be with his hair, followed by the skull, the rupturing of brains, a splattering of blood, and then…only blackness.

They say a person's life flashes before him in moments like these, but not Rig's. For him, time divided into thousandths of a second. The mouth rounded, eyes widened, and the words, "Holy shiii…." tumbled out.

Unexpectedly, a gust of wind added sideways momentum. It pushed just enough; the rock fell off-center The granite slammed down, bending the back of his hat brim, its sharp edge leaving an eight-inch gash between the victim's shoulders. A moment later, the only evidence of the mishap was the trickling line of blood soaking into his shirt.

He broke the silence with a loud scream of "Jeeze!" Illogic ruled as he thought, *Why in hell did I have to bring her along?* Struggling against reason, the blame was shifted on Lyra instead of his lack of planning. *Lord only knows, she can't handle a winch. Plus, the imbecile is dropping me way too fast. I'm sure she's nearly burnt out the brake. Damn! Why didn't I make John come?*

The piercing shriek blasted through his partner's earphones. Instinctively, she jerked the headset away. After a second to regain composure, the young woman tentatively asked, "You sure you're okay?"

"Hell no! I'm frickin' facing death, and you're asking me if I'm okay?…*Get a life*!"

Displeasure turned to sarcasm. "Do I sense a slight bit of hostility, Mr. King?" she half-shouted into her microphone while frantically working to stop another problem, the way the winch was feeding out rope.

Not sure the umbilical cordage wouldn't jam in the pulley, Rig's companion didn't want to distract his concentration with another mishap likely in progress. *One thing at a time*, she quietly reasoned. *He has enough to handle and doesn't seem to be doing that all too well.*

"Hostility?" he screamed into the mike, his strained voice beginning to splinter.

"Yes, hostility! You have absolutely zero concept of how much anger you constantly give off. In fact, Mr. King, you are the most enraged person I've ever met. Yours is an…an explosive, cowboyish…She paused for a more accurate description before continuing, "barbaric rage."

Inching downward, he returned the shout, "So now I'm barbaric?" Seething, he became further embroiled in the argument.

Distracted by his anger, the explorer was oblivious to the situation overhead. With every few swings, threads continued to sever, bringing him ever closer to a stunning instant of undoing.

Equally unaware of the unraveling crisis in progress, Lyra continued to concentrate on averting her partner's attention from the dangers of such a difficult descent. This obfuscation involved deep-frying Mr. King in an artificially heated exchange. As he passed the 1,300-foot mark, the young woman's condescending Manhattan upbringing and attitude further yanked his chain. "Forget that I said 'barbaric,'" she said, trying once more. "Can't you at least acknowledge being a little angry? We'll talk about the degree later."

Furious, Rig's ability to intelligently communicate shrank with each tick of the clock. "Hell yes, I'm angry," he roared, wanting to crawl through the mike and strangle his rim-side helper.

"Would you like to get rid of it?" she queried, this time in a soothing tone.

"Are you nuts? I'm dropping like a rock, probably to my death, and you—you're bugging me about being upset? *Give me a break*!"

Seeing no headway, she changed tactics. "Say, I've been meaning to ask, how did you get such an unusual first name?"

"I can't believe you want to chat; I've got better things to do."

"Oh, relax! Since you're stuck, we might as well pass the time by talking."

It took a moment, but he reconsidered. "Ahhh, what the heck! Why not? Actually, it's one of those asinine family traditions. Started with my grandfather, a Brit on Mother's side. He...."

As they talked, the stockbroker lowered past a raven, perched on an outcropping. Munching a pine nut, the startled bird panicked. Flapping and cawing furiously while gaining altitude, it attempted to warn the rest of the universe of the obviously odious intruder.

As one with a constant chip on his shoulder, it seemed to King that now even animals were laughing at him. While the feathered nuisance frantically distanced himself, He yelled, "Hey! What are you cackling at?"

Again Lyra's velvet voice filled his headset: "'Cackling?' I didn't say a word. Come on now. Wouldn't you really like to get rid of that rage? It has to be awful, carrying it around all the time." Thinking to herself, she mused, *Parents must have mated during a solar eclipse with Mercury in retrograde.*

"Are you still pushing the anger thing? Because if you are, this is one helluva poor time for a self-improvement course."

Shifting gears again, and with an even throatier reply, she said, "And why not?"

Unknown to his male ego, Rigden King, III, was an unofficial card-carrying member of the fraternity of men who become hypnotized at the sound of a sultry female voice. As dulcet-toned words flowed, the listener fell captive under the young woman's influence, much the same as a basketed cobra bobs and weaves to the flute of a Hindu fakir. Like the reptile, he too was mesmerized, unaware of his trance.

"What do you mean, would I like to get rid of my anger?" he returned, this time at a cognitive level slightly above one who has had a lobotomy.

"Just that. Would you like to lose that temper?"

Before he could answer, the cave's ledge came into view. As usual, Murphy's Law was in full effect; miscalculations left him twenty yards to the left of the target. Irritated, he commanded, "Not now!" while pushing off the facing in an attempt to swing over.

To Lyra, her partner's growing state of anxiety was obvious. "What's happening?"

"Nothing! I'm busy. Don't talk unless it's necessary," he ordered, typical of a person under extreme pressure or with a controlling personality. In Rig's case, it was both.

"Okay, okay."

It's strange how mountain climbers can dangle from a precipice and then, just like a spider held by a lone thread, scurry back and forth along the vertical facing. Each time coming a little closer to the goal, he added more force, trying to get enough scuttling sideways movement to compensate for his error.

Above, unseen by either party, the blade-like edge of the outcropping continued fraying the rope. Thus far, an alarming quarter of its filaments were severed.

"Give me twenty more feet! I'm still too high."

With a sudden plummet the line slackened, then jerked. Again, he felt his pounding heart crammed up into his throat. After being reeled out 1,506 feet, the rope had the elasticity of a rubber band; the slightest drop had him yo-yoing up and down. To a passive observer, the sight could appear almost comical. To the dangling stockbroker, it was one more hair-whitening experience.

According to the outfitting shop that sold the gear, climbing cordage of this weave and thickness was certified for up to eight thousand pounds. Once sliced, however, it could carry but a fraction of that.

"No, that's thirty feet. You've given out too much! Pull me up twenty or so, and, no, I can't tell you how much that is. You've just got to estimate."

A natural purity, unusual in its clarity, radiated from Lyra—most apparent in the soft glow of her face and the silken sound of her voice. Normal individuals would have struck back at King's acerbic tone in like manner, but not her.

Seconds later she responded gently, "How's that?"

"Okay, I think. Maybe I can just make it." He grunted, winded from exertion made worse by the furnace-like sun.

Streams of sweat ran down King's face as his analytical mind mulled the predicament. *Damn! If I hadn't spent until late last night modifying the winch on the Bronco, I could have been here this morning when the temperature was only ninety.*

Rapidly tiring and dehydrated, the treasure hunter knew he didn't have long to make it, or the attempt would have to be postponed until the next day. With steely determination, he launched a final, gut-out scramble for the ledge—dust, sweat, blood, and banged knee all ignored. *Still five feet below the lip,* he calculated, *but at least I can get a handhold and pull myself up.* The internal complaints continued: *Should have worn gloves; those rocks will tear my hands up.*

Closer, closer, two more feet and....The mind chatter flowed on as he caught the branch of a small tree growing a foot below his objective. "Ughhh! Got it," he groaned. Almost simultaneously, his other hand grabbed the flat rock outcropping leading to the cave. Out of breath, the rapeller was forced to pause and recharge.

Looking around, only now did he discover the partially eroded, chiseled indentations resembling steps. They descended thirty yards down from the ledge to the worn line of an ancient riverbank—one that was two thousand feet higher than that down in the canyon. "My God!" he whispered. "How long ago was water up to this level?"

The whiny voice in his head responded, *No time, stupid! It's late; we need daylight. That can be answered later.*

Back to work, part of Rig's balance shifted to his left boot, resting where a wide step was once carved. With another groan, he maneuvered his right leg up to the level surface. Without warning, soil around the tree crumbled. Falling back, the explorer's weight dislodged his wooden mooring.

"Whoaaa!" was the only sound he made while deftly switching his left hand to a jutting rock—none too soon. More earth gave way around the roots. The tree started its descent. Lost was a silent sentinel, a living witness that had overlooked this sacred scene for more than 281 years. It bounced against the cliff, slammed by a burst of wind as it continued to drop.

The adventurer's concentration was elsewhere. Oblivious to all forms of life except his own, he gave a final moan of fatigue. His mind was empty, save for a single thought: *Stud, you're getting way too old for this.*

With one leg again up on the outcropping, he was safe at last…but not quite. Half of his body still dangled off the ledge. A needle-like jab ran up his right thumb, the one wedged in a crack between two rocks. "What the hell?" he screamed, letting go of the precious hold while desperately clawing for another.

Quickly pulling himself onto the flat area, Rig felt two more jolts, this time to his left hand. "Ahaaa, Jeez!" he yelped, as a pair of scorpions scurried under the shadowed safety of small boulders.

Extremities began to tingle, on their way to going numb. Catching his breath, the adventurer sat, dizzy and lightheaded. After unhooking the harness, he clumsily fumbled as he removed the backpack. Exhausted, and starting to collapse from an allergic reaction to the venom, a fourth sting was felt from inside his left pant leg. "What the…?" Stomping his foot, in a blurring flash, the last enemy was nailed with the heel of his cowboy boot. Disheveled, sweating, looking like something "rode hard and put away wet," he sat, gasping for air, staring vacuously at a rock by his feet.

"What's happening? Are you on the ledge yet?" a worried voice called through the earphones.

Slumping, the adventurer's Jell-O'd body lost its last bit of rigidity as he replied, "Yeahhh…jus' got here." As the body collapsed, his hat falling to his side went unnoticed. Following a minor pause, the sheer raw force of willpower lifted Rig to his feet.

"Sounds like you're drunk," squeaked a fearful voice. "What's the matter?"

"Shcorpions."

"Scorpions? How many are there?"

The poison momentarily affected the broker's ability to think, let alone speak. He miscounted, "Threeee."

Disoriented as to the direction of the cave, he took a step toward the cliff's edge, just inches away. He froze, interrupted by a frantic call, "Rig?" Turning, as if responding to a person behind him, he tied to answer. Words wouldn't form. Swaying, he took two steps forward, staggered backward toward the canyon, and teetered—again barely missing plunging over the side.

"Were they big black ones, medium brown ones, or the little crystal-clear type?"

"Li'l clear ones…a whole nesht…they're all over," he said, slurring and reeling more than ever.

"*Oh my God*! Are you out of the harness?"

"Yeah, sunnder a rock."

"Good. Pull it free; I'll be right down."

King's headset went silent as his helper reeled in the leather chair and line. Disappearing off the shelf, the rope, like a long noodle, was sucked upward to the waiting Bronco.

In a daze, he was oblivious to the backpack's absence as well as unclear about which way led to safety. One false step, and another visitor would be added to those who annually vanished from these cliffs. Lucky or guided by higher forces, Rig headed in the right direction—toward the dark entrance to the cave, his body moving with a choppy gait.

The befuddled explorer looked up, humorously imagining the jutting rock above the portal to resemble a giant grotesque nose above a gaping mouth. Directly below the "nose" dangled a scraggily bush, which his drunken mind further labeled as un-plucked nasal hair. Taking no more notice, the trek into blackness continued.

For the moment, he had no feel for time. "Mus' be night… all those stars…Wunner where what's-er-name is? "A shifting, amorphous figure back in the cave caught his attention. Vaguely aware of what appeared to be some sort of moving mist, he muttered, "How can fog be in Arizona? Damn, this is the strangest state. You never know what to…."

The form, slowly taking shape, floated toward him, stopped, pointed to the cave wall, and faded.

Seconds ran into minutes, until, in the dark, he felt Lyra touching his cheek, urgently whispering. Even in the Phoenician's bewildered condition, he experienced a gloating satisfaction in the moment—confirmation of what he'd been imagining, that familiar, male-female chemistry.

A slobbered mumble declared, "Knew it…I knew it! Girl's finally showing her true feelings…but Lord, wish she'd change her perfume. Well, maybe it's the sweatiness. Even so, she's a keeper; guess I shouldn't get too critical."

Coming from him, this comment represented a radical shift in policy; many who knew him would say, "True, Rig's standards in dating were low, but they were strict—preferences always ran to flashy, trashy, and not too bright."

Not motivated by a chivalrous heart, to him the hunt for "luv" had always been simply a game—a lustful safari in constant pursuit of what he liked to call "the two-legged jaguar," an elusive quarry, whose sylph-like powers frequently had less accomplished sportsmen carrying flowers and running in circles.

Avoiding the role of either knight or pawn, King always approached dating as so many of his gender. Once at a singles club, five martinis down and leaning on a polished teakwood bar, he drunkenly compared this pursuit to playing Dungeons and Dragons, except his version was ruled by four archetypal dwarfs: Caesar, Squeezer, Hump'er, and Dump'er.

But that was then; the seasons of this man's thinking were changing. No longer in the youthful days of summer, he was entering fall with an eye to winter. And while this wasn't planned as a romantic trip, he was becoming increasingly attracted to this strange female…and yet, paradoxically, repulsed. Such a push-pull dichotomy had him perplexed; culturally, he and she were from opposite worlds—Arizona and New York—vinegar and oil.

Unknown to his outer self, the radar of Rig's heart always searched for such an exotic creature: Nefertiti-shaped eyes, lush red lips, shoulder-length auburn hair, and high cheekbones that further embellished her already sensuous body.

A further facet, he strangely found her level of intelligent conversation a refreshing detour from that of his past companion choices. On the long ride north, for the first time He noted it oddly enjoyable to be hours in the company of a female who spoke in more than monosyllables. Those who fawned over his lifestyle and giggled at his every joke were good at an earlier stage of life, but the coming snows had him wanting the warm blanket of a more mature affection.

Lying flat on the dusty floor, the stockbroker forgot where he was, the reason for being there, and any reference to the hour, unaware that darkness would soon slide into the canyon.

"Don't move," Lyra commanded in a low, penetrating tone.

"Huh?"

"I said don't move; you've got a snake slithering across your cheek."

Rig's eyes popped wide open as the end of a Mojave's smelly tail—the source of what he perceived as Lyra's scent—glided over his mouth. Mind-hand coordination out of sync, he could not manage the gravity of the situation. After what seemed a torturously long time, the reptile moved off, heading toward the entrance, into the late afternoon sun. Shaken, he sat up in one quick but awkward movement.

Vigorously rubbing his mouth, he managed to spit out, "Ptew! How'd…how'd you get down here?"

"Boy, are you spaced! Used the radio control to the winch, just like we planned. I guess you're too out of it to remember our…."

Interrupting, as was his habit, he said, "No, how…how did you manage to swing over the twenty yards?"

"I'm not stupid. You told me you were off and by how much. I just moved the tripod and the truck, then I dropped straight down." With her arms akimbo, the clarification came with an obvious, but well-earned smugness.

"Okay, okay. Let's see if I can stand." Effort alone was not enough; knees buckled. Falling to the floor, a weak explorer acquiesced. "Maybe we need to take a minute till I get oriented."

"Here, have some water," she offered, pulling a plastic container out of the backpack.

King looked off into space while taking a long swig. "Had the strangest dream a minute ago; at least...yeah, it was....But he didn't finish the sentence.

"What?"

"Remember Willie's story of Archie Madbear and the hidden chamber?"

Rocked by the stupidity of his remark, Lyra swallowed in disbelief before replying, "How could I forget? We discussed nothing else but that on the seven-hour drive up here."

"Oh yeah." Glancing around, he spoke to himself, "Darn, guess I left my hat outside. I'll pick it up when we return."

"Look," she suggested, "we have to hurry; there are only a couple more hours of daylight. Let's focus on Madbear's message: 'Go back of the teeth, through the right cheek, behind the right eye.'"

"I'm ready," he replied, picking up the backpack and awkwardly flipping it over his shoulder while attempting to maintain his balance. His bravado didn't work. Once more the ground rose up to meet him.

"You know, Lyra, I've been on a couple of these treasure expeditions, and hell, just once I would like plain instructions, like 'Head five feet south of such and such painted rock and dig.'"

"There goes the anger again."

"Damn it; I am not angry, just upset."

"Oooh...so that's what you call it. Certainly glad you cleared that up." She delivered her comment with a smile, although he couldn't make it out because of the shadows. Nonetheless, the stockbroker sensed it there by the self-assuredness of her tone.

"That floating thing was probably just a figment of my imagination, but if it was real, and I don't think it was, it pointed to that area."

Using her flashlight, Lyra made broad, sweeping movements across the wall. "Looks solid to me. It's fascinating how this cave was sliced out of solid rock. The level of technology needed to do something this massive is simply incredible."

Still in his own world, a recovering King mumbled, "That dream must have been an hallucination." Louder, he added, "Anyway, the ghost indicated over here, and there's certainly no statue, drawing, or anything like what the old goat talked about. I think we need to go deeper until we see something that has cheeks and eyes. Give me a second more to get my bearings, and we can get moving."

CHAPTER II

KINKAID'S STORY

Since we're waiting," Lyra suggested, "let's go back over highlights in the article. This way, clues will be fresh in our minds…Here it is, 'April 5, 1909, the twenty-ninth year of the *Phoenix Gazette.*'"

"Oh crud, woman—get on with it. Forget the dinky details. Just hit the important parts."

Rig's partner was one of those who mainly focused on the humorous notes in the ballad of life. Others would have returned his rudeness with a well-deserved verbal smack, but Lyra seemed unaffected. She glanced up playfully and commented, "I may be wrong, but you don't really work and play well with others, do you?" Before he could return with another of his salvos, she quickly tacked on, "I am; I'm getting on with it. Be patient."

"Not if you're reading every damn comma," he barked. "We'll be here forever. For Pete's sake, try to keep to the main text, will ya, huh?"

Momentarily, her even temperament again snapped. "You and your…your *misogynistic T. Rex mentality.*"

"Well, unlike current company, Princess, my jaw doesn't *unhinge when swallowing*!"

As another fight ensued, the cave's echo lent a strange, acoustical dimension.

Inflamed to the point of exploding, a still uncoordinated King tried standing, only for the third time to fall on his derrière.

This is the fourth melee they had gotten into since leaving Phoenix. Wanting to save face, at least with his own ego, he leaned on the axiom, *A good general knows when to retreat.* "*Enough!* Go ahead; read every damn word. That way, we won't miss anything."

Finding a chink in her companion's armor, Lyra couldn't help but make one last thrust. Her reply barely covered the sarcastic intent. "*Like a clue*?"

"Yeah, yeah. Don't be funny, just get on with it."

She started with what they covered twice before, jumping over insignificant data, such as the cave was found by G.E. Kinkaid, a Smithsonian Institution employee, during a mineral exploration trip down the Colorado.

While looking for the more salient points, her treasure-hungry companion broke in: "Let me get this straight. The writer says this cavern somehow connects to either the Orient or Egypt. Well, sorry. I just can't buy this daffy world-tunnel theory. It's imbecilic."

"Hey! No one's asking you to accept anything....Although, it is odd."

"What?"

"How you take some things on blind faith and reject others that are backed by physical evidence."

"Such as?"

"You won't even consider the global tunnels concept. Yet, look at this stupid trip from a sane person's point of view. Here you are, a grown man, running around the desert, dangling over a cliff, hoping to find supposedly long-lost treasure. All based on some tip from a friend of a friend. And you call my theories 'imbecilic'?"

"Absolutely."

"At least they're grounded in fact." An icy silence descended. Sensing a line may have been crossed, in a more calm voice she ventured, "Shall I continue with the article, Mr.King?"

"*Whatever.*"

Hearing his dig, the reader goadingly took her time by repeating the paragraph heading, "'*A THOROUGH*

INVESTIGATION,'" before continuing. "'*Under the direction of Prof. S.A. Jordan, the Smithsonian Institute is now pursuing the most thorough explorations, which will be continued until the last link in the chain is forged. Nearly a third of a mile underground, about 1,480 feet below the surface, the long, main passage has been delved into to find another mammoth chamber from which radiates scores of passageways like the spokes of a wheel. Several hundred rooms....*' "

Patience not being King's strong suit, Rig blurted, "See if you can find where they talk about the weapons." Noticing a silence, he splashed light in the young woman's direction; irritation was evident by the look in her eyes. Quick to cover his rudeness, the Phoenician backtracked, "Sorry—go ahead. I promise not to do that any more...unless it's necessary, that is."

Locating the requested part, she continued, "'*War weapons, copper instruments, sharp-edged and hard as steel....*'"

This time the reader paused, asking, "What type of military things were these?"

"No way of knowing. Indians didn't have the technology to make metal that hard. Anyway, let's get on with it. And reread that part about the mural with the dinosaur drawing."

Rig's partner wanted a little more civility. "Could you at least say *please*, just once in a while?" Without waiting for a reply, she restarted. "This is interesting. Listen to this next part. It's called, '*MR. KINKAID'S REPORT*.' I'm going to leave out the less pertinent areas. Here he says, '*First, I would impress that the cavern is nearly inaccessible. The entrance is 1,486 feet down the sheer canyon wall. It is located on government land and no visitor will be allowed there under penalty of trespass.*'"

Not a conspiratorialist, per se, but recently growing more suspicious of the government's integrity, King was baffled by the tunnel being off-limits, even today. In addition, he found it strange that the Smithsonian's head of natural history confessed in a phone call, "Kinkaid and Jordan did indeed work for us during that period," but in the same breath, admitted, "Their files have recently come up missing." Even more suspicious, a lower-ranking female museum employee, over lunch, quietly told him, "All documents concerning this cave have recently vanished."

Thinking he was probably getting fired up over some bureaucratic oversight, the treasure hunter mused, "Well, they certainly covered their tracks....Oops, sorry! Go on. I'll be quiet."

Doubting his ability to remain silent, Lyra began again—reading about how Kinkaid was looking for mineral deposits when he saw stains in the sediment approximately two thousand feet above today's riverbed. Inching up the steeply sloped escarpment and farther up the vertical face, he subsequently discovered the rock shelf, which obscured the tunnel from boaters on the river. But according to the article, what astounded the geologist even more were the chiseled steps in the cliff, going from the ledge down a number of yards to an ancient waterline.

The newspaper further related that back several hundred feet into the main passage, the explorer came to a crypt where Egyptian-like mummies were stored. Several of these, along with various artifacts, were taken to Yuma, then shipped on to the Smithsonian.

"Lyra?"

"What?"

"You've seen *Raiders of the Lost Ark,* right?"

"No. Why?" she laughed. "Was that a prerequisite for getting into your Treasure Hunting 101 class?"

"Real funny! Hmmm—strange. I'd assumed you would have. I mean, considering that you're writing a movie script and all. Anyway, listen to this. The last scene has this workman in the basement of the Smithsonian, pulling out a box and then shoving it into one of the seemingly endless rows of other crates. Unlabeled, it looks identical to the rest. Turning out the lights, the guy leaves and the audience sees this light coming out from the cracks between the slats."...Her quietness prompted a follow-up, "Don't you get it?"

"Get what?"

"You're kidding? It's obvious! Only the people in the theater realize the Ark of the Covenant, one of the most sacred objects on Earth, is lost in one of your Washington, D.C. basements. Now that's just a story, but guess where Kinkaid shipped all this stuff?"

"Rig, I'm reading the same piece as you—the Smithsonian."

"Bingo! Like Yogi Berra said, 'Déjà vu all over again.' I smell some sort of cover-up."

"It may," she responded, "just be a paperwork error. Although I do find it beyond curious that in the late 1800s, in the middle of nowhere, parts of this canyon were given mystical names like the Tower of Ra, Osiris Temple, Tower of Set, Shiva Temple, Cheops Pyramid, and the like. I mean, what weird event prompted a Wild West Billy the Kid population to give these places occult names?"

"Yeah, for cowboys to come up with those, way back then, is more than strange. But the reason I think this really smells fishy is that the museum is trying to pass off this article printed on…get this…the fifth of the month, as some 'April First, Fool's Day joke.' Surely, they don't think we're that dumb."

Ignoring his comment, and skipping past less interesting parts, the D.C. representative began reading the segment titled, '*THE SHRINE.*' "'*Over a hundred feet from the entrance is a cross-hall, several hundred feet long, in which was found the idol or image of the people's god, sitting cross-legged, with a lotus flower or lily in each hand.*' Here it gets into stuff that isn't too interesting, like the statue resembling Buddha."

"Good, jump over as much as possible. Say, could that be it—the carved idol?"

"Big enough that you can crawl in the mouth, go through a cheek, and get behind the right eye? I doubt it."

"Slow down. That's not what I mean. If that's there, maybe a larger figure is carved out of the wall or something."

Rig's teammate was skeptical. "Possibly, but let's read the rest for things more germane to finding this fabulous treasure of yours. "'*In the opposite corner of this cross-hall were found tools of all descriptions, made of copper. These people undoubtedly knew the lost art of hardening this metal, which has been sought by chemists for centuries, without result.*'"

"Lyra, hold it. I find it hard to believe these metallurgical techniques originated here, in the Southwest; if they were, I'd probably have seen something like them at the Heard Indian Museum in Phoenix."

"Then, Mr. King," a tinge of humor coated her voice, "do I understand you are now agreeing with my global-tunnel concept?"

"No way—one doesn't necessarily prove the other. There's got to be a more plausible explanation."

Ignoring his closed-mindedness, she read further, "'*On a bench running around the workroom was some charcoal and other material probably used in the process. There is also slag and stuff similar to matte, showing that these ancients smelted ores, but so far no trace of how this was done has been discovered, nor has been the origin of the ore. Among the other finds are vases or urns and cups of copper and gold, made very artistic in design. The pottery work includes enameled ware and glazed vessels.*'"

"Stop! Stop!...I forgot about that part. As far as I know, Indians in this area didn't have enamel ware, either."

"Tell me then, why it's not possible their technology came from other parts of the world."

Not wanting his partner garnering too many points at one time, the response was subdued. "I don't know. But I will give you this much: it had to have come from somewhere, and this godforsaken region certainly doesn't seem the likely point of origin."

A lively discussion ensued. He asserted that while the inhabitants obviously had some highly evolved knowledge, a cave connecting to other parts of the world was an idea too harebrained to entertain.

"Where's your proof?"

"Rig, are you blind? This cavern alone as well as its artifacts demonstrate a high level of scientific knowledge. And these had to have come from somewhere else."

Knowing the debate wasn't going anywhere, the treasure hunter attempted breaking the deadlock. "That's not important. Let's finish. What's next?"

Her arm tired, she lay the open newspaper on the floor. From out of the darkness, a tarantula made its leisurely way across the unfolded pages. Glancing up, Lyra saw her partner, flashlight poised, about to squash the arachnid—sending it into another dimension.

Shining light in his eyes, she yelled, "Rig! Don't you dare! He isn't hurting anyone."

"I just don't like...I don't like spiders."

"Stop being silly. Here, listen to this next part. The columnist goes on to say, '*The tomb or crypt in which mummies were found is one of the largest of the chambers, the walls slanting back at an angle of about thirty-five degrees. On these are tiers of mummies, each one occupying a separate hewn shelf. At the head of each is a small bench on which is found copper cups and pieces of broken swords.'*

"Since the next couple of paragraphs seem unimportant, I'm skipping ahead."

"Fine…fine. But, Lyra, what's really weird is nowhere in this region did natives use either swords of this type or that form of burial. And I wonder why females aren't mentioned in the article."

"Probably an all-male contingent used to mine the planet or…."

Rig sliced across her hypothesis, "What do you mean, 'used to mine the planet?'"

"Well, that's my supposition. Let me go on. *'Among the discoveries, no bones of animals have ever been found, no skins, no clothing nor bedding. Many of the rooms are bare but for water vessels. One room about 40 by 700 feet was probably the main dining hall, for cooking utensils are found there.'*"

Once more overriding Lyra's reading, he interjected, "The size of that room blows my mind."

"Here's another point," she continued. "*'Upwards of 50,000 people could have lived in the cavern comfortably.'* Now I'll hop over to some more…aahh, this part is where Kinkaid talks again.

"He says, *'One thing I have not spoken of may be of interest. There is one chamber to which the passageway is not ventilated, and when we approached it, a deadly, snaky smell struck us. Our lights would not penetrate the gloom, and until stronger ones are available, we will not know what the chamber contains. Some say snakes, but others boo-hoo this idea and think it may contain a deadly gas or chemicals used by the ancients. No sounds are heard, but it smells snaky just the same.'*"

"You know, Lyra, this could be the room we're looking for; it just smells like it."

With one eyebrow raised, she quipped, "Oooooh, Mr. Spock?! And they say Vulcans don't have psychic ability."

Always in war-mode, King's mind had a hair-trigger; the gauntlet was picked up and flung back. To him, there was no such thing as 'psychic ability.' His opinion about what made this nation great rested in Yankee ingenuity, not airy-fairy myths.

Pushed too often, and unable to regain her usual placidity, Lyra felt an overwhelming urge to stuff facts into that huge hole in the middle of her partner's fatuous reasoning. "It's just the opposite. As an example, most would never guess the Declaration of Independence was not only written but signed, mainly by your so-called *airy-fairy* mystics. So there!"

His combative mode ratcheted up two notches. "I didn't know The Amazing Randy was that old."

"Hey—you're so smug, like you know everything. People don't realize that *most* of America's Founding Fathers were either members of the Ancient and Mystical Order of the Rosy Cross or high-level Masons. How about that?"

"Oh sure, like who?"

"Benjamin Franklin, for one—he was a Rosicrucian. And...."

Feeling they are wasting time and growing angrier, King again butted in. "Will you *please* finish the article? I want to get on with the hunt."

Exasperated, she quickly paraphrased the rest. "Here's the part about the Hopi legend of emergence from caves deep in the Earth after the last world flood. Now, can you see how that fact in and of itself supports my global-tunnel theory?"

"Girl, you're one-of-a-kind. How did we ever get paired up?"

A low groan was followed by her semi-serious quip, "For me, it's definitely the working off of some ancient karma." She went back to her point. "Anyway, the article says these caverns are supposedly linked to those in Egypt—which suggests they and the Hopi are one culture. But since the rest isn't too interesting, I won't finish this last part."

"That's stupid. As if the Hopi and Egyptians are the same...Say, Lyra...Hey, are you listening?"

"Hmm? Not really. I was just thinking about how the typical American doesn't have a clue about any of this."

"About any of what?"

The Washington D.C. representative explained that not only did the Hopi go underground to escape the world flood, but that their tribe had ancient artifacts showing they originated from the Seven Sisters. Seeing her partner's uncomprehending look, she had to make a clarification of the astrological reference: "That means, from the constellation Pleiades."

About to comment concerning the absurdity of her statement, the stockbroker instead screamed, jumped up, and did a strange form of dance—yanking off his shirt and swatting his back. Light revealed yet another tarantula. Having fallen down his neck, it held on for dear life. In a flash of movement, the arachnid lost its hold, becoming crushed under an already gut-stained boot.

"Yuck! Rig, why'd you do that?"

The arachnophobe offered no answer.

Although repelled at the death of an innocent, Lyra found her partner's hopping up and down humorous. Chuckling, she jibed, "Not bad rhythm—do you also do ballroom?" Sensing a frown, she cleared her throat and continued, "Anyway, you asked about the tunnels. That's why the Foundation sent me here, or at least part of what they want."

"Part? What's the rest?"

"Oh, you know; nonprofit organizations always have several things going at once; helps them get more out of their budgets. Plus I told you, I'm also here on a data-gathering mission for my movie script." Trying to help her companion off the floor—a difficult feat—she added, "Can't you stand yet?"

"Uhgggh, I think so. At this point, I need a laugh; tell me more about these tunnels that supposedly go around the world. Where's the proof?"

"There's plenty. Although the public's in the dark. Simply bring up the subject and the guy on the street thinks you're a nutcase. Facts are there—if people would just put two and two together—like tobacco and cocaine showing up in autopsies of ancient Egyptian mummies, both plants at that time were only available here in the Americas. So while I agree some explorers came from the Middle East by boat, these caves could definitely be another route."

"Get real! I mean, you would assume that if we can put a man on the moon, NASA would have information about these alleged subterranean paths of yours."

"*I said, they do*. Satellites have both identified and mapped over a third of the underground global grid. In fact, U.S.

military forces have not only explored a number of these, but also they are actually creating more."

"Oh yeah? Then why haven't I heard about it? I read two newspapers a day."

"Don't be so naive. Everyone knows Washington keeps people away from what it wants hidden. I mean, for how many years did the government label everyone a kook who tried exposing just one of the connecting tunnels—the secret hideout beneath the Greenbriar Hotel in West Virginia—nicknamed Hotel Armageddon? That is, until it was finally reported by *The Washington Post.*"

"Doesn't make sense. I still ask, why hide them? I mean, if actual proof really is out there."

"Since the media's controlled, everything that doesn't fit the master plan gets quashed. Like when Vice President Cheney's neighbors tried reporting the underground explosions below his house which were occurring twenty-four hours a day, and the coming and going of excavation equipment for a year and a half—nothing. A total news blackout. And that specific tunnel ties into other evacuation routes that crisscross Washington. Don't you ever wonder where the Vice President disappears to for months on end?"

"Not really."

"He's coordinating…ahhh…never mind."

"Girl, what *are* you talking about?"

"Forget I said that. Although, if you like to solve mysteries, it's a matter of public record; worldwide, sixty-nine biochemists, the ones who can create antidotes for the coming pandemics, have been murdered or vanished *over the last two years*. Think you can connect the dots?"

"What dots? We're supposedly talking about tunnels."

"I'm just showing a pattern of media blackout. There is a lot of other tunnel evidence. What about the satellite pictures showing caves from South America connecting to the Salisian tunnels outside of Cairo? Or…."

With the subject wearing thin, at least in the treasure hunter's mind, impatience set in.

"Let's get going. We can get into this trans-world tunnel thing later."

Still wobbly but able to move, the poisoned explorer rose to his feet. Without fanfare, their search began.

CHAPTER III

THE ANCIENT SAGA

Heading into an unrelenting blackness, the two shined lights back and forth. Their pace quickened—skipping most of the forty barracks-like rooms, which lined both sides of the tunnel.

Rig paused, looking back over his shoulder. Just below awareness something was bothering him. "I want," he stopped short, mulling the possibilities, "to go as far back as we can."

With a flashlight, Lyra directed her companion to look up. "See that?"

"See what?"

"Anything missing or wrong?"

"What do you mean, wrong?"

"There's no soot from torches. How do you think the inhabitants got light in here?"

"How would I know? Bet you've got a theory."

"Think about it. Remember the mummies the article talks about?"

"Yeah, so?"

"Possibly this was illuminated the same way the Egyptians lit their pyramid chambers—with mirrors."

"Wait a minute. I get the idea you're trying to tell me they crossed the world and came up through this tunnel by using some sort of reflective light, right?"

"All I'm saying is there are a lot more strange things out there than most people know."

"Okay then, just how did they use these reflectors of yours?"

"I'm not saying mirrors were used. But if they were, the sun from outside bounced a shaft of light from one to another, ending up way inside. Anyway, that's how it was done in the time of the pharaohs."

"I suppose anything's possible." His answer was nothing more than a polite rejoinder. In truth, the stockbroker was more focused on finding his secret chamber than discovering how this cave was lit, thinking, *Frankly, my dear, I don't give a damn.* To which he audibly added, "I will say this: If your tunnels are unending, your mirror theory is shot; reflection can't project some beam through tubes that circle the globe; something else had to have been used."

Lost in her own imagination and in a barely audible register, his companion answered, "Exactly."

"This must be the Shrine Room they talk about," exclaimed Rig as he flashed his light, trying to get a sense of the dimensions. "See these sloping racks? Here's where they stacked their mummies, along with those goblets and swords. Wonder if they took the two cacti statues back to Washing—*Whoa! Lyra!*" This time the treasure hunter excitedly interrupted himself. "*Look at this!*"

Silently, the pair stood before three intricate eight-foot-long paintings—the wall drawings, mentioned in the *Gazette.* Only partially described in the article, where the middle panel had been mistaken for Egyptian hieroglyphics, the first section was composed of horizontal lines, resembling a page out of a giant notebook. The words, if it was writing, were in some sort of Morris code—each row made of red dots and green dashes against a white background.

The second picture showed a dynamic flow of stylized humanoid figures—raw, animated, each in action (some of it bloody), and all depicting what appeared to be important events. Compensating for the artistic crudity, dry desert air had preserved the brilliancy of its colors: blood red, emerald green, fiery orange, blazing yellow, and an iridescent cobalt blue, like the wingtips of an exotic Amazon parrot.

The third mural was made of vertical rows of various yellow designs—geometric patterns whose apparent intricacy and fanciful beauty defied description. Differing from both other segments, this drawing was painted on a soft green background with no symbol repeated twice.

"What on Earth?" King's voice faded as he traced back and forth on the wall with his flashlight. His eyes caught something so incredible it struck him dumb. Overwhelmed, he sucked in his breath, then loudly blurted, "Lyra!" His voice echoed off the walls, shocking him to a lower register. "My God! What do you think this is?"

The beam of King's flashlight partially illuminated the second eight-foot segment, the one with curious, humanlike representations. Entangled in her own thoughts, the Ra representative remained mute.

This was one of those climactic moments for which all males subconsciously yearn. Each carrying this primitive gene—a primal drive to roam the seas and jungles of the world, hoping to someday stand before a mystery that precedes the dawn of known civilization. In awe, the treasure hunter was now before such an antiquity.

Lyra flashed her light to the opposite side of the cave, then swept it to the ceiling. Although interest was still riveted on the panels, Rig momentarily glanced up to see if his partner had discovered something else. She had. The domed room, above what once was an altar, caught the beam and rippled with a sparkling quality.

"Know what that is?" she queried.

"Crystal deposit?"

"Crystals, yes…but strategically placed."

"What do you mean, 'strategically placed?'"

Downplaying its significance, the answer was sidestepped. "We might go into that later; the explanation is rather lengthy."

"Then why the hell bring it up?"

She didn't answer. Taking focus away from the ceiling, her flashlight quickly shined back to the far-left rectangle. "Look. Here you have an eight-foot picture of binary dots and dashes. What do you think it means?"

Out of his technical depth and faking it, he suggested the panel was possibly of Mayan origin. Countering, the

Foundation's expert disagreed. While changing shutter speeds, she explained this was similar but more ancient in form, one which the later Mayan culture altered into a more simplistic style. The intensity of camera's flash caught her partner off guard.

"*Jeez, girl!* Give me some warning next time. I'm blinded."

"Sorry."

"Well," he asked, assuming she was probably only guessing, "then what do *you* think?"

"Ahhh...can't say. I'm familiar with Olmec, Mayan, Aztec, and a number of other Latin American societies. It's certainly none of those."

Surprised by her knowledge, King glanced over. Illuminated only by flashlights, he saw the silhouette of his companion's head. For the briefest of moments, overridden by an even stronger lure, he forgot the promise of treasure.

Now it was Lyra's turn to become excited. Breathlessly, she exclaimed, "Look...here, where I'm shining!" With both beams lighting the center panel, at last the picture's message could be seen in its entirety. "This must be quickly brought to the Council's attention. I suspect each of these three rectangles tells the same story—The Ancient Saga."

"What do you mean, 'Ancient Saga?'"

"Maybe this is a new Rosetta Stone. That's...."

Rig's mind wandered while his companion talked on. He was particularly drawn to an image in the middle picture. Beside himself with excitement, the stockbroker cut her off. "*My God!* Look at that—*a dinosaur!* That's the one reported in the *Gazette*. They were supposed to have died out sixty-five million years ago." Lowering his voice to reverent quietness, he whispered, "How could these Indians possibly have known about their existence?"

"What makes you think only Indians lived here? Would you believe that in 1925, archeologists from the University of Arizona in Tucson unearthed a short sword inscribed with a similar picture—one of a brontosaurus? Now, don't tell me that was from Indians, too."

"Are you saying Earth was inhabited during prehistoric times?"

"As I said, there's evidence man's been on this planet for at least three hundred and possibly as much as six hundred mil...."

"*Whoa...stop right there!* I really hope you aren't going to say 'millions of years.' I mean, come on; where's the evidence?"

"I would have, if you hadn't cut me off...again. Look around. How about this cave? It's real. Even you can't deny its existence."

"Ahh ...."

"Quit stammering. Face it, there's a whole body of archeological remains out there. This is why its existence was hidden from the public. What you're seeing here is far more ancient than those Anasazi we're always hearing about."

"So now you agree—I mean about the cover-up and all?"

Lyra paused from note taking. "I guess; it's obvious someone wanted to throw the public off the trail. I think that's the real reason they made this part of a national forest off-limits."

"Yeah, and this *Gazette* article must have been printed before they could shut Kinkaid up."

"Absolutely."

"I'm getting dizzy again. I've got to sit for a minute." Ignoring the dust, Rig lowered himself to the cold cavern floor. Wearing shorts, his companion chose to remain standing. Both continued scanning sections of the wall with their flashlights.

Leaning back on one hand, he felt a soft, almost undetectable breeze moving across the darkness. The air carried an earthy, underground rock smell. Minutes passed while each mulled private agendas, oblivious to the stagnant silence.

The Ra representative, too, was becoming aware of the strangeness felt earlier by her partner. So much so that her skin broke out in goose bumps as she mentally concluded, *Something...something's not right!*

Snapping the silence, King burst forth, "*Damn! Who were these people?* Where do you think they came from? Think these pictures are dream records, like those of Australian Aborigines?" While continuing to stare at the array of images on the middle panel, he mused, *A few somehow...seem vaguely familiar.*

Heart racing, the treasure hunter could not help but be overwhelmed by the discovery. His left hand lightly brushed across the center mural. It was an automatic reflex, a subconscious—though futile attempt—to somehow gain a fragment of its deeper meaning.

Astonishment mounted as fingers continued sliding from one painted figure to another. "See this one? It's almost like out of a comic book; the guy looks like a type of Mad Max apocalyptic road warrior; head resembles a lizard—probably some sort of mask. And what about that tail?" Without waiting for a response, he rambled on, "And look here—the armor and sword he's wearing." Rig traced the pointed ears on what appeared to be another individual. "Doesn't this one look like that Anubis or whatever he's called? You know, the dog god? No wonder the Smithsonian boys thought these were Egyptian."

Observing his reactions, she softly answered, "Similar, but as I said, these go back several hundred million years."

The recipient of this wisdom wasn't listening. Attempting to decipher the picture's origin, he gushed, "And this other figure, the guy with the curls in his beard, resembles those Babylonian statues I've seen at the Metropolitan Museum of Art, in New York. My God, I can't believe all this! See over here? This figure has the body of a human but the face of an insect." He gestured, using the beam of his flashlight as a pointer. "These are too weird to be real."

"Oh, they're real, all right. Our Foundation research confirms it."

"*Go away!* How do your people know this? Where…where do you get your information?"

"We have our sources. This last one you're referring to is actually half-human, half-insect. Each of these represents not only different species, but separate time periods. What they're showing goes way beyond Earth's recorded time. Here," she pointed, "is where humans came into existence. As it states in Genesis 1:26, '*Let us make man in our image, after our likeness….*'"

Unfortunately, the treasure hunter missed most of Lyra's explanation. Shocked by the half-human, half-insect comment, King slid into another private thought. Mired in contemplation, he continued to shine his flashlight, rapidly skimming from right to left, top to bottom.

"Tell me again, how do you know all this?" Before she could answer, another drawing caught his attention. "*Get outta here!* They even had pornography!"

"I can't believe you see perversion in this. That isn't pornography."

"You don't date very often, do you? Just look at him! Dog boy's wearing a mask and he's...."

Hoping to avoid his sordid interpretation of the entwined figures, his companion cut in, "Again, you weren't listening. I said they're not masks; and like most males, you see pornography in everything."

The lie was thin. "I was too listening...to your every word. But, and I'll say it again, if you don't consider this serious sex, you certainly haven't...."

"*You're such a clod*. This isn't perverse, at least not in the context of that era and culture. You should try reading the Bible sometime. Take a look at Genesis, chapter six, verse four. It says, '*There were giants on the Earth in those days; and also after that, when the sons of God came in unto the daughters of men, and they bore children to them and they became giants who in the olden days were mighty men of renown*.'"

"You're kidding. That's in the Bible?"

"Absolutely. Often what mankind considers myth is merely a recounting of something that actually happened. Up here—these acts...." she pointed to a different section of the panel, "were exactly that—the result of which you would term 'star-matings.' Hercules, Cyclops, and Goliath are three good examples."

"Those were just legends...You *are* joking, aren't you?" The Phoenician kick-started the awkward pause. "You mean to say these actually existed...like the minotaur?"

"No, it came later; that was an Atlantean experiment. They crossbred humans with animals to create drones to do their grunt work." Shining a light on her watch, she added, "This is something we ought to get into some other time."

"I always thought this Atlantean thing was pure fiction."

"Don't count on it. Apparently you haven't read about the excavations going on in the Canary Islands and Jamaica."

"Hey, Lyra, look down here, toward the bottom. If I'm not mistaken, these seem Mayan, while the ones above are like Hopi kachinas. Wow, I can't get over this long parade of weird figures."

"Except, the one you're pointing to isn't Mayan; it's Olmec. See how it has thick lips and slanted, Oriental eyes. That group came from the Congo region in Africa. Look over here. Your Mayans surfaced in this period."

Her flashlight moved to the next scene. "See those in the kneeling position? They are being beheaded by...."

"Yeah, geez! The guy with the lizard mask is doing a Mafia-type whacking."

Shaking her head because her obtuse partner still couldn't process the information that these figures weren't wearing masks, the Ra agent shined her beam toward the earliest part of the saga. "As for these, they do bear a slight resemblance to kachinas...or then again, maybe kachinas resemble them."

In the darkness, her smile went unseen. Pointing the light past her companion and onto the wall, she used its secondary illumination to observe King's reaction. It was blank. Swimming in fantasy, he was once more too busy to listen.

"*Damn!* I'd like to know what this is all about!"

First drawing in a big breath, she said, "Okay, but we don't have time for the whole story." Spellbound, he listened intently as Lyra gave a brief explanation. "This wasn't expected. This cave is far older than we assumed. It has to be one of the main trunk tunnels connecting with other parts of the globe. It tells...." Shining the light at her watch, she frowned. "We should look for your gold and get out as soon as possible."

"Why? Don't you want to gather data about your tunnels?"

Ignoring his questions, her answer went in a different direction. "It'll be night soon; I don't want to be hoisted up in the dark."

"Okay, but can you just give me a brief version of the thing?"

"All right, although you probably won't believe a word of it; and it'll have to be fast if you want to find your treasure."

This second mention of treasure shook the stockbroker's brain back to its primary objective: "You have a point. Maybe you'd better take some more photos. We can discuss them later?"

"That's what I was planning on doing."

"Good. While you're busy, I'll walk around and see if anything else jumps out at me."

Lyra changed her thinking. Curious to see if that fortress protecting Rig's closed-mindedness could be scaled, she said, "*Wait!* Before going off, take a second and examine the designs on this third section. Don't they look even a little familiar?"

"I guess...but I can't seem to place them. Why?"

"You aren't really current on anything outside of the financial world, are you?"

"*Woman!* You starting with me again?"

"No. It's just...It's all right in front of your eyes. Look at this last part, here. Earth has reached the most critical time in its history; the planet's dying, mankind is about to be driven to extinction, and nearly everyone's standing around allowing it to happen."

"I doubt that. But what's that got to do with your ancient story?"

"Quite a bit—it relates to hidden information the government's withholding. You see, these pictures show a progression—a linking of events. But to give you the full overview might take longer than we have at the moment."

Curiosity piqued more than ever, he played on her good nature. "Can't you just give me a hint—something?"

"All right, look at these, over here. They set in motion the apocalyptic future this planet is now entering."

"These cartoons don't tell me squat. And what do you mean, 'now entering'?"

"See this? This part prophesies coming events. The terrorism back in 2001 was just the beginning. Soon the world will witness tsunamis like these—ten stories high. Then over here it shows volcanoes erupting, blocking out the sun." Pointing to another panel, she added, "And these appear to be massive earthquakes, like the ones that sunk Atlantis. Even now there are about one hundred plant and animal species becoming extinct every day and...."

"Aw come on! Wars, tsunamis, volcanoes, earthquakes—they've always been here. As for your three or four hundred thousand species dying off every ten years, so what? We've got enough creepy-crawlies as it is! I don't get how all this ties in."

"More than you know. Mt. Toba erupted seventy-four thousand years ago, and that one thing alone nearly wiped out mankind; only two to ten thousand people on the entire planet survived. As for your 'so what' when species vanish, so will humankind. It's all linked—totally interdependent. In fact, within the last fifty years, *ninety percent* of the oceans' big fish have disappeared. And according to a United Nations study last year, twenty-five percent of all wildlife will be extinct *within the next four!"*

While Lyra talked, Rig searched his knapsack for a candy bar. He held one up, asking, "Wanna piece?"

"Of what?"

"This."

"No thanks." She picked up his discarded wrapper and put it in her pocket.

The broker thought it was dim-witted of his partner to be policing litter in this remote cave. Guiltlessly, he went back to addressing her point. "I don't know where you get these far-out theories. Look, man won't disappear just because a few animals are dying off."

"*A few*?! I can't believe you're saying that. Did you ever stop to consider that one species, *just one species* alone, may perform something essential that keeps the Earth's entire ecosystem in balance?"

"What you bleeding-heart liberals don't admit, is that given enough money, we can cultivate and breed anything. All our needs will be met. Ever hear of soilent green?...Just kidding. Seriously, we can manufacture little pellets to feed half the world. Anyway, we're wasting time. What you're talking about hasn't anything to do with these panels."

"Yes, it does! It's all interconnected, and The Saga explains it."

"*Come on!* Let's get out of here; we've got to get going."

"Rig, take a look at the last figure in this central mural. Can't you see what he's doing?"

"Him?" His beam met at the spot where she had hers shinning. "I see but don't understand the symbolism. Why?"

"Actions up here, earlier in the story, molded much of society as it is today. As an example, there is a direct correlation between the problems they set in motion and, say, why today frogs are being born deformed."

"What?"

"You know, the pollution crisis—like the news stories in 1997 about frogs having only three legs and no eyes?"

"*Oh, Lord!* Here we go again."

"No, *you listen, Mister!* Frogs are a *serious* ecological barometer. And the problem's being swept under the rug—like it doesn't exist."

"Look, since I don't usually order frogs' legs when I'm out to eat, they aren't a part of my area of interest; I just forgot... not that I thought it was ever a serious issue."

"*Forgot?* I can't believe you don't know about any of this! And it's getting worse than ever. Pollution alone is wrecking the climate. That's...."

"We're losing precious time. Next you're going to be preaching statistics about the ozone layer. None of that junk has anything to do with this saga, or whatever you call it."

"You don't have a clue about the impact of these things, do you? If you *materialistas* weren't so blithely immersed in all your goodies, you'd be frozen in fear."

"Like what, your deformed frog thing? *Ooooh*, I'm shaking in my boots."

"*You're impossible!* Here," she said, poking at a particular image in the panel, "to the far right. At least some of these are symbols you must have come across before, somewhere."

"Not really."

"Yes, you have. They've been all over the media for the past twenty years. This is a form of language that uses left-brain, neuro-activating pictograms."

"Wha?"

"They awaken the ancient memories of the viewer; they're preparing mankind. Doesn't that make sense?"

"Not in the slightest. And you're wrong; I still don't remember seeing these before. Even if I did, no big deal."

Annoyed, the Ra representative's voice changed octaves. "*Theeese, Mr. King, these are crop circles!*"

Ignoring his companion's answer, he focused on her insult. "Your voice is beginning to sound like my second wife's."

The returning jibe was flung with the zeal of a sailor harpooning a whale. "*Second?* How sad, and with all your sensitivity, too."

Her point whizzed past, missing its mark. The treasure hunter had already turned his attention away; fights like this took too much effort. Wanting to conserve what little energy he had, the response was an exasperated, "Oh, never mind. We're burning up precious minutes. Let's get back to the hunt. Otherwise, we're going to be chasing each other around your creation story for the rest of the day."

For him, the next fifteen minutes felt like seconds. Gold on his mind, the stockbroker furiously poked about, looking for any clue. In contrast, the Foundation's agent quietly concentrated on photography. In rapid succession, she took nearly twenty pictures. Then, with her flashlight tucked under an arm, she began scribbling notes.

Finishing her last entry, she offered, "Well, I got what I came for. Now I'll devote my attention to your project."

Disappointed at not yet finding the statue leading to the hidden chamber, they retraced their way back to the oval doorway. After a brief discussion about the next move, both stepped once more into the main tunnel.

Another wisp of air caught his attention. "Feel that?"

All the tension went from his partner's voice, her reply was soft.

"What say we follow? Might lead to someplace important."

At this juncture the cave split into a number of shafts resembling the spokes of a wheel. One opened into a gigantic, apparently endless void.

Caught off guard by its size, astonished, King mumbled, "This must be the Great Hall, the one that can accommodate fifty thousand people."

"I doubt it. They said the whole complex was able to support fifty thousand. That doesn't necessarily mean this room by itself. You make it sound like they were all in here having a sit-down dinner. Besides, I can't fathom anyone making a secret chamber off the eating hall. But if you want, let's go in and satisfy this curiosity of yours."

"I'm just hoping that maybe there's that big statue or carving somewhere in here."

Inside the massive cavity, their flashlights were almost ineffective—pointing into, but not illuminating what seemed a solid wall of blackness. The room's immensity took Rig by surprise. "*Dang!*" is the only sound he made before it echoed, bouncing back and forth and ultimately dying in a whisper. Ignoring the reverberation, he spoke again, this time in a more subdued tone. "Hard to imagine where this bloody thing ends." He recalled from the article that the space had a forty-foot width and a seven-hundred-foot length—spanning approximately two and one-half football fields.

"Truly amazing," whispered Lyra.

"Imagine," he mused, "aboriginal man chipped all this out of a mountain of solid rock."

Miffed at her partner's continual lack of logic, which caused her to flash, "Oh really—you think cavemen carved this with just Stone Age hammers and chisels?"

"Well, something happened here. They probably...."

"*Did what?* . . Tell me, just what tools could they possibly have used to hollow out a room the size of an airplane hanger? Explain that if you can."

"Do you have some sort of hormonal imbalance you want to tell me about?"

"What?"

"Or maybe you just need to cut your caffeine intake; seems like you're maxed out for the day."

"Unlike you, Mr. King, I didn't require three coffee stops on the drive up here. Besides, you saw me; I didn't drink that much coffee. Are you always this rude?"

"*Mellow out!* No need to get hostile; I was just kidding." he tried to change the subject. "To answer your question, I suppose Indians had to have some sort of cutting equipment. They...."

"*Impossible!*" Her searing blast almost seemed to raise the temperature of the cool chamber. "Science says that forty thousand years ago, man had only stones tied to sticks with strips of leather. And these walls...these were, Mr. King, these were *sliced.* How could you possibly think primitive hammers could have achieved something this monumental?"

"Okay, O Wise One, then how'd they do it?"

The Ra representative offered a time-line, suggesting when the cave was first inhabited. The day he installed the winch for the trip, Lyra was busy calling geologists who specialized in the area around the Grand Canyon. According to them, erosion from the rim down 3,500 feet to today's water, took roughly six to twenty million years; exact dates were hard to pinpoint because the Colorado didn't even flow through here until 5.6 million years ago. And below the steps, the final 2,000 feet down to the river became etched out, at least in geological time, just recently—over the last one and one-half million years. Therefore, based on the high watermark near the ledge, many experts concluded the cave was most likely occupied somewhere between 1.5 and 5.6 million years ago.

"Nahhh. That I can't swallow."

"Strange, I would assume you've swallowed all sorts of unusual things in your time."

"What's that supposed to mean?"

"Forget it."

Another flurry of bickering ended with Lyra declaring, "The mind is like a parachute; it doesn't work unless it's open. Yours never considers anything beyond its dogmatic little comfort level."

"Dogmatic? Try me; let's hear this grand theory of yours. That is, if you have one."

"All right, I will. You see, caves like this are actual proof of ancient civilizations. Yet paradoxically, their existence causes an incredible problem that society refuses to consider, let alone accept."

"I don't get it. Why?"

"Besides dissolving Christianity's story of creation, they warp science's timetable of mitochondrial evolution. And those who do suspect these truths are afraid to take a close look. As Carl Jung said, 'Man can't take too much reality.' That's why the majority ignores the evidence—turning their eyes away as if it doesn't exist. As an example, do you know that Fundamentalist Christians still argue that man has been on Earth for only six thousand years?"

Rig shined his flashlight upward to the ceiling before responding. "Fundamentalists are strange; they're like members of the Flat Earth Society."

"No, they're not. It's just that a few take the Bible too literally—refusing to accept facts that would expand their concept of God."

"We've got to get moving. Where's your point in all this?"

Lyra let her mind wander before replying. "Of the entire universe, Earth…Earth is simply one of the Creator's many gardens. This planet alone goes back billions of years."

"And?"

"During that time, there have been many cycles in humanity's physical and spiritual evolution. Each of these growth eras was then followed by an involution, or a major cleansing. If you want to call it that."

"Cleansing?"

"As I said, these were times when most of humanity died out. Take the Great Flood I talked about earlier as an example."

"The what?"

"Noah and his ark? Come on, certainly you know about that, don't you?"

"Don't be ridiculous."

A noise sounded three feet ahead. Both froze. Instinctively, Lyra grabed her companion's arm. Cloaked by blackness, the intruder was invisible. Not thinking he would need a pistol, King swallowed hard; he was unprepared. Their beams darted back and forth, trying to illumine the darkness. Impossible. Still, they knew there was a sound…one they did not make. Suddenly, laughter broke the moment. Inspection of the floor reveals the culprit—a golf-ball-size rock that had become dislodged from a crack in the ceiling.

Calming down and matching his companion's earlier conciliatory tone, he offered, "Okay, if what you say is true, and I only say 'If,' then why can't we find evidence of these supposed million-year-old civilizations? Hell, that hominid skull found in Northern Chad shows that six million years ago man was still half ape. And I don't think humans could have evolved this much in such a short span."

"So you think they were Earth's only residents? Just because anthropologists have come across a few bones, does that speak for the whole planet? These …."

Picking up the stone, Rig threw it into the darkness. It bounced off the opposite wall as he interrupted her answer. "Then why haven't we gotten proof of an earlier man? I mean, besides Leaky's four-million-year-old half-woman, half-ape skeleton found in Kenya, that's about it. This alone shoots your technologically-advanced-race concept all to hell."

"Must you always swear?"

"*Hey!* Some of the greatest men in history swore. Besides, by tonight back in Phoenix, we go our separate ways. Stop being so controlling, okay?"

Walking, talking, and still searching, they can't help continuing the conversation.

"Rig, listen to me. What most people don't know is that there exists actual archeological evidence pointing to highly advanced civilizations. Problem is, the concept is always disregarded."

"*Yeah, right!* Like I said, where's there any evidence?"

"It's there, but the findings are always discredited. As an example, in the June 5, 1852, issue of the *Scientific American,* they report discovering a metal vase near Dorchester, Massachusetts, which tested over six hundred million years old. Now that's something tangible."

"Oh, sure. Like, back in 1852, they could date something that old."

"*The analysis was done recently*."

"Probably by the staff of *The National Enquirer*."

"*See, you're just like the rest!*" Her voice trembled. "Okay, let's say that somehow the calculations were off. Then explain these: a 505-million-year-old shoeprint found at Antelope Spring in Utah; or the 408-million-year-old iron nail at a quarry in Scotland; or the 312-million-year-old iron pot from Wilburton, Oklahoma; the 320-million-year-old gold chain found in Morrisonville, Illinois; or that iron hammer found imbedded in 85 million- year-old cretaceous rock...Shall I go on?"

Scratching his head, the treasure hunter sighed, then answered indifferently, "If you want, but I still can't believe it. As far as I'm concerned, this is La-La Land. Sounds like the person who gave you that research is suffering from Boundary Deficit Disorder—obviously having a rough time telling fact from fantasy."

"*You're such a jerk!*" She continued her efforts at prying open her partner's clamshell mind. "Look, for the third time I'm telling you that advanced races have been on this planet for hundreds of millions of years—actually longer. And since you're so negative...."

"Why not go for trillions?" he volleyed while stopping, bending over, and thrusting a finger into a crack on the floor to gauge its depth.

"That's it; I'm done. I'm not expending the effort of going into twenty or so other pieces of proof."

An ancient earthquake had left a raised edge on the floor. The toe of King's boot caught its lip. Stumbling and yelling "*Ahhhh jeez,*" he tried to appear collected by calmly responding, "Thank you; a more reasonable topic of conversation would be highly appreciated."

"See? That answer just proved my point."

"What point?"

"Regardless of the evidence, you and everyone else refuse to believe anything that doesn't fit into your rigid Judeo-Christian or Darwinian framework."

Amused at the anger, her partner tried a humoring approach. His technique was none too smooth. "Oh, go ahead. We've got time. Tell me what you've got, before your pH level gets more out of kilter."

"What's that supposed to mean?"

"Never mind. Just get on with it."

"Then let me give you an example closer to home. Which do you want to discuss—a 170,000-year-old artifact dug up near Flagstaff or a copper coin found 114 feet below the surface at Lawn Ridge, Illinois?"

"A real coin?"

"The Foundation thinks so. It's either a coin or a medallion; we don't know which yet.

The drawings and language on it are still being deciphered."

"How old do you think it is?"

"Relatively young—somewhere between 200,000 and 400,000 years."

"Let's pick up the pace," he injected. "Walk faster. It's getting late. All right, say your Ancient Man Theory is true. Why haven't we seen any reports on the evening news? I mean the Ted Koppels and Larry Kings could keep something like this going for weeks...maybe months. Or have you forgotten what they did with O.J., Clinton, and Michael Jackson?" Rig saw another stone on the cave floor and couldn't resist giving it a violent kick. "And this is way bigger. Besides, human life didn't exist in our solar system ten million years ago, let alone hundreds of millions."

"Try billions," she responded, her face turning a bright, unseen pink.

"Oh, sure. By the way, how long did you say you are going to be in town?"

"Several days. Why?"

"I've got this swamp property near Yuma. You should consider it for an investment."

"*That's enough!* You and your group are so arrogant. The embarrassing fact is, you're all huddled together, terrified to go into anything unknown. And don't give me this, 'Well, we're exploring outer space,' thing either. In terms of distance, NASA hasn't even made it off Earth's front porch."

"Slow down. Do you ever take a breath? You're wound up tighter than an eight-day clock."

Ignoring him, she pushed on. "Answer me this, then: How old is God? What's this stupidity that makes people think they're the firstborn in the universe?"

"Come on, woman, you're getting hyper."

As they journeyed into inky darkness, a wave of cold that some would call a vibrational shift rippled through the Great Hall. It passed unnoticed by the explorers who were immersed in their heated discussion.

Finishing an earlier point, Lyra added, "Unfortunately, the church and science communities are stuck. One won't accept the evidence; the other can't."

"Why?"

"Because of their self-imposed rules. Take religious groups, for example. They need to control. If mankind ever finds its direct link with God, churches and synagogues are out of business. Then in an almost parallel way, you have the scientific community with the same dilemma; should the world begin to rely solely on God, they're also out of work."

"I don't see the correlation."

"Surely you know scientists are primarily motivated by research grants. To keep from being ridiculed, most are forced to work only within traditionally accepted guidelines. I mean, if someone proposes an ultra-revolutionary idea, they've usually taken too radical a step out of the circle and face being ostracized by their peers. Because of this type of pressure, few in either the religious or scientific communities want to explore concepts that go beyond their established paradigms."

"Seems like you're exaggerating a bit."

Nearing one end of the room, Lyra commented, "Not in the slightest. Case in point: just ask your Leakys about this evidence I was mentioning and you'll get laughed out of the room. Still, it does exist. Remember what happened to Copernicus and Galileo?"

"Refresh my memory."

"People of that time believed the sun and the stars revolved around the Earth. Yet, these two dared to teach the truth, and look how they were persecuted."

"So you're saying scientists are ignoring available facts?"

"*Afraid to examine* would be a better phrase. Let me prove the point. Another example is their refusal to acknowledge the body's aura."

"The aura?"

"You heard me. For thousands of years, many societies around the world have understood that the physical body radiates an electromagnetic field. Still, most Western medical science refuses to recognize it as a bona fide diagnostic tool."

"For good reason—it's psychic nonsense."

"Oh, really? Then how could there be documented photographs of it since 1939?"

"When?!"

"Nineteen-thirty-nine, when Semyon Kirlian invented a camera showing a pulsating current of energy around all living things."

"Photographs. You're kidding?"

"Actual photos."

Momentarily silenced, King pondered her statement.

"And if society can't handle such a simple fact, the real truth about ancient civilizations could never be accepted. That's why the Foundation has to work quietly."

"The *real truth*?" Rig, with his usual causticity, retorted, "Here we go. Okay, try me; see if I'm intelligent enough… No! See if I'm un-dogmatic enough to grasp this hypothesis of yours."

The representative from Washington ignored the sarcasm. "Well, this cave is a perfect example. Admitting that some several-million-year-old culture had the technology to carve this out of solid rock, knew dinosaurs, and interfaced with alien beings would…."

"*Whoa, whoa!* What do you mean, *aliens*?"

"See, I knew you weren't listening. Do you think these drawings are of civilizations that simply died out?"

"If they're not cartoons, they have to be. After all, we know a lot about, say, the Mayans—and they're extinct."

"No, they're not; they still exist down in Central America."

"Really? So maybe that wasn't a good example. Look, no one's going to buy this kooky dog-boy or insect-alien idea."

"Why not?"

"Too weird."

"It is not. Don't you get it? That's the joke. These panels don't negate the existence of God—they add a much deeper layer." She gives a muffled chuckle before adding, "It's humanity that's weird."

"How so?"

"As I've said, most people won't face the truth, regardless of how blatantly it shows itself; but they blindly accept stupid things that aren't even provable."

"Like what?"

"Oh, like…Tell me, what proof do you have that the Garden of Eden actually existed?"

"*Newsweek* magazine did a special," the explorer reported with mock seriousness. "Showed an apple tree with some snake talking to this semi-nude chick. I gotta tell you; right then and there, that picture made me a true believer."

"No, get serious for once. What actual physical proof do you have that angels, heaven, or any of that exists?"

"Come on, Lyra. We have thousands of years of their validation. Of course they're real. Why? Don't you believe in them?"

"Absolutely! I'm simply trying to break through your rigid belief system. What I'm hearing is, you're willing to put trust in things you haven't seen, and yet you deny this mural that your hands just ran across."

The listener fell silent as he tried to figure a way of countering her argument.

"Hey, Mr. King, anybody home?"

"All right, all right—take a moment and try to see this from my perspective. We just saw some drawings of…of what you are telling me are alien beings, maybe even a dinosaur. Can't you see how all of this is a little too radical?"

"How old do you think intelligent life is? I mean, out of trillions and trillions of stars, isn't it the height of conceit to think Earth is the only planet with an intelligent population?"

"So, you don't take the Bible story of creation word for word?"

"Those who really know, don't—like the Catholic Church. As far back as 1943, Pope Pius XII issued the *Divino Afflante Spiritu*—a formal position saying the Bible shouldn't be taken literally. He wrote, and I'm quoting, '*It's to be interpreted in the simple context of the time in which it was written.*'"

"That logic has more holes than a colander; ranks right up there with David Letterman's list of the ten ways that Democrats tricked Rush Limbaugh into getting hooked on drugs. Or…or maybe since I'm not a student of the occult…."

"*Occult?!* Occult simply means 'hidden,' 'obscured,' or 'secret'—not 'insidious.' Then why do you think even Jesus spoke in parables?"

"I'll bite; why?"

"At that time, people were less educated. They didn't have the knowledge to accept the complete truth—in some ways, much like today."

"I want it."

"The truth?…You can't…Oh, *never mind*!"

He gritted his teeth, mumbling, "Crud, doesn't it ever end?"

CHAPTER IV

FOOTPRINTS IN TIME

A third of a mile underground, moving through the bowels of Mother Earth, it was normal for one's nerves to fray. Here, the only thing giving the explorers slight solace was a pair of bobbing flashlight beams.

Except for miners and spelunkers, few ever experienced such extreme visual deprivation. Without light, placing a hand even within a half-inch of one's own face gave no indication of its existence, except for the radiating warmth.

To many who probe these depths, horror seems to take physical form—conjured by a part of the mind that delights in playing the most ghoulish of games. The engulfing blackness fostered a helpless, naked feeling, causing some to go so far as to imagine dripping fangs just a few scant inches away.

Add to this one more terror: The millions of tons of rock and dirt overhead created a psychological compression—the mental weight from realizing the actual possibility of being buried alive. This or some lesser degree of claustrophobia afflicted all who came here. Most coped. With others, it overwhelmed, making any movement, even breathing, a forced, mechanical effort.

With his next step, Rig reeled. There was the weight of a foreign hand upon his shoulder. Overcome by fright, he gave minimal attention to the trickle of warm urine flowing down his leg. But stop! In truth, there was no hand, no urine…only a cruel fantasy made real by sheer panic. All had been an illusion—a sick delight from that dark side of his thinking. Tormented by this internal trickster, the treasure hunter had to summon every ounce of will to continue moving forward.

Minds occupied with such thoughts barely noticed a nearly indiscernible, unnatural odor. The fleeting scent came and went, riding on subtle currents. Its indefinite effect left both explorers vacillating, wanting to say something and yet inwardly denying the smell's almost phantom existence.

At the far end of the chamber, there was real—not imagined movement. From its direction came a hissing noise. Too low. The ears of the trespassers were not close enough to hear.

Also shoving fright below her containment line, Lyra clarified her theory. "Think of it this *wa…yeeeeeee*!"

The piercing yell jolted Rig into a defensive stance. "What is it?" he shouted, trying to be heard over the scream's repeated bouncing off the cavern walls.

"Something touched my hair!"

"Oh," came a relieved, half moaning sigh, "that's probably just a bat. Getting toward evening, and they've been flying out of here for the last few minutes. Can't believe you didn't hear them."

"Guess I was too distracted by our conversation." Her quivering voice, ringing with doubt, asked, "Are you sure that's what it was?"

"Yeah." Wanting to get back to work, Rig changed the subject. "Then where in your saga is this 'Big Bang Theory' scientists are always babbling about?"

The answer betrayed a still quaking voice, "Those people really upset me. Notice they never have a decent answer to what or who started the bang, let alone who created the material that made it happen? They always hide behind something so…so totally illogical, saying, 'Well, it always was.' As if that's some sort of brilliant answer. Their half-witted platitudes clarify nothing…absolutely zero!"

Without letting her partner get a word in edgewise, the diatribe continued. "I remember right after the millennium, science came up with what it calls the Ekpyrotic Theory. It announced 'The Beginning' was actually caused by twin, parallel, three-dimensional universes called 'membranes,' less than a millimeter apart, that periodically collide. And you know what?" Without waiting for an answer she fired on, her voice cracking under the mounting irritation, "Those nincompoops were so excited about their dumb 'Big Bang' concept that concentration was on the hole and not the doughnut. Get this—they…they admit the existence of at least two universes. But by definition, the 'Universe' is all—one hundred percent—the entire cosmos! So by stupidly fixating on just this single point of creation, they lose the more important realization that there are really not two, but an infinite number of realms. As the Bible says in John 14:2, *In my Father's house are many rooms*, meaning existence is like a stack of a million sheets of paper, each universe being a separate page—all coexisting separately but simultaneously. I mean, how stupid can these academicians be?"

In anger, she tacked on another thought. "You know, there are all sorts of things science refuses to accept, or turns a blind eye to."

"Such as?"

"Well, chances are you've never heard of the Nordic runes that were discovered strung from the Gulf of Mexico to Illinois. Have you?"

"What's a rune?"

"See what I mean? The average person hasn't a clue." She pulled out a gold chain hanging around her neck. From it dangled a small rectangular pendant surrounded by bezel, set with rubies. The little block bore a strange inscription. "These are clay tablets whose designs make up the Viking alphabet. Believing the symbols have mystical powers, the enlarged versions were frequently used as, sort of, magical boundary posts."

"Interesting," he acknowledged, accepting her offer and bending forward for a closer inspection.

"Anyway, the smaller size is still used as a tool of divination."

"You're saying some of these boundary markers are still around?"

"Absolutely. And the Kensington Stone, found in 1898, contradicts what's taught in schools—irrefutable proof that Vikings came up the Mississippi and Missouri Rivers."

"That puts the Scandinavians here hundreds of years prior to Columbus!"

"Plus, before the Norse, there were the Chinese, Japanese.... There's even evidence of Minoan settlements all the way from Massachusetts to Iowa."

Unable to stay quiet, he interjected with a laugh, "Well, don't tell the public; I like taking off on Columbus Day."

"True, most don't want to hear about things that dismantle their belief systems—such as the discovery of Toltec pottery and the rock writings of Canaanite sailors in Ohio, of all places. So you're right—the public psychologically needs to keep this myth of 1492 going, even if they have evidence to the contrary."

"Lyra, calm down. So what if some property markers mean Norse explorers came here first?"

"You aren't listening. I said they were *not* the first."

Walking along, the treasure hunter brushed a hand against the marble-smooth wall, searching for some deviation in its surface.

"Why...why are you doing that?"

"Oh, I don't know. It's just, we keep walking and nothing seems to vary. I'm hoping for something...anything that might lead to a clue."

The Foundation's agent continued, "As another scientific fact, we know the end for most of the world is starting to happen. A lot of groups besides Christian societies prophesied this—like, say, like the Hopi."

"The Hopi?"

"Sure, they teach we are entering the Fourth Cleansing. There were three worlds before this one. The first was destroyed by fire, the second by ice, and the last by water. You also might find it interesting that their planetary flood story coincides with Christianity's Great Deluge."

As they proceeded, she talked more about Hopi, Christian, Incan, Mayan, and other related prophecies, each declaring that the Earth was beginning a period of massive upheaval leading to its destruction. Alarmed by the use of the word "cleansing," King demanded clarification.

"This planet is at the tipping point. Unless there are immediate changes," her voice dipped as she spoke, "this will be the end for most of civilization. Signs are everywhere." Citing another Hopi legend forewarning the terrible commencement, she added, "They say a dark star will be seen in the sky and an unknown blue flower will bloom in the desert at the beginning of what many call the Apocalypse."

"Lyra, we've gotten this comet scare thing a number of times. So? Big deal."

"That's what you think. An unknown blue flower has just been discovered in New Mexico. As for the dark star, you might consider Nostradamus's seventy-second quatrain."

"Ahhh, jeez, don't drag Nostradamus into this. Until now, you just about had my attention."

"No, many have come true."

"And?"

"One deals with a random asteroid that came in September of 1999."

"*Pssssst*! I don't want to alarm you, but that was five years ago; we're still here."

"What you don't know, Mr. Smarty-pants, is that it was deflected. The general public never even knew of its existence. They...."

"What do you mean, deflected?"

"There's more. While the mile-wide asteroid coming on March 14, 2014, is frightening enough, the Foundation has proof of a gargantuan one, slated to arrive in 2011. Although, to keep the public in the dark, they are only talking about the one in 2028."

He yawned. "I'm still not worried. We'll somehow take care of them...with missiles or something."

"Not the way they're going about it. The Star Wars shield certainly won't. That whole program's a joke. In fact, the Pentagon has to put homing devices into the incoming rockets...and," she laughed, "most of the time, the outgoing rockets still miss." Smiling broadly, she threw in, "Now that's a confidence builder...at least for the North Koreans, since their missiles can reach Los Angeles."

Her companion's sarcasm was unmistakable. "Oh, great! So I'll have to cash in my stocks and head for the hills, all because someone found a flower and there are a few asteroids headed in our direction. *Get real!*"

Lyra saw no hope for her recalcitrant companion. *He's like all the rest.*

As for the treasure hunter, he was tired of doomsday talk, thinking, *This female is strange, real strange.*

Both were silent for about ten feet, working their way down one side of the room. Nearing the end of the Great Hall and discovering nothing, they crossed over. Starting back, they quickened their pace. Flashlight beams swept the wall as their conversation continued.

"Lyra, try me again. I still don't get it. What's this hidden reason you think people don't want to hear about earlier civilizations?"

"They'd be too frightened. It's easier to ignore the facts than to realize you're not in control and never have been. This planet has been used...."

She bumped into Rig who was frozen, mid-stride.

Pulling the young woman near, his lips nearly touched her ear as he whispered, "Hear anything?"

"Like what?" her response was equally low, cautious.

"Nothing. I...I guess I'm on edge. The combination of this blackness and the silence is getting on my nerves. I need the sound of machinery...a bird, or at least something."

"I'm nervous, too. Someone could steal the four-by-four, leaving us stranded down here. We would vanish without a trace."

"*Lord! Thanks*, I needed that."

The noise Rig thought he heard was still absorbing most of his concentration. Not wanting to frighten his companion, he felt the need to keep a dialogue going. Choosing the first topic that came to mind he asked, "What's your screenplay about?"

"Galactic alliances—power struggles manipulating man's evolution since his inception, and how one group is seeking total domination over time and space."

Attention focused elsewhere, King listened for the sound. With superficial lightness he added, "So what's this film going to be called?"

"*The Council of Nine* or *The Omega Protocol*. I don't know yet." Lyra's mood brightened as she discussed her project. "I'm still trying to choose. Anyway, they're just working titles. Which do you like?"

"First isn't bad. Sounds mysterious. Yeah, I like it. *The Omega* thing is a bit too...vague. Hey, look at this," he says, shining his light down…"could it be? Darn, it's definitely a set of footprints. There is a line between the feet, as if something has been dragged.

Rattled, the Ra representative became serious, ordering, "*Shhhhhh!*" as she instinctively put an unseen finger to her lips. "Can't you feel it?"

"Feel what?"

"*Be quiet!*"

Both had become aware of another sensation—one of great danger. Sight, sound, feeling, everything in their nervous systems pulsated. Internal voices screamed, *Danger! Run!* But to where? The enveloping blackness blinded them. For the moment, nothing was said. Senses strained—trying to hear and see farther into the blackness than humanly possible.

Whispering in her ear, he asked, "Does the cave seem colder than before, or is it me?"

Although near, she pulled him closer. Even with lips touching his cheek, the young woman's voice was barely audible. "I think you're right, but there's no breeze."

The proximity of Lyra's mouth shot a blast of heat through King's body. For the moment, her presence and radiating warmth had the treasure hunter forgetting any fear. Seconds passed as his mind tried to refocus on whatever made the noise.

Breaking silence, she again whispered, "I have goose bumps."

Leaning over, he moved her hair out of the way. Lips grazing the curvature of her ear, he took a long, deep breath—pulling in that fading hint of fragrance applied early this morning. "Stay here, I'm going about a hundred feet ahead to see what's up."

Bravery had nothing to do with his volunteering. This offering of himself as a sacrificial lamb was inspired by that ageless game of male-female role-playing. Regardless of King's personal fear, by virtue of having that singular, masculine appendage, Rig knew he was shamed into being the protector.

After twenty feet, a slight waft of something unusual caught his attention—that snaky smell referred to in the newspaper article. It wasn't there when they entered the hall. Then again, maybe it was. *No way to know*, he reasoned. *My mind's been on tilt ever since finding that damned mural.*

What with the unexplained sound and now a strange smell, the Phoenician realized there might be not one, but two potential problems. *This may be one of those mines with the poisonous gas I've heard about!*

Although confused as to the direction of danger, and wanting to run for the nearest exit, he continued searching, using his flashlight to grope the dark. Even with the temperature a cool sixty-eight degrees, beads of sweat popped up on his forehead, which he absentmindedly wiped away. Not wanting to be alone, Lyra stayed never more than an arm's length away.

At the opposite end of the hall, unobserved, a creature, seven-feet-tall, tail dragging on the floor, crept stealthily in the direction of the duo. It stopped at the chamber's midpoint, the entrance. For nearly a minute, an intense, fiery-eyed stare locked onto the intruders before the being slunk out the doorway, back into the main tunnel.

For no apparent reason, as if their fear never existed, the worry of the explorers inexplicably vanished. The stockbroker turned to his companion saying, "There is probably no treasure here since the government picked the place clean. We ought to go home now."

Also speaking as if in a daze, the young woman mechanically responded, "I think you are right; anything valuable would have been found long ago. And I don't feel so good. Let us get out of here."

Devoid of further conversation, and with the mannequin-like expressions of two soulless beings, they turned and slogged toward the entrance. Minutes later, far ahead, the cave's opening broke into sight.

Overcome with sickness, Lyra began to stagger. Dizziness and nausea further clouded her thinking. Her body didn't want to function; every step took intense effort, as if a concrete block was attached to each ankle. Even the weight of camera and notepad seemed more than she could carry. Without breaking her shuffling stride, the flashlight and tools of recording, slipped slowly from her hands. Feeling lighter now, she laboriously placed one foot in front of the other, plodding on to freedom.

This time, it was her tennis shoe that snagged on an uneven section of the floor. Lacking energy to stop the fall, she stumbled. One of her knees hit hard. The pain was excruciating. In shock, rocking back and forth, she lay on her side in a fetal position, grasping the injured leg with both hands. Inches from the cave's wall, the young woman's eyes gradually refocused. It was here that rays of incoming light from a crack along the floor, helped her make the discovery.

"Ahhh, oh! Rig...*Rig, look at this!*"

King slowly turned, glancing back as he continued to amble forward. Another fifteen feet and he would be outside, safe. "What?" he asked, without slowing down.

His partner was insistent. "*Come! Look at this.*"

Zombie-like, he could only mumble, "Time to go. Have to get to the top before dark."

"*Rig! Rig, turn around!* I'm talking to you. What's with you? I'm hurt!"

At last able to comprehend, he replied, "Uhah...Okay, I'm coming."

The agony increased. "*Ahhhh, oooh—the pain!* My knee is bleeding. Please help."

As King bent down, and with the blinding speed of a released coiled spring, she slapped him. The force was such it made her fingers tingle and burn. In his semi-crouching position, the stockbroker was caught totally off balance. To him, everything went into slow motion; his body spun and completed its drop.

Stupefied and half-shouting, he yelled, "Damn it! I didn't mean what I said about the Indians. *Chill out! Don't get so violent.* Lord, I believe you; I believe you! Prehistoric people carved these caves with lasers—yeah, that's it—they all had lasers. Really, they all...."

"*Just shut up for a minute*! I may have found your treasure, but we've either been poisoned or mind-printed. We have to work fast!"

He began to sit up, still confused. "You found the treasure? By the way, how did we get from the Great Hall to here? And what's...what's this 'poisoned' or 'mind'-something?...Why do we have to work fast?"

The evening shadows from the cave's entrance provided far less illumination than when they arrived. Taking a flashlight, he shone it on her knee. "Here, let me have a look. It's skinned but nothing serious," he said, taking a handkerchief and gently wiping the blood and dirt away.

"Forget my knee for a moment. You have to see this."

"Huh? What?"

"This. See the crack, this line that runs along where the floor meets the wall? It goes for about four feet. Now look at the cave's opening."

The Ra representative, using the beam of her flashlight, pointed to a number of jagged rocks protruding from the floor at the entrance. She showed how the setting sun cast shadows, giving the visual effect of a row of teeth. To someone outside looking in, the cave's opening might suggest a mouth. Turning back, he watched as she traced an almost invisible, irregular outline on the wall with his flashlight.

Silently, each came to the same conclusion—why the tunnel was left rugged for the first twenty yards. A smooth appearance would have revealed what needed to be kept secret. The builders obviously wanted the door's outline to be hidden in the pattern of nonconforming rocks.

Lyra asked, "See any type of handle or knob?"

Examining the potential opening from about a foot away, he answered, "If they went to this much trouble, they wouldn't show one."

A silence began, lasting but a moment.

"Let's try sliding something around the crack to see where the mechanism is. Maybe we can figure out how to open this thing," he suggested. Digging into his knapsack, the Phoenician pulled out a Hostess Twinkie™.

"Oh great, snack time?"

Ignoring her, Rig took the cardboard from the wrapper and began shoving it around the crack.

"You're not a total loss after all," she murmured.

"That's the closest thing to a compliment you've given me yet. But I am pretty good."

"Don't get your hand stuck back there."

"Huh?"

"The one you're using to pat yourself on the back." Her joking tone abruptly changed. "We'd better hurry." Standing and brushing off the dust, she said, "I'll return in a minute; I'm going to retrieve my things."

King's mind was all aglow. *Wow! The Holy Grail! This must be the same high Carter felt as he broke the seal on Tutankhamen's tomb.* The explorer's mind flashed fantasy pictures similar to those he had seen illustrating the Boy King's burial chamber. Both hands began to quiver as his adrenaline-to-blood ratio tilted nearly off the scale.

Talking over his shoulder while slowly maneuvering the cardboard around the door's asymmetrical curve, he called out, "You're right. The sun's setting; we'll be stuck here in the dark if we don't hurry."

Under her breath, Lyra's reply was so low her companion didn't quite hear. "That may be the least of our worries."

Acoustics magnified her comment, prompting Rig's "What?"

"I agree. We have to hurry."

As he reached the top, the stiff paper snagged. "This could be it! Let me see if it stops at the same place below."

On his hands and knees, an anxious treasure hunter slid his thin probe along the crack abutting the floor. Excitement mounted as he touched a second protuberance an equal distance away from the side as another one at the top. They deduced that if there was a push on the locking mechanism, the wall should swing open…maybe.

Again following the door's outline with her flashlight, Lyra pointed to a slightly worn rock. "How about this?"

Unknown to the pair, the slab was delicately balanced—able to swivel with the slightest tap of a finger. Rig depressed the only stone that seemed somewhat polished. The bolt holding the door slid back. With great force, he threw himself against the slab. It flew open, his momentum propelling him well inside. Landing hard, the Indiana Jones wannabe lay spread-eagle, mouth kissing the dust-covered floor. Smashed in the fall, his flashlight flickered. Two blinks and the beam disappeared. "Damn!"

"You all right?" Lyra called, still standing at the opening.

Sputtering inhaled dirt, the answer was more of a grumble. "Yeah!"

"Then what's wrong?"

"Flashlight's out." Rubbing his shoulder, a prostrate King took stock. "This has been one frickin', painful trip."

The door opened to a large room. A faint orange glow came from a single shaft of light. Rays of the setting sun, shone through a thirty-inch-wide hole in the wall—invisible from the outside, hidden by a bush of sage. At this moment of sunset, the beam crossed the floor, touching what appeared to be a long table. Wiping the dust from his face, the treasure hunter couldn't help but notice the round window-like opening in the wall. His enthusiasm was uncontainable. "Hey! Look! That must be the eye!"

As the dust began to settle, through the haze the remaining flashlight illuminated two ten-foot-tall bronze statues. Guarding the entrance, they resembled the earliest figures depicted in the center mural. Standing on marble pedestals, with arms raised upward and out, they faced each other. Where their hands met, the metal giants created an ominous formal arch.

"Lyra, come here. The table—it's a sarcophagus. Inside should be jewelry and artifacts!" Intoxicated by the promise of wealth, the treasure hunter bolted between the figures, to claim his prize.

"*Arughhh*!" He staggered backward, pushing one of the works of art off its base. Having followed and reflexively jumping aside, Lyra was only brushed as the enormous bronze crashed. An instant later, it was all over, the tall figure ending up leaning against the door.

Doubled over with convulsive pain, King weakly called, "Help! I've been stabbed!"

Crouching, his companion quickly shined her light into every corner. The beam, darting back and forth, revealed no enemy. Cautiously, without moving, she looked for tripwires and a hole in the wall that might house a second projectile.

"Can you stand?"

Still folded in half, he replied, "I…I think so."

Arm around her neck, he hobbled to the rectangular slab. Ordering her partner to lie `facedown, Lyra pulled up his shirt. The earlier blood-dried cut confused her.

"*No, not there!*" The pain intensified. "Over a little."

The victim guided her along a two-inch vertical red line to the right of his spine.

"Just as I thought. You were lucky! A bit to the left, it would have severed your spinal cord and you'd have been crippled."

In agony, he had trouble mouthing the words, "Whaaat is it?"

"Shamans have used this since the beginning of time; it's a kind of energy dart. You would probably call it an invisible spear. Here, lie still. Stop squirming."

The Ra representative gently placed her hands on his back, one on each side of the wound. Leaning over, applying all her weight, she forced her palms together toward the point of pain—a motion similar to extracting a giant sliver. Next, she placed her mouth over the wound and began sucking, periodically turning her head and spitting on the floor. The young woman repeated the process over and over. Suddenly, he groaned. Contorted, his body arched, then fell back.

"Good. I think I got it. Feeling better?"

"There's still a stinging sensation but nothing like it was. What'd you do?"

"Something I picked up in Kenya. You should be all right now."

Finding it hard to move, King rolled over on his side, examining the surface of the table with his fingertips, and giving it a rap with his closed fist, to see if it was hollow. It was. "Just as I thought; this must be some sort of coffin or treasure chamber."

"It's a sacrificial altar," she said, shining her light on its surface. "See these grooves running from where would be the victim's heart area, past the throat, and going all the way to the end?"

Her wounded companion traced one of the two ruts with his finger. "Oh. I thought this carving was simply decoration."

"This is how the blood was channeled to flow to a receptacle on the floor."

Lyra's explanation sent a jolt through the Phoenician's body. Ignoring the psychic wound, he immediately rose to a sitting position. With an energy born of shock, the mind overrode any pain, enabling him to vault completely off the slab.

Growing shadows and only a single flashlight between them, Rig strained to see what mounds of golden goods were possibly piled against the walls. Intently, his eyes followed Lyra's beam as she again scanned all directions. Her body tensed. Free from the distraction of her partner's wound, the young woman now sensed a powerful vibration, one that radiated throughout the room. Her light rapidly swept everywhere—the floor, ceiling…finally stopping at the far wall.

The entire chamber was bare, save for the statues, the table, and cloth-covered objects ensconced in an alcove. But no bulging chest of treasure.

Like a child finding a Christmas tree without presents beneath, Rig's disappointment was overwhelming. No stranger to frustration or pain, Lyra sympathized. She had been hoping her companion's dream was about to be fulfilled. Wallowing in self-pity, the stockbroker's anger flared. Rather than berating himself for running after a fantasy, he voiced irritation. "Damned old bastard. Guess Willie was just full of so much BS."

Seeing with her third eye, the Ra representative adjusted her vision to locate the source of power. Emanating from the ledge, it prompted her to respond, "Not necessarily. Look over there."

Using any convenient pretext, Rig again pressed close to her body. Gazing over his companion's shoulder and once more taking in a hint of perfume, he asked with pseudo-innocence, "Find something?"

Lyra inwardly scolded herself that preoccupation with a partner had overridden years of training; her observations had been far too sloppy. Strenuously refocusing, she now spied two distinct, ethereal colors flowing outward from the wall. Their variations indicated that each was a separate point of energy. In the dimming light she concentrated on the stronger glow that bathed a curiously shaped object in purple light as it rested among the other items. Closer scrutiny showed it to be a connected pair of silver-colored discs, about eighteen inches in diameter, sandwiched together with a half inch of space in between. Through the center, protruding from both sides, was a strange, double-ended, terminating crystal. Adding to its mystery, on one side, around the rim, were arcane symbols.

"Rig, look here!"

Taking the twin objects in both hands, he looked stupefied. "Wonder if these markings mean anything."

A disgusted glance went unnoticed. "Of course they do." Dismay at the idiocy of his question was detectable in her tone.

"How do you know?"

"Think they're just artistic designs?"

From the valley of despair moments before, the treasure hunter now soared over mountaintops of expectation. Since neither was familiar with the object's function or how to translate the writing, they turned their attention to three indentations on the discs' underside.

"Perhaps," she surmised, "these are receptacles for those five-foot-long rods over there against the far wall. Maybe they're used as a tripod."

The more pragmatic of the two, Lyra checked her wristwatch and voiced the urgency of their situation. *They must get back to the rim*. Moving as if in a daydream, the boy with his toy had already tuned her out. Alone with his thoughts, Rig proceeded to place a stick into each of the holes.

While the poles were assembled in their proper alignment, Lyra took several photographs before focusing on the second glow—one emitting a golden light. Her hand reached out, touching a rectangular container, wrapped in an opalescent linen. Opening the lid, they were amazed to find an emerald shaft, stuck through the center of a golden scroll. With surgical precision, King delicately began the unrolling. The flashlight revealed some sort of inscriptive style, different from the one on the discs.

"It's in a Biblical format, but I think it can be translated," she whispered in a tone of reverence.

"For Pete's sake, what is it? Is it like the Dead Sea Scrolls?"

Paying no attention, the expert from Washington slowly began to interpret. *"In the now, before the concept of time, there was impenetrable blackness in every direction...."*

A cold shiver ran down her back; she understood the ramifications of their discovery.

To the stockbroker, any non-business application was of secondary interest; the smell of money was far too enticing. Awestruck, he said, "If these are actual ancient writings, they'll be priceless. Quick, shine the light on this other stuff!"

Frustrated and without control of the flashlight, King was at his companion's mercy. Ignoring the command, Lyra methodically scanned the alcove, lifting another cloth to examine the items beneath. The first to catch her eye was a pendant. At the end of a chain dangled a crystal, and a medallion of unusual amulet design.

Nonplused, the weekend warrior blurted, "Wonder what these are!"

"Power-attunement objects would be my first guess. But I can't fathom what's in those small bottles over there." Removing the plug of one small, cobalt-blue container, and not knowing if its contents were poisonous, she took only a cautious micro-whiff. Her response: *"Fascinating!"*

"What?" he mechanically asked, as fingers continue to skim across the raised markings on top of the discs.

"This liquid, although similar to a perfume, changes your intuitive capabilities. I want to try the rest when we get back."

"Be my guest; I'm into hard assets." Stuffing two more charms and a bracelet into his knapsack, Rig's eyes lit on yet another treasure. *"Wow, look!"* he cried, hefting a thirteen-inch, wand-looking device with a crystal attached to one end.

Taking it from his hand, she offered another expert opinion. "I feel this is some sort of ceremonial object, or maybe a medical laser."

"How do you know?"

"Looks like something I've seen in temples down in the Yucatan. We'll know better after I examine it later."

Light had all but faded from the wall's round opening. With a number of unfamiliar pieces before him, King settled on one that caught his eye—a ring. Slipping it onto his finger, the treasure hunter became too excited to notice the subtle wave of energy rippling throughout his body. Distracted by glitter, he picked up a golden headband resembling a tiara, set with the same stone as that in the ring. Next to it lay two upper armbands, each encrusted with an identical gem.

His announcement radiated ego. "These ought to buy me a rundown castle in Scotland! Maybe Madonna and I can be neighbors."

A moment passed before she spoke. "I've seen drawings of something similar; I think it's a brain-wave modulator. Probably will work better if I put on those armbands. Together, they seem to form an energy triangle, turning the entire body into a kind of transmitter."

"English, girl. English!"

"Whatever they're called," she continued, her eyes rolling back into her head, "they can send and receive distant cosmic wave patterns. Oh, golly…."

"*What?! What?!*"

Lyra fell silent. A blissful look swept over her face.

"What?" He tugged at her arm.

"This is incredible. Just as I thought! It lets you penetrate different vibratory dimensions—maybe into the very heart of the Nous, if you have enough practice. So far, I've only been able to get to the eighth dimension, and that was under laboratory conditions."

"What do you mean, eighth? Last I heard, there were only four or five."

Removing the band from her head, she continued, "Uhhh… no." The Ra representative rubbed her fingers lightly around the curve of the device as she added, "We know of eleven. Some believe there are eighteen, maybe more." Handing it to him, she instructed, "Rig, imagine for a moment being able to peer into the smallest atomic particle and, within that one grain, see an entire universe—in infinitesimal detail. This is the origin of the Hermetic saying, *As above, so below.*"

Overwhelmed, he dismissed her suggestion. With daylight fading, King's only thought now was that they must hurry. "Shine the light here while I put these things away. We can go over the rest of this stuff back on the rim."

Each was quiet for the moment. Especially the entrepreneur, who wondered how to market such strange objects, conceivably worth untold millions. *Lyra better not be planning to turn them all over to some damn antiquities museum!* A sweet silence pervaded the room. The only small sounds were the rustling of their clothes and the Velcro straps being tightened on his knapsack.

A deafening noise shattered the stillness, magnified by the crystal-like resonance of the nearly empty room. Instinctively both flinched, spinning in the direction of the sound. Once more…*Chuunng*!

"What the hell's that?" he shouted as his companion shined the light on the still vibrating source, the gong-sounding statue.

It was clear something was attempting to force its way into the room—banging the door against the leaning bronze.

At the top of her lungs Lyra screamed, *"We're trapped! There's no way out; it's going to kill us!"*

Each time the hinged slab slammed against the hollow bronze, it continued to create a nearly deafening bell-like reverberation.

"Quick! Shine it over there!" he yelled.

Misdirected, the beam failed to catch a scaly arm pulling the door shut for another thrust. They glanced at each other, then back at the statue. *Chuunng*! The ancient work of art moved another half inch. It was obvious that with only several more shoves, the assailant would be in.

The Phoenician screamed, *"My God! What is it?"*

Trembling, frozen in fear, she couldn't answer.

An idea came. "Lyra, quick! Shine the light over here!"

His companion's arm still paralyzed, Rig grabbed her wrist, forcing it to point at the targeted area. Pushing as hard as possible, he bore down on the second statue. It didn't fall as easily as the first. King's mind went blank as a Sampson-like strength, born of adrenaline, surged through his arms. Rocking the work of art back and forth, with one final shove it fell—further blocking the entrance. The rhythmic banging continued.

A loud, indefinable growling came through the door's crack. Although this added statue helped, the thing's progress had only been slowed; a breaching was inevitable…a minute or two at the most.

Trapped in this forty-by-forty-foot dungeon, with no exit, the pair were driven by a single emotion—hysteria. Even if they tried going through the window-eyed opening, the drop was nearly straight down, and they had no rope. The function of the room had become transformed. Fate had placed its seal on the outcome. Each realized…*this was their tomb.*

Stuttering, the Ra representative had a hard time forming words. *"R-R-Rig, what do we do?"*

"I don't know!" he screamed. *"Damn it—I don't have an answer*!"

As the forced entry continued, the treasure hunter ripped the flashlight from his companion's grip. The beam flashed on the door. Once more, timing was slightly off, by only a second they missed sight of the intruder.

Nonplused, his only words were, "*What the…?* What kind of animal is this?"

Waving the flashlight, Rig searched frantically for a solution. Nothing. The walls were cleanly cut—seamless. Except for the statues and table of death, the room was bare. Grasping at straws, he rushed to the alcove, hoping against reason to detect some sort of hollow sound, indicating a hidden panel or trap door. Wildly, the explorer slammed his fist against the stone, only to receive skinned knuckles. *Failure*! Knowing they were doomed, knees buckling, he nearly collapsed, held up only by leaning against the wall.

But then…."*I have an idea!*" he yelled over the incessant noise. "If we can just shove that tabletop over to the statues, it may be heavy enough so the thing won't be able to push the door open."

"And then what—*die of dehydration?*" Her scream filled the room.

The growling and banging grew louder with every thrust of the slab.

Seizing her by the shoulders, he spun her around. *"Look! We've gotta try*!"

Having no other option, they gave the thick tabletop a massive push. Wisdom suggested the slab, resting on the surface, would slide off and be broken in the fall. In fact, he was counting on it; smaller pieces would be easier to carry and stack. To their amazement, instead of separating, the whole altar pivoted. The flashlight revealed a hidden staircase.

Across the room the blocked door was now open a full six-inches. Neither prisoner knew how much longer before the being would enter.

Without hesitation, Lyra, flashlight once more in hand, descended first. One step behind, Rig stopped. Grabbing her again by the shoulder, he pulled her to a halt.

"What on Earth are you doing?"

"*Ahh damn!* I forgot the knapsack and poles. Quick, I need the light."

Against all instinct, it was handed over. Unable to flee, the young woman stood shivering in the darkness—waiting. Having retrieved the treasure, King scurried back, bounding rabbit-like into the hole. The beast, if Rig had turned and pointed his flashlight, would have been seen squeezing through the door's crack.

Starting their descent, he thought out loud, "If this is an escape route, the priests must have had some reverse way of blocking the passage."

Again, King made an abrupt halt, ordering, "Here, follow me!" Changing direction yet another time, he retreated back up the stairs. Hesitantly, slowly, Lyra complied; her feet, having a mind of their own, took but half-steps.

Peering up into the hallowed table, he screamed, "*Hurry, damn it!* I think together we can move this thing back and seal the hole. Look, there are loops attached to the inside, and here are wooden pegs."

Almost clear of the room's door, the creature let out a shriek of frustration. Terror manufactured missing strength as the escaping duo pushed against the heavy table. It slid more easily than its mass would suggest. Inserting the spikes, Rig, while Lyra pointed the flashlight, tried to block any further sideways movement. Goose bumps rose on his arms; only inches away, the creature was violently pounding against the lid. Not knowing if the pegs would hold, their only option was to flee.

Turning, the two disappeared down the stairs, blindly heading into what, they didn't know. Shaking, Lyra let her partner assume the lead. Without ceremony, reaching out, Rig took her hand. Following a short spiraling descent, the tunnel intersected a natural cave.

Few were aware that the region around the Grand Canyon is a honeycomb of underground passages. Rarely do they terminate at the surface. Of those that do, most exit twenty or so miles out into the desert.

The pace of their escape slowed. Exhausted and barely moving, King began to mumble, "It is wrong we took these things. We must leave them here. We must leave...."

"Rig!"

"What?"

"I want you to close your eyes for a moment."

"Why?"

"Just do it."

"Okay, but…."

Again with lightning speed, Lyra's slap caught her companion off guard. He staggered two steps, trying to keep equilibrium.

"*Owww!* Why'd you do that?"

"I was helping. I'll explain later. *Hurry!* Let's get out of here."

Perplexed, he half-yelled, "*Well, damn it, woman!* Don't help me anymore! With friends like you, I don't need enemies."

A few minutes later, he was calm enough to inquire, "What do you think that beast was?"

She ducked giving an answer by reversing the question. "What do *you* think?"

By her tone, the stockbroker knew something wasn't right. He stopped, turned, and issued a challenge. "Hold on a minute. You know, don't you?"

The Ra agent's response was a red herring. "Could be a bear. There are a lot of them around here."

Total disbelief dominated the Phoenician's face, but for once in his life Rigden King, III, decided it was far more important to leave than remain and argue. Unfulfilled, his mood became sullen.

Rounding a corner, the duo were forced to a halt. A cave-in had blocked their path. Luckily, after pushing a few rocks out of the way, there was just enough space at the top to squeeze through. Rig went first. Maneuvering over the rocks, he paused to retrieve the poles and pouch. Crouching on the other side, the light was shined back to ease Lyra's passage. After gingerly crawling through, both started the ten-foot descent to the cavern floor. A loose rock caused her to stumble—the momentum sending King sprawling. The remaining flashlight smashed to the ground.

In the pitch-black, "Lyra…Lyra…you okay?"

"I…I guess so. Let me stand and I'll see…Rig, where's the light?"

His tone was low, just above a whisper. "It's dead. Sure you're okay?"

"Dead?"

"Yeah, *kaput…dead*. Are you hurt?"

"No, I...I think I'm fine."

Panic-stricken, but not wanting to further alarm his companion, only his mind was allowed to scream, *We're trapped! We are going to die!* Their circumstance was beyond desperate—lost, without light, and out of water. On top of everything, his claustrophobia was worse than in the main tunnel—and there, it was nearly unbearable. Unable to see, Rig was in the vise-like crush of suffocation; his lungs barely worked—making it nearly impossible to draw in air.

To him, the outcome was inevitable. The adventurer's imagination flashed a picture. Years hence, someone would stumble across two dust-covered cadavers—empty eye sockets, leathery flesh, and contorted, tooth-gaping mouths...shrieking in silent horror.

Right now, however, he had to deal with a more frightening issue. In the pitch-black, the cavern walls had come alive, and worse...they were moving. Their peristaltic action seemed to be at work—rhythmically contracting—closing in. The mind raced out of control, as more demons of his burning imagination left Hell and flew about freely in his imagination.

Lyra made no sound. Surprised, he assumed that by trusting in her male protector, she was better able to handle this than he. In the dark, a hand reached out, seeking the comfort of his touch. Groping, her fingers rapidly traced the lines of a washboard-hard stomach under her companion's shirt.

Finally speaking, a tremor in her voice betrayed mounting panic. "*What do we do?* The tunnel may be a dead end, and we can't go back."

Allaying fears of his own, Rig demanded his thinking to clear. An idea came. "Lyra, *calm down*! Can you feel where the poles dropped?"

"Yes...I believe so. Why?"

"I've got a couple cans of lighter fluid in my knapsack. We can make a torch."

Still shivering from fright, she responded, "Even so, are you sure we can get out?"

He lied, "Of course. Now feel around for one of those sticks."

Her reply relayed a growing recognition. "You're quite resourceful. I'm impressed. Where'd...where'd you learn all this?"

Unseen by his companion, a look of satisfaction crossed the stockbroker's face as he feigned a British-accented voice. "The name's Bond…James Bond."

"Why do you carry lighter fluid?"

"Quick way to start a fire. Never know when I'll be on a camping trip. It's also the reason I have a first-aid kit, compass, snakebite kit…all sorts of little things."

For cloth to wrap around the pole, he took off his *Carpe Ditus*-logoed T-shirt, cutting it into strips with a pocketknife.

"I've been meaning to ask, what does *Carpe ditus* mean?"

"It's a takeoff on *Carpe diem*—Latin, for 'seize the day.'"

"And *Carpe ditus*?"

"My personal motto…a colloquialism; means, 'Seize the money.'"

Without light, the Wall Street trader couldn't see the disappointment in his partner's expression. Unbeknownst to him, King had just lost all of his newly gained points. Striking a match, he lit the makeshift torch. Once more, the two moved on. Rounding a bend, they gagged as they were met by a foul stench wafting down the tunnel—each nearly overcome with nausea.

In a choking gasp, she asked, "What is that?"

Nearly unable to breathe, he coughed before responding, "Not sure. But it's definitely gross."

Following an "S" twist in the passage, they approached a slender, rickety bridge spanning a narrow chasm. Here the stench was strongest. So much so, it took tremendous control for either not to vomit. With each step, the air grew increasingly putrid. Peering into the crevasse, they saw only darkness—the depth was such that the torch's light could not penetrate its mystery. Halfway across, the Phoenician saturated an extra strip of T-shirt, igniting and dropping the fiery piece into the void. Nothing this day had prepared either for the next sight. At the bottom was a bone yard—a ghastly heap, swollen with human skeletons, bleached by age. Quickly, he lit another, sending it down. Once more, the same scene. Except this time, they could make out the source of the smell—a naked, decomposing, female body with much of its flesh missing.

Landing next to the purple corpse, the flame momentarily illuminated the full scope of the carnage before flickering out. Gripping the rope railing, the two stood in revulsion, neither able to speak. Their horror was abruptly broken by a noise—rocks hitting the cavern floor not far behind.

"Quiet!" Rig ordered.

Hardly breathing, they listened intently. The bridge softly swayed with the shifting of their body weight. It was the same growling they heard on the other side of the door in the sacrificial chamber. The sound was very near, and moving closer.

"It must have gotten into the passage," Lyra croaked, her words punctuated by fear. "*It's at the caved-in area! This flame won't protect us, and we don't know where we are or how far to the surface…or even if this has an exit!"*

Mind churning for a solution, King commanded, "*Here, grab the torch!"*

Having maneuvered his companion to the other side, the explorer proceeded to cut the ropes holding the bridge in place. Neither gave thought to the conclusion that if ahead lay a dead end, they'd just bought a one-way ticket.

As the linked planks fell toward the opposite side, Lyra exclaimed, *"Run! We've got to get out of here!* Maybe it can jump."

After they went a few paces, the torch sputtered and went out. Distracted, Rig hadn't been paying attention. He fumbled in the blackness, feverishly wrapping another strip around the end of the pole. A loud, bone-rattling cry came from somewhere close. The being had reached the chasm. Doused with lighter fluid, the torch was relit. Her hand in his, the two scurried off in a broken gait. The uneven cave floor made running difficult. From out of the darkness, the beast's howl grew louder. Its unearthly, piercing sound echoed everywhere, drenching the pair in terror.

Had it gotten over? each wondered. Stopping to find the answer was out of the question.

The tunnel forked. Lyra ordered, "*This way!"*

Her partner didn't argue. Wild with fear, they were practically running. The chamber widened, narrowed, then expanded. The climb became steep. Much to their relief, the screams behind them seemed to be subsiding. *Maybe,* each hoped, *It was still stranded on the other side.*

Passing a small, underground waterfall, Lyra knelt, scooping up water from the turquoise-colored pool. The flickering torch cast a romantic ambiance. Unexpectedly, Rig gave her wrist a quick, forceful push.

"Why'd you do that?" The anger in her voice was softened by a parched throat.

"Sorry—try to hold out a little longer. You never know in Arizona; a lot of the desert water carries deadly levels of arsenic."

"But I'm thirsty."

"It's up to you, but many a miner has died this way. Case in point—look over there. Those are animal bones."

"Rig! Animals! The surface!"

At the edge of light, the torch's glow revealed steps neatly carved into a rising passageway, partially hidden in the farthest corner. The discovery moved both to ecstatic shouts.

As they ascended, the air took on a different quality. Maybe it was due to their reprieve from death, but the treasure hunter noted that the higher they rose, the sweeter the smell. Night came early to the shadowed bottom of the Grand Canyon. On the rim, it arrived more slowly. Straining, each attempted to glimpse the end of the tunnel and the first signs of sunset.

King needed to stop and catch his wind. Not breathing hard, Lyra laughed to herself before announcing, "You know, age is strictly a figment of the imagination. There really is no reason to grow older." He gasped for air while the female, exuberant about exiting, chattered on. "I find it amusing how people believe their lifespan is determined by this planet revolving around some other rock. Aging is simply a program made up by your personal belief system."

Plodding on, not answering, the broker continued puffing, mumbling, "My God, now she's Deepak Chopra!"

"Think of it this way," she blithely continued. "Most of man's cellular structure regenerates every three months. That means your body becomes renewed four times a year. So whatever picture we hold of ourselves, the atoms mobilize to fit that mental image; when we change our beliefs, the physical form has to follow. In fact, this has been scientifically documented by the medical community; often when a person with multiple-personalities has switched from one identity to another, some people have instantly changed eye color, shoe sizes...even weight."

Worn out, winded, King didn't want any more of her metaphysical claptrap. The weekend warrior had a rough enough time gathering his next breath, let alone carrying on a conversation. "Lyra, I…I can't talk. Let's do this later. Hey, there's light!"

With the tunnel's end in sight, at last they felt the danger lifting. But then…a high-pitched buzzing came from their right. Like an echo, it was met by an identical answer from the left. The two froze. A den of rattlesnakes! And they were past a point of no return. Rig's eyes darted back and forth, looking for an escape. The walls here were narrow and roughly hewn. Of itself, that would be okay. However, several more vipers were near, poised, coiled on the jutting rocks to each side. From the sound of it, more lay ahead, basking in the fading sun. The noise became louder. The growing cacophony left little doubt that this was a massive colony.

Instantly, the intruders realized the seriousness of their entrapment. In Arizona, seldom does anyone die from a single snakebite. But with this many potential strikes, death would be certain.

Torch in hand, Rig whispered, "Here, take it." He tipped the flame downward, tilting the back end of the shaft upward for her to grasp. Hands now free, in ultra-slow motion, he removed the knapsack. His tone was hushed. "Okay, now give it back."

From the faint light of the cave's opening, King strained to see if there was any possible way of maneuvering to safety. The mind was emphatic in its answer, shouting, *No!*

Without warning, another *whrrrrring* sound came from an outcropping within a few feet of Lyra's head. Turning ever so slowly, she strained for a better view while crying weakly, "*Riiiiig!*"

Twisting just his upper body, he waved the torch as a distraction. Enraged, the snake buzzed even louder. Focused on the flame—a strike buried four fangs into the fiery ball of cloth. Singed, the reptile released, fell, and retreated into the shadows. Swiveling back, Rig spotted yet another coiled obstacle on the path. Completely surrounded, both knew that with just one bite, jerking reflexes of the victim would turn the air into a flurry of fangs. And the viper a few feet ahead was likely to be the one that set it all in motion.

Cautiously, he lowered the tip of the torch. Sensing movement, the reptile flew at the heat, burying his fangs deeply into the pole. Writhing, the snake remained attached—a victim of its own anger. Strangely, defying all odds, this did not trigger the colony's onslaught. Burned to death, twisting ceased. Its limp corpse dangled from the rod.

Acting as a shield, the knapsack was now waist-high. Unfortunately, that only blocked from one angle. With such limited protection, Rig was frantic in his attempt to find the best way of saving Lyra.

As sunlight faded, darkness was within degrees of becoming absolute. Adding to their problems, again the sputtering torch was about to go out. And with trespassers in their midst, the reptiles' agitation was mounting. It's intensity was such, the air carried an engulfing sense of hatred.

In a nearly inaudible voice, he spoke, "We have only one small chance. Run as fast as possible—on three. Ready?"

Lyra pled in a low, yet defiant tone, "*No! Don't!* That's certain death. I need you to trust me."

"What?"

"Trust me!"

"Oh Lord, what now?" The furrows on King's brow deepened.

"You're radiating fright. That's irritating them more. We have to do two things. Begin by focusing with everything you've got; see yourself filled and surrounded by a blinding white light."

"Woman, you're crazy!" he growled barely above a whisper.

"For once in your life, shut up and listen! If you run, you'll be committing suicide. Let go of all fear, every last fragment. Then force yourself to feel love for the snakes."

"You're insane!"

"*Don't argue!* I can calm them. But if you don't do this, we're dead."

"We're dead meat anyway."

"*Be quiet!* Concentrate on those two things and walk... *slowly*."

To the stockbroker, what Lyra suggested was not only counterintuitive, but seemed beyond asinine. *Dumb woman's gone nuts. We've got to make a dash. Maybe one of us will make it… but I doubt it.*

As if reading his mind, she responded, "If you're thinking about running, that'll be our death warrant. Look, if you can't let go of fear, flood your mind with pictures of sex. For you, that shouldn't be too difficult."

The colony's increasing agitation had reached a virulent crescendo. Rig's inner voices pled for some other option… any option. The dilemma was, he couldn't leave Lyra. To bolt would mean her certain death, although using his companion's stupid method, it was already guaranteed; they'd both die in unspeakable agony. In his mind, this triggered another picture—them writhing in pain, snakes attached to their faces, arms and legs, all pumping venom.

The more mature voice went off in his head: *I guess we die; nothing else to do but go along with her harebrained scheme. Life's a bitch!* He paused, took a deep breath, and was about to start. Then, mysteriously, as if by mutual consent, a wave of calm began spreading over the den. The loud buzzing of rattles diminished to only three or four. The businessman's analytical mind assigned this to the fact that light had nearly disappeared.

"*Go!*" she whispered. He didn't move. Nudging his back, she issued another order: "*Now! Slowly!*"

The torch's flame flickered and was gone. Holding his breath, King gingerly took a first step. Proceeding in ultra-careful motion, he anticipated the needle-sting of fangs to begin at any moment. Driven by caution, the most minor movement was painstakingly calculated—such as ignoring the stinging sweat flowing into his right eye, which he didn't dare rub. Like a shadow, Lyra was right behind. Finally, out of breath, more from fear than exertion, the two emerged from between several gigantic boulders.

The Phoenician rejoiced. "*All right!*"

While pausing to calm their nerves, Lyra coyly asked, "What were you concentrating on as we were walking out?" He looked sheepish. "Racecars."

A smile formed on the young woman's lips. She knew better.

CHAPTER V

YIN and YANG

There is something magical, almost tangible, that occurs during the fleeting last moments of twilight. But that time had just passed. A few minutes before, a full moon rose. Breaking free of the horizon, the orb shifted the area's vibrational pattern, blending its soft power into the desert night. An indiscernible cloud of dust magnified the luminescent body, giving the sphere a bloated look—the illusion of being double its actual size. This filled the landscape with such brightness that one could almost read without the aid of additional light.

From the position of the moon, the weary adventurers knew in which direction to head. Their truck was only a half-mile away. A rabbit scurried unseen out of the sagebrush near Lyra's feet. Emotionally and physically spent, the two proceeded in silence.

Thinking about the stockbroker's fixation on wealth, the Ra representative wrestled with a nearly impossible problem: How to persuade someone so blinded by greed to set aside personal gain and share these artifacts with humanity? She glanced at her Wall Street companion as he walked, mumbling, lost in the calculation of a perceived fortune.

Lyra remembered it was but two short days ago that Rig came bounding into that hospital room. Separately, she and the stockbroker had just been informed that William Jennings, or Willie J. as he was known, was about to make his transition to the hereafter. At the patient's request, each had been summoned to the dying man's bedside.

This patient was no ordinary man. Among that strange breed of lone miners who still roamed the Old West, the crusty ol' dog stood out like a page from history—a throwback to the Gold Rush of the 1849.

Despite today's broad media coverage, few outside his small circle knew of the unusual lifestyle of this group. While not publicized, disputes, disappearances, and even murders were still quite common in the Arizona hills. Whether going for gold or silver, every rock hound believed he was on the verge of discovering the mother lode. Most carried a gun—still pulled when tempers flared. This paranoia was the core of a hard-rock miner, a part of his mental makeup. Willie J., with his Colt revolver always strapped to his side, was no exception.

Suspicious by nature, Jennings always liked keeping to himself—coming into town usually only once a month. From his shack, twenty miles southwest of Flagstaff, the desert rat could search for gold far from prying eyes. And yet, this seclusion did not leave him uninformed. Ever resourceful, he ran an electrical cord from his pickup truck, through the chain-link fence and into his cabin window. Comforted by television and a radio, the miner remained versed in current events, yet safe from the outside world.

Looking at the man, one would assume he didn't have two quarters to rub together. Nothing was further from truth. With meager expenses and never paying the IRS, the crafty codger had salted away over $500,000—hidden at several locations—just in case claim jumpers decided to use torture.

But during the previous three months, what started out as a minor chest pain was keeping him from sleeping nights. Without insurance or any living relatives, he determined to cover medical expenses by changing his cache into something more liquid.

On this morning's trip to the Grand Canyon, Rig recounted to Lyra that it was one of those chance meetings the day he found the old coot, stranded high up on that mountain road. There Jennings was, sitting on the tailgate of a broken-down truck, smoking a pipe, analyzing his predicament.

As Willie J. entered Rig's vehicle, the Phoenician noticed his dusty passenger turning around to the back seat, suspiciously taking note of the shovel, pick, and lumps beneath a blanket. In these hills, you didn't accuse someone of something unless you were prepared for the ramifications. Knowing this, Jennings took a cautious tack. Rather than suggesting his driver was illegally looting nearby Indian graves, the wary hitchhiker nonchalantly started talking about people who invest in gold bullion and rare coins. Circling slowly, he then casually broached the primary topic by suggesting that a friend might possibly want to acquire Indian artifacts.

Woven into this conversation, the prospector asked what his chauffeur did for a living. That opened the door. Bouncing along on the two-hour trip through the mountains, the passenger was treated to a seminar on Wall Street power. Actually, Rig was simply passing time, humoring the cantankerous old fart. For Willie J., though, it was more than a blessing—it was an entrée into a world he'd never known. By the time the stockbroker had finished his impromptu pitch, the Dow Jones seemed an intelligent place in which Mr. Jennings should temporarily park his money.

Taking pity but also enjoying the flavor of his wizened passenger, King offered what he assumed must have been the man's first hot meal in months. Four bourbons later, the tight-lipped miner loosened up. He confided his need to secretly launder nuggets into cash, and was open to investing the proceeds in stocks.

Not until this very moment had Rig imagined the disheveled-looking bum could ever qualify as a client. However, within thirty seconds, the Wall Street veteran had calculated where to invest and how to churn his new acquaintance's funds. Forgetting his buyer's needs, the plan to flip Willie's money in and out of the market would assuredly get enough commissions to buy that Porsche the broker had been eyeing. Not that he wanted his client to lose his money. But like many in the equities field, profit for the investor was usually a secondary issue. Thus, similar to the tick-bird on the back of a rhinoceros, Rig began a lopsided, albeit symbiotic relationship.

According to King, it seemed like only an hour ago that he got a call about Willie J. being terminally ill. Racing to the patient's room, the stockbroker clutched a pad of stock powers. He had hoped his facile tongue could convince the dying man to transfer ownership of his entire portfolio as a final act of friendship. *Since there are no living relatives,* Rig reasoned, *what could be the harm?* Turning the corner and opening Willie's door, the anxious broker slammed into a wall of shock. A young woman, who didn't appear to be a nurse, was leaning over the patient. Immediately King made a logical and alarming assumption—she had to be some long-lost relative.

Not so. For the past week, Lyra had been in the Southwest, conducting research. Her East Coast nonprofit Foundation had assigned her the task of tracking down the validity of an Apache legend—a supposed major tunnel complex somewhere in the Superstition Mountains.

While lying in his hospital bed, Willie J. had heard of her organization from a radio interview with the Foundation's director on Art Bell's "Coast to Coast AM"—a talk show dedicated to exploring such offbeat subjects as paranormal phenomena, government conspiracies, space aliens, and other unconventional topics. From Washington, D.C., a Ra staff member notified their field scout that while in Arizona, she had a second task to perform; one of Mr. Jennings's nurses called, saying her patient possessed vital information about some hidden cave.

Probably a blind alley, Lyra assumed, *but I'm supposed to check it out.*

Arriving at his side, she found the dying miner barely able to speak. Chest pains and the coughing of blood had graduated into something far worse. His voice was low, unsteady. It was at the precise moment that she bent down, trying to understand his words, that Rig burst into the room.

Bristling, the intruder jockeyed to find out just what this female's relationship was with his client. Devoid of respect for the dying, the broker blurted, "Excuse me, Miss. My name is Rigden King, III; and you are…?"

His arrogant demeanor and chaotic vibration instinctively set off the young woman's alarms. Underlying the superficial cordiality, a noticeable tension permeated the room. Each stared, sizing up the other.

"My name is Lyra. I'm here from the Ra Foundation. Are you family?"

With a wave of relief, King answered her query with a return question. "Then I take it, you're not a relative?"

"No. And by your response, you are…?"

"Actually, I'm Mr. Jennings's financial advisor. I've come with a paper for him to sign. Could you give us a minute… alone?"

An eyebrow raised, Willie's female guest was suspicious of both this person's timing and his intent. Nonetheless, she acquiesced. "No problem."

As the emissary from Washington arose, the old man made a feeble gesture with the only arm still under his command. Obediently, she sat back on the edge of the bed. Again the dying patient motioned. This time it was meant for Rig. Dutifully, he took his station on the opposite side. Unable to speak loudly, primarily using wrist and finger movements, Jennings signed for each to lean closer. Like a fish out of water, the old man gasped for air; the end was near.

With great labor and halting speech, a twisted tale of lost treasure unfolded. Less than a year ago, Willie J. had come upon the prostrate figure of a Piute medicine man, Archie Madbear, up on the north rim of the Grand Canyon. Out searching for eagle nests on a scorching July afternoon, the aged Indian had fallen, breaking both legs. Four days he had been lying there, on the verge of expiring, in the high-desert sun.

Blinded, tongue swollen, the elder lacked even the life force to form the word for water. Setting up camp, the miner nursed him, until it was evident Madbear was going to live. Eventually, Willie was able to leave long enough to hike back and bring his truck closer. In thankfulness for saving his life, the Piute confided a vision he had during the ordeal.

The Indian's spirit had traveled to a nearby cave. To Madbear, it was obvious the tunnel had been created by the Ancient Ones—because of the wall drawings, and that he saw it could be used to travel to far parts of the world. Moreover, he intuited that within the subterranean passages were some sort of great riches.

Hearing these words the broker eagerly leaned closer, becoming increasingly frustrated as the story's details grew incoherent. According to the miner, to get to the treasure, one must go through the right cheek, and behind some sort of eye.

The two listeners looked up and across the bed, seeing if the other made any sense of the story.

With attention split, Rig strained, trying to figure out what the hell this girl was really doing there. After all, he reasoned, *I'm Willie's friend, sort of; the entire treasure should rightfully be mine.*

A crucial moment: Hacking, the dying man whispered, "Get the article, 'Explorations in The Grand Canyon,' *Phoenix Gazette*, April 5, 1909." Wanting to say more, the patient's lips moved, but no words formed. For a second, his body trembled. At last, his mouth remained still, his eyes glazed.

The buzzer beside his bed went off. William Jennings's monitor in the hall nurses' station flat-lined. Over the loudspeaker an urgent voice cried, "*Code blue! Code blue—stat!*" In half a minute, an emergency team arrived. With choreographed precision, the beehive activity became intense. Defibrillator in place, electrodes were pressed to the dead man's chest and the warning, "*Clear*," shouted. The jolt made the miner's body contract, momentarily rising before dropping back. No response. The doctor again bellowed "*Clear!*" Several times the process was repeated. The outcome was the same. At last, a long-needled syringe was readied. With eyes staring at the ceiling, there wasn't even a flinch as the pointed metal penetrated deep into the patient's nonpumping organ. Again, the defibrillator. The standard cry. Once more, nothing.

The doctor and nurses feverishly continued working over the still-warm corpse. It was too soon to give up. Finally, head bent down in resignation, the physician slowly took a step back. Ignored and away from the focused commotion, no one noticed Lyra, turning toward an unoccupied corner of the room. Making a small, farewell wave toward the seemingly empty wall, she smiled gently as Willie slipped away.

Out in the hall, Rig paused for a moment. On the one hand, he was exasperated at not being able to transfer the miner's estate to himself, but at the same time he felt elation at hearing the secret of a fabulous fortune.

His nemesis approached, saying, "Since we seem to be into this together, do you want to look up the newspaper article to see what Mr. Jennings was referring to?"

The comment shook the broker back to reality. His mind sped in several directions, trying to find the most efficient way of cutting a new enemy out of the equation. Feigning disinterest, he replied, "I don't know. Did you really believe all that garbage? The guy sounded delirious…at least to me."

The ploy was too thinly veiled. "Mr. King, I am not interested in your treasure, if there really is one. As a representative of the Ra Foundation, I'm in Arizona solely to investigate various caves—nothing more, nothing less."

"That's fine, but I really don't need a fifth wheel tagging along, especially a female. It can get pretty dangerous out there."

Annoyed by his attitude, the D.C. visitor's winsome look vanished. Clenched teeth made bones on both sides of her cheeks protrude. "*Forget the lecture, Sparky!*"

"Name's Rig."

"*Whatever!* Look, I've seen danger from the jungles of South America to the deserts of Mongolia. And believe me, this cave isn't anything new."

Walking toward the elevator, Rig's pit-bull mentality continued trying to argue the stranger out of going. Momentarily outgunned by the woman's logical responses, he had little room in which to maneuver. Thus began their first verbal scirmish. As the elevator door opened on the ground floor, the heated exchange raged on.

Lyra played her final ace. "You want a treasure; I only want to fill out my report and hopefully add some notes to my screenplay."

"How wonderful."

"Don't get smart, Mr. King. I'm going to see that cave with or without you. Because of the terrain, it will be better if we go together. But I'm prepared to proceed alone, if need be. However, I'm warning you—don't try to exclude me, or by tomorrow I will plaster this information all over the Internet: before sunset, you'll have hundreds crawling over your precious little pile of gold. *Got the picture?*"

In defeat, he sighed a feeble, "Okay."

"Now," continued Lyra, "I suggest we go to the library and look up this article Mr. Jennings was talking about."

Rig's bachelor mind was working overtime. Attempting to appear nonchalant he suggested, "I don't know where you're staying, but since we're joined at the hip and my apartment's on the way, why don't we park your car at my place and go in mine?"

Shooting him a side-glance, the answer came cautiously. "If you realize this is strictly a business arrangement—nothing more."

Caught off guard by her directness, the salesman forged an insincere smile, throwing in a "Fine, no problem" but thinking, *You're not my type, anyway.*

Driving along, Rig mulled, *There's something off-key about this girl.* His intrigue stemmed from something he couldn't quite put a finger on. The only thing that vaguely equated with his feeling was a mustang mare he once saw, trotting across the desert—the wind whipping through her mane, head and tail buoyed by pride rather than arrogance. Roaming free, this majestic animal was simply in touch with who and what she truly was. Unused to being on equal footing with such a female, King found himself caught off stride—although he would never admit this point, especially to himself.

Both cars pulled into his complex. The Ra representative parked while he suggested the need to briefly pop into his condo—to drop off a briefcase and change out of his suit.

Going up the stairs, he paused and asked, "Why are you smiling?"

"Oh, I was just looking at the numbers on your door."

"So? It's twenty-two. What about it?"

Stepping through, the answer was casual. "Nothing. Mine's thirty-three."

"Are we in competition about addresses? What's the big deal?"

"No, no. It…uhh, has nothing to do with that. There's no competition, really. I was just looking at the synchronicity of your being a twenty-two and mine a thirty-three, from a…well, shall we say a Chaldean mathematical perspective. It's really not important. Can we go?"

With Rig in the bedroom, Lyra glanced about. The decor: eclectic. A samovar converted into a lamp cast light on a French-cuffed shirt thrown over the back of a Queen Anne-style chair. On the floor by the couch, a half-empty bottle of imported cabernet next to a Wolfgang Puck pizza box. Lid open, it covered a sauce-stained *Wall Street Journal* obscuring part of an Italian necktie, dirty silk socks, and a half-eaten banana. Over the couch on the wall, a fake Matisse. On the coffee table, an empty Turkish coffee cup and yesterday's Phoenix newspaper—August 5, 2004. "Reasonable taste," she murmured, concluding with, "but the housekeeping skills of an orangutan."

The phone rang.

"Lyra, could you answer that? It should be John from the office."

"Hello. King residence. May I help you?"

On the other end came an amazed, then demanding, female voice. "*Who is this?*"

"My name is Lyra. Are you calling for Mr. King? I can get him."

The reply was less than warm. Its chilling tone, however, had little impact upon Rig's guest—although Lyra was quite playful by nature. Normally, she would wait until a friendship bloomed before revealing that aspect of her personality. Then again, Rigden King, III, was an egotistical balloon just begging to be popped.

Covering the receiver with her palm and in a foreign accent, she called out, "Riggy? Oh, Riggy?"

The stockbroker stuck his head out of the bedroom while still fastening his shirt. "What's this Riggy thing? Is it John?"

Continuing in her foreign impersonation...."No. I do believe it is Darla, asking for her Riggy. What do you wish I should tell her?"

Shirt still unfastened, King made a mad dash for the phone. Stumbling over his words, he began unleashing lies as flimsy as those used by Clinton when he swore, "I did not have sexual relations with that woman," or George W. Bush, when he emphatically stated that he didn't really know Kenneth Lay. (The first, simply a mincing ploy used by most post-pubescent males, and easily exposed by anyone with a dictionary. Dubya's lie was to surface more slowly; he didn't really know Kenneth Lay. (The first, simply a mincing ploy used by most post-pubescent males, and easily exposed by anyone with a dictionary. Dubya's lie was to surface more slowly; "Kenny Boy," the ex-head of Enron, was not only one of George W's largest financial campaign supporters going back to 1996, but whose personal jet was used throughout the 2000 Presidential election. Seemingly predestined for conviction, Lay became the subject of many hushed conversations in the dark corners of Washington's upscale restaurants; where D.C. Belt Insiders took odds that the dangerous canary might mysteriously die before singing—a throttling that would stop the forcing of a Presidential Pardon.)

After a few agonizing minutes of slippery explaination, the Lothario put the phone down, wiping sweat from his brow. He shot a stabbing glance at his guest, who could no longer contain her mischievous laughter.

Rig's mock appreciation mingled with mild anger. "Thanks! You're a big help."

Still in her accent, "Anytime, Riggy," she cooed, all the while smiling. "Believe me, anytime."

As they left, the Wall Street trader saw a way of impressing this strange, alluring woman. On the verandah, he made an exaggerated gesture of picking up and stroking a neighbor's Himalayan cat, jostled from peaceful sleep in a flower box.

"Like cats, do you?" she asked.

"All my life."

"Know much about them?"

With his usual arrogance, the answer was a smug, "Of course."

"Then you agree that the round, hairless spot on the back you're patting is the classic symptom of ringworm."

King's hands instantly pulled apart, leaving the bewildered feline momentarily suspended in midair.

Lyra again chided, "And of course, you already know that an exposed person should immediately scrub with soap and hope they don't get infected, right?"

She hadn't got past the 'scrub with soap' part before her companion was fishing keys from his pants pocket, inserting one into the door. Trying her best to remain serious, a Cheshire-like grin began to illuminate an angelic face.

But all that now seemed like a very long time ago. Covered with dust, Rig tried to recall where he put his spare shirt, as the emotionally and physically drained explorers trudged toward their vehicle. Lyra sighed with relief, seeing it was still parked where they left it. Dehydrated and on the verge of collapse, they'd have a long, hard trip back to Phoenix.

Just before reaching the Bronco, inspiration struck the Ra representative—a plan that would enable Rig to disseminate these devices throughout the world, rather than letting them be under the control of the government or corporate giants. Casting with a fly fisherman's skill, making only a small ripple on his consciousness, she deftly placed her proposal before the unsuspecting explorer. Deep in thought about his treasure's value, Rig mistook her words for his own. In a flash, he rose to the bait.

"That's it! Whatever these things are, I'll file patents and license the rights. Wow! This way, I not only make even more money through their marketing, but still also retain ownership. What an idea! Am I brilliant or what?"

CHAPTER VI

POISON ARROWS

With few signposts, desert roads can be confusing, especially at night. Used unrelentingly by weekend four-wheelers, they continuously crisscrossed. Resembling the entanglement of spaghetti on a plate, the options were confusing. To worsen matters, the moon had risen to a point where true east was strictly a guess. Handicapped by darkness, finding a quick way back might be nearly impossible.

Moreover, on this particular evening, unclouded but heavy desert air held an ominous pall. Pricked by intuition, Lyra sensed the negativity of something or someone—and that they were its target.

Frowning slightly, she glanced at Rig, knowing that he too had the ability to be aware of such phenomena—indeed, everyone did. Most simply suppressed their innate abilities. This young woman, however, had been trained to know that *all thought is power*—a force in motion. Every idea, be it good or evil, was a form of prayer radiating outward. Without a specific objective, it went forth in all directions. Aimed, it was a bullet that could seek out anyone, anywhere.

"Rig, something's out of sync. I can feel it."

Shrugging off her worry as some sort of post-traumatic shock, he replied smugly, "Hey, lighten up; it's just your imagination. Your Foundation got its tunnel information; you have some movie ideas; I found my treasure. Frankly, it can't get any better than this. So, mellow out for once!"

"Stop the car for a second."

"Why?"

"Please, just stop."

He slammed the vehicle to a halt. Momentarily, the engulfing thick cloud of dust made visibility nil. There was a period of silence before the demand, "All right, all right, damn it. What now?"

"Take a second. Try to feel it. Let go of your thoughts."

"Feel what?"

"Make your mind blank. Pretend you're a balloon, expanding both mentally and physically, beyond the horizon."

"Ah, do I have to?"

"*Please*, just for a moment."

After the stressful events of the day, the treasure hunter was not only tired but exasperated. Running out of patience, he barked, "Come on, Lyra. This is stupid."

"*Pleeease*, try it!"

With a heavy sigh he agreed. "All right, how?"

"Take a deep breath. As you let it out, clear your mind; don't think of anything. Let your body react, not your brain."

Believing it was a waste of time, he complained, "Is this really necessary? I mean...."

Emphatic, she pleaded more strongly. "*Please!* Yes, it is important and it'll take but a moment."

Bending to the emotional demand, her companion reticently agreed. "Okay, one minute. Then we go. Right?"

"Only for a minute."

Doubting, Rig made a minimal effort at following her instructions.

"Feel anything—anything different?"

"Oh, I don't know. My skin tingles. It's...it's hard to explain. It's like...oh, never mind."

"No. Go on. You're doing fine."

"Well, it's as if my body's gone electric. I feel a heavy, prickly sensation all around, or something like that. I don't know what I'm saying. It's...."

"That's it. I wanted you to feel it, too. Now you understand we have to get out of here—*fast!* They're still after us. *We have to hurry!*"

"Wait a minute. What's this, 'They're still after us'? 'They,' who?"

"I'll explain as we go, but we have to leave here immediately."

Unknown to both, for several minutes, two glowing dots had been hovering eight thousand feet overhead, camouflaged by the star-dotted sky. As the vehicle began to move, the blips, resembling twin meteorites, streaked across the horizon, finally disappearing from sight.

King wasn't sure what Lyra was referring to by 'they,' but reasoned, *Guess I can find out on the way.*

Hurrying at thirty-five miles per hour, dodging toaster-sized rocks and deep ruts while also maneuvering through washed-out arroyos took tremendous concentration. As the minutes passed, his mind kept churning. Reaching critical mass, King exploded. "*Damn it, Lyra!* I want to know...*now!* There's a lot you're not telling me."

Before the words had left his mouth, another crucial decision loomed as once more the road forked. Skidding to a stop, they were surrounded by another billowing dust cloud.

She spoke first. "I'm being told to go to the right."

"What do you mean, being told?"

"Uh, I mean, I think the right fork is the most logical choice, based upon the position of the moon. And if I remember correctly, that's how we came in."

"*No!* We're going to the left."

No changing a Taurus's thinking. They went his way. For fifteen minutes his companion sat quietly, more in fear than anger. As they came over a rise, one hundred yards in the distance the moonlight revealed a group of thirteen figures standing around a fire.

"Hey—a bunch of campers. They can give directions."

"I don't think so. This...this doesn't feel right."

"*Right—shmight!* I'm only asking the way to the highway. This isn't the big city; it's safe out here."

Adamant, she voiced her opinion more strongly. "I just don't like it!"

"Look, I've been all over the Southwest and never had a problem."

Stopping the vehicle, Rig stuck his head out the window… only to be met by dead silence. Within moments, the sleeping desert was shaken, jolted awake by a heartbeat sound—the booming cadence of Indian drumming. By unseen command and in mysterious synchronization, a ghostly dozen begin dancing counterclockwise around the fire. They appeared to float, swaying slowly, moving to the rhythmic tinkling of ankle bells. Starting in a falsetto voice, the lead singer wailed, speaking in an unearthly dialect. The others followed a half-beat later, lending an eerie echo to his words.

"Rig, I'm really frightened. Let's turn around and go back. I'm sure we can find our way out by ourselves. Please, roll up the window and let's go. We've got to get out of here!"

"*No!* We wait."

The Ra representative recognized the familiar, dead look in her companion's eyes. Worse, he was once again conversing in that flat monotone. With no other option, she raked the back of his right hand with her comb. The scraping was so hard, blood began to flow.

"*Yeeoow*! That hurts. *Damn it, woman!* What the hell are you doing? You mad at me personally, or just psycho?"

"Rig, quick! Roll up your window. *Now!*"

Shaking his head in disbelief, he began to comply. *This is one strange girl,* he thought. *I've got to ditch her as soon as—*

Without warning, the SUV was rocked with tremendous force. Slamming against the driver's door was the biggest wolf either had ever seen—twice normal size. Lyra let out a piercing scream as the beast forced its snapping jaws and one paw through the last few inches of the driver's-side window. Hearts beat wildly as the two instinctively dove toward the passenger door.

There was a strange insanity to the canine's lunges. Its eyes burned with unfathomable zeal—something born of pure evil. Accompanying the creature's frenzy was a high-pitched whine—a sound that, like a paper cut to a finger, sliced the explorers' souls. Again and again, the gigantic animal tried thrusting its head into the crack.

The beast's breath flooded the cabin, a steamy stench somewhere between putrefied meat and sulfur fumes. Even from Lyra's side, there was no way of escaping the rank smell. Once more, the animal's body slammed against the window.

"*It's going to break!*" she screamed.

Rig hit the gas. The vehicle surged.

Hysterically, Lyra cried, "*No!* We have to turn around. We're heading straight for them!" She was referring to the circle of dancers who remained absorbed in their night magic.

Driving off the road and making a wide loop, King attempted to retreat in the direction from which they came. Bouncing over rocks, dodging cacti, and hitting jackrabbit holes, top speed could only be sixteen miles per hour. His head smacked repeatedly against the roof as the vehicle bounced uncontrollably. At this reckless yet relatively slow pace, the animal ceaselessly kept up its attack. Steering with one hand and pushing buttons with the other, he finally managed to fully close his window. Beyond busy, neither noticed the red drool smeared on the glass. In a frenzy, the creature had bitten its tongue. But the smell of blood, even if it was the beast's own, only increased its demonic ferocity.

Glancing to the side and knocking over a Saguaro, King mumbled, "*Oh God, no!*"—his subconscious attempt at keeping cactus tines from puncturing the tires.

Bewildered, he added, "*Did…did you see that?* Damn thing's gotta be rabid! And what about its size? The thing's monstrous."

But now the beast had disappeared from view. Assuming the animal had retreated back into the desert, the driver eased off the gas. From out of nowhere, it sailed over the SUV, landing on Lyra's side. The four-by-four immediately sped up, but to no avail. As if possessed, time and again the thing hurled itself against the glass.

Catching his breath, Rig stuttered, "That's…that's…My God! That's impossible. How could it do that? Jump over us, I mean."

With the wolf slamming against her door, Lyra was too frightened to speak. Leaning into her protector, who was barely able to keep the vehicle on the road, she finally managed to cry, "It's a…a skinwalker, not a wolf."

"Skinwalker? What the hell's a skinwalker?"

Again the road split. This time, where they turned was not as important as keeping the animal from crashing through, and getting inside. With the creature's mega-size and its powerful assaults, driver and passenger were both terrified and amazed a window hadn't yet shattered.

As the barrage continued, the Ra representative managed a brief, semi-screaming response, "Shape…shape-shifter!"

Her companion was too busy to ask for clarification, not that Lyra would have been able to respond. Had she, it would be said that some people can change physical form—shape-shifting themselves into wolves and birds, as well as assorted other animals—all possessing supernatural attributes.

With constant thudding against the door, the rest of her explanation was also short. "We were lured to this area by that group! Our fear pulled us here."

Too busy driving to listen, Rig yelled, "Reach into the glove compartment and hand me the pistol."

But how to dodge potholes and rocks that can rip out the oil pan while also getting off a shot before the animal landed in someone's lap? If he missed, a second try would be impossible; the wolf would instantly be in the front seat, ripping out their throats.

"We're bouncing too much. I'll never hit it. Here, hold the gun. And don't touch anything or it'll go off."

Giving someone you don't really know a loaded semi-automatic, especially when that person was being thrown all around the front seat, was an enormous gamble. But it was one King had to take—the wrong one. Before his passenger could hand it over, the gun exploded. In the confines of their small area, the blast was deafening.

With most accidents, there is that instant when you freeze, wondering if you have been injured but too numbed by the moment to know. Regaining their senses, there was good news and bad. The bullet had only lightly grazed his cheek. The bad—it blew out the driver's window.

He slammed on the brakes. Again the van was enveloped by choking desert dust. Stunned and without thinking, Lyra pivoted—now pointing the pistol at her partner's chest. Mortified at what he had done, her entire body tightened… including her index finger—which was slowly pulling on the trigger.

King's reflexes made his body a blur. As he wrenched the gun away, his thumb was impaled by the descending hammer. One hundredth of a second later and a bullet would have made a pencil-size hole in the driver's chest.

Standing in front of their headlights in the settling cloud, the silhouette of the massive canine became visible. It was a one-time opportunity. Quickly, Rig switched the weapon to his left hand. Never having practiced as a southpaw, the chances of his hitting the target were ridiculously slim. In rapid succession, three clumsy shots were squeezed off. On the third, a cry. The beast spun and fell. Before a fourth, it was up, whimpering, limping, disappearing into the darkness.

"It wasn't a solid hit. I think I just nicked him. Here, hold this and try not to shoot me again. Okay?"

"Let's get out of here!" she yelled, half-pleading, half-yelling.

Rig instructed Lyra to get the compass out of the backpack. Surprised that he hadn't thought of this solution earlier, he placed the blame on being mentally and physically exhausted.

Based on the possibility of another discharge, he began to realize it would be prudent to first return the gun to the glove compartment rather than leaving it sliding back and forth on the seat.

"Will you stop fishing in that bag for a moment? I don't want any more accidents."

After some discussion, she couldn't find the compass. They conclude it must have tumbled out in the cave when he was digging for the lighter fluid. Ever resourceful, King came up with another solution: they could get bearings from the North Star. With their direction finally clear, the two breathed a sigh of relief.

Driving and gingerly attempting to push the remaining glass outside, the driver worked carefully as some pieces of the window fell inward, landing on the floor. After sweeping the chunks aside with his foot, he took a long swig of water from an extra bottle as Lyra, kept apologizing profusely, while inspecting the graze-mark on his cheek. Satisfied it wasn't serious, she also drank. The only problem now was the wind whipping in through the glassless hole, which both tried to ignore.

Crises subsided, the Phoenician demanded answers. "What's a skinwalker?"

Fear thawing only slightly, Lyra was slow to reply. "A skinwalker is...Actually, I better start with the overall concept. Creation is simply a series of thoughts held in concentration—a myriad of overlying, interconnecting holograms. They...."

"*Woman, what the hell* are you talking about?"

"There's no need to get angry. Just look at the primary difference between...say, skin, metal, wood, or water. Generally speaking, the difference is all in the molecular structure, right?"

"True," he answered, not having the vaguest idea as to where the conversation was heading.

"Rig, many people are adept at mentally holding a different picture of themselves so strongly that their molecules conform to that shape; and...."

"*Hold it!* You seriously expect me to believe people can change their shapes?"

"I don't care if you believe it or not. The fact remains that shape-shifting is done all over the world. You can turn into anything, even a mouse. Like up on these Indian reservations, the practice is very common; you have hundreds of eyewitnesses." Seeing his expression, she laughed, "You look stunned." Without waiting, the answer continued. "Most anyone who works at it can do it."

Confused, he wanted to know why this, like the other weird things she'd mentioned, wasn't publicized.

"It's a mind block. Today's audience can only accept television-type magicians. Shape-shifters who fly or can run several hundred miles in a night are thought to be disciples of the Devil, rather than adept practitioners of theoretical physics; it freaks people out."

"Can you kill them?"

"You wounded one, didn't you?"

"I guess I hit something. Plus, it did bite its tongue. Incidentally, now tell me the truth. What do you really think was after us back in the cave?"

Looking out across the moonlit desert, she spoke softly. "There's a lot more to this than I want to go into right now."

The Wall Street broker slammed his hand down on the steering wheel and growled, "*Woman*, why are you so *bloody damned secretive*? Who died and made you queen? *You're*...."

Lyra jerked her head toward the inquisitor. Responding with fire almost coming from her nostrils, her gaze was like a blast furnace. "You always have to push, don't you? That's the way it is with most people. *Push, push, push*—that's all you do. Maybe it comes from being a stockbroker—how you make sales, by bullying and manipulating."

"*Look, lady,* I didn't invite you here. *You*...you forced yourself on me—not me onto you. So let's not talk about pushing."

CHAPTER VII

TRIBULATION & DIS-EASE

Forty-five minutes later, lost again, they spotted a cabin. Though it looked innocent enough, both were becoming more wary with every passing hour.

Unexpectedly, the Phoenician did the unthinkable, possibly to allay his partner's anger. Turning, he asked, "What do you think? Should we go up there and knock or what?"

"I don't know…It…it feels okay."

Leaning across her lap, he removed the pistol from the glove compartment.

"What are you going to do?"

From between clenched teeth, the response was less than sweet. "Nothing—if they're nice."

Rig checked the gun's safety, making sure it was on. Bending forward, he slid the weapon under the belt behind him, into the small of his back—barrel pointed into his underwear.

Feeling uncomfortable about its location, he pondered, *I wonder what would happen if it accidentally went off?*

As the Bronco got closer, the cabin door opened. A slender, seventyish-looking man appeared. Standing in the doorway, the figure was haloed by the cabin's light. Weary and frightened, neither traveler knew what to expect.

A Bavarian-accented voice called out, "Are you here, lost?"

"We sure are, partner. Can you help us?"

The man's answer rang with common Western openness, but again, overlaid in a European tone. "Certainly. I'm John Kimbrell. Come on in. What are you two doing way out this far?" Without waiting for an answer, the host added, "By the way, this road is a dead end. It stops a mile up farther."

"Name is Rigden King and this is Lyra. We were just, uh, exploring, and got turned around."

"Well, that happens. Other than the State Department boys, that's the only reason I get visitors occasionally."

Cautiously stepping into the cabin, the two surveyed their surroundings. Aside from a messy desk and a thin layer of pervasive dust, indicative of one otherwise occupied, the main room was clean but sparsely furnished. There were also what appeared to be six diplomas on the wall, three of which were doctorates. Accompanying them are several autographed pictures of U.S. presidents—George H. W. Bush, Bill Clinton, and George W.—each shaking hands with Dr. Kimbrell. Under the grouping was nailed a small crucifix. Stacked on the floor were piles of books that could no longer find space in the bulging, ceiling-high bookcase. In the middle of the room, before a fireplace, sat a leather sofa draped with a beautiful Navajo blanket. A breakfast table was against the far wall. Seeing and sensing nothing out of the ordinary, the visitors, ever so slightly, lowered their guard.

Not noticing the diplomas, the tired salesman misread their host. "What are you doin' out here, old-timer—prospecting?"

"Young man, I am neither an old-timer nor a prospector. I'm a physicist, semi-retired."

Surprised at the answer, Rig checked his companions take on the situation. She seemed quite at ease.

"You two look like you've been through an ordeal. Been out hiking?"

"Ahhh...yeah, hiking—all day."

"Well, have a seat. Can I get you some coffee or tea? Or maybe something stronger, like schnapps?"

The Ra representative was the first to answer. "Tea would be good."

“I’ll have both the shot then coffee, if it isn’t too much trouble.”

“No trouble at all. In fact, I need the break.”

As Krimbrell got busy in the cooking nook, the agent from the District of Columbia voiced her curiosity. “Doctor, why does a physicist retire way out in the middle of nowhere?”

“A little gift from the government for my past and hopefully future contributions. They let me use it to do my research; I need the solitude. Besides, this is nowhere today. But in a few years, it’ll probably be oceanfront property…or close to it, if my calculations are right.”

King again looked at his companion, seeking visible confirmation that they’d stumbled upon a crackpot.

“To answer your question, Miss, ah…What did you say your name was?”

“Lyra.”

“Lyra? Unusual name.”

She smiled before responding, “So I’ve been told.”

“To answer your question, I get royalties from a number of patents. Being up here gives me the quietude I need to pursue my passion—an area of theoretical physics dealing with string theory. Maybe you’ve heard of it, eh?”

Only Lyra nodded in the affirmative.

”And, I’m away from the electronic chaos of the city.”

Immediately, Rig noticed his partner becoming more serious than expected. Interest piqued, she asked, “What type of theories?”

“How man’s collective thought patterns create scientifically measurable forces that actually control weather, trigger massive climatological shifts, Earth changes, that sort of thing. And frankly, since my wife died six years ago, I simply enjoy the peace.”

Not paying attention, the stockbroker’s restless elbow sent a bowl flying to the floor. In innumerable pieces, the ceramic was beyond repair. Embarrassed, stuttering, King made every effort to offer payment. Their host, however, dismissed it as a relic he didn’t want anyway. Like a schoolboy, the awkward guest sheepishly sat again as the physicist swept up shards.

Bending down to help, Lyra added, “Rig, I think the doctor is saying that out here, he’s away from the high-density, electromagnetic areas—those that scramble thinking and cause cancer. Plus, here you have a greater concentration of negative ions."

Kimbrell stopped. Looking her in the eyes, he asked, "Young lady, where did you learn this?"

"Oh, I had special schooling."

"Which university?"

Like a matador, the Ra representative sidestepped the question, redirecting the conversation by pointing to the many degrees on the wall. "I'm sure it wasn't as prestigious as these. Do you personally know these presidents?"

"Yes, of course." Wanting to keep the topic away from herself, the young woman quickly inquired, "Doctor, you mentioned Earth changes. Could you explain what that might entail?"

The old man described an increase in world volcanic activity, global warming, diminishing breathable oxygen—fallen to 21.6%—and other advancing catastrophes. Within seven years, he asserted, volcanic ash would cut out enough light to reduce global crop yields by twenty-three percent—plunging even developed countries into starvation.

Pronouncing deaths from these as minor compared to the next development, their host pointed to a drawing on the wall detailing the Yellowstone Park Caldera. A giant crater whose mouth was forty-three miles in length and nineteen in width, it is one of the world's six mega-volcanoes. Erupting every six hundred thousand years, and well overdue, it was ten thousand times more powerful than Mount St. Helens. In the past, each such explosion had created a nuclear winter, blocking out the sun and making an acidic rain, wiping out most life on this planet.

With other Earth problems too numerous to address, what primarily concerned this physicist was that at Yellowstone, scientists had recently observed the center of the crater bulging—an upward thrusting of more than twelve feet. With such a massive buildup, many calculated the next explosion was likely to happen at any moment.

Speaking of another killer, gigantic sunspot eruptions, Dr. Kimbrell told how, in the near future, this solar radiation was forecast to send a "kill-shot" to Earth, literally cooking a significant percentage of the planet's population...at least those above ground.

As if lecturing to a classroom of Heidelberg students, and with more catastrophes to go, the physicist unveiled yet another horror: devastating world droughts caused by global deforestation, as in the Amazon where twenty percent of the forest had been removed. To which the doctor emphasized, "Fewer trees…no rain; massive droughts; it's that simple."

While he continued, Lyra quietly moved closer to inspect her host's degrees. In mid-sentence, the scientist stoped to ask if Rig had ever heard of hypercanes. Drawing a blank, the guest was told that these were storms with wind velocities of 250 to 450 miles per hour—Hurricane Andrew only clocked 152 mph. The doctor explained because of changing weather patterns, such almost-supernatural phenomena would soon be common occurrences.

He also spoke of another problem burdening man's survival—global warming—"a more serious threat than terrorism," according to an official Pentagon study which stated, "Climate change is happening so fast, forecasting models have grown ineffective."

But the worst was yet to be spoken—a flipping of the North and South Poles. A map on the far wall illustrated how, as temperatures increased, the planet's magnetic force decreased. Coupled with global warming, which had begun melting both polar icecaps, the combination of these was forcing a redistribution of planetary weight—causing the Earth to wobble. The end result would be tsunamis, followed by a sudden global flip…one more factor hastening man's ultimate demise.

Looking at the titles of his books, Lyra kept one ear tuned in to the conversation as their host talked on. "Here's one place where science and religion cross-verify each other. Unfortunately, this flip is probably the Biblically referenced 'rapture,' the switch that will happen in the 'blink of an eye.'"

Turning, the Ra representative added, "The doctor's right. Sometime check out the 24th chapter of Matthew. '*At that time two men will be working in a field; one will be taken away, the other will be left behind. Two women will be at a mill grinding meal; one will be taken away, the other will be left behind.*'"

"You know your Bible," marveled a surprised Kimbrell.

"A little."

"Then, you might recognize another passage from the 4th and 5th chapters of St. Paul's first letter to the Thessalonians. '*There will be the shout of command, the archangel's voice, the sound of God's trumpet, and the Lord himself will come down from Heaven. The Day of the Lord will come as a thief comes at night. When people say, "Everything is quiet and safe," then suddenly destruction will hit them! It will come as suddenly as the pains that come upon a woman in labor, and people will not escape.*'"

"I know that passage but I find it could also suggest colliding with an asteroid."

Cup to his lips, forgetting to drink, the stockbroker turned even more attentive. Transfixed, he listened as the two cited a string of other prophecies relating to current times. Throughout the next half-hour, Rigden King, III, sat mute, too numb to speak.

Finally butting in, he asked in an incredulous tone, "You… you both really mean the Earth will be…like, going upside down?"

Seeing he'd opened Pandora's box, the physicist tried calming his worried guest. "Don't be shocked. It's sad, but man has brought this on himself. Trust me, you won't feel a thing."

"Why?"

"At the time of rotation," Kimbrell replied, "the planet's spin will reach up to twenty-four thousand miles per hour. You will be thrown like a straw in a tornado."

Rocked nearly off his chair, Rig shot off a question, "*How? My God!* When did you say this will be happening?"

"Eight to ten years from now, according to unbiased authoritative sources. By my calculations, however, in seven years we should be hit by a truly major asteroid—larger than the one which we nearly collided with just before the millennium." He chuckled. "Oddly, that one and Earth crossed at the exact spot, only six hours apart."

"Do you mean," Rig questioned, aghast, "that we were at the same point in space?"

"Separated by a slim three hundred and sixty-three minutes, young man."

"This…this is the first time I'm hearing about it."

"You weren't supposed to know. It was another governmental cover-up—like when the White House kept secret that it prevented a near nuclear bomb explosion in New York City, back in October of 2001."

"For real?"

"Young man, Earth has *twenty times* more asteroid craters than the moon; we're long overdue for a hit. Tell me, Mr. King, what good would it do to alert people to such disasters—for the highways to be clogged and the stores to be looted? Plus, being hit by a space mass of that size would cause six months of jet-black darkness—a nuclear winter, killing roughly seventy-seven percent of the planet."

"But...." mumbled Rig.

"Oh, but don't worry about that! The current two-degree change in the temperature of the oceans is guaranteeing something far worse." Kimbrell pauses to reflect. "Anyway, for some strange reason, the asteroid swerved at the last moment." Shrugging his shoulders in disbelief, the physicist added, "That's something I still don't understand."

In shock, the adventurer slowly sct his cup down, absentmindedly chewing a thumbnail while contemplating the forecasted doom. Staring at the ceiling, he came back, wanting proof: "Doc, since you have this in-depth knowledge about the climate, let me ask you a question. Lyra was telling me about these frogs being born without eyes and legs? Does that somehow fit into your study?"

"Of course. Like the vanishing populations of butterflies, bees, and bats, frogs are also a critical, ecological barometer. Their deformities are simply another sign of planetary destruction."

"Then why doesn't someone do something?"

"Industry can't. If it did, the cost would be so great, it would lower their stock values. That's why a number of Fortune 500 companies created Washington think tanks, such as the Kino-March Institute and U.S. Legacy Foundation—brain centers that feed politicians false information. And since no one outside learns who funds the studies, John Q. Public never realizes that it's those hidden companies that are really responsible for most environmental problems. As I said, the government doesn't want you to know. Like the ABC television documentary that revealed that the White House had the 2003 EPA report altered to make global warming seem not as serious as it really is."

Seeing his guest empty the last bit of coffee from his cup, the gracious host asked, "Would you like some more?" Turning to Lyra, "More tea?"

"That would be nice."

The Phoenician chimed in, "Thanks. Another cup would be great. Pardon me, but do you have any artificial sweetener?"

Getting up, Kimbrell responded, "No, will sugar do?"

"Thanks, I'll pass. Black's fine."

The physicist continued, "Young man, this isn't propaganda. These things are scientific facts."

Obviously agitated, Rig stood, stretched, and began pacing. Tripping over a throw rug, he caught his balance. "*Oooops!* This just isn't my day!" Addressing the last statement, the doctor's male guest casually remarked, "Don't worry, Mr. Kimbrell. These environmental glitches can't be all that serious, and even if they were, they can be fixed." Before wrecking something else, the clumsy adventurer headed back to the table where he again could sit quietly.

"That's just it; these situations are so critical, you barely have the time, Mr. King. You're just at, and about to cross the line of no return. Let me show you the fallacy of your assumptions." He directed Rig's attention to another chart on the wall. "See here how the growing population crisis means less farmland and more pollution? Immigrants are now flooding America's borders—every year, *one million* cross here into Arizona alone. But just wait several years. That's a drop in the bucket; with the advancing famine, it'll become a tidal wave."

"Ah ha! Now that's where we've got you!" the broker rejoined with his usual smugness. "We've got plenty of land. Science has, and always will, find ways of feeding more people with less…just wait and see."

"Mr. King," Kimbrell countered with Prussian sternness, "*wrong!* So far, your science can't eliminate leprosy, cancer, or…or even the Black Plague, for that matter."

"Wasn't the Black Plague eradicated back in the Middle Ages?"

"Heavens, no—it's alive and well. All you have to do is look for it up on the Navajo Reservation—just another of the numerous problems this government doesn't want to broadcast too loudly."

Under his breath, the stockbroker mumbled, "First, Lyra, now him; I must'a found their nest."

"Come here, young man. I want to show you something." Pulling out research for an upcoming book, the doctor pointed to one of his charts. "Look," the physicist demanded, "these problems are growing almost exponentially, and you say science is fixing them? See here." He pointed to the graph with his pencil. "Until 1990, there were only ten major earthquakes per decade. But from that year to 1998, there were *three hundred*. Add to that, now the world has *fifty percent* less fresh water than in the 1960s. *The 1960s!* What people don't grasp is that without forests, the world has far less oxygen for breathing, not to mention decreased rain. Lack of moisture, in turn, causes weather patterns to shift—creating massive droughts and bottled water costing $1.69 per liter. And this is just a small part of why world farm production is dropping so dramatically. But...."

Scanning one of her host's books, Lyra doubled over, as if being stabbed. Reeling, knees buckling, she grabbed the bookcase with her other hand to keep from falling. Out into the night...eight thousand five hundred and sixteen miles away, wildlife on the eastern shores of the Antarctic were also struck by sudden change. On the ice shelf, on what would normally be a frozen, peaceful, moonlit evening, something was wrong...terribly wrong. Confused, animals awakened and milled about. Without warning, a loud crack—the sound of a small explosion. The noise, however, didn't subside. Like rolling thunder, it continued for five long, frightening minutes. As in the year 2000, when a 183-mile-long chunk of ice, the length of Delaware, broke off (and a piece bigger than Jamaica in 2003), now one the size of California was being set adrift. A tear softly rolled down the young woman's cheek. The Ra representative was saddened—one more sign heralding the beginning of the "Tribulation."

Back at the cabin, their psychic senses in hibernation, oblivious to the subtle shift of the planet's auric field, the two males continued conversing. The physicist stood, this time to take the cups over to the sink. Focus shifted, Rig noticed a bread-box-size instrument on an end table beside the sofa and started to absentmindedly fiddle with it, twisting one of its dials.

From the sink, their host turned to continue the conversation. "*No! Halt!*" The scream was almost deafening.

Startled, Rig jerked back his hand. The doctor apologized, explaining that a catastrophe could have resulted. He rushed over to make the readjustment.

"Young man, this is a radionics machine. Know anything about the subject?"

"Never heard of it."

Going back to her inspection and half listening, Lyra continued leafing through the doctor's books. Their host explained that radionics was a mechanical way of taking a thought, amplifying it, and beaming it out to a specific point. It can be aimed at an individual, a group, or even a geographical location. "In this case, by changing the dials," Doctor Kimbrell explained, "you could have accidentally killed my patient."

He gave the example of a time when, back East in the Cumberland Valley, a farming community that had a massive moth infestation. "The Psy-tronic Foundation in Pennsylvania was asked to take aerial photos of that region's most highly infested areas to see if they could find a solution. These pictures were then put into a machine similar to this one. A setting was established at a vibrational degree impossible for moths to tolerate and continue living. The scientists only turned the device on from 8:30 to 11:00 each morning. The result should have gone down in the annals of history. By about the eighth day, every corn borer, Japanese beetle, and nematode on that one property was dead." The doctor continued, "Here, young man, I want to show you something else."

He handed Rig an old, weathered envelope, ordering, "Open it."

The guest took out a faded letter and several pictures. "What's this?"

"Never mind reading. Just look at the pictures, and I'll tell you. This is from Dr. Terrence Dale, Chief of Dun Chemical Company back in 1985. Using a cotton swab, he smeared pesticide on the photos of every other row of those citrus trees you're looking at before placing them in a device like this."

"And?"

"A week later, all the nematodes and every insect in the rows that were painted were dead. In the untreated rows, however, they were thriving, continuing on as if nothing had changed."

Rig handed back the pictures and letter. "Incredible. But if it's that great, why isn't your radionics thing sold at Sears, or by that guy who peddles those bread-making machines on TV? Seems like people would be breaking down his doors to get one."

"Mr. King…Mr. King, I find it hard to believe that you, a man of the world, and I'm assuming one with a college education, with so much naïveté. Why would pesticide companies want you to have it? What would the multi-billion-dollar chemical manufacturers sell if this inexpensive machine were used by all the farmers of the world?"

"They'd go bankrupt."

"Maybe they need to. Now possibly you can see how Big Business manipulates the government into making laws protecting their interests. If farmers had this machine, world markets would be flooded with inexpensive, organic food."

"Doc, I don't get the big need for this organic thing."

"Don't feel bad. Most of the public doesn't either." Pulling a sheet of paper from his file, he asked, "See this graph? These studies prove that because of depleted soil and the heavy use of insecticides and herbicides, regular foods have lost seventy-six percent of their nutritional value. That's why you need all those vitamin supplements."

Kimbrell rolled his eyes to the side as if receiving an epiphany. While his male guest thought of another question, the old man jotted down an important note for a new project.

"Excuse me," said the scientist. "I got off the subject. What I really want you to know is that all disease is simply a thought pattern. Something which often materializes on the physical plane. The String Theory of physics proves this. Each second of every day, billions of thoughts, much like television and radio programs, are flying through the air. Every person on the planet is a sending and receiving station—constantly manifesting and transmitting, or the opposite—absorbing others' thoughts—mostly the negative ones, like sickness."

"And poverty," Lyra puts in.

"True," the doctor continued. "We are constantly being influenced by a broad array of beliefs. And when our mind allows these into our thinking, they affect our actions, often materializing in our physical self."

Lyra joined the two. Sitting at the table, she listened intently.

Her companion queried, "So, Doc, in your belief system, disease is caused by the mind?"

"Of course. Here's a better way of looking at it. The word 'disease,' when broken down, is 'dis,' meaning 'not,' and 'ease,' or ' at peace.'"

The Ra representative chimed in. "Meaning, not in a healthy harmonic."

"Exactly," Kimbrell concurred. "For each disease, there is its opposite or state-of-wellness frequency. So all radionics does, after diagnosing the type of illness, is to beam into the patient the healthy vibrational equivalent. What you were about to do was to change the setting. To what, I don't know, but as with the moths, it possibly could have killed the recipient."

"Sounds like a kind of transmitter. Is that all there is to it?"

"Well, that's the simplified version. Here, this is a good book to read, *The Holographic Universe* by Michael Talbot. This, to you I give," the doctor said with twisted, Germanic syntax.

As the stockbroker began leafing through the pages, his host continued, "I originally bought it for one of my nephews, but he died in a fire last year. You should find it fascinating. It scientifically proves not only that there is really just one cosmic mind, but also that much of this phenomena people term 'psychic' is simply the laws of physics set in motion."

"Doctor," Rig asks, "looking at your radionics machine from a money-making standpoint, it seems the medical community would want it in a flash."

Kimbrell sighed. "There's so much illogic out there; most won't even give this device a second glance. And that's a shame, especially when you consider that virulent disease strains have left our precious antibiotics ninety-three percent ineffective. We constantly have to create even stronger drugs, but the germs are also mutating—into more resistant forms. So, it's an upward spiral. But something else—there are growing signs pointing to a pandemic like the world has never before seen."

"What?" The doctor's statement startled Rig.

"Think of it as, for the secret families truly in charge of the planet, a way of quickly decreasing world population—more efficient than gas chambers."

"Like...sort of like Nazi Germany...no offense," Rig mumbled awkwardly.

"None taken, young man. Just know that there is far more afoot than meets the eye. However, by using this little machine and taking a map, a single practitioner could actually nullify an entire pathogenic outbreak in a given area...anthrax, smallpox, even nuclear radiation. Unfortunately, few except the manufacturers can make money with it. The medical industries are so afraid of radionics decreasing their revenues, they've gotten laws passed in a number of states making it hard to even buy one."

"Then, why don't *you* do it? I mean, if it really works, you could stop the effects of chemical and bio-terrorism!"

"Frankly, my time is being consumed, if you can believe this, by even more pressing problems. But anyone can get involved. Then again, no one is, to this, paying attention."

Lyra leaned forward in her chair. "Dr. Kimbrell, you might explain to Rig how radionics can be used in a *deadly* way. I mean, over and above making an error with the settings."

"Indeed, you're right, young lady." As he put papers back into his valise, their host added, "Think of something that, while invisible, has actual tangible density. Like...I guess a poor comparison would be a bullet. With this machine, the projectile or belief sent out is both strong and continuous, at least until it's turned off. So if the operator has a doubt or negative thoughts about the patient, that too is implanted in the recipient. You see, it's imperative that the practitioner not only be positive, but that he or she keeps the device protected from curious dial-twisters." The doctor waited a moment before continuing, "You don't laugh, young man? I...I make joke."

Rig forced a smile and injected, "Then a sloppy operator, with improper intent, could actually cause harm?"

"Of course—even death!...Look at this." He handed the guest a hollow bone etched with mythological figures.

"In Australia, for instance, it's well documented that some Aborigines can simply point this toward a person hundreds of miles away, and if the thought is to kill, the victim dies. The whole secret is in getting an emotionally charged intent set in motion and letting it, like an arrow, fly. In fact, for years, both the CIA and Russian military used radionics to assassinate. That is, until they finally understood that it had a nasty way of bouncing back to them! As cosmic law states, 'What is given out, you always get returned'—only greater."

"It's a prayer," injected Lyra.

While their host continued to talk, the Phoenician wondered if Kimbrell, with his knowledge of physics, might be able to shed any light on the mysterious things found in the cave. Before exposing his fortune, however, the suspicious businessman wanted to know how quickly the physicist could possibly turn the information over to the wrong people.

"How do you stay in touch with the outside world, Doctor, by phone?"

"As of yesterday, I don't. Look here." Their host pointed to a pile of parts on the kitchen counter. "I dropped my cell phone—smashed it to pieces and there isn't another neighbor within forty-five miles."

Relieved and reaching for his knapsack, Rig commented, "I've got something I would like your opinion on, scientifically speaking, that is."

"By all means. What do you have?"

Lyra was amazed—her partner exposing his fortune!

With obvious pride, King pulled out the twin discs. The moment they become visible, Kimbrell's smile dropped. As the device was set on the table, the physicist jumped up to dig into a box near his bookcase for a clean pad of writing paper.

Looking at the metallic object, excited to the point of shaking, the German lapsed deeper into his accent. "Hmmmm. Vhat on Earth have you here? And vhat is dis vriting? You two veren't just around driving, vere you?"

Hearing the mispronunciation, the doctor's male guest suppressed a smirk.

Rig and Lyra begin answering at the same time, with him overriding her softer voice. "Well err…No, we…."

Again, Dr. Kimbrell voiced an opinion. "I'm guessing the vriting is pre-Sumerian; but…I don't recognize it. In fact, I vonder if it is possibly from some civilization unrecorded." The physicist held the artifact up toward the ceiling light, turning it slowly, examining it from every angle. "Vhere did you say you found dis?"

The treasure hunter's response was guarded. "We didn't."

"Do you two know vhat function dis ting has?" Nonplused, King responded, "Don't have a clue. We're hoping you might."

Without waiting, Lyra jumped in. "Doctor, please don't ask any questions. Think of these as things to help humanity. That's all we can say at the moment."

Surprised, King glared at his partner. Stunned by her aggression, he stumbled for words. "Yeah, that's all we can say." Ingrained greed got the better of him. Unable to leave it alone, pointing to the discs, the stock-and-bond salesman pushed for information. "Doc, what do you guess this might be?"

"Can't tell for certain." Kimbrell used a magnifying glass as he studied the raised lettering around the rim. "Dis ting…dis, vhatever it is, appears to be some sort of photonic resonator. I…."

Always impatient, the broker wanted more. "What's a photonic resonator?"

"I tink I'm looking at something dat pulls in cosmic energy, screens the signal, possibly using dis preprogrammed crystal to scramble the energy pattern and den refocuses the molecules. Beyond dat and mitout any experimentation, I can't say." In a calmer manner, their host asked, "Do you have any idea what metal this is?"

"We believe it's platinum or silver."

The physicist voiced his scholarly opinion. "I don't think so. The color is slightly different. See this reddish hue?"

"Then what do you think they used?"

"Mr. King, who are the 'they' you refer to?"

"Uh, we're not sure yet."

Lyra turned away so Kimbrell wouldn't see her disgusted expression, thinking, *Rig just can't keep his big mouth shut*.

Still examining the discs, the physicist took a spoon from the table and gave one of the discs a hard rap. The pitch and intensity of vibration hurt everyone's ears.

"Whatever this metal is," the doctor concluded, "it vas probably used for its specific frequency—one that has an especially high resonance."

Again, the Phoenician pressed, "So you really don't know what this could be?"

"As I said, not without testing. But I'll be glad to do so if you want to leave it with me."

"Thanks for the offer, but that won't be necessary."

Over an hour had passed at the cabin. With the honed instincts of a wild animal, Lyra was ever alert, constantly scanning for danger. Although feeling none, the cautious Ra agent suggested it would be best to get going. Disappointed, but seeing no more information to be gleaned, her companion reluctantly agreed. After expressing appreciation for the hospitality, the two listened intently while getting directions. Again outlined by the light of the opened door, the old man watched, waving until the Bronco could no longer be seen through the dust. Bouncing along, they knew that Flagstaff was still a long three-and-one-half-hour ride ahead.

Time passed, the silence a welcome relief, until Lyra let out a startling *"Oh, no!"*

Nearly jumping out of his skin, Rig anxiously looked from side to side while scanning the road and shouting back, *"What?"* Before his passenger had a chance to answer, he blasted with increasing volume, *"What?! What?! What?!"*

"Fooy!—I broke a nail! Why tonight? And I had them looking so good too."

"Okay, that's it!" he snapped. "We nearly get killed in a cave, and according to you, someone or *something* is, as we speak, zeroing in on us. Then, we barely escaped this skinwalker thing. If only half of this is true, don't you think we should keep on the lookout instead of filing nails?"

"We're okay now. I don't feel them anymore."

Patience shredded, the driver branded his passenger with a searing look. For a long while, the two remained quiet. The unwinding dirt road ahead appeared desolate and boring. Neither noticed, by the side, a glowing pair of eyes briefly illuminated by the momentary splash of headlights. Continuing on, the two adventurers silently hoped that danger was far behind.

In the high Arizona desert, even brilliant moonlight wasn't enough to diminish the crystal-clear sharpness of the heavens. Overcome by its beauty, Rig and Lyra rolled to a stop. With a minimum of noise, they stepped out and looked up…stars, stars, billions, trillions of stars.

Unlike in cities, where only the brightest of celestial bodies are discernible, here the sky was a pure black canopy dotted with multitudinous twinkling lights. Most were white, while a number shimmered in other shades: red, ice blue, yellow, and orange. And flowing across this speckled heaven, a portion was overlaid with a slender band known as the Milky Way—as some would explain, "A river of souls journeying home, returning to their beginning."

The night was hushed. Silence here was so profound, visitors often believed they could hear minute ribbons of sound. The jaded dismissed the notion, accusing the wind or blaming their imagination. In actuality, these gossamer notes were nothing less than celestial melodies…the singing of ever-present angels.

Every aspect of this place came together to offer a sacred feeling, one of being in the center of an infinite cathedral. So much so, many a traveler with eyes shut and heart wide open, swore they could even detect the smell of incense.

In rapt attentiveness, a man and a woman, two souls, stood next to each other. No word was spoken. None was necessary. This was a moment when God was not merely a bearded man on some distant cloud. There was an ancient stirring, a feeling of oneness with the Divine Presence—the All-in-All. From the depths of one's being, a knowingness arose that humanity was, is, and always will be gently swaddled in the Creator's sustaining love.

Without conscious thought, Rig reached over, entwining his fingers into Lyra's. Not moving, his companion slowly glanced down then back to the stars. Distracted by a shortening breath and rapidly beating heart, she became oblivious to the overhead splendor. Closing her eyes, the young woman's focus went within, caught up in a whirlwind of emotions.

Heading back, Rig's circuitry was overloaded: a found treasure; a strange beast or group trying to kill them; and then…then there was Lyra.

CHAPTER VIII

FOCUSED POWER

Lyra…You awake? I need to find out about this skinwalker thing…Lyra?"

Though sitting up, she appeared to be sleeping. Rig assumed that after an exhausting day, his companion needed to catch a quick nap. This, however, was not the case.

"What?" she asked, slowly opening her eyes.

"Sorry. I can't wait any longer."

"You didn't wait any time at all."

"I know. I know. I'm sorry, but…."

The Ra representative spoke softly, yet with a powerful resonance. "Rig, *I need to finish*. You just have to be patient." Again her eyes closed.

"Finish what? Come on, finish what?"

No answer—silence.

By the time the lights of Flagstaff came into view, both acknowledged they were in a state of exhaustion. Regardless, it was agreed to press on to Phoenix rather than stay over. To keep awake, he turned into a truck stop for sandwiches, coffee, and a soda. She remained in the vehicle—adding to her movie script while the day's events were still vivid. Disheveled and grouchy, he wove his way around parked trucks and gas pumps before disappearing inside.

The Bent Spoon café was quiet. Ignoring customers, a gum-chewing waitress next to the far end of the room chatted with her boyfriend. Growing impatient, the out-of-towner stood at the counter, shifting his weight from one foot to the other. Minutes passed that to King seemed an eternity. Used to faster attention, he drum-rolled his fingers on the cash register and began to seethe.

Sensing mental darts, the woman glanced up. This abrupt, mood-dampening caused her boyfriend to hurl an insult. Finding its mark and with adrenaline flowing, the newcomer lost focus—his mind driven by primitive logic. As if in a battle involving spear-throwing, the challenge was instantly picked up and re-flung. Soon, and with deadly intent, the boyfriend's Neanderthal-size frame slowly rose. Frowning, and with the appearance of a two-story earthmover, he lumbered toward the cash register. King's fingers slowly closed—each hand forming a rock-hard fist.

Toe-to-toe, faces a few inches apart, the antagonists' eyes locked on the other. As they exchanged epithets, a sudden blast of spittle from the Teamster's chewing tobacco spewed forth—an enormous gob landing on the treasure hunter's lower lip. Veins in both necks bulged, looking like strands of rope beneath their skin. Within moments, the deadly flurry of insults ended, speaking ceased.

Activity in the café had already frozen. Mid-mouthful, like ice-entrapped prehistoric beasts with food un-swallowed, customers were encased in the moment. A Norman Rockwell picture: the fry cook stood on tiptoe, trying to look out the pass-through window, straining for a ringside view. Hearts of even small children beat faster; they knew something bad was about to happen. Each fighter waited for that single spark—any small reason to ignite their excuse.

Slapping check and bagged food on the counter, the nasal-toned waitress broke the deadlock. Coffee in hand and without a word, Rig tossed several packets of artificial sweetener into the open sack, and headed for the door.

Behind him, the enemy's voice rose, allowing the stranger to catch the end of that familiar phrase, "…and the horse you rode in on."

For the outsider, a crucial decision—should he set his food down and make this nitwit eat his words, or just walk away? Refocusing, logic returned. The truth, this stockbroker knew he wasn't the world's greatest fighter. Nor was he in any condition to even start. Then again, he was no coward, either.

Somewhere in the back of his brain, a thought cried out… that familiar, shrill little voice screaming, *Are you crazy? Keep going!*

Faced with a no-win situation, even if he lucked out and didn't get seriously hurt, a brawl would surely mean ending up in jail. As his second boot touched the floor, the normally sage internal aspect growled, *Ahhh…what the hell!* King stopped, and set the sack and coffee by his feet. The turn toward Bubba was unhurried. With cold intensity, he again stared into his adversary's eyes.

The newcomer allowed this grand gesture a twelve-second duration. Outwardly, he was ready to do battle. For a moment, it seemed the only option. But inwardly, he knew this was a really dumb way of proving a point. Sufficient time having passed, and hopefully achieving a degree of vindication, he turned away. Bag and coffee once again in hand, King left at a slow, deliberate pace. Every eye in the eatery bored into his back. Boiling with anger, he opened the screen door with a forceful kick. It slammed behind him, making a sharp crack. Two steps and he paused, noticing the night air seemed thicker and dirtier than when he entered.

Getting into the SUV, he was still shaking. So much so, some of the steaming coffee spilled, running over the tender back of his hand. A mind still locked in battle, ignoring the pain, Rig stared straight ahead—as the area of skin in question turned pink. Overwhelmed by the force of his grating vibration, Lyra retreated as close to the passenger door as possible.

Looking into the reddened face, she meekly asked, "What happened in there?"

Caught up, unable to override his emotions, the answer was a hard "*Nothing! Let it go!*"

Her softness flowed out to him. "You really need to get control of your anger. When fighting, rule number one is to never lose focus. If you do, you give your power away."

With clenched jaw, and in the staccato rhythm of his seething state, he repeated, "*I…said… let…it…go!*"

Again her voice almost sang in that melodic tone. "All right, but you're really such a nice person. I hate to see that anger controlling you so."

"Lyra!"

"Let me say this one thing more, and I'll be quiet. All right?" No answer...."*All right?"*

The reply was sullen. "Okay."

"There's a technique I'd like to share with you. It'll dissolve that anger problem of yours. Once that's tamed, you'll overcome all those chaotic thoughts that set up blocks in your life. It's called the Sedona Me...."

Peeling out of the parking lot, he snipped, *"Get off my back!"*

The answer was almost whispered. "Okay...Okay."

"Just not now, damn it...maybe later."

"Promise?"

"Yeah, yeah; I promise."

"All right. We'll talk later then."

Looking into the sack, she came across his artificial sweetener and made the wrong suggestion. "You really should try to drink your coffee black. Did you know a number of these brands are carcinogenic?"

An ego still bruised over the café incident, he exploded, *"Woman, I said...give it a rest!"* As soon as the words left his lips, they seemed to have put him in a less offensive mood. "Thanks, but now's not the time."

Snapping on the radio, Creedence Clearwater Revival's song, *Bad Moon Rising*, filled the cab. Getting his mind off his recent near brawl, King joined in singing the song's foreboding message.

"Do we really have to listen to this? Can't we have something else? *Please?*"

"Then you choose!"

"Thank you, I will." She turned the dial and a radio voice said, "Hello! This is Coast-to-Coast AM, and I'm Art Bell. Tonight, we'll be talking with the famous psychic Sven Johanson about the 'New Millennium' map—the one given by angelic beings showing our country's coastline after the coming disasters. And I don't mean these terrorist problems, either. You know...that's when much of the land from Washington

State to California, as well as parts of the East Coast, fall into the ocean. So hold on, this promises to be quite an evening. Hi, Sven, welcome to ...."

As soon as the driver recognized Bell's signature voice, he blurted, "Oh crud! Not that moron! He and his sidekick, Noory, pander to every crackpot this side of Mars!"

Giggling, the Ra representative couldn't help but interject, "I know a few in the Vega sector they've missed."

"Huh?"

"Just joking...just joking," she insisted. "You're always so serious."

"Out of curiosity, do you really listen to this garbage?"

"Sometimes."

"And here I thought you were genuinely intelligent."

With Rig's constant downpour of insults, Lyra's dam was again breached. Poorly chosen words once more flooded his passenger's high ground. The row, over as quickly as it started, ended with her folding her arms in disgust. Sullen, the young woman stared out the side window.

Unaware of the degree of icy tension and not knowing when to shut up, King blundered on. "No need to get mad; *I'm right, ya know?* I can't fathom where Bell and Noory find these wacko guests. And their audience, my God—they're loony! They get the nuttiest screwballs calling in." The stockbroker cracked a smile. "I have this mental picture: Bell's listeners, all fluttering around their radios like a bunch of moths at a porch light...getting lured in by the guy's razzle-dazzle." He laughed, then continued. "And talk about paranoia! I mean, look! These were the crazies who thought Y2K was going to be the end of civilization."

He hazarded a quick glance at Lyra...still a shell of silence.

King tried to backpedal. "Come on, you know it's true. Once I heard this caller insisting that she's the ambassador from Venus." Observing his passenger growing more irritated, he stupidly continued digging his hole. "What's spooky is that the kook used enough logic, I guess, and in a peculiar sort of way, she actually sounded credible...sort of. No wonder Coast-to-Coast listeners get fooled."

Pausing, he looked for a thawing in the sheet of ice between them but was met by a cold look.

Able to take only so much of his ongoing idiocy, Lyra lashed out. "There you go again. You and your grand opinions, going off in the wrong direction…as usual."

"Like how?"

"So what if a few of Mr. Bell's and Mr. Noory's guests push the envelope? That's show business. What you, in your infinite lack of understanding, don't acknowledge is that many of these experts often give out incredibly advanced, scientific findings."

"Oh, yeah. Right. Like the guy who sent in a photograph of a small toy in a cage, claiming he had captured a miniature alien. Now that's high science."

"Mister Know-it-all, your problem is that you constantly make statements when you haven't even the tiniest speck of knowledge on the subject."

"Sure, and like you do?"

A gale of emotions unleashed, the driver had a rough time squeezing in another word. "Look, their experts talk about what mainstream scientists can't."

"Or wouldn't be caught dead talking about."

"Rig, you people are such control freaks. Heaven forbid that society questions any of the constant lies you've been raised on." As he tried to interrupt, his partner forced her point. "You people like to think everyone who listens to this type of program has the word *nincompoop* stamped across his forehead. The irony is, your group is so closed off, it's pathetic! These listeners' only crime is they want a few honest answers—for a change." Her voice rose several decibels. "Look, Mister, of all the people on this planet, these are the very few who at least have the nerve to examine ideas outside the box. It's a good thing somebody has the courage!" Energy expended, the Ra representative turned once more to look out her window.

Putting on the turn signal to pass a U-Haul towing a Toyota, Rig couldn't resist one more frontal assault. "Outside the box? That's putting it mildly. The ones I've heard must be calling from *within the box*—of their padded cell!"

"There you go again with the sarcasm. Tell me; what's the big deal if their guests are a little entertaining? This show is one of the few places the guy on the street can get unfiltered information. Not the censored pap you're normally fed. I mean, you do agree most news is heavily altered, right?"

"All I can say is, his program's like reading a rag-mag at the supermarket checkout counter. You know? They're always printing something about the secret prophecies of Fatima, or how Satan was spotted working at a Burger King in Boise, Idaho."

"Now you're being ridiculous."

"No, I'm not! Lyra, get off it. As anyone with more than a single marble in his head will tell you, talk shows like this cater to guests who have trouble rubbing their only two brain cells together."

She boiled, *"You insufferable hypocrite!* You're putting them down while it's patently obvious that you have tuned in to the program more than once! Who held the gun to your head and forced you to listen?"

"Settle down! This is one of the few stations I can get while driving across the desert. It's just that these supposed experts spew things about, like…like aliens having access to the Pentagon or…or this anti-government crap concerning mass-mind crowd control, concentration camps being erected right here in America…and a thousand other crackpot ideas."

"And a lot of what they expose is one hundred percent fact."

"That's absurd!" he laughs. "Lemme tell you how stupid all this is. One night, as I was driving to Vegas, there was this supposed Ph.D. astrologer predicting that Earth was going to have some sort of major space alien contact in 2002. Well, I hate to tell ya, Babe, it never happened."

"*Babe?"* she spit. Enflamed, her words were paced. *"Don't…you…ever…call me that again! Got it?* And how do you know? Governments, and I don't care what nation, treat their citizenry like mushrooms."

"Jeez, relax! What do you mean, mushrooms?"

"You're kept in the dark and fed, for want of a more descriptive word, manure. Rig, these experts you label *wacko* often explain scientific anomalies and situations the government either doesn't know of, or the higher-ups forbid being divulged."

"I don't see any of these supposed *catastrophes,"* he roared, "other than the occasional freaks of nature we spoke about earlier. *Wait!* What do you mean, they're *forbidden to*?"

Head resting back and eyes shut, King's companion was growing more tired. "This thing is too complex to give you a quick answer. How about later?"

"Oooooh, dreadfully sorry!" Feigning idiocy, he added, "Guess I'm so dense your complexity would be way beyond me, *O Queen of Great Intellect."*

"That's not what I meant. I'm just tire…."

"Well then, try me; we'll be driving for several hours."

To placate her partner, the Ra representative launched into a broad, technical explanation. She insisted many of these catastrophes had already been triggered by super-secret projects, such as climate-altering H.A.A.R.P in Alaska, or other machinations so shocking they're known only to a handful of those in power. According to her, much of this was classified information cloaked above 'Top Secret.' "It's so protected," she finally concluded, "that even most presidents don't know everything that exists out there…and certainly not this one."

"Okay. If these guys are that good, which I don't believe, why can't they even stop simple acts of terrorism?"

The emissary from Washington let out a long sigh before replying. "You are the most…pig-headed individual I've ever met. Can't you fathom that there are *volumes* the public isn't being told?"

"Such as?"

Again sighing, she tried to pacify her companion's curiosity. "Such as the fact that news of the asteroid that Kimbrell was talking about that nearly crashed, *was* leaked to the press…a number of times. Though, by international agreement, governments kept everyone unaware so as not to cause global panic."

"And you know all this for a fact?"

"Absolutely." Arching forward, stretching a back aching from the long ride, she continued, "We're off topic. I want to first finish my point about Mr. Bell."

"Point? What point? It's simple; you like him, and I don't. Guy's an idiot."

"If he is," Lyra recoiled, "there should be more like him, except…."

"Except? Ah! Gotcha! Here it comes. Okay, except what?"

"Well…the only thing wrong is some nights, he and Noory get millions of their listeners all worked up, visualizing planetary catastrophes."

"*Wow!* Lyra, did you see that driver nearly hit that pickup? Guy must be drunk or his meth just kicked in." He refocused. "So Bell and Noory have large audiences. That's no big deal."

"Of course I saw it. And there you go again, pooh-poohing everything you don't read about in your precious *Wall Street Journal,* or see on CNN."

"Poo-pooing?"

"*Rig, stop it!* You know what I mean. If they're not careful, both he and Mr. Noory are in a position to trigger worldwide disasters."

"Those two? Hah! Little Artsy Fartsy and Georgie Porgie? Nah…I don't think so. This isn't Ming the Merciless and Aleister Crowley we're talking about here. Art's simply a talk-show host, sitting in a trailer house-radio station out in the middle of the Nevada desert, and Noory's broadcasting alternates between two locations—the land of 'fruits and nuts,' and 'OZ.'"

"Where?"

"California…Guacamole country, and Kansas."

"Ming the Merciless? I see you've elevated your reading material from those with centerfold pages to comic books. And, you're wrong…again."

"How droll. Now who's being sarcastic, and what do you mean, wrong?"

"Wrong! Their listening audience is in the millions of people. Imagine what power is generated when all these minds are brought to a clear, pinpointed focus. Believe me, individually, each of these men can set whole disasters in motion. In fact, in a way, Mr. Bell did."

"Ahhh, here we go—voodoo. I knew it…I knew it! Arthur's into voodoo!"

"Will you *stop it?* I simply…."

Before Lyra had a chance to finish her answer, the radio host's voice overrode their conversation.

In this segment, call-ins are being taken rather than interviewing guests. Bell jumped right in: "Hi. On my time-traveler line, you are on the air. Hello!"

"Hi. I'd like to ask Sven about the earthquake predicted for the New Madras, Missouri, fault line that's going to split the country from the mouth of the Mississippi up to the Great Lakes. I…."

As a car passed, King's attention was diverted. He pointed to its bumper sticker. Gleefully savoring every word, he read the sentiment out loud, "Oh God, please protect me from those who think they follow you." He chuckled. "Don't know who owns that car, but I could grow to like that guy."

"Who's to say it's a he?"

In a rare display of mutual agreement, the two burst out laughing.

Pondering his companion's premise, the driver was confused and sought clarification. He recalled a time when Art Bell spoke of scientists digging up a cadaver from the 1918 flu epidemic, the one that killed over twenty-one million people. That night Bell said, "Now this seems to me to be one of the dumber things that we have ever done. And we have done a lot of dumb things. But as I said to the earlier audience, I can close my eyes and see the Level IV containment. I can see the guy in the white lab coat. I can see the magnification of the 1918 virus into its teeming, teeming, teeming…I can see a glass—ahhh, full of it—a test tube full of it all. I can see the fingers slipping and the glass hitting the floor. I can see all of that."

"So according to your focus theory," Rig continued, "if everyone visualized that picture, the plague should have been reactivated and wiped out half of the United States by now."

"That's not what I'm saying. The flu wasn't reawakened, because his audience was divided. One group thought it could happen and the other knew it wouldn't. Do you see how each canceled out the other?"

"No."

"To create miraculous happenings, millions aren't needed. With just *one or two people* and no opposition, anyone *can do anything*—move mountains, if need be."

Holding the coffee cup in his left hand, Rig extended it through the smashed-out window. Whipping wind caused some liquid to fly back on his arm, with a slight stream landing in the car. An especially large droplet dangled from the tip of his nose like a miniature ornament. Coming up to a hill and using his index finger as a pointer, he roared, "Move, mountain, move!" Feigning astonishment, the unbeliever turned, joking, "Darn! My finger must be broken; it didn't budge."

"Finger's not broken. It's your brain."

"Funny, very funny…Ha, ha."

"Rig, the reason the hill didn't move is that, at least on a subconscious level, you feel what you're asking is impossible. Seeing the outcome already *in a state of completion is the key.* If you had turned your prayer over to the Infinite, without resistance, that hill would have gone anywhere you directed."

"*Come on!* If that's true," he bristled, "why didn't you use prayer back in the cave?"

"I was too frightened."

After a slight pause, he felt calmer and answered, "Makes sense, I guess. You know, I still wonder what that thing was down there, and why it was after us."

"In a minute—let's get back to focused power. Do you see what I mean?"

"Not really. I think you're saying that if someone prays for a thing to occur and another is against it, nothing will happen. Right?"

"Yes and no. It depends. If some are stronger in their thinking, certainly they can override the prayer of another. Take the 2000 Presidential Election for example. It's a fact that forty days before voting, a segment of a major Christian faction got over one million people to fast and pray for Bush to win…And remember the confusion that caused? Even with the *Miami Herald*'s official tally showing Gore winning in Florida by twenty-five thousand votes, W. still became president. So, don't tell me prayer doesn't work."

"No kidding…one million?"

"It's true. But what's more ironic is that when anyone tries to force a specific outcome rather than seeking God's will, even though they call it 'holy prayer,' what they're really performing is *black* witchcraft. Think about it. Isn't demanding a particular result—whether by prayer or by guns—the strategy of the bin Ladens of the world?"

King craned his neck toward Lyra. More in a defensive mode than trying to learn, his cynicism was obvious. "*That's it…that's it.* Then what you're asserting is that, say, groups praying for Hitler to die were wrong."

"Actually, yes. In Hitler's case, the proper spiritual prayer would have been seeing the world delivered from evil and war. In the case of the 2000 Election, had those who prayed and fasted wanted to follow true Christianity, they would have asked for and trusted God's will being done to elect the most qualified candidate. Rig, regardless of whether President Bush is the best man or not is immaterial. The point is that in the car of life, you should be the passenger; let go and let God drive."

"Then," the broker countered, "back to your point. The stronger-minded person or group wins, even if the results will hurt the other side?"

"On one level—absolutely. If the being or group is unified and laser-focused in one direction—look out! It's a cosmic law: 'That which is thought, is ordained to manifest.' Like…."

"Wait a minute. I'm confused. So you're telling me, the side with the highest number of prayers wins?"

"No, it's the *quality* of prayer, not the *number* praying—the tapping into the Universal Mind or Consciousness and allowing that to flow through you. That power is unlimited. Successful results depend on only four things: clarity of thought; the force behind it; releasing without attachments; and *knowing it's already done.*"

"Give me an example."

"Remember that drought down in Texas back in '98?"

"Yeah, do I! It affected the grain market all the way to Ohio. Really lost my shirt that season."

"Well, it was the worst the state had ever known. Went on for months. Personally, I think Mr. Bell started his experiment out of curiosity—some sort of quasi-metaphysical test using mass-consciousness. Anyway, everybody in the audience was asked to focus their thoughts—to see lots of rain falling down there."

"And?"

"I'm getting to that. After a few days, it poured. Such a deluge, not only was there tremendous flooding, the storm seemed like it would never stop." The Ra representative smiled. She knew the radio host made a classic mistake in his unintentional prayer; he asked everyone to see a huge amount of rain falling, rather than simply just what was needed.

"Lyra, that's...that was just a coincidence. Get real. Rain was bound to come. I mean, sometime."

"Oh, ye of little faith! That's exactly the problem. Few comprehend the infinite amount of power one is able to access. Mr. Bell tapped the Universal Force and accidentally channeled it through his listeners."

"What about the release part of your formula?"

"Since most people weren't emotionally connected to the state, they prayed and let it go without fear and—most importantly—with no attachment."

Knowing they were both hungry, she changed the subject and asked, "Want a sandwich?"

"Sure, I'm starving."

Finishing his coffee, Rig flipped the plastic cup out the broken window. Seeing the litter, his passenger's mouth dropped. In further horror, she watched as he used his left knee to steer while both hands unfolded the sandwich wrapper. Finally open, and with his right hand returned to guide the vehicle, she breathed an audible sigh of relief.

Seeing apprehension on her face prompted a, *"Whaaat?"*

Forcing a large swallow, she said, "That's...that's just one example of Mr. Bell getting miraculous results. Then there was the time he asked his audience to meditate on the healing of Richard Hogland's heart."

"Who?"

"Their space expert—the man who sees the outline of a face carved in a rock on the surface of Mars."

"Oh boy," Rig opined, "now there's another flaky one...Okay, okay. Don't look at me like that. So then what happened?"

"Instant healing."

"Spontaneous remissions happen all the time, at least according to the AMA. They're just flukes of nature."

"That's what you're supposed to believe. How can the medical community admit something being beyond science? They'd be giving credit to an unknown outside of medicine; and if the public were to ever understand these principles, it would take away the doctors' prestige and diminish their livelihood."

"Nahhh! We just like a little scientific evidence—something that's provable—not the now-you-see-it, now-you-don't, rabbit-in-the-hat trick."

"Rig, even scientists agree that every action must have a cause, Right?"

"So?"

"Well, logic dictates that *all healing* must have some starting dynamic or impetus; things just don't spring forth without reason. And your medical community is the first to admit that no cure can happen without something first setting that process in motion."

"Then these spontaneous healings are…? *Hey!*" He points. "See that cactus coming up, one with the center, the vertical part, missing?"

"Which?"

"Phooey, you missed it," he grunts. "I wanted to show you something. *Look!* Quick, *look!* There's the other."

"What? Where?"

"That cactus there. See its middle?" Pointing, King explained, "Out in the desert the Spaniards had a secret way of marking mine locations. They lopped off the center spire, leaving just the arms that stick out to the side." He slowed down for a better view.

"Oh, now I see it."

"When you find one of these missing a center, always look for a similar cactus nearby. Line the two up like sights of a gun and a gold or silver mine will invariably be at one of the ends." Speeding back up, he finished, "Thought you might find that interesting. Anyway, back to this prayer thing."

"I do. Thank you. Okay, there are a couple more examples I could give about Mr. Bell but you probably wouldn't be interested. Anyway, he quit asking the audience to focus on things shortly after that. I guess he became worried what could happen if he wasn't careful—something akin to handling nitroglycerin, only infinitely more powerful."

"Ehhh, these are all simply flukes of nature."

"Rig, I can't understand how you could think there are catastrophes beyond God's ability to fix. Okay, smarty-pants, I'll really give you something. And I'm not going to go into the husband and wife who were half an hour off the California coast when their plane's engine froze. By using the technique

I'm about to explain, they did what's scientifically impossible—flew a full twenty-eight minutes before landing at an airport. Come to think of it, there were a number of similar incidents recorded during World War II and Korea, for example, but you'd of course demand, 'Where's the proof?' And it is there, but I'll tell you about a more recent incident that's equally impossible, yet fully documented." She chuckled. "Even today, this confounds the scientific community."

Turning the cab light on, Lyra pulled two articles from her briefcase. Quoting the first, she told of a time, back in 1993, when an oil tanker sank off the rocky coast of the Shetland Islands, west of the United Kingdom. The visitor from Washington was quick to emphasize this spill was the twelfth largest in history, reminiscent of the 1989 Exxon Valdez catastrophe—that infamous Alaskan petroleum slick that stretched for 1,240 miles and took 11,000 people to do a cleanup that wasn't completed to that day.

The driver listened as his passenger explained the Shetland spill's threefold threat. First, the primary livelihood of the islands came from Scottish salmon, caught offshore. Those fish, of course, were completely decimated. Second, not only was there an enormous toxic danger to the human population, but one that could wipe out nearly all local wildlife. Reports indicated 1,542 seabirds died almost instantly. And with the spill fanning out, oil-sodden feathers and the inability to breathe assured thousands more were soon to follow. Exacerbating the catastrophe, stormy winds and monstrous waves made cleanup impossible. Scientists were at a loss—helpless.

"What are you taking all this from?"

"Here—this is an article from February 21, 1994, by a Shetlander named Dawn Lambert. It's called *Environmental Tragedy is NOT Inevitable.*'

"The piece relates how Ms. Lambert and a friend in England were almost paralyzed with fear about the devastation to all that area's wildlife. It was such a gruesome scene, and throughout the British Isles the story became so talked about that the topic was nearly inescapable. Increasingly scary pictures kept popping up on every BBC news bulletin.

"But this is where it gets interesting. I'm about to speak of a method by which these two people actually made that incredibly huge slick disappear. Or said a better way, they changed focus and saw it vanish, as did everyone else."

"Oh, come on!"

"No, it's true. Let me explain how the miracle happened. Rather than working to clean up the problem, these two went in a radically different direction. They strove, instead, to gain a deeper understanding of the qualities and perfection of God. Now this process may seem vague, but bear with me. Their goal was to arrive at a point where each had zero doubt that any crisis or illness, even one of this magnitude, was beyond the Creator's ability to heal. After all, if God is God, every difficulty can be fixed. Right?"

Without waiting for his opinion, she continued. "Three days passed. But, as with many problems or physical illnesses, the emergency only seemed to worsen."

He dodged lumber in the road while his companion recounted, "And yet, both women ceaselessly strove to gain a clearer understanding of who and what God really is: the all-knowing, all-powerful, Father-Mother. On the fourth day, something strange happened. Simultaneously, though they were miles apart, each was overcome with tears of joy, followed by a deep sense of peace. Accompanying this was a profound understanding: God can and will make perfect even the most seemingly impossible of situations."

"Look out!" Lyra screamed.

Rig again swerved, barely missing a jackrabbit darting across the road. An unleashed temper once more clouded his reasoning. *"Damn rodents!* Think they own the entire desert."

Both were quiet for a few seconds before she proceeded. The story was abbreviated for expediency. "Calling across the channel, Ms. Lambert found her friend was equally calm. An impulse came that compelled each to turn on the news—only to discover an extraordinary thing being reported. Against all scientific understanding, the slick had totally vanished. In panic, environmentalists concluded it had sunk to the ocean floor. Still a problem, experts foresaw the next development would be the complete devastation of all fish, shellfish, and sea plant life. But soon after, the winds died down and the water calmed. Mysteriously, however, divers and their cameras found everything normal. Even the sand was pure white.

If you research it," she said, "BBC archives record a British television commentator's conclusion as, 'No sign of any oil sinking to the seabed; the oil has virtually disappeared.'"

The Ra representative told how the TV program also showed the birds being treated in the cleaning-up process, mysteriously fully recovered—and ready for immediate release. Unfortunately, Lyra added, "it's true that ten gray seals and four otters perished—two from being run over by a camera crew's truck, several from oil pollution, the others from old age. But those deaths happened prior to Mrs. Lambert and her friend delving into and putting all their trust in Divine Principle."

"I don't remember any of this."

"Where were you? News of it was everywhere. Like here in *Discover* magazine." The Ra rep holds up a second article while continuing, "Back in January of 1994, these people also did a Shetland Island oil story entitled, *'A Disaster That Wasn't.'"* She finished by saying, "Rig, using this ancient method! Anyone can make miracles happen."

"Wait. So you're telling me these women made the oil slick disappear?"

"Yes and no. They did do the opposite of what's done by your church groups, metaphysicians, or even shamans."

"Like what?"

"Well, in most religions, you plead or bargain with some deity to...*Watch out...There's another!* By the side of the road—over there."

"I see him...I see him; I only brake for investment bankers. If that fur-ball doesn't stay put, he's going to that Great Carrot Patch in the Sky."

"As I was saying, the first group prays, hoping their god will fix the problem. Which sometimes seems to work. But most of the time, it doesn't."

"I'm with you—so far."

"As for the metaphysicians and shamans, by using spirits, crystals, rituals, and whatnot...and this is their trick...they try to manipulate or mold the outcome."

"And they do, don't they? I mean, I watched a PBS documentary where this medicine man guy did some pretty far-out stuff."

"Yes, but what I'm talking about is a higher level of spirituality. Controlling objects, people, or events is simply a redirection of matter. These are parlor tricks. With enough practice, they can be pulled off by any amateur. What Dawn Lambert and her friend did was something different; they simply let go of fear and looked at the situation from the Creator's perspective."

"What do you mean?"

"Each didn't attempt to alter, manipulate, or control a thing. In fact, even God didn't. Both women simply came to the conclusion that if the Creator is this perfect All-in-All, there can be no error or what you would call 'a problem.' In God's flawless world, opposite of the chaotic life or dimension we see here, no spill can exist—sort of a Heaven on Earth."

"Oh, brother—you must have your Ph.D. in this stuff, which translates to what I call, Piled Higher and Deeper."

"Stop being nasty! Answer me this: If God is this perfect, all-knowing, everywhere being, how could He have an accident? How can this omniscient, omnipresent, all-loving entity wreck the climate, kill animals, make wars, and destroy human lives? He…She…It can't. The Creator is incapable of error. It only demonstrates two things: *perfection* and *love*. Once each woman understood this, they changed their focus. Looking past or through the illusion of the problem, they concentrated on the truth—the true reality. And as they tuned into this perspective or zone of understanding, the negative situation or lie vanished—like fog touched by morning sun."

Still doubting, Rig suggested maybe waves broke up the oil, or possibly it disappeared by the use of chemicals. In rebuttal, she again pointed to the Valdez spill and reminded him saltwater doesn't dissolve petroleum. "Up in Alaska, they're still cleaning gunk off those rocks." As for the chemical agents at Shetland, she noted, "A little was used, but that means the oil would have sunk to the seabed. And as the BBC reported, it just wasn't there."

Absorbed in thought, her companion mumbled, "Amazing, but what else can you do with this technique?"

"Oh, there's teleportation, not only of yourself but of objects. Or the manifesting of things out of thin air, as in the Biblical loaves-and-fishes story. Then there's the raising of the dead and…."

"*Whoa!* Are you kidding me? You mean like in the movie, *Night of the Living Dead,* where these corpses rise out of their graves and head into town?"

"No, silly. Like what Jesus did with Lazarus."

"I can't believe you or anyone else can animate a corpse. This sort of thing just doesn't happen."

"Not true. I myself have seen...."

Without warning, a rock, thrown by the wheel of a passing truck, left a fracture in the windshield. Driver and passenger, recovering from their instinctive flinching, continued their conversation.

"*Ahhh, damn!* Now I've gotta buy John a windshield *and* a window! Crap! This just keeps getting better and better."

"Rig, the raising of Lazarus and other people is well documented. Even today there are...."

"I've never witnessed it, so I can't form an opinion. But even if it is possible, which I don't believe, I certainly don't see *me* doing it."

"You don't realize who man really is, do you? Haven't you ever read Jesus' admonition when he was talking about his miracles, saying, '*These things and greater shall they also do'?* The *they* means you—modern man. You just have to re-remember how."

Although talking to the stockbroker felt like explaining something to a rock, Lyra attempted to show that Divine Law would always be immutable. She stressed that limitations imposed by physics were nothing more than illusionary hypotheses built on the fabricated dreams of man. The Shetland Island oil spill was just one more event disproving yet another scientific myth: *For every action, there is an equal and opposite reaction.*

"What I'm explaining are cosmic principles, which haven't changed from the beginning of time. *Those miracles done by the ancients, the average individual can and is now being 'expected' to perform.* Such demonstrations, what some might call 'supernatural occurrences,' aren't strictly for the chosen few—the supposed elite. Remember, *however hopeless and frightening your situation may seem, there is always a solution...* within your grasp this very moment."

She paused to gather her thoughts. "This is an especially crucial time in the evolution of man—a period when a quantum leap in spiritual understanding is occurring. Humankind is being urged to drop its violent, manipulative ways, rediscover its Divine connection—and to reverently apply these ancient mystical laws. That done, the picture of death, destruction, and poverty will disappear—miraculous solutions will unfold before your eyes."

Too tired to talk on, she slumped back in the seat. As they headed on toward Phoenix, bleak scenery and monotonous miles add to their weariness.

CHAPTER IX

WHITE-LIGHTING

Fifteen minutes passed. Amidst her nail-filing, Lyra mused, *Too bad Rig's so wrapped up in that little world of his. Cut through those layers, and he's kind of cute.* Glancing over, her mouth opened in shock. Once more her partner had that glassy-eyed stare. Turning back, she saw they were sliding over the double-striped centerline…toward an oncoming cement truck. Its headlights, decorative nose-like wreath on the grill, and polished chrome bumper, conspired with Evil to form a macabre smiling face.

"*Rig*!" Lyra jerked the steering wheel hard, simultaneously stabbing him in the leg with her file. Unfortunately, she pulled too hard.

Pain wrenched the driver from his hypnotic state. Correction was instinctive. Hands and feet moved in blurring motions; everything seemed happening in some sort of hyper-speed—a place and time where driver and passenger had that sinking feeling of being simply spectators—with little or no control over the outcome. Again hitting the brakes and yanking the wheel in the opposite direction, King, worked with feverous desperation, trying to keep from going over the cliff's edge. Tires screeched. The rear of the Bronco slammed hard, clicking against the bolts of the flimsy metal railing.

Fishtailing, their vehicle spun out of control, careening once again into the oncoming lane. Whipping wildly, it tilted up on two wheels before falling back, finally stopping—pointed toward Flagstaff.

Ashen-faced, they sat without speaking. With his white-knuckled hands still gripping the wheel, the treasure hunter didn't notice that the blue stone in his ring had turned a dark gray. Finally talking and shaken to the core, the pair concluded they needed to pull over and spend the night. Phoenix wasn't worth the risk.

Rig now felt his right leg throbbing from the stab wound. "Damn it, woman! I'm sick of you poking and punching me!"

Ever a stickler for details, the emissary coolly responded, "I never punched. I've only stabbed, slapped, and raked...but give me some time and we'll see what develops."

"*Lady*, what is your problem?"

The answer came in a form of fire: "What *you* don't know is you keep getting under the mind control of those who use the cave."

"*Wait!* What do you mean, those who use the cave?"

"I'll get into that in a minute. First...."

"No!" he exploded, his temper flaring to new heights. "I want to get into it *now*, damn it!"

"*Okay, okay.* Calm down. Your face is getting tomato red. I'll explain everything, but first you have to learn to protect yourself. If you don't, this might happen again, even as we speak. I've been doing it for you all day, but your continuous anger, combined with exhaustion, tends to make it wear off."

"What are you babbling about?"

Emotionally raw, tired of being put down, Lyra lashed back. Going for the jugular, she recounted all the times her companion has been too stupidly unaware to know when someone had saved his life—when his mind was controlled by someone else. The concept being far beyond radical, at least in the mind of Rigden King, III, he rejected what he believed to be one more of his passenger's harebrained pipedreams.

"All right then, do you believe in telepathy?"

The answer oozed condescension. "Not really, although I've seen a few mental-case mentalists on TV."

Irritated, Lyra's mouth formed a tight circle. So much so that her words, *"Okay, pick a number between one and ten,"* barely made it through the opening.

"Are you for real about this?"

"Just do it!" she yelled, her whole body beginning to vibrate.

"All right, all right! Calm down, girl! I've got one."

"Six!"

"Lucky guess," he said with his usual smirk. "Wanna go for double or nothing?"

"Then pick one between zero and one hundred."

A slight pause. "Got one."

"Fifty-seven."

"How'd you do that?"

"Don't be ridiculous; I just told you—it's called mind-reading. Now let's take it a step further. I'll think of a color and send it to you. Ready?"

Disbelieving, Rig didn't know what to make of the demo. "This is really stupid. Tell you what. If I play your stupid game, will you finally say what you think that thing was in the cave? That is, if you really know."

"Fine, fine. First tell me what color I'm thinking of."

"Well, it's kind of hard while I'm driving, but I think it's... ahh, green."

"Good. That's right."

"How do I know that was the color, and you're not just lying?"

Trying hard to remain civil and still talking between clenched teeth she replied, *"It...was...green."*

"Unplug, for God's sake! I believe you. It was green, already."

"Listen to me. You, I, or anyone can send an idea to someone else, anywhere, anytime. And if you don't know a thought's origin, you can easily mistake it as your own, just like you did back in the cave. That's what makes mind-imprinting so insidious. Any trained person can easily control an unsuspecting victim, especially when the receiver is tired, frightened, or angry. Remember what I said? When you give your power away, that hands them the advantage. Trust me; I've been studying these principles for years."

"This is too much. Sorry, I can't buy it. It's all a bunch of psychic hogwash."

"Well, Mr. Wall Street, you'd *better* believe! Your lack of understanding has nearly gotten us killed—several times."

"Then if you know so much, how come whoever they supposedly are, how come they also affected you back in the canyon?"

"Remember Star Trek? Like you, I didn't keep my shields up. As I said, focused power can be blocked in several ways. White-lighting is just one technique. Think of the mind as your home; in most areas of the world, you wouldn't go to bed with the front door unlocked and the windows wide open. But whether you're aware of it or not, the majority of people try to break in by reading your mind, even if they do it subconsciously. Prove it to yourself sometime. Try asking a banker for a loan when you desperately need the money." She rummaged through her purse while talking. "He or she will pick up on your desperation even as you're entering the room. So I white-light myself, rather than letting someone wander freely around inside my head.

"There's another thing. Did you ever come back from a movie or a shopping mall feeling drained?…Yes! Here it is! Thought I'd lost my lipstick."

"Sure. Shopping, for me at least, is always exhausting. And come to think of it, I sometimes do come home from the theater feeling pooped."

"Many people, like salesmen, consciously or subconsciously try to mentally manipulate you into doing something against your will. And a few in every crowd even act as psychic vampires."

"Psychic what?"

"You heard me. They rob you of energy."

"You're kidding? And what do they do with it?"

"By siphoning your energy, it gives them a power boost. Haven't you ever noticed that being around a particular person tires you to the point of being fatigued?"

"I used to date a girl like that."

"That figures; she was probably a succubus."

"Cut it out." Suddenly excited, King wanted to learn more. "Tell me, when should I do this white-lighting thing?"

"Oh, I usually activate it in the morning when rising and at night before going to bed. Today, however, because of all the stress, I had to do it several times. Although apparently not enough."

Her companion's frustration burst forth. "So damn it, why don't you teach me? Getting killed isn't high on my list!"

"Do you always have to be so domineering? You're such a classical sociopath—thinking everybody owes you something. I can't believe it."

"No need to get insulting." Restating it as nicely as possible, the stockbroker tried again, this time adding a stretched-out, "*Pleeease?*"

"That's better, but only slightly. All right. Light, or I should say *blinding white light,* is a visible and very physical aspect of God—something that gives the actual power of protection. For example, when Moses went up to receive the Ten Commandments, remember he couldn't look into the Creator's face? The light was too bright."

"Guess I skipped that chapter."

"Rig, the first step in protecting yourself from the negative thoughts or energy draining of others is to get your mind quiet. For you, that might take some doing."

"Thanks a lot."

"Now see a brilliant white light filling your entire body… so much so that it overflows several feet outside. Then ask the Divine Essence, or whatever name you use for the Father-Mother, to protect you from the negative thoughts of some specific person or group. And that's all there is to it. Just remember to close with, *It is done,* and *thank you*."

"And that's it? That's all there is to it?"

"That's it—simple, yet immensely powerful. Although as I said, that mantle of protection wears off under stress and over time. So to be the most effective, it should become an automatic part of your daily routine."

"Now," he queried with the impatience of a little boy, "can you tell me about that beast in the cave? *Hey, look!* There's a rest area." He points to a road stop ahead. "Maybe we should pull in and get some sleep. My vision's beginning to blur."

CHAPTER X

VISITORS

This stretch of the highway was a dismal place. Except for the rest stop, other conveniences were miles away. The parking lot was half-full of the usual travelers: campers; a pickup pulling a boat; assorted cars; and a semi, loaded with propane. While weary sojourners milled about stretching their legs, a mother changed a diaper, and a truck driver was tapping each of his tires with a metal bar, determining if one was going flat.

Exiting their vehicle, Rig noticed a sign with three bullet holes warning visitors not to wander past the asphalted areas—rattlesnakes. Ahead, a small poodle strained on its leash—attempting to pull a ten-year-old girl over to a dying bush in the middle of a scorched, urine-soaked patch of ground. Chuckling, not only at the little dog's enormous deposit but that its stool had fallen in the form of the letter "X", the treasure hunter wondered whose unfortunate lot it was to pick up after the thousands of canines who annually graced this same smelly spot.

Moving the SUV to a far corner of the parking area, Lyra and her companion made two beds by putting their seats into a reclining position. it had been a long, hard day. Somewhat cooler, it was still warm enough that there was no need for blankets. Out of habit, even with a window missing, Rig flipped the switch, locking all four doors.

As they settled in, he remarked about the quietness. More than one would expect, it was broken only by the occasional noise of vehicles speeding up and down the highway. Facing each other, lips inches apart, conversation needed to be only a soft whisper. Between the sexes, this was one of the most intimate times of communication—lilting sounds of tenderness, the type normally shared by lovers and married couples, moments before sleep.

In an unplanned harmonic, their breathing fell into a synchronized, undulating pattern. After a few minutes, the Phoenician was amazed and a little embarrassed—surprised at catching himself trying to inhale the smallest suggestion of his companion's breath.

Tired, he was oblivious to the tingling beginning to course through his body. His heart pounding, waves of energy were giving his skin a decidedly pinkish cast. Lyra too, was falling under the moment's magic—failing to perceive the soft, auric glow that enveloped them both.

Guard down, and unknowingly outclassed in the art of brinkmanship, the equities salesman began his strategy. "Lyra?"

"Yes?"

"You…uh…are you writing your movie from personal experience?"

Gently came the reply. "If you're asking if I've used fact-based situations rather than it being all fiction, the answer's yes."

"Right, that's what I mean. Ahhh…am I included?"

Flashing a grin, she said, "For the moment. So you'd better be nice." Her sentence ended with a slight giggle.

"You know," he continued, "I was thinking. If I'm in your movie, my part should be played by, ahh…say, Rob Lowe."

Trying to suppress laughter, she choked out, "That's a possibility, but I was thinking, if we achieve budget, a better choice might be Jack Nicholson. However, if we can't get all the funds, then you'll be…."

Immediately propping up on one elbow, the stockbroker radiated irritation. "*Nicholson? No way!* And who plays me if you don't raise enough?"

Knowing it would set him off, Lyra's mischievousness overrode her better sense. "Well, if we don't reach our goal, I think we'll have to settle for G. Gordon Liddy. He's a pretty good actor. What do you think?"

Attention deficit disorder at full tilt, King's mind had already flitted elsewhere—going from thought to thought, much as a bird changes branches high up in a tree. Seconds went by without an answer. Picking up the thread, she talked on, unaware that his devious brain was plotting a more immediate objective.

Having come back, he said, "May I offer a small suggestion?"

The answer was a throaty, "Absolutely."

Before speaking, heart jack-hammering out of control, Rig hesitantly reached out—gently laying a hand on one of her breasts…hoping his next move would open that narrow window of opportunity—through which he yearned to enter. "You know, Hollywood isn't usually as interested as much in a story as it is…well…ahhh, in order to be a major hit, movies have to have… uhh…have some form of…how shall I put this?"

Perceiving the oasis for which her companion was headed, and in her sultriest voice, Lyra responded, "You mean…a love scene?" Taking a long breath, she piled it on. "You want to see the sort of passion where the walls of the room seem to melt and…."

As his companion continued, Rig's mind shifted into overdrive: *And our bodies become so sweaty, we slip and slide! That when we come together, there's a slapping sound.* His eyes held an intent gaze as he edged closer—testosterone building toward a Mt. Saint Helens' moment.

With a teasing, cooing tone, she added, "That frenzied eroticism where you lose every bit of control? And after orgasm, you're so embarrassed, you refuse to ever think about the things you said or did? You mean that kind of love-making, right?"

Sighing, a wave of relief swept over the Phoenician as he responded, "Well, maybe not that torrid. I was just thinking this would be a perfect break for that obligatory…you know, skin-to-skin, plot-point in the narrative."

Lyra reached over, placing a hand directly on the one Rig had on her breast. Its additional weight made the softness of the young woman's body fold in between his fingers. King's heart redlined. Above the nervousness, he bathed in a fulfilling satisfaction; the ultimate prize was literally within reach…But no—her movement continued. Void of the slightest anger, the female gently lifted the offending hand, placing it back by her partner's side. Not speaking, she rolled over to face the passenger door.

With neither one moving, the silence in the SUV, at least to Rig, was deafening. Its roar was such that he heard blood surging through his ears. Elsewhere in his body, this same liquid ebbed—deflating more than ego as once again the mountain god retreated, collapsing into dormancy—awaiting resurrection at the libido's next invocation. Ashamed, he turned to face the driver's side.

After what felt like a long time, the stillness of the night was broken by that silken voice. "In your dreams, Riggy…in your dreams."

Moonlight shown through the shattered window. Frustrated, the Lothario twisted and turned. Pride in shreds, he yearned to wrap himself in any form of comfort. There was none. Tonight, at least for Rigden King, III, the curtain of sleep would descend all too slowly. Wide-eyed, staring up at the vinyl roof, he emitted an almost inaudible moan. Still awake, his companion heard the pain of wounded ego—reminding her of the pitiful sound made by a male lion that night out in the Serengeti six months ago. A sympathetic smile formed as emerald-colored eyes fluttered shut.

At three a.m., a pair of silver-domed spacecraft floated above the rest area. Everyone in the parking lot was in a state of profound hypnosis, save for one aging, deaf dachshund whose vocal cords have been severed to silence its incessant barking. Unknown to most, aliens could employ techniques that make their spaceships invisible, even at close range. Another was the ability to place an entire group of people into a somnambulistic state. Barking frenziedly, but achieving only a pathetic, muted gurgle, the dog stood on his hind legs. Its two front paws feverishly scratched the car's side window. Sensing danger and fulfilling his job as guard, he tried frantically to awaken anyone who would listen. No one heard. No one could.

Projection of false pictures to influence large audiences is another ploy commonly employed by extraterrestrials. A steady stream of cars and trucks flowed along the highway, ignoring the rest stop as if it didn't exist. And to them, it didn't. No one entered the parking lot; no one exited. Nothing stirred, except the mime-like barking of a fearless sentry.

Without a sound, a ray of blue light engulfed the SUV. All four door locks popped up. From a cloud of light, a statuesque male emerged and stepped forward. Unhurriedly, the being reached for the handle on the driver's side.

As morning rays of sun shown in his face, King's eyes blinked open. He was still embarrassed. Next to him, Lyra quietly combed her hair. Up for some time, she'd allowed her companion to awaken within the timing of his own rhythm. As he stretched, she noticed a reddish mark over a small, dark, BB-size bump on the underside of his upper left arm.

Grinning sheepishly, he greeted her with, "Good morning."

The returning answer and cherubic smile allayed all his fears. "And good morning to you! Sleep well?"

A troubled look swept over his face. "We should be getting back. Damn, I hadn't planned on being out of the office on a Monday. I've gotta check in."

Getting out, he stretched and made a visit to the restroom, assuming Lyra had done that earlier.

A half-hour down the road, she asked, "Could we pull over at the next stop?"

"Didn't you go already? I wish you'd spoken up earlier. There aren't any more of those until we get to Sunset Point… Wait a minute. That's strange. I see…huh? This must be new. I didn't know they built another one along this stretch. Well, with all this influx of out-of-state traffic, I guess they had to."

Turning into the parking lot, the treasure hunter kept mulling over last night's hazy vision. Heading toward their respective bathrooms, they ambled down the concrete path to where it forked. Still troubled about his dream, he was oblivious to the surroundings. Flashing back to his boyhood, Rig dwelled on the many times shimmering beings were… imagined…standing at the foot of his bed. Going deeper in thought, even the mephitic chemical odor of the park toilets failed to penetrate his concentration.

As he sauntered back to the Bronco, the thought surfaced: No hurry, she'll probably need more time. Takes 'em forever to line the toilet seat.

Ripped from his reveries by what he saw, King paused. Under his breath he murmured, "*Oh man!* That dimwit came down here and shot this sign, too. *What a psycho!*—even aimed at the same frickin' words. I'd like to get my hands on that sorry son of a bitch and.... "

Something else caught this traveler's attention. To the left seemed to be the exact configuration of rocks, the same urine-soaked patch of ground, and the same dying bush as at last night's stop. The first conclusion, *Naw, can't be! This is too weird*, was upset by irrefutable evidence—the dog's X-shaped deposit next to, what looked like, a replica of that dying plant. Confused, the mind denied what appeared all too real. His mature, internal voice, seeking an explanation, was drowned out by its little counterpart which began humming the theme to *The Twilight Zone*. In a muddle, trying to make sense of this discovery, he slowly wandered back to the SUV.

Speeding down the highway, his furrowed brow inspired Lyra to ask, "What's bothering you?"

"You're not going to believe this, but we just...we just came...." Scratching his head, the Wall Streeter found it difficult to articulate the unfathomable. "Somehow, this rest stop was a duplicate of the earlier one. It was like we came back." Nearly breathless, his spewed forth. "But...I know it can't be! We went forty miles toward Phoenix. And there's more." King excitedly explained the bullet holes in the sign, the identical shrub, some canine's gift to the universe in the same spot; and more unbelievable yet, the dog's deposit was in that same "X" configuration.

"Rig," Lyra urged, "you'd better pull over. We need to talk."

A man of the world, this male had had enough relationships to know that when a woman uses the words, "We need to talk," something bad was about to happen. Gravel flew as they skidded onto the shoulder.

Turning and expecting the worst, he blurted, "*What now?*"

"I didn't really want to get into this."

"Into what?"

"Do you believe in flying saucers?"

Subconsciously, that's what'd been nagging him. Although a Doubting Thomas, his response was amazingly open. "Honestly, I've never seen one, so I can't say whether I believe or not. Why?"

For the Ra Foundation's representative, the next question was a major leap. "What if I told you that *I…I am an alien?"*

The calmness of the SUV was broken by a rocking motion made by the sucking wind as an eighteen-wheeler whipped by, passing within a few feet.

Now that he knew his companion was truly loony, King dryly interjected, "This brings to mind Arthur C. Clarke's comment—you know—the author of *2001, A Space Odyssey*—about the possibility of other life in the universe. He said, to the effect, *'There are only two possibilities: Either there is, or we are completely alone…and to me,'* Clarke concluded, *'both scenarios are equally frightening.'"*

"No, I really am!"

The driver searched his passenger's eyes. "Are you serious?"

"Totally. I'm from the planet Eeliopal."

"Oh my God! That's a relief."

"Why?"

"For the longest time," he shot back, "I've been wanting to tell you a secret."

"What?"

"That I'm Batman. *Whew!* Glad I got *that* off my chest." Rig's sarcasm mounted. "Now I feel a whole lot better." Flooring the gas pedal, he yelled over the pounding of gravel and squealing tires, "That's it! I'm outta here! This was just way too much fun for one weekend."

The alien grabbed him by the arm. "*Listen to me! I am from another planet!* In fact,from another galaxy."

Turning on the radio, the Phoenician divided his attention, screaming over the music, "What a coincidence! I've got these neighbors from Venus you should meet. Well, actually they just moved here from Malibu. Like to barbecue a lot. Suppose that explains why all the neighborhood cats have been disappearing. And to think, everybody's been blaming those poor Vietnamese families that moved into the area."

Her index finger hit the radio's off button. "*Stop it! Stop it right now! Pull over!* We have to resolve this."

King did his best to ignore the crazy woman next to him. Finally she grabbed the steering wheel, touching off a major tug-of-war. Weaving down the yellow line, the driver realized it was far safer to take a few minutes and placate this nut than to get into an accident. Angrily, he hit the brakes. Once more the tires skidded, sending them back to the road's shoulder. Minutes ticked as Lyra attempted to explain her secret.

The adventurer in him would have liked to believe, but the skeptic couldn't quite leap over his mountain of doubt. *Perhaps if I let her talk long enough,* his mind turned, *something's going to give and I'll see she's lying.* Playing along, the broker asked a simple question. "If what you say is true, why are you telling me…me, of all people? Why not the President?"

"Had the trip gone as planned, I wouldn't have said a word. But you and I have stumbled onto something. And they want us dead. I…."

"Who wants us dead?"

"It might be clearer if I first explain who I am and just what the Foundation really is. Our office in Washington is a cover so we can be near your political center. We actually function under the Council of Nine, The Guardians."

"The Guardians?"

"Don't interrupt. I'm getting to that. Ancient ones who watch over various galaxies. My group's been assigned here, because Earth faces a special problem."

"Which is?"

"*Shhhh!* Stop breaking in and I'll tell you. The Council is attempting to keep your planet from self-destructing."

"Except for terrorism, everything looks fine to me."

"That figures. it was the same thing your people said just before the sinking of Atlantis. Had The Guardians not intervened, your planet would have gone nova—upsetting the entire holographic grid."

"The what?"

"I'll explain. Due to the interconnectedness of the universe, havoc would have rippled across the full time-space continuum. What you don't realize is that when something like this happens, it takes the hyper-dimensional matrix eons to realign."

Again stopping her, the earthling probed for flaws in the, supposed, alien's logic, "Do all of your people look like us?"

Although an arrogant question, the extraterrestrial explained, "Aside from a few internal differences, we are both quite similar."

"So you do look exactly like us?"

"Well, this actually isn't my birth body; I'm a walk-in."

"A walk-in?"

"That's when a soul finishes its mission, its life on Earth, and the individual is getting ready to die. Occasionally, but only by mutual consent, another is allowed to occupy that person's shell when the first spirit exits."

"You're kidding!"

"Rig, to us, death is only a minor transition, not a finality—simply a changing of zip codes."

"You mean you take over that person's identity?"

"Sort of—to a degree. As I said, these are people already preparing to pass on. It was not technically correct to say their personality or identity is taken over. That soul simply leaves. Oh, you may live in their house, drive their car, even work at their old job, but you're still the original you. You try to fit in to as much of their daily routine as possible while fulfilling your assignment."

"*God!* Maybe that's what happened to Bruce."

"Who?"

"Guy I used to know from college—shy, introverted. You know the type—never drank, real straight-laced. Died on the operating table. After they revived him, it was like he was a different person—a real Mick Jagger—sorta…you know what I mean."

For an hour, which to the listener seemed but a few minutes, they continued. His questions flowed nonstop. Every conceivable pent-up thought, from vague childhood memories of spaceships to bad sci-fi movie myths, flooded his mind. Spellbound, the earthling's attention was riveted on the supposed alien …or at least, a great storyteller.

Happy to have someone to confide in outside of the Council, Lyra talked passionately about her planet and its three moons—Alpha, Beta, and the smallest, Omega. She explained that the larger two were chunks which split off when her home was hit by an ancient asteroid, and recounted a myth often told to Eeliopal children.

The story goes that, in the time before time, Alpha and Beta, as they later were called, were in fixed orbits on opposite sides of her planet, so they couldn't see and didn't know of the other's existence. This is how it remained, until one day Beta began humming a beautiful lullaby. Alpha knew the sound wasn't coming from Eeliopal, since the old rock was grouchy and never talked much—making Alpha totally confused about the music's origin. Finally, he questioned the elder sphere as to who was singing, but the cranky planet refused to answer. Perplexed, the moon called out, "Who's making that song?" Shocked that someone else beside Eeliopal was nearby, Beta answered, "It is I, the Beautiful One. I sing. Who are you?" Straightforward, Alpha replied, "I, the Strong One, that's who." And that's how it began.

Every so often, they would call out to each other, and, over time, became friends. Lyra pointed out that on one level the story taught children how the strongest love relationships frequently began as friendships. She went on to say that as their closeness grew, each longed to get a look at the other. One day, they decided to petition the Great One, maker of all that was, is and ever will be. Prayer granted, each was given the force to meet halfway around. But in their joy, the speed was too great and they collided. It was here that Omega spun off and became a minor or baby moon, as it remains to this day.

Lyra took special pride in describing Eeliopal's landscape and the architecture of its beautiful cities. The alien also rhapsodized over how pristine their countryside was, with its pure mountain streams and clear air. Most of all, she lamented missing the telepathic interaction her people shared with animal species...and was aghast that on Earth, these poor creatures were actually eaten.

The Eeliopian then asserted, "While many on your planet already do this man-to-animal mind-linking, or interspecies telepathy, the majority of Earth people scoff at it—some erroneously believing that animals don't even possess souls ."

"Lyra, excuse me. I really appreciate this domed-city stuff and all...and don't misunderstand, I do find it fascinating. However, I think it was more important that we focus on the *beings trying to kill us*. Don't you?"

"I'm getting to that. I'm just giving you the full picture so you'll understand the tremendous importance of the artifacts you found." The Ra representative's smile turned into a frown. Her voice dropped, sputtering, "Those…those you are interested in are pure evil—nothing more than scum. They've always lusted to be overlords of every dimension. And for traveling in hyperspace, their ships need a rare element, available only on a few far-flung planets. Earth is one of them."

"What's its name?"

"Your people don't yet know of it. Discovery will be made in about eight years. Dr. Cortez Franco will name it 'T-5'—an anti-quark, xeondrite particle for plasma stabilization necessary when they traverse wormholes. Without it, their anti-matter reactors and gravity amplifiers destabilize—disintegrating their ships into atomic goo. We have a different design that they haven't gotten their claws on…yet. Anyway, to obtain this element, they enslave earthlings, using them for mining, breeding, and as a supplemental food source."

Anger mounting, Lyra described their warlike mentality and many galactic colonizations. On Earth, they first settled on the continents of Atlan and Poseidon, as they were then known. She spoke of their Atlantean priesthood and its high refinement in the magical Black Arts. "Their god, Baal," she added as an aside, "and his followers are even referenced a number of times in the Old Testament—known today as 'The Illumaniti.'

"Prior to Atlantis's sinking, those continents were also inhabited by The Children of the One or Children of Light, as they were also known. The opposite of The Followers of Baal, they worshiped the one true God, but were subjugated into slavery, as well as often used for grotesque medical experiments."

The alien remarked the world would be shocked to learn this very same evil priesthood also had airships, submarines, and nuclear weapons…as well as cloning. As proof, she said that detailed descriptions of these and even battles involving nuclear arms still exist, clearly recorded in a number of ancient, but easily found, East Indian texts.

She spoke of a period of corruption on Earth 10,532 years ago, a point that coincided with Christianity's Great

Flood—erroneously pinpointed by many Biblical scholars as occurring at a much later date. In Atlantis, inflated egos led the Followers of Baal to overload their power supply—resulting not only in the destruction of that continent, but the flooding of most of the planet. Although, this pivotal event was often confused with less dramatic inundation stories, such as those recounted in *The Epic of Gilgamesh,* the Nez Perce telling of a world flood, or the Mayan deluge as recorded in the *Popol Vuh,* to name a few. Those were simply regional, and at different dates; the only true planetary flood was that which sank Atlantis.

She went on to say that after blowing up Atlantis, this evil group had been given another chance by being allowed to reincarnate—some recently participating in the rise of the Third Reich, with many of those souls again recycling right after WWII.

As a spiritual test, these beings had been placed in similar levels of past power in governments, religious orders, and key industries. That alone, she stressed, explained some of the self-serving, cruel, evil actions of many now in authority—such as the use of black magic through a cabal of diabolical societies that secretly promulgate "The New World Order" under the guise of globalization.

"The Flood! Now that's one event that, regardless of your timing, I do know something about."

"So you think. But as your Paul Harvey would say, 'Here's *the rest* of the story.' Because both the Followers of Baal and the Children of the One were psychically adept, many had prior warning of the coming disaster. These two opposite groups fled to five locations around the Earth."

"Five places?"

"*Five!* Do you have any idea where?"

Engrossed, the earthling hadn't even blinked in several minutes as he listened to the fascinating story. For Rigden King, III, the boundaries of what was once considered "impossible" were rapidly receding. But the alien's last sentence tugged him back.

"Uhhh…the five? No, I don't have a clue."

"Egypt was one," she asserted. "Prior to that, people there lived in mud huts. Then, almost overnight, they mysteriously evolved into a sophisticated society. Incidentally, Atlantean records are still buried within a chamber called The Hall of Records, accessed through the right paw of the Sphinx. What's more, it was prophesied that these will soon be made available to mankind."

"When?"

"When the vibration of those who were the priests in that lifetime, the ones who did the encapsulating, come together for the unsealing ceremony—using six sacred crystals. Interestingly enough, back in 2000, even your *Arizona Republic* newspaper ran an article about a team discovering that very opening. It said that the Archeological Department of the Egyptian government *acknowledges* knowing of this hidden door and even the chamber that lies behind it, but irrationally forbids any exploration."

"Why? And say, where are these underwater, glass-domed Atlantean cities I've heard about?"

"*Underwater cities?!* Where on Earth do you people come up with these cockamamie concepts?" She didn't wait for an answer. "Most of this lunacy you read about or watch in the movies is the creation of some stupid, drug-hallucinating, low-paid, sci-fi writer—nothing more. At least what I'm telling you is based upon fact!

"And to answer your first question, Egyptian archeologists have been mind-printed to leave this chamber untouched until the right time—when the crystals are brought together. But that period is just around the corner."

"*This is too much!*" he exclaimed, his heart beating faster. "What are the other four…areas?"

"The Yucatan."

"The Yucatan?"

"Absolutely. Scientists are discovering burial sites down there where they can even piece together the fact that ancient Yucatan brain surgeons were over eighty percent successful. The third place was in Mongolia—the location of Shambhala—but it is in a different vibratory range only visible to spiritually developed individuals. Contrary to the reports of failed expeditions, however, this supposedly mythical land does exist. And the fourth…the fourth group relocated to the Pyrenees."

"You mean that little area between Spain and France?"

"One and the same. Rig, don't you find it rather coincidental that people there speak neither French nor Spanish, but a strange, unrelated language? Incidentally, as the Atlanteans were warlike, so are the Basques—as I'm sure you've noticed from their repeated terrorist attacks in Spain. Now I want you to guess where the fifth group relocated. Where do you think they went?"

"Haven't a clue—Australia?"

"You're way off. You'd never get it, so I might as well tell…Arizona."

"Get out of here!"

"It's true. They settled in two places—a little south of Flagstaff and in the Superstition Mountains. We have relics to prove it. But this fact is known only to a very few people. You…Oh my! Rig?"

"What?"

"My guides are…."

"Your who?"

"Guides…think of them as angels. Anyway, they are…Boy, I hope you realize what they're offering."

"Offering? Offering what?"

"*Shhhh!* They're still talking. It is being suggested that you be brought into the Ra's inner circle, *The Ancient Order of Light.*"

"The what?"

"A handful of people who work directly with the space brotherhood, helping keep Earth from self-destructing." The alien explained that all this and more was conditional—contingent upon the decision of her monitor.

Unable to contain his excitement, King blurted, "Who or what is this monitor person?"

"Our people assign a few from our planet to live here among you. My specific coordinator is something like a regional director, if you will. He helps me and others to acclimate to the rules of your societies…that is, before we take on individual assignments."

"Who is he—or is it a she?"

"I'm forbidden to say, let alone give you a name. The only thing I can tell you is that this is a person in upper management with a major pharmaceutical company on the East Coast. Sit still, and I'll make contact."

Rig reaches to hand her the cell phone.

"No, silly. I'll do it telepathically."

"Sorry."

"Be quiet a minute!" The alien closed her eyes and took several long, deep breaths before entering an altered state of awareness.

Rig watched in fascination, not knowing whether all this was real or if he was being taken in by a psychotic liar. Still, the broker felt strangely certain that in some way her story contained more than a fragment of validity. How much, if any, he wasn't certain. Several minutes passed before she reopened her eyes.

"My monitor says he will test you."

"He?"

"Okay, he."

"Test me how?"

"Don't worry; just relax."

Unaccustomed to psychic phenomena, King noticed a massive physical shift, a glowing throughout his entire body. More specifically, there seemed to be an intensity, especially within his chest area.

After the initial shock, and as it became stronger, he thought, *Seems okay; guess I can handle it.*

Within sixty seconds, the pulsation decreased.

Lyra looked over, smiled, and added, "He says you'll do."

"What do you mean, I'll do?"

"He was testing your intent and honesty factors. Don't worry about it. You're a fraction over. You weren't graded from A to F, but from pass to fail. And you passed—one toe over the line, so to speak."

"I have just one question."

"I was expecting several."

"C'mon! If you're so telepathic, why were you so fearful in the cave? Couldn't your people have rescued us?"

"I was too rattled to mentally transmit and receive. Plus, due to the depth, they didn't know where we were, and couldn't have gotten to us in time. By the way, I think you now understand that it wasn't a bear chasing us. It was a DAK warrior, one of the Aryan-SST group."

"What's this DAK-SST thing?"

"Remember the reptilian-looking pictures on the mural? As I kept telling you, those aren't masks. Some are carnivorous warriors from the Aryan Alliance. Do you recall the line between the footprints where you thought something was dragged?"

"Yeah."

"It was—his tail. The DAK are an arm of the Aryan-SST—part of the hierarchy of the rebel cosmic overlords I mentioned earlier—directly under Baal and responsible for war as well as all aspects of physical coercion. So you can see, *this is real*; it isn't some child's wizardry book about make-believe kingdoms, dragons, and pretend spells. This is deadly, and involves your entire planet."

Excited, fascinated, completely blown away—the Phoenician had never had a rush like this. Her story transcended every fantasy he ever imagined. Hundreds of thoughts flowed through his mind as he pulled onto the highway, heading south.

Momentarily leaving her contemplation, Lyra complimented him on doing his white-lighting properly. Then, almost nonchalantly, she added, "By the way, you have a tracking device inserted in the underside of your left arm."

"A what?" The raised tone of voice showed that his shock meter had gone off the scale.

She smiled sweetly. "You're such a worrier; it's one of *ours.*"

Speaking of tracking reminded Lyra of a precaution that needed to be taken. While her companion was otherwise engrossed watching the road, and before she could take the battery out of the cell phone, it rang.

"Must be John, wondering why I'm not at my desk."

It wasn't. The voice, although human-sounding, was low and methodically paced as it said, "You must turn around. What you took is wrong. Those things must be returned. You—"

Rig's reply was indignant, slightly below a controlled scream. "*Who the hell is this? Who are y-?*"

The line went dead.

"I wonder how they got my cell phone number?"

Lyra asked if he still had his wallet. The response was that it was lost. Other than a money clip he carried in his front pocket, it had everything—even business cards with his cell phone number. The Ra representative suggested it probably dropped out when she fell on him in the cave. In the confusion, it would have been easy to miss its absence.

At least the stockbroker-turned-warrior felt some satisfaction in knowing that he was able to protect himself from the mental control of others. Passing vehicles and going around curves, once again the driver didn't notice his passenger removing the phone's battery.

As they descended from the high country, lost in conversation, neither observed the tree-covered mountain scenery gradually giving way to a cactus desert. But with a fortune in the back seat, a lost wallet was a minor inconvenience; Rig's attitude turned cheerful. "By the way," he said with a simpering look, "You know you've got a cute little snore... kind'a like a root hog?"

Before the last word had left his lips, she returned with an equally playful, "Oh...slept with many root hogs, have we? Sounds like you've spent too much time at the watering hole."

The sun was almost blinding as King added ten more miles per hour to the speedometer. Hot air, as if from a hair dryer, continued to boil through the missing and rolled-down windows. Unfazed by his companion's retort, the Phoenician flashed yet a bigger smile and crooned, "*Mon chère... laissez le bon temps rouler!*"

"What?"

With even greater, self-satisfying emphasis, he repeated the phrase more slowly. "*Laissez...le bon temps rouler!*"

"I speak French, but that's...well, maybe it was your accent. Why don't you simply tell me what you're trying to say?"

"It's Cajun, *Mon chère*, Cajun. Means, Let the good times roll."

"Oh."

"You do not approve of theees, *Mon chère*?"

She wasn't smiling. The somber reply, in Arabic, lacked her partner's jubilance. *"In-sha 'a-llah."*

"Meaning?"

There was an uneasiness to her tone. In a barely audible voice, the Ra representative translated the ancient wish. "God willing."

CHAPTER XI

CIRCLING THE DRAGON

Overloaded by all that had happened, Rig subconsciously yearned for the comfort of a normal, daily routine. Lapsing into its business mode of decision-making, the left brain kicked in, analyzing the situation. On the positive side of the ledger, in his possession were things that would bring immense wealth…maybe. On the negative side, it was a fact that several times in the past twenty-four hours, he had nearly been killed—once or twice, possibly by space beings. Still from the left lobe, his reasoning went: *If this alien stuff is real…Lord! I could actually be traveling with one. Then again, maybe all this is just so much crud…But what if what she's saying is true? Is it really possible I've been invited into some group to help save the planet?* Then his nagging, whining voice kicked in. *Hey, stupid! Reality check! About this last thing, who are you kidding? You, of all people? Yeah, right.*

Once more, the stockbroker mentally scribbled a note on the ledger's negative side: *How is all this possible with a six a.m. to three p.m., five-day-a-week career?* Conclusion: *Insufficient data! More—much more input needed.*

A sobering thought hit. *Damn, ol' Farley's going to be pissed—me, not showing up for one of his stupid Monday morning pep talks. My only hope is that John will make up some plausible story and fill me in later on what to say. That's it—call home; Johnny-boy will have left a message.*

Unobtrusively, Lyra slid the battery back into his cell phone, with the admonishment: "Get on and off as quickly as you can, so our position won't be pinpointed. That's why I took the battery out. Leave it in, even if the phone's off, and global positioning satellites will still be able to establish our exact location."

As they whizzed past a flattened Gila monster, cell phone to his ear, Rig glanced at a hawk by the side of the road. Oblivious to traffic, the raptor was busy jerking intestines from the lizard's belly.

The answering machine spit out a frantic message. "Hey, buddy, where the hell are you? *Stupid ass!* What've you gone and done? There're FBI agents swarming all over the office, asking all sorts of questions. And to top it off, the SEC's here. Pardner, I'm afraid your securities license has been jerked. In fact, Farley stormed in and cleaned out your desk; took your entire client base. Man, you're persona non grata around here! I'm comin' over during lunch. If you're not there, I'll be back after work. *Wait for me!* Whatever you've stepped into, you'll need my help cleaning if off."

There was a second message, one from Darla. In a whiny voice typical of one who had lived a pampered life, she said, "*Love, you have to call me*. Two men from the FBI—well, they said they were from the FBI, but I don't recognize credentials—anyway, they asked a lot of questions. Father is going to be *supremely* irritated; he was about to nominate you for that open-chair position for the October Planned Parenthood Ball; but now, I don't know. You had better phone me. it's that *girl,* isn't it? Second thought, don't call! *I never want to hear from you again*." *Click*—the line went dead.

The next message, again from Darla, was maudlin and sugarcoated. "Sweetheart, I'm sorry! *Please* tell me what this is all about. *Love you to death! Bye*."

Turning to Lyra, and with a disbelieving, glazed look, he said, "I've been fired from my job and…and the FBI's looking for me. I can't figure out why, unless it was one of my Mafia clients." His piercing glare accompanied an angry question. "Or is there something you're holding back? And here, you might as well take the battery out."

Sympathetic, she responded, “Not that I’m aware of. I’ve told you everything. Let me check with the Foundation.” Once more, Lyra closed her eyes. In the next twenty-five miles before arriving in Phoenix, the now ex-stockbroker had to make some critical decisions. Minutes later, his companion emerged from her communiqué with a report. “The Director is in Europe at a conference. He gets back in three days. We are being told to lie low until he sees what can be found out in Washington.” Looking over and touching his upper arm, she said, “You hurt your shoulder.”

“Yeah, smashed it when you fell on me in the cave.”

“Why didn’t you say something?”

“What’s to say? I just hurt it. How do you know? I mean....”

“By the color of your aura. Can’t imagine why I didn’t see it sooner; tired, I suppose. You need to have it examined. Say, sometime today I have to see a person in Phoenix, Dr. Xiao-Fan Chu, who, incidentally, is an excellent acupuncturist. You should come along and let him have a look at it.”

A vastly different idea popped into Rig’s mind. “If we can coordinate the timing, but first I need to swing by Arizona State and talk with my old university professor, Dr. Miller. The guy’s really versed in the noetic sciences; maybe he can shed some light on the discs’ language. That’ll give me a hint as to what these things might be worth.”

“Can I make a suggestion?”

The answer was punctuated by caution. “Sure.”

“Take this film and have it developed in one of those while-you-wait places. Only show the pictures to the professor. Don’t leave the discs. While you’re doing that, I need to go back to the resort and freshen up before seeing Master Chu. In fact, if you feel all right about it, why don’t you leave the knapsack with me? Go to the university; then pick me up later.”

Twenty-four hours had gone a long way toward securing Rig’s confidence in this girl. A day ago, this normally untrusting businessman wouldn’t let anyone hold his wallet, much less a potential treasure.

“Okay...but understand that my going is predicated upon whether or not Miller has a free period.”

“To keep from being tracked, why don’t you call from a pay phone?”

A few minutes later at a Texaco station: "Operator, Dr. Miller's office, please...Dr. Miller, this is Rigden King. If you remember, I was on the team helping with that archeological dig near Banja Luka, Yugoslavia, seventeen years ago."

As the professor answered, Lyra listened to her companion's side of the conversation. "You do...not so much for the project but for the incident with the pig, the farmer's daughter, and my consumption of *sljiovica*. Yeah, that brandy does carry quite a kick. I'd hoped you had forgotten all that. Anyway, I've got a relic here you'll be fascinated with...No, no, it is not Yugoslavian. It's...well, it just may be from a different planet...Yes, that's what I said, from another planet. I'm about an hour from the campus. Could I possibly swing by? Great. See you soon."

Considering her friend's penchant for business, Lyra wondered out loud, "Of all places, why Yugoslavia?"

"Ehhh, part of my checkered past. As a student, I wanted some excitement. While everybody was learning French or German, I picked Serbo-Croatian." Rig shook his head in disbelief. "*God!* Considering what the Serbs did in Kosovo in'99, I'm embarrassed to admit I even speak the language." With a shrug he added, "But I did all that in the '80s. Back then, who knew?"

In the distance, the familiar brown haze of Phoenix came into view. City Fathers would have visitors believe it was simply a dust cloud brought in by desert winds. And to some extent, this was partially accurate. Pocketed between two mountain ranges, the area was actually a frequent victim of a polluting air inversion. Just ask any jogger in the winter months. When the temperature dropped below fifty-five, Phoenicians acted as if it was freezing. That's about the point at which most residents justified lighting their annual Yule fires. Many evenings the smoke was so thick the air looked more like fog.

Having dropped her off at her room, King went back for the photos and then off to his alma mater. As he pulled out of the resort's parking area, Lyra came running. The Ra emissary's parting warning was delivered with extra emphasis. "Be careful! Don't trust anyone...*not anyone!*"

Not having been on campus for a while, the former student noticed things seemed slightly changed. Reflecting back, he found it amusing how various levels of education seemed to have their own distinct aroma. For example, walking through the front doors of any grade school, one cannot escape that particular perfume found nowhere else—something akin to a blend of angelic joy, Elmer's glue, and peanut butter sandwiches. In stark contrast, wafting down the dark halls of most high schools were the smells of hormones, chem-lab experiments, and residual cigarette smoke, all mixed with an overtone of less-than-clean gym clothes. Colleges, too, had their odors—though far more subtle. There, it was usually only the philosophies that were in need of purification.

Rounding a corner, the visiting alumnus spotted a size thirty-eight, double-D-cup blonde in a tightly tailored blouse, talking to another girl. With his attention on twin-distractions, the tip of King's shoe caught on a piece of sidewalk previously buckled from the intense summer heat. Arms flapped with the ungainly grace of a goose landing on a sheet of ice as he struggled to regain balance.

Although knowing the building's general location, an excuse was contrived for an introduction. "Pardon me. Do you two gorgeous creatures know the way to the Science Hall?"

Interrupted, but polite, they paused to scrutinize. By look and smell, this creature's appearance was of one who had spent last night dumpster-diving. Discounting that, the obnoxious ploy was not only less than suave, it was crude--an affront. Their disgusted facial expressions spoke volumes, which only female, literary majors could manufacture. Beyond disinterested, the young women pointed in the appropriate direction before turning and walking away.

Thick-skinned, the Don Juan mused in a W.C. Fields imitation, "My boy, it is like selling insurance; it is only a matter of numbers. The more 'No's' you get, the sooner you'll land a 'Yes.' Ah well, and besides…they're probably lesbians."

Knocking on the professor's door, the graduate heard a familiar voice. "Enter!"

"Dr. Miller, thank you for seeing me on such short notice."

"Not at all, my boy, not at all. it has been a long time. Rig, I would like you to meet someone from the State Department. Hope you don't mind."

Standing next to the doctor was a quintessentially bureaucratic-looking individual. Dressed in a dark suit and wearing shaded glasses, the official's micro-trimmed haircut and anorexic face (as if the skin had been stretched over a wire form) lent an uncomfortable air to the meeting.

"What you don't know is that for the last several years I've been consulting with the Hamilton-Biggs Group in Washington—a think tank utilizing my anthropological background for…."

"Excuse me," the man in black cut in. "Dr. Miller, I'm afraid you can't go into that."

"That's right. I forgot. Anyway, it was good to see you, my boy. What have you been up to?"

In a stern voice, Dr. Miller's guest abruptly took over. "Mr. King, explain what you found, and where."

A slap in the face! The Rig was taken aback by the interloper's boldness. Not only was this meeting to have been strictly with the professor, it was clear this outsider was taking control. The ex-student ignored the official, directing his conversation solely at his old teacher. "Dr. Miller…."

Again, the man in black broke in. "Mr. King, I suggest you address your findings to me. What exactly do you have?"

At this point, the treasure hunter was truly thankful for Lyra's forewarning about only bringing pictures. Seeing no way out of some sort of show-and-tell, he set the photos in front of the instructor, ignoring and, he hoped, insulting the intruder.

The astonishment on the professor's face was obvious. "*Oh my. Oh my, Rig.* This is indeed something. I have a special decryption program the government is experimenting with. I'll run these symbols immediately. How about you coming back, say four this afternoon? That is, unless you want to wait. But I'm afraid it will be awfully dull."

As the alumnus groped for an answer, the Washington official spoke. "Mr. King, this is *far more serious* than you know." Picking up the pictures, the intruder demanded, "Where is this device?"

The response—surly. "*Safe!* Why?"

"What you don't seem to know is that the Patriot Act makes having such an artifact a felony, punishable by twenty-five yea…."

As the State Department representative continued his intimidation, Rig's mind was whirling. *Let 'em think they've got me. All they have are these stupid photos. Damned if I'll turn over my fortune! Guess now I've got to sell overseas.* This time, it was the treasure hunter who interrupted. "Okay, checkmate! Look, I'll cooperate—whatever you want. Is there a reward?"

"I'm sure something can be arranged," came the agent's humorless reply from thin, barely moving lips.

Nervous, totally out of his element, Dr. Miller stood a mute observer to the tense exchange. Academia had not prepared the addled scholar for the strain of such high-stakes negotiations.

"Good, how much?"

"Mr. King, we will get to that when you come up with the artifacts."

"I'll bring them to you, anytime, anywhere. How about my pictures?"

The reply was cold, calculating, though tipped with a sweetener. "You can pick up your photos and your money when we meet."

"All right." But not for one second did Rig trust this encroacher to give back his pictures, let alone answer questions concerning the deciphering. Hoping the score was enemy one, himself two, he attempted an exit gambit. "Fair enough. Well, Professor, thanks again for seeing me. Guess I'll come by at four, then coordinate the rest of this through...ahhh, what did you say your name was?"

A face still void of expression, the government man replied, "I didn't give one."

With that, the score was now two-even. The game in overtime, Rig tried for a bonus point. "Well, don't I at least get a business card?"

"We are in an agency whose representatives do not carry cards." The agent, for a third time during the meeting, shook his head as one trying to throw off a confusing thought before coming back to the point. "I won't be asking again, Mr. King, *where is the device?"*

"It's buried near Bisbee, a town near the Arizona/Mexican border." The government official again seemed momentarily disoriented. Though when he spoke, his tone was clear and condescending. "*I know* where Bisbee is."

"Then you know it'll take me the entire night to go get it and come back. So how about nine a.m. tomorrow?"

"No. I'll send along one of my people; we'll recover it tonight."

Indignant, Rig raised his voice. *"Hey! Nobody—and I do mean no-body—goes with me if you want the damn thing. Got it?"*

"You're in over your head, Mr. King. This deals with national security. As I said, not turning the item over is a treasonable offense; you legally disappear...*forever!* So don't think we won't play hardball. *You...got...that?"*

This last statement was the only time the treasure hunter saw Mr. Black eek out a faint smile.

Incensed, the reply was fiery. *"I got it and you'll get it. So get off my back, or you won't get it at all! I don't care what you threaten!"*

The Washington, D.C., representative calmly added, "Then be at the corner of Monroe and Central tomorrow at nine a.m.—*sharp!* And I strongly suggest you fulfill your promise."

"Nine a.m. I'll be there."

"See that you are. Now give me your driver's license."

"Why?"

"Just give it." The unnecessary request was simply for effect—similar to that of a canine, lifting its leg and marking King as his personal territory.

"I lost my wallet in an accident, but I don't see the reason you need it."

"*You* don't *need* a reason. *Hand it over!"*

"I told you, I don't have it."

Moving around the desk, the agent slammed Rig into the wall. "*Spread 'em!*" he commanded , kicking his captive's ankles apart. Pockets were probed—nothing.

While groping with one hand, the agent's other forced his victim's face into the wall. Through mashed lips, the ex-student barely managed saying, "Next time, could we at least have dinner and drinks first?"

"Cut the wisecracks!"

"*See?* Told you I lost it. Hey, if I get pulled over without a driver's license, we might miss your deadline."

"Mr. King, whether it is known or not, you and every person in this country belong to us. We'll put the word out. Regardless of how many traffic laws are broken, you won't be stopped. Count on it. Be at that corner. On time. *Or else!*"

Ignoring every speed limit on the way back to Phoenix, the treasure hunter was lost in thought, until he glanced into the rearview mirror. Even though there have been several changes of direction, a familiar car seemed to be on his tail. Testing his theory, he made two quick turns.

The prey exploded, "*Those bastards! They're following me.*"

Flooring the gas pedal, bobbing and weaving, the escapee intentionally headed west instead of north. Swinging up a narrow alley behind Tierman Auto Werks, the fox lucked out. A split second after he passed, a customer backed up, blocking the alley. The hounds couldn't pass. Safe at last, heading east down Indian School Road, finally turning left on 44th Street, it was off to pick up Lyra.

King's mind buzzed, calculating options. *Wonder how I can slip past that ass from the State Department when I go see the professor? Guess I'll cross that bridge when I come to it.*

Playing more mental chess, he thought, *Damn goon-squad probably even has someone waiting at the apartment. Even so, there isn't time to change before meeting the acupuncturist. We can drop by later. If it's clear, I can get cleaned up and settle things with John. That is, if he's still there. No way to know.... Shouldn't call the office; they'll listen in.*

Relating the ASU incident, Rig was more than amazed when the Foundation's rep wasn't shocked. "Lyra, I don't think you've told me everything." Angrier than ever, he demanded answers. "I want to know what's up, and I want to know *now,* damn it!"

The alien took a moment before beginning. "It's the Order of Baal. But I can't give you more specifics because I don't have any. Honest. All I can do is assume they're still after us and will go to any lengths to get these things in their possession."

"Lyra, come on. Spill it. Is this everything?"

"I told you; I don't know what more I can say. These creatures have an agenda, and they've infiltrated every layer of your society. Unless stopped, and soon, they'll control nearly every man, woman, and child on your planet. Sad thing is," she continued, "it won't be hard; free will here is almost gone."

"What do you mean, 'free will here is almost gone'?"

"Humans are being imprinted—indoctrinated and manipulated by a whole bunch of control programs. As an example, this has resulted in things such as…oh, worldwide terrorism and smaller events like the Atlanta bombing, or the Columbine shooting, employee rampages, et cetera."

"I still don't get it. How do these correlate?"

"As I said, mankind's free will is being molded. Subliminal programming through TV, radio, and movies are just a few of the ways. And in addition to the telepathic imprinting you already know about, there are even more odious mind-control techniques. For example, one percent of Earth's inhabitants have been tagged with tracking and behavior-influencing implants. I swear, some of your people are so gullible, they're even paying for the privilege."

"*Wow!* Maybe I read about that in one of those magazines like *Forbes* or *Barron's*. It said something like, *'In today's competitive world, a mnemonic computer chip enhances your intelligence AND heightens your sex drive. Get one today, before your competition!'*"

"Exactly. Incidentally, can you imagine how easy it is to do mind control on someone who has *a receiver* stuck in his head?" Without pausing, she added, "Did you ever see the film, *The Manchurian Candidate*?" The extraterrestrial skipped over to another thought. "If the chance ever arises, you might find the x-ray of Lee Harvey Oswald's head rather interesting."

"Can't say I'm familiar with your film, but my God, you're right. I do see how someone in business would do anything to stay ahead of the guy down the hall."

"That's only one example of control. Here's something far worse. Without knowing it, a number of your females have been forced into an alien breeding program."

"*A what?* Wonder if that explains an article I read—about these women who reported mysteriously becoming pregnant, supposedly without intercourse. I thought it was some sort of feminist joke."

"Not in the slightest. Did they also mention that in the ninth month, the fetus disappears from the womb? Under hypnosis, many of these surrogates reveal that they are later reabducted—taken up to view their," she grimaced, "deformed and half-human offspring."

"This is difficult for me to swallow. Even in light of what's just happened, I...."

"If it was hard for you, think about the general public. If they knew, they'd go berserk. Societies would break down—fall apart."

"Who's the ringleader of all this?"

"Baal himself. That's the real issue the Council's working on. We're operating at full speed, especially with the prophesied showdown between Good and Evil starting to take place. Trust me. Everything's coming to a head in just eight years. This is why we're in such a hurry." She paused and then added, "If you only knew what your prophets have seen, it would chill you to the bone."

"What you've already told me is a mind-blower. Anyway, before we go to your acupuncturist, I need to stop in at the bank for a moment; I'm broke without my wallet."

"Fine with me."

Five minutes later, Rig emerged from the building—his stride brisk, jaw clenched, aura crimson. Slamming the door, he yelled, "*Can you believe those sons a bitches?* Now the IRS has gone and frozen my account! I have twenty-six thousand in cash, sitting there; and I can't touch it."

"Twenty-six thousand?"

"Yeah, I keep it handy for insider...uhh, let's just say, for stock tips. *Damn*!" he mumbled, slamming a fist on the dashboard. "You know, I can't understand it. None of this makes any sense. My taxes are current and I'm only four measly months behind on alimony. Hey! Would you believe, that stupid manager even threatened to call the cops on me if I didn't leave?" Chuckling and looking rather sheepish, he revealed, "Guess I was screaming at the top of my lungs. Wonder what this is all about?"

The answer came dryly. "The Followers of Baal."

"Give me a break, woman. We're talking about the IRS here, not some stupid alien group."

"That's what you think. You still don't understand mind-printing, do you? As I said, if a person isn't protected by white-lighting, almost anyone can be controlled by thought projection. And those with brain-chip implants are totally helpless."

His frustration mounts. "So, you think they're guiding my little bank manager, the IRS, and everybody else in town? *C'mon! Get real.*"

"Rig, remember how I said that they don't need to manipulate pawns, like your branch manager? They only go after the key players, like, say, the regional head of your bank, the FBI, or…" Lyra paused, deciding whether or not to throw out her next point, "key players, like your nation's president." She smiled, waiting for the other shoe to drop.

"This is ridiculous!"

"Can't you see that all this is being done by the Followers of Baal? Look at what happened today. The Feds are after you; you lost your job, and your securities license was jerked. Even your checking account's frozen."

"So?"

"When will you wake up? All this was accomplished by simply imprinting three or four people, at the most."

Exasperated, the treasure hunter was beside himself. "*Damn! This is too much.* I don't know what to do or where to go."

"Does the swearing really help?"

"*Hell, yes!* I'm fighting for survival here, and you're worried about my frickin' vocabulary."

The reply was soft. "There are always options."

"Oh sure, right. Like, I have no job, no friendly relatives, and forget John; he blows all his dough as soon as he gets it. I see tons of alternatives coming at me from every direction." The ex-stockbroker sighed, slumping over the steering wheel. "Wish I had about $10,000 till I get back on my feet. You seem to have all the answers. Where's that coming from?"

"I would gladly give it to you but I'm not exactly wealthy. We're given only a subsistence salary; I live mainly on the Foundation's credit cards. But you're welcome to use them as much as you like."

Sincerely touched, he began to calm down. "Thanks, but that's not quite going to cut it. I have to find another way, and fast."

Crossing the Salt River, that invisible line of economic demarcation into South Phoenix, Rig wondered why this

Master Chu had chosen the poorest area of the city for his practice. Pulling up to the building, he noted that even the clinic was shabby. Located on a side street off Central and Southern, the business lay in the heart of a gang section known as "Uzi Alley." Instead of a reasonably modern office as anticipated, the two entered a dilapidated building with a dimly lit waiting room, pungent with a smoky cloud of incense. One entire wall was lined with what seemed like a hundred glass jars containing various exotic barks, berries, and other strange compounds, none of which he could identify.

Hearing a noise over his shoulder, Rig spun. The doctor had appeared, as if from nowhere. Dressed in old Mandarin-style attire, the Asian seemed out of place in modern America, even more so this deep in the barrio. Golden-skinned like Lyra, tall, and soft-spoken, Chu carried himself with an air of unmistakable authority.

Without explanation, the Ra representative turned and asked King to wait a few minutes. Quickly, she and the old man disappeared behind a beaded curtain into a back room. Uncomfortable, the ex-broker got one of those mental tics; something nagged just beyond the range of recognition, slightly below the cognitive level. Not quite able to put a finger on it, he concluded that whatever it is, it was nothing compared to what had been happening lately. The feeling was swept under his mental rug—the need for a solution relegated to a less frenetic period.

Returning, Dr. Chu invited his new patient to take off his shirt and lie on a table in an adjoining room. A few minutes later, the explorer's shoulder was porcupined with needles.

"How you feel now, young man?"

"Frankly, if you can believe this, Dr. Chu, the pain seems to have moved across my back; it has, like gone, to the other side. I'm not making this up."

"I know you be serious. We have saying, 'Pain is living thing—alive. Like ego or evil, no want die.' It smart. I put needle here; it run over there and hide. I put needle there; it go down here. The only way to kill this type of pain is by Circling Dragon."

Rolling eyes indicate the patient's level of skepticism. "What's that?"

"You see; I now no put needle in pain but all around in circle, like fence, so pain cannot flee. Then I put last needle in center, into pain itself. It cannot run or hide; must die. This is Circling Dragon. Same way as how man eliminate ego or destroy evil. You cannot run; must look straight in eye with all doors of escape closed."

As Chu's inscrutable pearls of wisdom rolled off the table, onto the worn linoleum floor, the ex-Wall Streeter's Occidental attention was miles away, wondering, *How do I get fast cash? Bank account's frozen, and it will take time to replace the credit cards. The only alternative is to sell one of those alien things.*

Spinning each needle between his thumb and forefinger, the Oriental voiced an idea. "Mr. King, Lyra tell me you need to sell instrument to get money. I have friend—chiropractor in Flagstaff. He pay much. I give you his number and address. He good man."

"Huh, what?"

The suggestion was repeated.

Forty minutes later, about half a block down the street, the now-healed Rig was pensive. "Say, did you notice where that Chu guy came from when we first entered? It was like he appeared from out of nowhere."

Trusting more in her companion's loyalty at this point, the alien confided, "If I tell you, it can't go any further. Promise?"

Pleased by her offer, the answer came quickly. "Sure. What?"

Rig learned that Master Chu was actually a delegate of the Council—Lyra's local contact. She explained that in addition to a regional monitor, her people had other representatives all over the globe, in most cities, in every walk of life. In this case, being an acupuncturist was simply his cover—and he appeared through a sliding panel in the wall.

The clinic was located above a side spur to one of the tunnels that run north under the river into downtown Phoenix. It was made by the Chinese back in the 1800s. When the city was being settled, a large Asian contingent was imported and used for cheap labor.

"Slave labor?" he inquired, speeding through a yellow light that turned red before they crossed the intersection.

"About the same thing, if you consider the starvation wages they received. To most Westerners at that time, the Chinese and Indians were simply animals. A rancher would often kill one just for the fun of it. Haven't you ever heard the expression, 'A good Injun's a dead Injun'?"

"Sure, I've heard it."

"To protect themselves, the Chinese formed a secret subterranean culture."

"I think," her partner responded, "I saw something about that on a TV documentary. It was…I can't quite remember the whole story."

"You probably did. Underground cities similar to this were all over the West."

"You're kidding. Like where?"

"Oh, San Francisco, Seattle, even Pendelton, Oregon. These tunnel areas had hotels, brothels, restaurants, jails—you name it. Anyway, then came the Tong wars—smuggling, opium dens, and, here in Phoenix, a system of underground escape routes."

"Why tunnels?"

"They needed to be able to go from nearly every major building to any other in the downtown area, even under the Salt River. That way, they could escape without being detected."

"This is really neat! I never imagined something like that could exist. But what does it have to do with Chu?"

"As I was hinting, we have a base in one of the passages. In fact, there are several tun…."

Overwhelmed, Rig's curiosity forces him to interrupt again. "A real base?"

"Uh huh—under your downtown area. From there it goes southwest, ending in the Estrella Mountains—at an area the local Gila Indians called, 'Gateway to the Stars.' Didn't you ever stop to wonder why there are so many UFO sightings over Phoenix?"

"This blows my mind. And these still exist?"

"A few. Most, however, have been blocked up and forgotten. One that's still in operation and connects with the one here is directly under the Federal Building on Central Avenue—where the FBI's located."

"So that's how Baal's people got the Feds to do a number on me."

"No, that's our tunnel. Besides, to do a mind imprint, the sender can be anywhere. A picture or clear thought of another person is all that's needed. You can be here and even affect your astronauts if you want to. In fact, the Russians and Chinese did that very thing on multiple occasions."

"I've got a question. If Chu's one of your guys, why is he wearing a costume that makes him look like an escapee from The Forbidden City? He sticks out like a sore thumb. I mean, if he wants to maintain a low profile, it isn't working."

She chuckled. "His real name is *'Gluck-ta.'* What a character! Loves playing a role. And he's absolutely fascinated with ancient Chinese culture. But instead of being stationed in Beijing, he got assigned here. And in this neighborhood, they're so thrilled to have an acupuncturist, no one cares how he dresses."

"Oh."

Backtracking north across the river, Rig wanted to clean up before again meeting with Dr. Miller. Pulling up to his apartment complex, they were met by the flashing lights of police cars in the parking lot. Pushing through the crowd, ambulance attendants were wheeling a gurney with a bloody sheet covering a body. Yellow tape cordoned off a section of the entrance. The two watched a police captain vehemently arguing with a tall man in a dark suit and sunglasses.

Tugging on his arm, Lyra implored, "Be cautious! You never know what's going to happen—especially with all the hassles today."

"Nah. No way they'd call attention to themselves like this. See the TV camera over there? Look, we've had lots of drug traffic in this area. Similar thing happened two weeks ago. It was getting real bad." He yawned. "I've got to move to Scottsdale."

Ever cautious, the warning was repeated. "Just the same, can we see what's going on first?"

Peeved, he made a disgusted face while thinking, *Woman's too paranoid*.

Tired of his put-downs, she wouldn't let him out of this. "I'm not paranoid. You still don't really accept what's happening."

"*Damn it, Lyra*! Stop listening to my thoughts."

"Rig, I've had run-ins with the Aryan-SST all over your planet. The only reason I've lasted this long is because of my caution. Trust me, fear is healthy. Let's park at the 7-Eleven over there and watch for a few minutes."

The realization that she knew what he was thinking all the time rattled him. *Dang! Now I have to watch my thoughts, too. Whoops! What about those sexual…?* He turned to see her expression.

Fortunately, his companion was too busy watching the police activity. A uniformed patrolman crossed the street in front of their car to enter the convenience store.

In his usual controlling style, the ex-stockbroker ordered, "Wait here. I'll see if I can find out what's up." Inside, acting as nonchalant as possible, he asked, "Excuse me, officer, but what's going on over there?"

Without turning around, the cop answered the voice over his shoulder. "Murder."

"Over drugs?"

"Probably, but don't know yet. Guy in one of the apartments likely surprised some junkie ransacking his place. Psycho must'a been higher than a kite."

"Which apartment?"

"Twenty-two."

Knowing that John had gone to meet him, Rig's knees started to buckle. He leaned against the counter in an effort not to collapse.

Shaking his head, the patrolman continued, "Strange, though. Never seen anything like it."

Numb, King could barely speak. "Wha…What do you mean?"

Turning around to see who was questioning him, the officer said, "Well, one thing's weird. Not only did the guy have a chunk out of his back over a kidney, but his throat's missing. Both pieces gone—like someone ripped them out and took 'em with him." Looking intently at his questioner, the official queried, "What's your interest in all this?"

"Ahhh, oh, I just live around the corner. That's all."

"Seen anything suspicious?"

"Nothing that stands out. What else happened?"

"That's all we have until forensic finishes. Still can't figure what the killer used; edges of the wound are jagged, not cut clean. And where's the back and the throat? What would some freak want with those?" Turning back to the clerk, the officer said, "Thanks. Need a quick-pick Powerball ticket and these antacid tablets."

Ending his purchase, the patrolman went back to his questioner as if the conversation had never ceased. "With that flesh missing, all we can figure is that he was being dissected. But that just doesn't seem right for a meth junkie. I'm telling you, the guy that did this is really sick." He sipped his iced tea and mused, "Anyway, whoever capped 'em must'a been frightened off because he broke the bathroom window and jumped out. What's really got us puzzled is why the FBI's here. Their horning in has got the captain really upset. Told me he's taking it to the mayor."

Barely able to move, Rig also bought antacids and headed out to the car. Trembling and with great difficulty, he told Lyra what happened. As the reality of his friend's death set in, King fell silent.

The alien interrupted his thoughts. "We have to get out of here. Want me to drive?" Her tone was urgent.

"Huh? What?...Uhhh, no. I'm...ahh, I'm okay."

CHAPTER XII

NEPHILUM

Back at the La Posada, still stunned by John's murder, Rig shook off his sadness long enough to remember the need to meet Dr. Miller.

"*Damn!* Lyra, it's 4:30. I told the professor I'd be back at 4:00. Jeez, I better ring the college and see if he was able to decipher any of this. That's assuming that S.O.B. from the government will even allow me to talk to him."

The receptionist picked up. "Science Department."

"Dr. Miller, please."

"Who is this?" came a worried-sounding female voice.

"Excuse me?"

"Who is calling, please?"

"Rigden King."

Stumbling over her words, the receptionist said, "I…I'm sorry to inform you, Mr. King, that Dr. Miller…Dr. Miller died this afternoon. Pardon me, but I'm still…."

It was obvious to Rig he was talking to someone in a state of shock.

"Died? Are you serious? How? What happened?"

"They're saying the doctor was murdered."

"Murdered!… Who did it?"

"No one knows. That's why the FBI's here." Her voice, now a whisper, took on an air of confidentiality. "But, if you ask me, I think it was a student."

"Look, Miss, what did you say your name was?"

"Walker, Kay Walker."

"Miss Walker, why's the FBI there if a student did it?"

"I don't really know. Maybe it was because the professor was consulting on some sort of federal project…."

"How do you figure it was murder?"

"One of the men said someone stabbed him from behind in the temple with a pen or something, while he was sitting at his desk."

"And?"

"Well, I was talking to one of the crime lab people…I don't know if I should be going into this."

"No, no, it was all right; I'm an alumnus."

"Okay…okay. The detective said being killed from behind like that means he probably knew the individual. Also, his room was ransacked. So Karen and I…. "

"Who's Karen?"

"She works here in the office."

"Oh?"

"Karen and I kinda think it was a student angry over a grade and looking for his file or who knows what. Here comes one of the detectives now. They want to talk to anyone calling in over the next several days asking for the professor. Mr. King, this is Detective Dorn…."

Rig slammed down the receiver with such force, it fell out of its cradle and onto the floor. Seeing his expression, Lyra could tell things had gotten worse. Trembling, he sat on the edge of the bed, head in his hands.

"What's happened?"

"Miller's murdered."

"Murdered? Were the photos stolen?"

"Didn't ask."

Under unbearable pressure, the ex-broker opted to focus on something trivial instead of facing the more serious problems at hand. "*Damn!* I've got to cancel my credit cards. No telling where they'll end up."

On hold for the Master Card representative, the two were silent for a moment before he spoke. "You know, when the cops discover that was John's body in my apartment, they'll assume I killed him."

"What do you mean?"

"Judas Priest, woman! Come on! Think! Finding my Lincoln in the parking lot, they'll figure I stole his Bronco. *Crud!* The whole police force will be out looking for it; our fingerprints are all over the thing. I've got to get a rag and wipe it down." He let out a false laugh, more like a sigh. "Man, this thing's getting worse by the minute. My complete life's turned upside down; it's gone insane."

Lyra's answer was calming, as if problems of this nature happened every day. "Rig, it is obvious. What you took are sacred temple objects. The Followers of Baal will do anything to get them back. Things like planting lies about you in the minds of the FBI, IRS, and Securities and Exchange Commission... even killing your friends, John and Doctor Miller."

"There you go again, with this mind-programming thing."

"I've seen the pattern before. It's my guess that a DAK assassin killed John, too. If he shifted shape to look human, it wouldn't have been any problem knocking on the door and mentally commanding your friend to invite him in."

"What about Miller's State Department guy?"

"He might be from the government, but I doubt it. Was he wearing sunglasses...indoors?"

"Yeah, so?"

"Lizard people have a light-sensitivity problem; their eyes find it difficult adjusting to brightness...even inside. By changing their form and wearing dark glasses or contacts, they can interface with any level of society. Just look at those guarding your president."

"But why all of this for a couple of relics?"

The representative from the Ra Foundation took a deep breath. "All right—we might as well get into that too. What you're witnessing is a microscopic part of a story...one more important than most could ever imagine."

"Try me."

"This is about more than just Earth. Your planet is simply a pawn in a massive, cosmic war; the stakes are literally all of creation."

"Is this for real?"

"Rig, look me in the eyes." Her voice lowered. "*I'm deadly serious*. Not only do The Followers of Baal want this as their primary base but, as I said, they don't have our ships' teleportation designs. For them, this rare Earth element is imperative. Unfortunately, the compound is semi-gaseous—highly unstable—making it available only in minute, nearly immeasurable amounts. Miles of rock have to be moved to extract a single ounce. That's why the maze of global tunnels."

"Makes sense, I guess. But why don't they just wipe us out—take over the planet?"

"They would. Except every so often the reptiles need humans as breeders; your bodies have certain DNA they've lost. You see, over the millennia, the DAK genome has developed a systemic flaw. Makes it impossible for them to reproduce solely among themselves over long periods. If they do, their race becomes crippled; they need to periodically bring in plasma links found most notably in humans. That's why an occasional crossbreeding is mandatory. But this is different from the other breeding program I spoke of."

"Lyra, is this DAK thing somehow tied to the cattle and sheep mutilations we hear about?"

"*No way!* That's the work of a sub-group—something we can get into later."

Not satisfied, her companion pushed—wanting clarification of a documentary he'd seen on TV claiming that cattle are killed as part of alien experiments.

After a minute's worth of continuous prodding, she gave in. "*All right, all right!* Haven't you noticed, every time a farmer finds a dissected animal out in some field, there's usually an unmarked, black helicopter nearby?"

"I never really paid attention."

"Well they're there. What your government's really doing is monitoring alien kill-quotas—making sure they don't go over their bag limits. The military then draws attention away by making the locals think it was them doing black-ops work. And if that's not believed, nearby they set up a rock pentagram, plant a few skinned cats or dogs, leave burned candles, and put pressure on the local newspaper to send out a press release pinning the deaths on Satanists."

"Quotas? Tell me, why do you hear about these mutilations happening almost exclusively in Colorado, New Mexico, and Texas?"

"In the U.S., those are the areas with the largest alien bases. Why travel farther when the Aryan-SST has what it needs in its own backyard? And as I said, all this is being done with part of your government's full cooperation—an aspect of that interplanetary treaty signed by Eisenhower back in 1954. And by quotas, I mean that to keep a low profile, they are annually allowed to take only so many human abductees, and dissect a given number of animals."

"A treaty? Sounds more like duck hunting."

"Ratified by every president…except Clinton and Dubya. The real powers didn't want Clinton to know the full truth. And your current president is simply a glove over the hand of key advisors, who, in turn, are manipulated by those even higher up. Incidentally, you might like to know, just before his assassination, J.F.K. was going to expose the treaty-contact program, but that's another story. Anyway, yes, your hunting analogy is reasonably accurate."

"So these mutilations are the work of the reptiles?"

"No, they're the work of the Zeta Reticulans, the group you call 'Greys'—the information gatherers. Sometimes they abduct, but mostly they're simply involved in dissections. Anyway—"

"Ah…."

"Let me finish. This is where that breeding experiment came into play. To colonize, the Greys have to reactivate their salivary glands so they can eat Earth food—awakening organs that have atrophied since they now ingest energy components differently. Plus, these dissections give the DNA that enables impregnation compatibility with earthling females—resulting in a hybrid race that can self-perpetuate if their primary colonizing effort fails."

"*Colonizing? My God!* Then if the breeding and mutilations are being done by Greys, how do your lizard friends fit in? You said they need our genes as well."

As if hit by lightning, Lyra recoiled. "*Don't you ever dare refer to them as my friends again!*" she fumed. "The thought's *revolting!*"

The response was contrite. "Sorry." He deftly changed the subject. "Do both alien groups suffer from the same genetic weaknesses?"

"No. As I said, with the DAK, their problem is blood. But they don't out-breed on a wholesale level. They're quite selective. Remember that quote from Genesis in the Bible about giants, or Nephilum, coming unto the daughters of men? Many of your supposed myths were built on stories of offspring that were left behind; they looked too human to take back. And the reason The Followers of Baal don't destroy your entire race is because besides being a gene pool and a food source, earthlings are a handy labor force used for working their mines. Where else do you think many of your runaway youths end up?"

"Stop! Living in Phoenix, I can kind'a accept this flying saucer thing. But your crossbreeding and a secret mining operation…those I can't buy. How's it possible without detection?"

Despite growing frustration, the alien tried to explain further. "This war has been going on for eons."

He jumped up. Pacing back and forth, the earthling's agitated response was almost a shout. "Okay then, how do all these creatures stay hidden? *Answer me that!*"

"I already did—mind control. Look at it this way: when a thought is projected into someone, the receiver accepts the idea as if it were his own."

"Such as?"

"Say you convince a farmer that his cattle are missing. Imprint their absence in his mind, and he can stand right in the midst of the herd without seeing or hearing a single cow. To him, they're invisible. Set up a continuous, circular, imprinting wave-front, and regardless of how many people pass, not one person sees an animal."

"Pardon me, Love. I know you're sincere but this is flat-out nuts."

Exploding, Lyra lashed back, "*Nuts?* And don't call me *Love*, either; *I don't like it!*"

Feeling caged, the ex-stockbroker continued pacing—reaching out, waving his arms as if trying to beat off an invisible enemy. "This is just too far-fetched."

Again, calmly, the alien replied, "You're wrong. If ideas are telepathed into a population, you can govern…oh, politicians, the media, the making of laws…everything. *Rig…Rig… look at me*. Can't you see that by this you can control the course of economies, governments, and eventually the world? Just look at what Jack Ruby, Timothy McVeigh, and Osama bin Laden were brainwashed to do, or some of the irrational decisions your politicians make."

"I'll buy that you can hypnotize people into not seeing something, but what about photos? They'd show something." He grinned smugly. "*Hah! Got you there.*"

"*Really?* And what makes you think we'd not have the technology to scramble pictures? There's something you would call a high-wavelength, fractional reorganizer. It distorts all types of photos and interferes with your most sophisticated electronic equipment. How do you imagine we keep our ships invisible over cities and off radar scopes?"

Still pacing back and forth across the room, the earthling stopped to pop one of the chocolates left by the maid service into his mouth. Again, under his breath, he mumbled, "This is too much! John's murdered and…." He paused, unable to finish his sentence.

The extraterrestrial went deeper into an explanation. She talked about their being seen only when they want, and how the DAK, under the guidance of The Followers of Baal, even penetrated the White House. To manipulate U.S. policy, the Lyrian explained, they had programmed presidents seventy-seven times in the past three administrations alone. She stressed, "Left unchecked, this insidious scheme would affect the future of the entire planet." The earthling halted and looked probingly into the alien's eyes. "If this is true, why in the hell aren't you people *doing* something? Isn't there anything you can implement to protect us from being imprinted?"

"As I told you, white-lighting. That'd be a big help."

"So teach 'em, why don't you?"

"Oh, sure—we should just land on the White House lawn and announce that you're in the middle of a cosmic struggle. Do you know how ridiculous that is? Your infantile-thinking public can't even figure out who's telling the truth on simple, political issues. And you want us to introduce all 487 space groups? Now who's being ridiculous?"

"So that's why you people stay hidden—to work behind the scenes."

"We have to."

"Say, tell me. Is DAK the full name or an acronym?"

"*It's Daku Aryan Kamei*—which in your language translates roughly to Warriors of the Dark One. As I said before, they are the militant types, the enforcers. But surprisingly, at times, their methods of attaining dominance are exceedingly sophisticated—often achieved by simply controlling economies. As an example, by manipulating the world banking system, you have the entire planet at your feet. And carrying out that plan, there are those from that Atlantean incarnation I mentioned, who are helping them seize control."

"Since these Illuminati stay in the shadows, does our little band of Earth helpers have an outward organization or structure?"

"In North and South America, they form the SG2."

"SG2?"

"Shadow Government."

"What's the 'two' stand for?"

"SG1's Europe; SG3's Asia."

"Why are humans helping Baal? It doesn't make sense."

Amazed at the earthling's continuing innocence, the emissary elaborated. "On the contrary. For example, at the outset of World War II, it was a well documented fact that a number of your rich and powerful in America funneled billions into helping the Nazis' rise to power. Go to the Web; do your research. You'll come across people like Prescott S. Bush, George H's father. His assets were seized under the Trading with the Enemy Act for blatant financial support of the Third Reich."

"No!"

"It's true. I can name more than a handful of prominent American personalities and present day major Wall Street corporations that funded Hitler."

Sliding another chocolate into his mouth, Rig tried, in his best hoopster fashion, to sink the wrapper into the wastepaper basket. He missed. Lyra's last comment had thrown off his concentration. Ignoring his failure, he blurted, "You're serious about this SG thing."

"Totally serious. All this is in your public records. That is, if you're willing to dig for it."

Pausing to stare out the window, King thought about his old friend John. Coming back to the present, he shook his body, like one who was chilled, trying to clear the cobwebs before replying to the last statement. "What?"

"You weren't listening, were you?"

"Yeah, I was. Go on. I'm focused."

"All right, there's plenty of information supporting this, and I don't mean from conspiracy nuts, either; hard data is easy to find. But remember, governments control most all of the media, and Baal's infrastructure controls governments."

He wondered, *How does this Shadow Government thing work?*

Hearing the thought, she replied, "These are the ones who secretly run your country—select government officials, old-money families, certain religious leaders, and people high up in the military." Tilting her head slightly, the alien looked into the Phoenician's eyes and questioned, "You still don't believe me, do you?"

"Sorry, I'd like to, but this is all too much within a twenty-four-hour period."

"That's exactly how they want you to react. All the while they're sitting back laughing. I can never cease being amazed at how people from this planet don't realize how easy it is to be controlled."

Feeling a hunger exacerbated by nervousness, Rig opened the refrigerator under the wet bar. Absorbed in his selection and without turning around, he answered her last remark. "Guess not; at least I certainly never did."

"It's the easiest thing in the world. That is, once you find a person's motivation. For some it was wealth and fame. For others, it was doing God's will, or what they're told is God's will…or…or a thousand other reasons."

Yesterday was rough, but the shock of today's events are overloading King's fatigued mind. Antsy, the treasure hunter couldn't sit still. He wanted to delve into her explanation, but maintaining a focused attention was impossible. Leafing through a complimentary book most hotels have in their rooms, supposedly engrossed in the pictures, he outwardly appeared to be lacking interest. Finally the silence snapped, "Oh, all right. Give me an example."

"Well, as you people in sales always say, 'everyone's got a hot-button.' Let's say we randomly picked a mother and told her to strike some man standing on a street corner. Chances are she wouldn't, right?"

Crunching tortilla chips and gulping Pepsi, he answered was a muffled "Doubt it."

"Fine. Now project into the mother's mind that this person has just molested her two-year-old daughter. And add the idea that a hard slap would stop all future sexual assaults—not only against her baby but all other children as well. What would she do?"

"She'd probably haul off and smack him with the first thing that wasn't nailed down."

"Exactly. Now assume you want a nuclear war between, say, Iran and Israel or India and Pakistan. Tell me. What steps would you take?"

"I don't know. Lemme think. I'd…ahhh…." He bent over to pick up a chip that dropped on the rug. Heading toward the wastepaper basket, the conversation continued, "I guess, first I'd promise generals on both sides wealth and power. Then I'd get at least one of the armies to overthrow its government."

She added, "As happened in Pakistan. And?"

"Of course, the focus would have to be religion, wealth, or some kind of land dispute—like Palestinians wanting the Jews out of Israel, or the Pakistanis trying to annex the Kashmir Province. Then I'd fire up the situation by using terrorists. Ahhh…finally, I suppose I would find the decision makers in each country in charge of nuclear deployment—the guys who give the orders to flip the switch."

"So far, so good. But there's another step."

"I guess it would be to convince each side that the other is about to launch its missiles."

"Excellent! Keep going."

"And, I'd put into everyone's mind that the only way to prevent their country's annihilation would be to strike their enemy first."

"See how easy it is to manipulate…even a nation?"

"But I've never heard of telepathy being used for mind control. What about a government's nuclear checks and balances?"

"Who do you think they imprint, janitors? Americans, Russians, Chinese, North Koreans, Japanese, and six other groups have all been using psychic warfare since the early 1960s. And not just for influencing decisions and gathering data. Among other things, it was a tremendous assassination tool."

Lyra stared intently at her companion, who was once again gazing out the window. Suddenly, as in sleep apnea, the earthling's body shuddered, unable to pull air into his lungs. Panicked, hands to his throat, horror flashed across his face. Luckily, it was only a four-second experiment.

Coughing and gasping, he managed, "Did…did you do that?"

"Ooops. Didn't mean to frighten you. I only wanted to demonstrate the power of the mind's telekinetic abilities. I simply stopped your ability to breathe. When a psychic assassin prohibits your breathing for an extended period, or forces a person's heart to stop, doctors blame the death on stress. And there's not a single mark on the body. If you don't believe me, look at this."

She pulled a newspaper clipping from her purse. It was a picture and article describing a powerful form of psychokinesis developed by the Russian military. Supposedly used solely for detonating incoming missiles, it showed a man projecting his thoughts, exploding a pumpkin fifty feet away.

"But this isn't a normal individual. It was one whose DNA links back to the Nephilum."

The alien explained that more than eleven million people on this planet shared this ancient gene pool. Fortunately, almost no one had a memory of who they really were. Of those who knew, few had figured out how to consistently tap this primal force. Today they are getting dreams and visions—by the next decade, power beyond their imagination. The Ra agent went on to say that each of these people appeared outwardly normal—the person standing next to you in an elevator, the clerk in a store, even the busboy clearing plates from your table in a restaurant.

"Next time, look into their eyes," she warned. "There's something different." Jokingly, she suggested that even he might have such qualities flowing through his veins.

A furrow developed across the Phoenician's brow as he pondered her hypothesis. *Me, Zeus? Hurling thunderbolts? I don't think so. These eyes just show too many drugs during college.*

"You'd never know," she dryly remarks, hearing his thought. "It's obvious your mind's an unexplored wilderness."

"*Ha ha!* Say, you brought up something. Since India and Pakistan are into this war thing and each has nuclear capability, why hasn't one of them already annihilated the other? I mean, they've come really close several times."

"You can't imagine just how close. Last July, Pakistan was only seconds away from pushing the button. Little do you people know how frequently Baal's warriors have almost gotten these two into an all-out nuclear conflict."

"That's scary!"

"An understatement. There's no buffer period. America has twenty-eight minutes to decide whether or not to respond to Russian missiles. India and Pakistan have only two. Our fear is that we may not find out in time to erase their mind imprints and stop a detonation. To make matters worse, nearly everyone's getting nuclear-strike capability…even fanatic countries like North Korea and Iran."

Rig had moved away from the window and was now pacing. "Lord! Maybe it was true; I mean about using thought projections. The Followers of Baal might be able to control just about everything this way!"

"That's what I've been trying to tell you. Start at the top. As they say, 'Plant a thought in the head and the feet will move at your slightest whim.' Think about it for a second. Baal's warriors are psychically manipulating the actions of thousands throughout the world—terrorists, heads of state, business leaders, church figures…even to the point of guiding the outcome of elections." She chuckled, before adding, "Remember Florida and the, supposed, dangling chad flap?"

"Why?" he asks. "For what purpose?"

"Silly, I already told you. How do I get this across? You're being set up for a total planetary takeover."

"I thought they were just creating small, invisible colonies to do their mining."

"Their plan was far more complex. And the amazing part is that Baal's strategy has been diabolically simple. So much so that your Shadow Government will shove a bill through Congress mandating deference to specific sectarian beliefs... After that, a push for religious supremacy as a method to control the population."

"*Religious supremacy?* What do you mean, religious supremacy?"

"That they no longer need to remain hidden as they erase the line between Church and State. You know, like using the carrot of government vouchers to lure students to more effective schools—ones that *just happen to* preach their brand of faith-based religion."

Without pausing, she wrapped up her point. "I'll tell you this: If Baal weren't so frightening, the whole situation would be almost comical. It's like in a movie, or theater of the absurd, where you see the feet of the murderer sticking out under the curtain he's hiding behind. I mean, camouflaged with trappings of high-sounding morality and religious dogma, the SG2 is definitely here—waiting in the wings, just off stage. Trust me on that."

Picking up a dropped bobby pin, she had an afterthought. "I can even give you documented proof as to how their plot is progressing."

"Do it."

"In April, 2001, President Bush completed the Shadow Government in the Western Hemisphere by taking one last crucial step. He brought together the heads of state from Canada to Argentina, calling for a single, no-barrier trade zone—a "North and South America without borders." With that single move, Baal's plan finally became a reality—the SG2 is firmly in place."

Ever the disbeliever, Rig interjected, "I...I don't know."

Deciding to wear her hair up, Lyra began to comb, twist, and braid, talking into the mirror as she continued. "I'm surprised you still can't see the whole picture. I mean, how The Followers of Baal are advancing. Next to greed and a lust for power, one of the primary weaknesses of people on this planet stems from their religious fanaticism—especially obvious in factions of Islam, as well as certain areas of Christianity. Both are taught to blindly follow instead of question. I mean, it is a well-known fact that the present-day Koran isn't exactly what Mohammed intended. Same thing with the Bible. What with all the additions and deletions following twenty-one Christian ecumenical councils, it's no wonder parts of God's message became distorted. So, based on both groups' explicit policy of not questioning religious authority, I'll show you how the Shadow Government, at least in America, rose to power. That is, if you're interested."

Pacing faster and wringing his hands, her partner injected with mock sincerity, "This I gotta hear."

"Well, first, Baal's followers want leaders to control the masses. As I said, these Lucifarians started with many of the wealthy Mayflower families who are captains of industry—the movers and shakers of society. To get the minions to follow and pull the triggers, so to speak, they sought out the most vulnerable, manipulable segments of society—those under both economic hardship and who fear not attaining spiritual salvation. Then, using propaganda like the Nazis did against the Jews before World War II, they…."

"Blame a scapegoat so as to divert attention?"

"Exactly—by combusting people's frustrations into hate, anger is increasingly directed toward nonconforming religious and minority groups. As I was saying, the plan is to have the white race in the SG2 unify under one religion—an umbrella opened by the Patriot Act and Homeland Security programs. That way, anyone outside that circle becomes an enemy of the state. Think of it: soon the store clerk, the person next to you in the grocery check-out line or at a ballgame will be looking for your one, small, politically incorrect slip so they can report you and collect a reward."

"No way!"

"If you don't believe me, read about the Spanish Inquisition: citizens were encouraged to offer rabbit and pork to *friends* to see if they'd refuse; neighbor spied on neighbor; lists were made of those suspected of being uncircumcised; you were also watched in church to see if you mumbled when saying, 'Father, Son and Holy Ghost,' and God help you if you failed to enunciate the hymns clearly! Some people were even turned in for simply giving undue importance to the Old

Testament. And, get this—there were those reported for just washing their hands too frequently. These and fifty-three other equally deadly transgressions got you tortured, flayed, and burnt alive at the stake."

"But—but— "

"There are no buts about it. You, Rigden King, III, fit the profile of a person who will definitely be red-flagged by the Patriot point-index."

"Me? Red-flagged? How?"

"It began as something that seemed quite harmless: airline passenger profiling, supposedly looking for terrorists; the same with reviewing the books you buy or check out at the library; and the little discount card you use at the grocery store that will soon finger you as one who suspiciously purchases certain ethnic foods; or your license plate might be jotted down as you leave a Middle Eastern restaurant. Then there's that enemy at your firm who covets your corner office. Or try this one on for size: the buyer who wants your house to come on the market—about twenty years before you're ready. Any one of these folks might be inclined to trump up evidence against you. And let's not overlook the lies told by that angry neighbor child you've made mad. Or how about the reward given to your mailman, drycleaner, gas station attendant, or the person delivering your new dishwasher, who snitches on you after observing 'suspicious activity'?...Of course, if you watch what you say and do and don't get anyone upset, you can always sidestep such unpleasantries." She smiled, knowing for Rig, that would be an impossibility.

King doubled over, as if on the verge of throwing up.

"But there's more. Thanks to the RICO Act that allows the immediate seizure of your assets, you will stand accused... penniless, unable to hire a lawyer. And don't expect friends to come to your rescue. Anyone even contacting a suspected enemy of the state will get points put on *their* index.

"Rig, as it says in the Bible—although I'm paraphrasing a little bit here: *Compared to the Evil One who is coming, the Spanish Inquisitors, Hitler, Stalin, and Idi Amin were like poets at a tea party*."

"I can't believe this! It sounds like George Orwell's *1984*."

"Well, actually it'll be far worse. Incidentally, you might find it interesting that Orwell was a remote viewer—one who can see into the future—like Sinclair Lewis, Da Vinci, Jules Vern, and those used by your CIA. But since time in the other realms is so confusing, he got his dates mixed." She laughed. "Anyway, Baal's plan is unfolding totally out in the open, if people would just care to look."

"How is all this being accomplished?"

"*Is? Was!* As I said, most of it was already in place." Turning, she says, "Hand me more of those bobby pins next to my pocketbook over there on the dresser. Thanks." Lyra puts all but one in her mouth as she continues talking, arranging, and pinning. "Anyway, by advancing with baby steps, the takeover was almost invisible. I'll explain. Their first move back in the sixties and seventies was to get their people elected to seats on school boards all across America."

Rig stretched his aching body before unleashing his sarcasm. "Oh yeah, like those are real power positions."

"Don't forget, smart aleck, that was only the beginning. Even in building a house, there's always that first row of bricks. Over the next thirty years, others were voted onto town councils, mayoral seats, even governorships. Stage three, however, was far more, as you would say, slick. That tier penetrated Congress, the Senate, the judiciary, and even the heads of Washington think tanks. Their people now occupy your highest levels of office.

"Plus, remember they have nearly one hundred percent of mainstream news media. Why do you think the real facts about the Iraq war aren't brought out—such as The Downing Street Memo, a document showing this administration fabricating a story about WMDs, so as to justify war—or that the death toll of U.S. soldiers is really 3,105, not the reported 1,200? And… oh, there are things far worse that mainstream America has no knowledge of. Now who do you think is behind all this?"

Without waiting for a response, she continued, " Fair and balanced? In 1981, fifty-one companies owned almost all the U.S. news outlets. Now, nearly everything is filtered through just five—all spouting the same, well crafted, party line."

King threw his companion a grimace while she flashed back that angelic smile.

"Their masterstrokes were putting people into Bush's cabinet, and controlling the Supreme Court—the last two nails in the public's coffin. Playing off the nation's preoccupation with terrorism, and with the SG2's power base complete, they now have the ability to pass any law—do anything. Just watch. Using *Mein Kampf* and Machiavelli's *The Prince* as their playbooks, they're silently controlling world economies—using prearranged wars, false news, oil-price manipulation, international banking, weather alteration, and a host of other things. Applying pressure from different directions, all these lead to that last stage I spoke of—the forming of a single, supreme religion. And when the final curtain lifts...taa daah!...*It won't be Christianity.*"

"What you're asserting is that America...America is no longer a democracy."

"You poor deluded soul. You people haven't had real freedom for a long time."

He gulped. "But how?"

"Think about it. Since 1981, your government's been using cable TV in reverse; with some models, they can see and listen through your television, even when it is off. Same with the Internet. Actually, *every electrical outlet* in your home can be used as a microphone...And speaking of snooping"—she pointed to his cell phone. "But how about the loss of civil liberties? It was not just in major cities. Big Brother is installing street cameras even in rural areas. In Florida, for instance, there's one town that photographs not only every license plate, but snaps a picture, and automatically does a police background check to boot." And get this: While the American public won't stand for being spied upon, marketing surveys confirm if it's called, "eavesdropping," all this becomes perfectly acceptable."

"That's absurd."

"Oh! You think so? Soon here, as it is now in England, the average U.S. citizen will be on camera over 300 times per day. In fact, the Patriot Act even allows the FBI, *without any evidence* against you, the right to enter your home and rifle through every drawer—all under a rule called *Sneak and Peek.*"

Adjusting an obstinate lock of hair, she made another point. "But what the public really knows nothing about is Homeland

Security's secret star chambers—acting as judge, jury, and executioner. They call themselves 'The Erasers'; you vanish without a trace, and every record of your existence disappears. And what about those concentration camps, called, "retention centers," that are quietly being constructed across the U.S.? Rig, get it through your head—*freedom is gone!* Your country has become a police state. Terrorism is simply the excuse; it makes the taking away of personal freedoms and rights seem perfectly justified."

"I...I...."

"Don't be so shocked. The Illuminati had these programs put in motion decades ago. Like the scanning devices that, when they're driving by your house or from a helicopter, enable them to see inside. And believe me, they are able to zoom in on everyone and everything...and I do mean *every thing*—from specific things you're doing while making love, to the magazine article you're reading as you sit on the toilet.

"Furthermore, that strip—and soon to be a chip—in money allows them not only to determine the denomination but to tally exactly how many bills are hidden in your house, and where. How's that for efficiency?"

"Lyra, come on!"

"I know this sounds like so much out of a spy novel, but these are just for starters; other *far more deadly programs* also exist.

"Oh, and I almost forgot—just saying a keyword or phrase on the phone automatically triggers a recording of your conversation. Which is then computer analyzed to see if you're a threat to the state. And you think Americans still have liberty?"

Stunned, the earthling could only reply, "Uhhh...."

Ignoring his astonishment, she continued. "The Prince of Darkness controls by promising rewards of power and wealth—even kingships. In turn, your shadow governments manipulate the frightened working classes—prepping them to blindly follow...do anything. Mark my words: you'll remember what I've said after you see the public's hysteria setting in, several years from now."

Staring, mouth open, the audience of one listened intently.

"If you don't believe me, look at Earth's history. Soldiers have always been duped into believing they're dying for some important cause rather than money or power. Follow the wealth; examine the real reasons for the Crusades, World War I, II, Korea, Viet Nam, Bosnia, or this second foray into Iraq to supposedly defeat the 'Axis of Evil'—while they simply shake a fist at North Korea with its nuclear missiles that are able to strike the West Coast…But I almost forgot —there's no oil in North Korea, is there?"

"What about Afghanistan?"

"What part of the word 'oil' don't you understand? Two-thirds of the world's reserves come from this area. It's *all about money!* Bin Laden was just an excuse. As I said, this whole thing has been on the drawing board for years. Have you forgotten? It was the United States…*the United States* that originally armed the Taliban, gave them their financial backing, and then provided specialized guerilla training. Get it through your head: *all of this was part of the master plan*. Everyone's been hoodwinked into thinking these military moves are all about September 11th. As I said, follow the money."

Rig's face reddened. "I don't know about most of this spy stuff. But that last point hit home. Does seem that every time there's a problem, a number of politicians and their biggest campaign contributors rake it in like bandits."

"Exactly. Just look at how the Gulf Coast will be developed into casinos and hotels for the rich and famous."

"Huh?"

"Never mind; that's months down the road. Simply be aware that Bush Senior and Dubya *still have ties to oil*. Making three for three, even Cheney's up to his nose in the stuff. Before becoming Vice President, your dear friend Dickie was the President of Halliburton, a global petroleum company."

"That's old news. So?"

"Instead of divesting himself, *as is mandated by law*, he slipped around it with a loophole—placing his stocks in a trust. And…."

"He's still connected to—?"

"Phooey! That's just the tip of the iceberg."

"Oh?"

She paused, giving a little smirk before continuing. "I mean, is anyone so naive as to think these three are in no way swayed, if only subconsciously, by personal gain in their decision-making? But they are just the marionettes. The real master magician is Baal…It's the age-old story—world leaders driven by greed and power. Baal then misdirects the public's attention by shifting focus to some distant, global conflict—as in the Latin phrase, 'Ordo ab chao'—Order through chaos."

"Let me get this straight. According to you, this Aryan-SST Alliance, under the Followers of Baal, supposedly control Washington?"

"And London, Tokyo, the Kremlin—everywhere. Remember, this is a necessary step in conquering the world. Oh, he'll come out in the open in a few years, after nearly all of your planet's been exterminated."

"Ex…exterminated!" he sputtered. "This…this is the most senseless pile of crap I've ever heard!"

"Stop it! You're being such an ass. It's time you people accept the fact that except for us and God, you're all alone."

Though arrogant in most matters, when realizing he's in the wrong, Rigden King, III, will eventually concede. Pulling it together, the voice was contrite. "Sorry. Try to understand. This story of yours is blowing me away."

"It was you who asked me who was after the relics and why. Actually, there are a few things I could add, but I see you can't handle any more at this point."

"Oh, Lord! Like what?"

"All right, just don't forget that you asked for it."

CHAPTER XIII

ORIGINAL DOCTRINE

Soon, there's going to be a cleansing of the entire Earth, just as there were several times before, only worse. Prophets of all your races have foreseen this. The few who do survive will sell out to anyone simply to continue staying alive. That's when Malek...."

"Malek?"

"Baal in Christianity, Malek, or Malik, in Islam. The angel in charge of hell. He's one and the same—his followers' supreme leader. Anyway, that's when he emerges to control your people with his New World Order. His second goal will be a re-attempt at capturing the Throne of Heaven."

"This Malek isn't Jesus, is he?"

"Heavens, no! Jesus and others have been sent to help."

"So I've heard. Although, I haven't met him personally. He's...."

"Must you always be so shallow about spiritual matters? You people are so far into the forest, you can't see the trees; nearly everybody on this planet seems to have missed Jesus' real mission."

"Which was?" As his companion talked, the Phoenician reached over and tore a sheet off a small notepad next to the telephone. With concentration split, he carefully began folding, finally ending up with a small paper airplane. Lightly launched, it made a slight arc around the room, landing next to the closet door.

"Rig, Jesus isn't some egotist who craves personal adoration. That's an invention of man's twisted belief system. He's simply one of the Way-Showers—a being sent to awaken you not to His, but to *your own* actual divinity."

Even with the worries of the day, the tired treasure hunter managed to make a joke. "Hey, Lyra! There's this guy at the office you need to meet...Harlow Moon. He's full of this Bible stuff, always warning me about you New Agers."

"*I am not a New Ager!* You're like everyone else—spouting these oxymoronic platitudes. Yet, you don't have the slightest clue what they mean."

Her comment went unheard. The earthling's mind had already skipped in another direction. As the alien's last sentence dissolved into nothingness, he faded back. Sitting with legs crossed, nervousness made him begin to wiggle a dangling foot. Refocusing, he heard Lyra demanding, "Well... tell me the definition."

"Of what, New Ager?"

"That's what we're talking about, isn't it?"

The ex-salesman stumbled, searching for an explanation. "I guess New means recent, and Ager implies someone from that age."

The extraterrestrial countered by pointing out the idiocy of his definition. "It's another one of those fear phrases churches use to keep people under their control. They know that when humankind finally realizes its ability to directly link with the Father-Mother, man will again have an unfiltered connection—one without religious heads giving you their own special translation."

Bored, Rig yawned before speaking. "Can you please get to the point before I fall asleep?" Tired of his airplane, he picked up a pencil and started doodling. Finishing a futuristic drawing depicting Earth's destruction and knowing it was something Lyra would probably revile, he held it up and asked, "What do you think?"

"You really have to lay off those artificial sweeteners," she rejoined playfully. "They're cutting off the blood to your brain. Cause hallucinations, you know?"

"Wish I was hallucinating."

"Listen, to keep power for themselves alone, nearly all religious leaders get individuals to forget that their personal connection to the Creator is a God-given birthright. See how all this got started?"

"Kind'a, although I'd still really like to sit back and watch you and Harlow go at it. He's the type that sees sin in everything. Like, he's even on my back for subscribing to *Playboy*."

"Spiritually speaking," she says with emphasis, "your Bible says there is only one true sin—one that God considers unforgivable—*the denial or the rejection of the Christ consciousness—The Holy Spirit.* But as for your idea about Jesus the Christ, yes, He still exists. In fact, you, I, he…we all have the same God connection. He's simply more in touch with it."

King reached for the television channel changer. "Mind if I flip on the news while we talk? Might be something about the murders."

The TV's volume blasted out as Rig scrambled to lower the sound. "*Damn kids,*" he mumbled.

Lyra shouted over the decreasing noise as he fiddled with the channel changer. "No, I don't mind."

Mingling with the newscaster's voice, a rhythmic banging on the wall came from the adjoining room. Assuming it was a couple having sex, the Phoenician gave a knowing smirk. Thirty seconds later and still clueless, Lyra wondered aloud why management was hanging a picture this late in the day. Seeing her partner's expression, she probed his mind, getting a graphic image of several things he imagined the couple to be doing. Taken by surprise, her eyes widened.

Seeing and attempting to soften her embarrassment, her partner diplomatically restarted the earlier conversation. "You know, in the past, these religious explanations of yours would have gotten you burnt at the stake."

"What do you mean, in the past? Nothing's changed. Just question the current White House administration and you're called, 'unpatriotic,' branded a terrorist, aren't allowed to board commercial air flights, your phones are tapped, and they monitor all your moves on the Internet…soon, you'll be rounded up in the middle of the night and hauled off to one of those concentration camps."

"This can't be happening; this is America."

"Rig, I'm simply talking about unquestioning fanaticism, regardless of where it comes from."

"Could'a fooled me."

"Most religions are like spokes in a wheel. Anybody can follow them to the center, to God, if they move past man's dogma and on to the core teachings. Unfortunately, most...."

Unmistakable screaming and moaning begin leaking through the hollow wall. The building passion of their neighbors became quite distracting. The last few moments before climax, the extraterrestrial reached over and increased the TV's volume.

Finishing her prior thought, almost yelling, she asked, "Know what the real joke is?"

"What?"

"Funny part is, it was those heads of churches who distorted the Creator's original messages. They, not us, changed the teachings and created this 'New Age.' Remember Jesus' quote about—"

"What quote?"

"Never mind; you don't read the Bible. When He said, 'No one cometh unto the Father except through me,' he wasn't referring to Jesus the *man* but to your realignment with the divine, Christ consciousness—a remembering of *who you truly are* within the God aspect, not who some interpreter says you are."

Staring right through her, the listener's mind silently reacted, *No offense, girl, but as far as I'm concerned, this is just so much worthless BS.* As the alien continued talking, the trapdoor in King's brain slammed shut. His thoughts were on more practical matters. *All this church-talk makes me hungry.*

"Lyra," he broke in, "even though I haven't cleaned up, what say we go eat?"

CHAPTER XIV

THE CLEANSING

The path to the restaurant curved around a pool by a waterfall. As its light spray touched her cheek, the alien jerked to a stop. In full alarm, her olfactory hypersensitivity was slammed by the undeniable, snaky odor of a DAK. Worse, with a shifting breeze, there was no hint as to its location. To her, with all the pungency of overly applied aftershave, the smell indicated the presence of an SST warrior, nearby, only moments before. The two stood frozen, not knowing where to flee. That is, until Rig insisted they return to the room. Having left the knapsack, he reasoned his fortune was vulnerable to being stolen. Vehemently, the alien pointed out that was exactly where the enemy was probably headed. After a heated but whispered debate, she finally acceded to her companion's obstinacy.

Looking back over their shoulders, the two halted in front of her cabana. Trembling, the Council representative took a high-risk gamble. She knew, being unable to escape, it was both their deaths if a DAK suddenly opened the door. Sealing her ability to flee, she closed her eyes to psychically scan the interior and decide if anyone was present. Slowly, tension melted.

Always traveling incognito, the Ra agent suggested the warrior may not, in fact, have been targeting her. The enemy was probably someone in the entourage of foreign dignitaries who stayed at these resorts when passing through town. Even so, both agreed it would be safer to order room service rather than to chance getting recognized. The only thing for them to do now was to lie low—lie low and wait for tomorrow. After a few minutes, she changed her mind. “If there are DAKs in the area, maybe we can learn something.”

Not wanting her to go alone, Rig reluctantly agreed to tag along. Stalling for time, he suggested, “Maybe I’d better take a shower first. Can you order me underwear, a shirt, socks, and pants from the pro shop on your credit card?”

“Sure. What sizes?”

“Socks 10; pants a 32 waist, 31 inches in length; and medium on the shirt. Oh, and tell them nothing with flowered prints.”

“Strange. I would have thought you’d prefer some wild Hawaiian motif.”

With the bathroom door slightly ajar, he heard her remark and called out, “Funny, very funny.”

Beginning to dial, she stopped and once more flashed that mischievous grin.

A baritone voice boomed out over the sound of the shower, “Let’s get back to my question about the leader; what’s his name?”

Resuming her dialing, she answered, “Malek. He’s….”

With the noise of the pounding water drowning out her voice, he shouted, “Never mind; I can’t hear! Wait a few minutes!”

Pausing, a strange twinkle came to Lyra’s eyes. Quietly, the receiver was placed back on the phone. Curious about a man’s naked body, she tiptoed to the bathroom. Peering through the door’s slit, the Earth visitor silently observed Rig’s lathered, muscular form through the fogged shower glass. Droplets hitting his face, he, in the Dalmatian dialect, absent-mindedly began singing an old folksong—about a land across the sea, a village, and a love he called his soul—left standing there, waiting for his return. The rich sound bounced off the bathroom walls.

A natural empath, the extraterrestrial attuned to her companion’s inner feelings as well as the song’s outward melody. Struck by the earthling’s tenderness, she stood transfixed—mesmerized by the sweet emotions he so cleverly hid from the outside world.

Came the shout, "Who is this guy…ahh, Malek?"

The spell was broken. Rocked to reality, Lyra quickly scurried back to answer from across the room. "The question isn't 'who,' but rather 'what.' You've got to give me a moment to order your clothes."

"I thought you already did."

"Uhhh…no, I got distracted."

Waiting what seemed long enough to have considered her words before speaking, he resumed, "About this Malek. What do you mean, he's not a 'he' but a 'what'?"

Excusing herself from the call, she placed a hand over the phone's mouthpiece, yelling, "I'm still ordering. Wait a minute!"

"Sorry."

As the purchase was finished, she, hung up, and, without missing a beat, started to explain in a louder than earlier volume. "This entity came into being right after the beginning of time. As the consummate form of evil, it is not human in any sense of the word. And to add to the confusion, it can take on anyone's form. That's what makes locating it so difficult." Her voice broke from the strain. "If the Council doesn't find him soon, it'll be too late."

"Why?"

"He's laying the groundwork for a twofold plan. As I said, in several years he will publicly surface to formally take over world leadership. After that, the next step will be to again attempt taking control of all interstellar dimensions. Everything is prepared."

"*Wait a minute!* If I understand you right, you're telling me that we are supposedly going to allow somebody to be crowned Emperor of Creation?" He chuckled. "And you said artificial sweeteners clog the brain. You should add your tofu to that list."

The Ra representative ignored his humor. "Think again. The way he's taking over Earth, the Evil One's rise to universal power is almost childlike in its simplicity. First, he offers brilliant solutions for survival to your dying planet. What you don't know is that life here is prophesied to be so horrific, people will make him emperor in the blink of an eye. And using this as his central base, Baal will then set out to conquer all of time and space."

"Ah hah! So that's the real reason your Foundation is poking around—going after this Aryan-Baal group."

"Partially, but I sense by your brainwave pattern that I may have slightly confused you."

The little voice in the Phoenician's head chided, *Wouldn't be the first time!*

Telepathically picking up the barb, Lyra graciously allowed it to float by. "Rig, besides stopping Malek, we're also here to help Earth maintain its balance in the universe—though with even a little training, a handful of your peple could turn this whole thing arond—by yourselves. But if the population continues the way it is going, you will self-destruct, even without Baal's help."

The treasure hunter raised doubts about the Council being able to capture such a needle in the world's haystack. Agreeing, the emissary added that it was going to be nearly impossible. Especially since DAK warriors had already inserted his elemental aspect into a human host. At least before, the Galactic Elders could recognize his evil form. Blending into the crowd, he was now but a single face among nearly seven billion.

"However," she disclosed, "we do know he's entered the body of a thirty-three-year-old redheaded megalomaniac male somewhere in the Middle East. And no, it is not who you're thinking."

Trying to follow his companion's story, the ex-stockbroker still had strong doubts. Even so, he didn't mind listening. Momentarily, it shifted his thinking away from overwhelming grief over the death of two friends. Drying off, he called out, "Say, if this guy's in the Middle East, why are you in Arizona?"

"I was ordered here." Taking out a laptop to make screenplay notes, she typed while answering, "I'm one of three the Council has sent to scout the planet for clues."

The tiled bathroom acted as a megaphone, making his volume increase. "Why only three?"

"That's out in the field; we're doing other things. I admit it'll be tricky finding him, but it isn't impossible. Say, have you ever heard of bilocation?"

Rig registered a blank.

"That's when a physical body can be in two places at the same time—frequently occurring in people who have highly developed vibrational sensitivity. Malek," she explained, "can replicate and be in an almost infinite number of locations simultaneously. He's totally divisible, except for the exact center of his soul—the core, or 'anchor point' as we call it. That's what we're looking for, somewhere in one of these tunnels.

"The good news is that with his center in a human form, he may actually be able to be captured. That is, if my people can trace these passages back to his command center. Problem is, it is a gigantic maze. So we're forced to follow every lead, Arizona being one of them."

The earthling balked at accepting her concept. "I'll say it again—this is way too bizarre. I'm beginning to think you're practicing your movie-line on me."

"*Bizarre?* With all you've seen in the last twenty-four hours? You remind me of Polynesians when they first encountered sailing ships."

His voice boomed, "Polynesians? What are you talking about?"

"What I'm going to tell you is a historical fact, but you'll probably deny it too." Shaking her head in disbelief, she said, "You earthlings have the most amazing capability for ignoring truth."

Pulling open a dresser drawer, Lyra proceeded to take out a blouse. Holding it up for inspection, she was deciding whether or not to change for dinner.

"Get on with it, already."

"You know, you are about the rudest person I've ever met!" Reversing her decision, she put the article away. "Make a little stab at being patient…*for once in your life.*"

"I am patient."

"As I was saying, before the white man came, Polynesians had never seen any boat larger than a canoe."

"Yeah…and?"

Gritting her teeth, she tried hard to suppress anger. "When sailing ships came into view, they had no reference for anything that gigantic. Forget about accepting them; those people had no concept that could even explain their existence. Vessels of this nature were beyond their conceptual framework." She added a slight dig, "Kind'a how most earthlings perceive their bearded God—sitting on a throne, taking out vengeance on anyone who steps over the line."

"*Oh, crud!* Just spit it out. What're you trying to say?"

"Since the islanders had no frame of reference, their minds wouldn't allow the picture of vessels to register in their brains; they blocked them out. Technically, it was called *'agnosia'*—a psychological ignoring or blind spot that prevents you from seeing something."

"You're kidding?"

"No, this is an absolute fact. To the Polynesians, the ships didn't have form or shape—complete mass denial. They were invisible. Only when the captain and crew got into their dinghies and started ashore did the islanders have a point of comprehension. To the natives, those rowboats appeared as if out of a mist."

"Because they also had canoes, something that small was conceivable?"

"Exactly. Only when they saw little boats did their minds break through their blindness, where the psyches allowed those rowboats to become part of their sight."

Then how did the people explain the strangers? he wondered.

She mentally heard, but answered out loud. "Thinking they came out of the sky, the natives treated the first few landing parties as gods."

With obvious irritation, he jibed, "And, the point to this whole thing is?"

"Your people do the same, especially with extraterrestrials. If you introduce cosmic facts, like aliens, that are beyond humans' comfort level, you people either pretend they don't exist, try to shoot our craft down, or treat us like gods. And you're no different."

"*Bull!* I don't…."

Deciding to wear her hair down and taking a comb out of her purse, she rebutted his half-made point. "Go ahead… ignore the writing on the wall. But mark my words: your planet is being set up for a one-world government…with a creature so evil, *nothing* in your imagination can even begin to describe the terror." While continuing combing, she listened to the shower door opening and closing.

What would make the entire world bow down to a king or whatever he's going to be called? Rig mused. *No way that's going to happen.*

Even though his dialogue was internal, the Lyrian heard and called out, "To get people to accept his rule, your planet is being forced to the brink of economic, climatic, ecological, and geophysical destruction. As I told you, this way Baal can appear at the eleventh hour when all seems hopeless, and offer miraculous solutions."

"What?" he stuttered, caught off-guard by the way she's answered a question he didn't voice.

"To really get an appreciation of that moment," the alien elaborated, as if a one-sided conversation was perfectly normal, "the world will be hit with multiple catastrophes. Hysteria will be everywhere—in every strata of society. People will be dazed, insane, screaming for answers." Her voice dropped an octave, "Like you'll soon see in New Orleans."

"Where?"

Again her volume increased. "Never mind. That's when the evil maestro steps out from behind his curtain. As I said, peace is the promise, but the end result will be the opposite."

She sat at the table, reapplying fingernail polish to cover the damage of recent developments.

"That's quite a story."

"Story? This is not *a story!* It's already happening! And your really big cataclysms are right around the corner. Any moron can see the trend. This was even laid out in your Bible, if you would ever read it."

"I'm not into this apocalypse thing. Look, if Earth is really being wrecked, and I don't believe it is, it is because of sheer avarice, not some airy-fairy, alien plot. Man's always been greedy. Girl, you're going to have to do better than that."

He exited the bathroom wearing only a towel. This time it was Lyra, who, fixated on his muscular body, was lost for words.

Trying to refocus, she stuttered, "I'm…I'm not just talking about prophecy in The Book of Revelation."

Seeing her embarrassment, the Phoenician broke into that self-satisfied grin.

Regaining composure, she continued, "These are documented facts. All I'm asking is for you to be logical. Start from events that have already happened. Then add future probabilities. Pay special attention to what your scientists who aren't in some big corporation or on a think-tank's payroll are forecasting. Use your head! *Think*!"

Standing in front of the dresser mirror, now it was Rig's turn. Finishing his combing with a jaunty upward flourish that only damp or moosed hair could hold, he affected a look of grave concern. "Lyra, I didn't know people like me could channel—I mean pull in messages from the great beyond." He put the comb down, and touched fingertips to both temples.

"Of course, anyone can if they practice. But what brought that up?"

"I...I'm getting this message."

"No, you're not. You're just acting stupid...again."

"No, no—I'm seeing the whole picture!"

"*Rig, stop it!* You aren't channeling."

"I tell you, I am. In fact, I'm getting this crystal-clear vision...*Oh my!* Everything's so vivid! It's...it's...like watching CNN."

"Go ahead, earthling—laugh. That's the problem with this planet; no one listens. All this is treated like some gigantic farce."

"Okay," he said, returning to his hair. "If I promise to be good, will you please tell me what's happening down the road?"

"All right," picking up the challenge. "Right now the world has changing weather patterns that are bringing hypercanes, El Niños, increasing volcanic eruptions, earthquakes over 9.4 on the Richter scale, tsunamis, floods, plus long-term droughts—all contributing to growing global famines. And this doesn't even take into consideration the millions who will be cooked alive when the coming massive solar flares hit."

"Flares?"

"Not the little ones that interrupt communications; these are gigantic death rays."

"Jeez! Okay, you've got my attention."

The extraterrestrial told her partner to put all these pieces of the puzzle into a giant framework. Only then would he understand how critical the situation had become—how far society and the environment had deteriorated. As proof, she pointed to a number of facts, such as the Earth's general oxygen level having dropped so low, that in places like Mexico City, unable to breathe, birds were dropping dead out of the out of the air while in mid-flight.

"Rig, listen to me. Carbon dioxide levels are higher today than they have been in the last million years!" She stated that heat-trapped CO2 emissions jumped 3.1 percent just in the year 2000, up nearly a full 14 percent from 1990. With terrifying clarity, Lyra related how this one single problem alone, could be the linchpin—the *fait accompli*, wiping out nearly *all* of Earth's inhabitants. "Even at the current level, this is *guaranteeing the triggering* of an ice-age within the next decade—give or take a few years."

To King, this last point failed to sink in. Waiting for clothes and wearing only a towel, the ex-stockbroker's attention was fully absorbed in carefully positioning his body in a stuffed chair. For one who was a habitual sloucher, his scant covering dictated a more formal posture. With no other option, Rigsat, feet on the floor, knees together. Uncomfortable though it might be, there could be no leg-crossing. As Lyra talked on, he thought, *How do women sit this way for hours on end? No wonder they prefer pants over skirts.*

Once more the Lyrian heard his internalizations but offered no comment, turning away to conceal her smile.

Countering with an opinion, he said, "I don't know about this solar-flare-CO2 situation of yours, but Wall Street sees all of these climatic changes as being only minor issues. We are a hell of a lot more worried about nuclear suitcase bombs in the hands of…oh, terrorists, and missiles from North Korea, and our debt with China than we are about your earthquakes, sun spots and carbon dioxide."

"What? Don't you think wrapping your house in plastic sheeting and using duct tape in case of attack, like Homeland Security recommends, will be enough protection?"

"Stop making fun. And let's even ignore the shoulder-fired surface-to-air missiles bringing down airliners, or nukes at shopping malls. One-third of America can be wiped out just by radioactive fallout from just two dinky nations squabbling on the opposite side of the globe."

"Actually," she injected, "a worldwide, nuclear holocaust may really be Biblically prophesied. Incidentally, as preparation for this very thing, why do you think the CIA, and other government agencies are quietly moving their headquarters to Denver, Colorado?"

"Prophesied?"

"Yes. The last planetary cleansing was by water. it was written that the next will be by fire."

"*Oh, good!* Thanks. Knowing that will definitely make me sleep better. Say, didn't you tell Kimbrell this burning will be from a lack of ozone?"

"In part. But my guess is if the primary problem isn't from that or sun flares, it might come from a nuclear war. You probably know that when the Soviet Union broke up, rogue officers sold over eight hundred atomic bombs—to anyone who would buy. And I'm not talking about the twenty suitcase bombs bin Laden's people trucked over the Canadian and Mexican borders. But if Wall Street thinks that a nuclear war, or even China invading because of America defaulting on its debt are their most immediate crises, they're wrong."

"If not those, what is?"

"I thought you would have guessed—biological and chemical terrorism. And forget the amateurish way it was been carried out in the past. I'm talking real terrorism—on a grand scale."

"How 'grand'?"

"Certainly not little envelopes of anthrax. Your concern should be of a global strike with organisms such as those causing smallpox or bubonic plague. For example, one way to create widespread genocide would be to place containers in balloons launched undetected into the Earth's jet streams over America and Europe. Using radio-controlled release mechanisms, pods could drop great swaths of disease. Within two weeks, one-fifth of all human life in these areas would be destroyed. And that's only one delivery system. Lobbing germs, chemicals, or bombs from submarines offshore into major U.S. coastal cities is another."

"I didn't know terrorists had submarines."

"North Korea and Iran already have. As for terrorists… soon—by seizing the port of Karachi and commandeering the several always docked there. But that's just one way. These fanatical groups have enough other weapons stockpiled to annihilate this planet many times over. They think the more unbelievers they take down, the greater their heavenly reward. To them, death in war is a victory—even more so if it's their own. Although another serious threat is this coming pandemic created by your reincarnated Nazi-Atlanteans, who want to thin the world's population—by eighty percent; the surviving remainder becoming slaves, of course."

The somber notes of truth began ringing in King's ears. Emitting a groan, he was totally lost in a new level of worry. Hand to forehead, as if warding off a headache, he screamed, "*Enough!* My brain's maxed. Let's change the subject. Besides, I've been reading that this whole scare thing is a sham created by tree-hugging, left-wing psychos—and a few idiot scientists."

"There you go again; everyone's in a state of denial. That's what Baal's soldiers have programmed you to believe. Okay, so let's momentarily ignore the catastrophe happening at the North Pole. At the opposite end, in the Antarctic, you have an ozone problem so large that since 1999, to avoid cancer, all the children in Australia have been forced by law to wear hats and long-sleeved shirts to school. *And hey!* The hole's expanding, regardless of the lies the think tanks are putting out. Do you really think the epidemic of skin cancer all around the world is just a coincidence?"

"Okay, okay—we can get to your ozone problem later. I suppose you're going to say all this is the work of Malek. Never mind, don't answer that. Just tell me what *your* people see in the future."

"You're not going to like it," she warned. "This is only the beginning. From here, it's on a fast track and going downhill... Take the problems created as a result of the greenhouse effect."

Squirming in his chair, King's body movements reflected growing agitation. The alien continued, telling how the oceans' warming as well as higher land temperatures were melting both polar icecaps. "Loss of ice will have world sea levels rising over twenty feet. And if planetary warming were to continue, by 2023, there would be no Arctic or Antarctic ice at all. That is, as I said, if it weren't for the coming Ice Age."

"I'm getting confused."

"You're not alone; so does most everybody else. Let me explain: This greenhouse warming trend is actually *ushering in an Ice Age*. As I speak," she punched her sentence with increasing power, "there's a three-mile-wide stretch of ocean where the North Pole should be. Rig, that area hasn't seen open water for *fifty million years!* And get this…*Over forty-eight percent* of Arctic ice has already disappeared—*in just the last four decades*."

"*Forty-eight percent?* Why hasn't this been major news?"

"When will you people wake up? The media's controlled. Kimbrell told you so, remember? The 2003 EPA report was doctored. What the White House knows is this: Global warming is an extremely critical issue, but except for the privileged ruling class, the huddled masses will just have to cope as best they can. Believe it or not—and I hope you're listening—each and every day there are those in the White House who consult something called the Rapture Index."

"The *what*?"

"I am not kidding. These folks believe that soon, most of their inner group will be pulled up into the 'Rapture.' And by getting most of the planet's 1.5 billion Islamists mad at America, as well as not taking care of the North Korea and Iranian nuclear problem, it looks like they just might get their wish."

"Whoops! There goes my aunt in Florida; she can't swim." King's lame attempt to change and lighten the subject fell flat—more so, with his second attempt. "And she was just getting the hang of that voting booth, too."

"*Florida?*" Lyra exploded. "*Where's your compassion?* I'm talking war with billions dying, and you're still back on melting ice. But…and this is a long-shot, assuming my people can stop those conflicts, and I don't think it's possible, with flooding alone, entire nations will be under water! Then you'll have world droughts brought on by those sunspot eruptions, and other problems making it nearly impossible to grow crops—such as the increasing cloud-cover and trapped heat caused by global industry and growing volcanic activity.

"Of course, the real irony is how this planetary heating trend actually creates an Ice Age."

"You mentioned that, but it doesn't make sense. How?"

"The process began when warming increased the water temperature in the oceans' upper layers. This relates to a stream or path of water, moving along the surface of the world's seas. At some point, this warm ribbon of current drops to the ocean's floor, whereupon it continues, but now moving as a river of cold along the bottom. Traveling this way around the globe, it loops back to where it began, ultimately rising to the surface—and starting the circuit all over again. Heated by greenhouse gases, the faster-moving warm water on the surface pushes the cold stream, forcing it to travel more quickly. And as the French would say, 'V*oilá tout*! The quickening rush of cold water causes a decline in overall land temperature. And there you have it—an Ice Age. Moreover, there doesn't need to be a ten- or fifteen-degree rise to have this happen. *Two degrees…just two…*and the seas have *already warmed by one degree*! Even without the temperature increase brought on by industrialization and the thickening volcanic dust cover, the way things are heating up because of methane gas buildup, your one-degree rise is slated in the next nine to eleven years."

"How will people eat?"

"Most won't. We forecast that of those left, the majority will starve…including massive numbers right here in America."

"Are you serious? I mean, we have to eat."

"Don't you get it? That's part of his plan. Grocery stores will be looted—empty. Even with gasoline at seven dollars a gallon, service stations will be closed—cars abandoned where they stop. All of the world's socioeconomic structure will be nonfunctioning—at a standstill--and half of the planet will be frozen in a block of ice. Living without TV, phones, and water to flush the toilet will be the least of your worries. *Get it through your head*; there will be almost no food…*anywhere*. Armed gangs will roam the streets like hungry rats, devouring everything they find. Some people, maybe your neighbor, will resort to cannibalism just to stay alive. "But hold your hysteria…This is only the beginning! You've still got the real mega-calamities to deal with."

Rig groaned, "Like what?"

"So much for Social Security and your precious stock market. Every family, even the Donald Trumps and Bill Gateses of the world, will be brought to their knees—huddled in dark corners, praying no one comes to their door. That's why the Bible says, '*Woe unto those with child during these times*.' It goes on to state that the, '*people will have to flee and live in the hills just to survive*.'"

"You really see that?"

"Unfortunately." Lyra lamented. "As I said, this is only the starting point. Nation will rise against nation. There is even a high probability for civil war right here in America. Bloody wars will be fought over such basics as water rights so farmers can simply tend their failing crops that they're trying to raise under blackened skies. And by the sixth year of the coming holocaust, we see your infamous World War III…if it doesn't happen sooner. Then your biggest problems really begin. As Kimbrell explained, there will be a planetary flip caused by loss of magnetism at both poles and tectonic…."

She stopped. Her sentence was broken by a knock at the door. it was a bellhop with most of Rig's clothes. Unfortunately, they were out of socks in his size.

Butting in while Lyra was busy signing the room receipt, Rig's comment was laced with doubt. "You know something? You sound like Chicken Little running around yelling, '*The sky is falling! The sky is falling*!' I'm not buying it. Like I said to Kimbrell, surely the scientific community would have already sounded the alarm."

Talking over her shoulder while adding a gratuity, the alien replied soberly, "They have, but you people are like ostriches. Believe me, responsible scientists are trying; all the while, your White House is lying and doctoring reports, so everyone dismisses the real experts as alarmist kooks."

"Then why haven't other governments responded?"

The bellhop, accustomed to being an invisible presence, took little notice of their conversation. With receipt and tip in hand, he left.

"Rig, you still don't understand, do you? The Followers of Baal are systematically pushing your planet to the brink of destruction." The emissary from Washington thrust her point deeper. "Look at it this way. Earth is like a giant mobile—with a delicate balance of plants, animals, climate, and a human population. Disturb just one, and the whole equilibrium goes askew. What I'm saying is, Malek, by mind-printing influential players, is presiding over the entire crisis. Every calamity you can imagine is being manipulated, allowed to go to the extreme."

"Can man survive all this?" he asked.

"The spiritual, who have done their homework, will. As it is written in Matthew and Mark, '*For then there will be great suffering such as has never happened in the world until now, and never will again.*' It goes on to say, '*And if those days were not shortened, no flesh would live; but for the sake of the chosen ones, those days will be shortened.*' Speaking of that, did you know time has already been speeding up? If you don't believe me, think of some news event that seems like it just happened recently, then research how long it's really been."

Placing clothes on the bed, the earthling sat down on its edge. Leaning forward, an elbow on one knee, he buried his head in his hands. "Even if I go along with your crazy assumption, and I'm not saying I do, I'm still not clear on how Baal's guys can accomplish something so monumental." Starting to take the sales labels off his pants, he exploded, "You're...you're talking about massive changes that affect the whole Earth...such as a polar flip. Ahh, come on. That's pure fantasy. Be real."

"I didn't say Baal's in absolute control—as in being able to make the tectonic plates move on a whim. But science confirms it has happened 154 times over the last 100 million years. And the way things are going, it will definitely occur—*very soon*. By capitalizing on man's greed, he's simply quickening the process--like orchestrating the destruction of the rain forests. The loss of these trees significantly decreases world oxygen. In turn, this creates severe planetary droughts—which, of course, helps destroy the ozone layer, which worsens global warming and melts the polar icecaps. See the dominoes falling? Everything's interconnected. That singular imbalance is forcing the plates to move. And this is only one example; he has a whole series of catastrophes in progress."

Delicately unwrapping a chocolate and hesitating, Lyra waited a moment before placing it in her mouth. Savoring the taste, seconds passed before she commented. "But as I said, many of your higher-ups already know this. Why do you think Washington has all those escape tunnels? They plan to be safe, while you'll be outside, pounding on the door to get in."

The dark cocoa, having slightly melted, left a telltale smudge. Sucking off the gooey residue from the tip of her middle finger, she added, “Remember, there’s proof that pockets of your government have been secretly coordinating all this with the followers of Baal since the 1950s.”

CHAPTER XV

SMOKE AND MIRRORS

The news over, Rig clicked off the TV. The room hung heavy with thoughts of impending doom. Driven by hunger, he too was distracted by chocolate, again taking the basketball approach to ridding himself of the crumpled wrapper. The toss went wide, just missing the wastepaper basket. Lyra, on the other hand, used the feminine method. Great care was taken in folding the bright red foil several times, creating the smallest square imaginable before neatly placing it in an ashtray on the nightstand next to the bed.

Within moments, the silence was interrupted. "Say,this Malek guy, where did you say he comes from?"

"At one time he was what we call 'A Chosen One'—high in the galactic hierarchy—leader of the planet Malduk. Allegorically speaking, this is Lucifer, the fallen angel who stood at the left hand of the Creator. That is, before he and his legions split away to conquer all of time and space."

"This is getting really surreal, like a bad acid trip."

"A what?"

"Skip it—not important. Keep going."

The Ra representative related how Malek and his followers became so drunk with power, they attempted to conquer the Divine Center—the throne of Heaven. In the process, their planet was destroyed, creating the dangerous asteroid belt through which Earth was currently passing.

Terrifying pictures of the end of the world flooded Rig's mind. Sweeping the images away, he retreated into denial. "Sorry, maybe climate shifts, okay; but I can't buy into this... this giant conspiracy thing. These are simply problems common to overpopulation. I mean, these events aren't necessarily related. At least, that's how I see it."

The Ra emissary let out a long sigh.

"Hey, turn around," he insisted. "I want to get dressed."

"You're bashful," she giggled, continuing to stare mischievously. "I like that."

Now it was Rig's cheeks that turned pink. He made his point again. "Come on, Lyra, turn around."

With her back to him, the Lyrian's smile spread into a broad grin. The glass on a wall picture reflected a nearly full-frontal view of her busy companion...whose towel had dropped to the floor. Blinking, she was forced to clear her throat before continuing. "Then here's another thought. Even you agree that the world has a population crisis."

"So?"

"This is a time bomb governments could have easily defused long ago, if they had really wanted. Even if Earth's other problems are solved, the number of humans is forecasted to increase *forty-six percent* over the next fifty years!"

"And you're telling me that some group of space beings is behind global population growth? *No way!*"

"You make everything a joke. India alone has bloated to one point one billion inhabitants. Ignoring the food, water, and oxygen consumption, just imagine their daily mountain of excrement! It's...it's staggering. Look around! Everywhere on Earth is polluted. DDT contamination has even been found on top of Mount Everest. Rig, this planet can no longer absorb all this filth. It...."

"I agree, population is something that needs to be dealt with. But...."

"More than that, this is part of Malek's master plan—one more rock on the heap of deadly crises...another reason to bow down to someone who comes along with solutions! With two billion people, this can be a paradise. You have nearly seven billion. And if you all weren't about to be annihilated, nine would be right around the corner. Look at the under-the-fence flood of immigrants from Mexico. *Ten percent* of that nation's entire population is *in America!* And if you think this is a big problem now, imagine the tidal wave when those back in their country start starving due to the drought. Plus, I can outline several worse catastrophic events looming just over the horizon."

"And I'm sure you will."

Multitasking, Lyra carried on the discussion while typing. "No, I'm tired of wasting energy trying to get even one point across. Most of you are either unaware of the seriousness of these things or simply won't face the truth."

"That's because we don't see it."

"I know these events seem unconnected. That way, the Followers of Baal are never perceived as the source. Everything is meant to look natural. And if I can't get *you* to understand what's happening, how can my people wake up your entire planet?"

"On rare occasions, and I do mean rare, when they are discovered, the Aryan-SST counters by sending out brainwashing messages to those in key positions. The targets are hypnotized into believing the issue is totally inconsequential or simply a figment of their imaginations."

"How? By going into bedrooms and imprinting?"

"We both come calling, but for different reasons. Malek's followers program. My people come to warn. In the morning, it's like everything was a dream. Most don't even recall the visitation. The crisis then loses its importance and simply fades."

"Can you give me an example?"

"Of course—like your two-mile string of lights over Phoenix in March of 1997. Not only was it seen by thousands, it was videotaped by more than a dozen residents. Yet top scientists, military specialists, and politicians have all been programmed to believe these were nothing more than military flares. They totally deny the facts."

"Such as?"

"Oh, like the fact that spectrum lighting analysis shows that flares the Air Force uses are of a totally different pattern than those filmed. Now do you see how Baal's strategy works?"

Having witnessed the UFO display himself, the ex-broker finally switched from flippancy to seriousness. “I don’t want you to get too excited, but I may be beginning to perceive a bit of truth in this explanation of yours. I mean, until this moment, all these things seemed like unrelated curiosities or news stories. But now…now they’re beginning to tie together.”

“Can I turn around now?”

“Oh, sure.”

“It’s hard,” continued the extraterrestrial, “for people to get the connection unless they stand back and view the whole picture.”

Rig momentarily retreated to the bathroom to recheck the bullet streak across his cheek. With the door slightly ajar, he called out, “Hey, I need a toothbrush, soap, and a shaver. While we’re hunting DAK, let’s go to the gift shop and then to dinner.”

Minutes later, the two were greeted by a hot, humid, Arizona evening—typical of this time of year. Proceeding slowly, each was on edge, watching for signs of the enemy. Every few paces, Lyra tested the air and inspected the aura of everyone in sight.

As they glanced around, as if by the wave of a magic wand, nighttime had brought a metamorphosis to the La Posada. Lit torches draped with ribbons illuminated its winding pathways. Combined with multicolored lights strung in all directions, there was a festive, almost ethereal glow to the area. In the swimming pool, increasing the evening’s enchantment, votive candles bobbed up and down, gently rocked by the cascading waterfall. Overhead, skyrockets exploded, popped, then crackled—their streamers of color falling back to Earth. Below, mirrored reflections from the water underscored the night’s beauty, a gentle encore to the many hues of the dazzling display above.

Adding a note of sophistication, men dressed in black ties, accompanied by women in diamonds, pearls, and evening gowns, gathered in small groups. Holding drinks to their chests, they talked quietly, occasionally calling attention to themselves with outbursts of laughter.

Coming closer, Rig and Lyra were nearly deafened by the raucous strains of a mariachi band. The Southwestern music was a perfect complement to the strong smell of an outdoor barbecue. More wary than ever, she fearfully recognized that the pervasive mesquite smoke masked any hope of scenting their quarry.

On their way to the restaurant, Rig popped into the gift shop, keeping busy while his partner made a stop at a clothing boutique across the hall. The necessary items purchased, he found the corridor swollen with revelers. The occasion was a senator's daughter's wedding, and it was time for the send-off. With such a compact crowd, it would have been rude to break through the stream of guests and cross over. Courtesy suggested he take a moment and wait until the newlyweds and party passed. Preceding the couple, the band, confined by the tight passageway, seemed to blare even louder. Slowly, the procession, led by musicians, moved down the hall heading for the limousine out front.

Scanning the crowd, King spotted the well-known face of the Washington official and his wife. A bodyguard with his back to the crowd turned, speaking secretively into the politician's ear. But that's not what had Rig's attention. It was night; they were indoors—and the guard was wearing sunglasses. Looking around, he saw two more similarly attired men escorting the young couple.

Not knowing whether they were DAKs or not, the treasure hunter made an instinctive dash for safety—back into the doorway of the gift shop. Moving first, thinking second, he stepped on an onlooker's toes. Glancing away from the senator, he started to offer an apology. Shock opened his hand. The bag dropped. Inches away, he was staring into the face of another scowling, sun-glassed guard. Wanting to run, he knew that he couldn't; it would be a dead giveaway. Triggered by the obvious fear on King's face, the suspicious DAK proceeded to start a mind-scan. Frantic, Rig knew it was only a matter of seconds; he and Lyra were about to be exposed.

"*Whoops! Ahh, sorry*!" is all that spurted out, given the deadly predicament.

As the bodyguard spoke into his wristwatch, he shook his head, confused, as if just having received a heavy blow. Before more than three words could be uttered, a commotion arose—across the lobby, near the bride and groom. Shouts were followed by screams. A shot was fired. Shoving his suspect aside, the guard waded into the crowd. Like a salmon swimming downstream while everyone else was going up, the man waded toward where the noise originated.

With nearly everyone fleeing, the corridor had thinned enough for Rig to finally make his way across.

Grabbing Lyra's hand, he said, "We have to get out of here. I think those are DAKs."

"I know they are," she confirmed, while both maneuvered to escape, pushing through the flood of people. "I just couldn't smell them over the barbecue. Besides, who do you think got the fight started that saved you?"

"You?"

"Little ol' me. I scrambled his brainwaves to rattle him as he radioed in. Then I projected to one of the wedding guests that the person next to him had picked his pocket. And boom! You had a fight."

Hurriedly, the two made their way back to her room. Both agreed the event in the lobby took place much too quickly for the DAK to realize who they were, let alone where they went. Even so, Lyra was thankful she wore a large-brimmed hat this evening; it hid subtle auric characteristics that a trained enemy would be certain to recognize. Walking briskly, the two continued the conversation where they had left off earlier.

"I bet you didn't know," she began, "your government gave the DAK, Greys, and Martians permission to have actual bases here."

"Nothing you say shocks me anymore." Or so he thought.

"In return," she continued, "the Followers of Baal threw your leaders a small bone of, what my people consider, insignificant technology."

"Like what?"

"Oh, space-time transport for one." The response was almost casual. "You call them flying saucers. Washington has gotten part of this knowledge from downed craft back as far as the late '40s. Maybe you heard about some of the testing at Area 51…You know, before the more advanced experiments were moved?"

Rig asked, his attention now riveted on her every word, "What else do we have?"

"Hyper-dimensional transducers."

"What's that?"

"Teleportation machines—far more sophisticated than your earlier Tesla model."

"Get outta here! For real?"

"It's no big deal. Your military's been experimenting with this since the famous Philadelphia Experiment during the Second World War."

"Famous? I never heard of it."

Shaking her head in disbelief, the Lyrian murmured, "That figures."

"What?"

"Nothing. Nothing. Rig, there's a mountain of published information documenting this. As I said, Tesla made the prototype. During the war, the U.S. experimented by teleporting Navy ships from one location to another. But there was a glitch—like uninformed sailors getting trapped halfway through the metal bulkheads on rematerialization. Then one machine failed to shut down."

"My God! I'm assuming that would have led to some sort of major explosion, or something. But I never heard of it. What happened?"

"After the war, the device was refined at Montauk, on Long Island. Then, they sent a person back in time—to change history by removing the malfunctioning part and turn the thing off. But that's another story."

"Is this documented?"

"It's a well-known fact, though your government keeps trying to debunk it."

"Incredible!"

"If you don't believe me, always go to what you do know. Look, for example, at the disproportionate number of deaths among witnesses to JFK's assassination. According to insurance actuaries, the probability of so many of them dying—in particular, those who saw a second shooter on the Grassy Knoll—within two years of the assassination was two billion to one. Even certain frames of the Zapruder film, proving another bullet's impact from a different direction, have been removed. You really should read a little more. This is all declassified.

"I find it amazing; evidence is staring everyone in the face but the majority are under such hypnotic influence that only a handful of you are able to recognize the facts. And of those who do see a pattern, no one knows what to do."

"Nah, this can't be! If…if what you say is…is really true…."

Rig's word trailed off. Arriving back at the room, too excited to sit, he once more began pacing. Like a caged animal, even a useless movement was this man's subconscious way of putting things into focus.

Rig's lower lip was fast developing a sore from being repetitively bitten. "I'm sure in your little way you mean well; but you're…you're making at least some of this up, aren't you?"

"*That's it!* Enough of your putdowns. Tell me then; why do you think your government still denies the existence of UFOs?"

In his case, he felt there was no tangible proof. The alien countered that government/extraterrestrial meetings and galactic treaties were being kept hush-hush; the official position that, 'There is no such thing as a spaceship,' was just one more Washington-fostered illusion. Literally tons of captured evidence from downed crafts as well as an unofficial museum of alien cadavers actually existed. The Followers of Baal simply didn't want to raise questions about their presence.

"A museum?"

"Think in terms of Malek's overall agenda. Your planet has begun to enter a period of massive change—referred to in the Bible as the Time of Tribulation; we call it, The Great Cleansing."

"You sound like one of those scare-slinging, left-wing, talk-show types, like Al Franken or Ed Schultz…Hey, with all this prophetic ability, who's going to win the next presidential election? Bet I gotcha on that one."

"Scare-slinging? Look, Mister…stupidity and arrogance are the only things keeping your type from being frightened out of your wits. Okay…If the elections were *fair,* my meditations show the Oval Office having a more feminine decor." Twinkling eyes lost their luster with a follow-up Earth-prophecy: "The Ancient Ones say, 'In the Age of Aquarius, while Ki and Mars observe, and Sol, Mercury, and Jupiter, joined by a faceless orb, become as pearls strung, and Lilith next to her brother stands, a Janus heart hoists the crown gained by sleight of hand—and sudden sadness on an ill wind flies. Along this path, double woe: As through golden arches, even the Earl of Sandwich should stumble were he to lean on this king's staff.'"

With an IQ actually higher than most, still the Phoenician's expression remained blank. Buried too deep, the riddle's truth was solved by few, except those with abilities far beyond the range of even the most gifted.

Not finished, Lyra's remaining predictions became increasingly dire. "Forgetting the 'October Surprise' in 2006—something that will curl nearly everybody's toes—unless the future picture changes, those Presidential elections *won't even be held*. With North Korea's missiles, the Iranian conflict, plus allowed terrorist attacks in the U.S., and the manufactured pandemics, the White House is planning to invoke Executive Order—creating martial law and establishing a permanent, wartime presidency. Bank accounts will be seized, curfews…I told you, read *Mein Kampf* and Machiavelli's *The Prince;* they give you a step-by-step of their game-plan. I…."

A banging on the door. They froze. Obviously, the two were followed. Having heard loud talking, the being knew someone was in the room. Rig scanned the walls for a window that opened. One did but only ten inches—not enough to squeeze through. There was no way out. The two stood frozen, barely breathing. Another knock, this one louder.

Then a voice, "I've got your socks, Sir." Hearing voices and realizing a man and woman were there, but assuming the guests did not want to be disturbed, the bellboy added, "I'll hang the sack on your door handle."

The duo gave a sigh of relief, burst out laughing, retrieved the delivery, then plunged back into the topic at hand.

"Rig, if you don't believe you're headed for one world government, why do the boys in the District of Columbia incessantly push for a New World Order?"

"They don't. At least, I don't think they do."

"*The heck!* Go back," she insists, "and examine the film clips of President George H. W. Bush's speeches in 1990. Number 41 started out slowly, almost imperceptibly, talking about the need for '*a new, global approach*.' Several months later, his speechwriters cleverly modified it to a need for a '*new order to things*.'"

"I don't remember that."

"No one does, unless they're looking," she concedes. "It wasn't long before his phrase changed to, 'the need for a *New World Order*.' Then along came Clinton, cramming the concept further into the subconscious of the American public. His steady refrain was, '*We are a global village; we are a global village,'* ad nauseam. And then you have this 'globalization' plan being pushed by 43. See how you have been systematically led down the path? The noose is tightening."

"All right, I'll admit; there does seem to be some sort of a pattern. Even so, taken all together, this is truly hard to fathom. Sounds more like Hillary and Bill's 'vast right-wing conspiracy' garbage. I mean, how could Baal's troops have slipped all of this stuff by us?"

"Mass hypnosis. What I'm giving are actual quotes from your presidents' speeches," Lyra reminded him, "not something I'm making up. This is all part of Malek's subliminal programming. And to top it off, the public's been imprinted to ridicule anyone who even attempts to expose his existence.

"If you don't believe me and want to ignore your own Bible," she drove home, "examine other religions. As I said, this apocalyptic scenario has been foretold in the prophecies of nearly every race on your planet."

"*Whew!* I've got to sit down again," he said, slumping into a chair. Carrying a load of nervousness too great to contain, Rig jumped up, mumbling, "Need a drink. Mind if I raid your wet-bar again?"

"If it helps, go ahead. But I suggest we also use room service and order dinner."

CHAPTER XVI

F.E.A.R.

With forecasted doom piled on top of the recent murders of his friends, King was awash in confusion. Knowing his life would be cut short by these prophecies was frightening enough. But learning of the enslavement and potential extinction of humanity was a weight heavier than this human could carry. His words came softly, as one who had accepted the inevitability of defeat. "I…I guess there's not much we can do."

"*Stop that!* You're wrong! Nothing, and I do mean *no-thing* or problem, is hopeless! *Even the most catastrophic of situations is changeable*."

Not a second was wasted unscrewing the cap of a mini Jack Daniel's. Forgoing a glass, the frightened earthling knocked back the bourbon straight—with a toss of the head, and a grimacing gulp.

Lost in dismal thoughts, the earthling sidestepped his sorrow long enough to ask, "What'd you say?" Before she could reply, King's mind replayed a scene from a Hollywood horror movie showing the destruction of the planet. Lines of strain creased his face as he suddenly blurted, "Wait a minute! What do you mean *things can be changed*? Seconds ago, you told me Armageddon is a sure thing. At least that's what your prophets said."

"Not my prophets—yours. That's the problem with you people; your concept of God is so small, everyone limits what the Creator can do."

The Phoenician's scrambled brain cast around for something—anything to hang on to—some promise of safety. "Huh?" he answered, resurfacing.

"Listen to me!" Lyra exploded, she hoped with enough force to bring him back to the moment. "Pay attention. Everything, and by this I mean every single problem, regardless of how catastrophic it seems, can be fixed."

"Fixed? How?"

"What I'm about to reveal to you is the most ancient of wisdom. Use it correctly and *there is absolutely nothing that even one lone person cannot accomplish."*

The alien told her companion she was about to pass on *The Law of The Old Ones*—how to access total power. She explained there were only a couple of steps. The first was: Regardless of the size of the problem, a person must *let go of every shred of fear*. In other words, he or she must step out in total trust. And although it sounded simple, this initial stage was the most difficult.

Hearing these words, Rig's face dropped. Never a big believer in God, the ex-salesman was lost. He had never known the restful sleep that came of true security. For him, life had been a constant battle—one of attack or defend—the hounds of debt, deceit, and competition always snapping at his heels. Like the majority of his fellow humans, for him, the idea of a continuous state of peace was like some fabled realm, for which occasionally a visitor's pass was granted, but a place where few but the spiritually enlightened, continuously dwell.

The Lyrian explained that there existed a cosmic law, one whose translation could not be found in any Earth language. The closest would be something like '*harmonia.*' It meant that when a thing was out of balance, if we moved out of the way, God, or whatever name you wanted to use, would restore the situation to its original perfection. In other words, you don't have to burn incense, make sacrifices, shout alleluia, or even sing hymns. Just step aside.

She reiterated that a person's fear was the single most powerful obstruction, preventing this law of equilibrium from automatically prevailing. From a spiritual perspective, the word translated to nothing more than an acronym: *False... Evidence...Appearing...Real*. So real, in fact, that when worried or frightened, people literally shut down their divine flow of good; and the greater their fear, the tighter they squeezed.

"But however you say this law works, I still can't see how one person could possibly alter worldwide catastrophes."

His companion sighed. "You people simply don't know how powerful you really are, do you?"

"What do you mean, powerful?"

"Anyone—a truck driver, a dishwasher in the kitchen of some backwater café, even a prisoner on death row—*everyone has it! And 'it' is the ability, equal in all of us, to tap into the Divine Principle."*

"What's the Divine Principle?"

"It's the 'I Am that I Am'—the Infinite Source—the Creator."

"Oh, gotcha."

"What I want you to understand is by using this law of release, the unending power of God will correct any situation that appears. To quote Jesus, *'It is not I, but the Father within me, that does these miracles.'"*

All of us operate on three levels, she said: the conscious, the subconscious, and the guardian of the gate—the superconscious.

Exasperated, he couldn't contain the comment, "Here we go again."

"Why can't you be patient for once and let me explain? Obviously, you know about the first two levels, but you probably don't know about the function of the third."

Arrogance unbowed, Rig rose to the occasion. "Try me," was the challenge as he used his bath towel to snap at a cockroach that was scooting top speed across the carpet—a clean miss.

"I really wish you would try to capture that poor little creature and take him outside."

"Hell, his group will be on Earth long after humans. If I kill one, that won't wreck your delicate balance of nature. Trust me on that."

"Trust? I find it ironic," she said with a puzzled look on her face, "that you'd choose that particular word for this situation.

Enough. Let's get back to what we were discussing. Explain to me the function of the conscious mind."

Throwing the towel onto the chair in the corner, the treasure hunter growled, "This is getting really boring."

The alien remains emphatic. "Stick with me a minute; you'll see how all of this comes together. Tell me."

"All right," he mumbled. "The conscious aspect is what I'm purposefully thinking about this very second."

"And," she added, "your subconscious governs the automatic functions of the body—making over two thousand decisions every second. For instance, as I'm speaking, my lungs are pulling in air, and my heart is beating, but I don't have to tell them to do it."

The Ra representative pointed out that the third stage was the superconscious—the key to accessing miracles. It was the guardian of the gate and knew only one word, *Yes*! She further asserted that on Earth, ninety-nine point seven percent of people have mountains of negative programs constantly going through their minds. Nearly everyone was saturated with thoughts and statements like "God doesn't hear my prayers"; "I'm not worthy"; "I can't because of my circumstances"; "People won't let me"; "I don't have enough time or money"; etc. These messages are playing nonstop in nearly everyone's superconsciousness. To which their soul or guardian simply gives that one-word answer."

"I don't get it."

"Say on a conscious level you want to win…oh, the Powerball. But deep down, these stronger, negative refrains of fear and unworthiness are playing, negating your conscious intent. So, of course you don't win. You've magically pushed good away. People confuse not succeeding with being unlucky, but they're mistaken. There is no such thing as 'luck.' The fact is, an individual is either allowing or choking off the good that's trying to flow into their life. Remember, God gives only good. By refusing it, man himself unknowingly sabotages the natural process. You've probably heard the saying, *'The truth shall set you free.'*"

"No."

"Well, it was out there. But a more accurate way of stating it is, *'You are…and always have been free.'* You've simply designed a program to refuse it. It was like you've put up a wall."

Rig headed to the wet bar for another drink while answering, "A wall, huh? Then I did create something? But let me get this straight; according to you, good's all around me… uh-huh…humm. That must be why the FBI's on my tail, SEC's jerked my license, and my bank account's frozen. To you, those are all good things." He didn't give time for a response. "Or in the opposite direction, I am a co-creator; not only did I make the wall that keeps happiness away, I somehow enabled these problems to filter through. Which is it?"

"*Neither!*" she replied with vehemence. "Wait a minute; I'll try to make it clearer. If what you say is true, that means you really are doing something. However, *only God creates*. He, not you, is the doer. More simply stated, there is only one Creator, not two or three or what have you. I hear this 'I'm a co-creator' garbage all the time. This grandiose thinking that the Little You is able to manifest is nothing more than ego talking. Sure, you can manipulate the *hologram,* but *only God authors reality—the true state—the one of perfection.* All else is an *illusion*. Understand it this way; there never was a barrier. it was only a trick of the mind. You haven't constructed a thing. You simply gave power to a lie, which now seems real. And so you are denying your perfect self. See?"

A yawn, preceding his answer, indicated her companion's diminishing level of attention. "I don't see anything, especially how this ties in with your 'fear' thing." But wanting to break the boredom of her explanation, he couldn't resist inserting a joke. "We have a saying in the stock brokerage trade, 'The meek shall indeed inherit the Earth….We just won't give them the mineral rights!'" Seeing his friend wasn't laughing, he continued, "Anyway, your explanation makes me feel guilty—like a loser."

"Absolutely not. Just the opposite—you're guiltless. Look at it this way. If you accept a belief that's floating around, say, like a cold, did you create the cold?"

"Well, I got it, didn't I?"

"What you got is an illusion that seems real but is only a hypnotic nonreality. God doesn't create colds and neither do you."

"How can you say that God doesn't create colds?"

"Easy. Do you think God can have a cold? Of course not. So, if He can't have it, it can't really exist; it exists only in the dream state."

The Phoenician flopped on the bed, propping up his back with pillows while listening further.

"However, if you accept someone's belief concerning a cold," she insisted, "I mean, claim it as your own in that trance state, you'll surely exhibit all the classic symptoms. The truth is, the cold doesn't actually exist. And yet, its illusory picture is so strong, you succumb to the lie. Granted, the runny nose, the high temperature, and achy feeling all seem absolutely real. But they're not. So how can you be guilty of accepting a lie that's really an illusion?"

"It always seems real to me."

"The same way," she responded, "on stage and under the influence of a hypnotist, you might momentarily believe you're a chicken. However, would crowing make you a rooster? So when you awaken to the fact that the cold is a mental fabrication, the symptoms melt away—like the morning mist when the sun comes up. Once the reality of your perfection becomes evident, you're instantly healed of a belief that never was. As I said, truth didn't set you free; *you have always been free*."

Scratching his head, it was obvious by his expression that this was a difficult concept to grasp. He asked, "Therefore, if life is only an illusion, someone can murder and rob and no one's really hurt?"

"Again, this is one of those 'yes and no' answers. To those who believe in this existence and accept evil as a part of their reality, yes; that person certainly has killed and stolen. It was like watching TV—all depends on what channel you are on. If you're viewing a gory horror show, that's your focus for the moment. However, if you change channels, you and the TV are still the same, but the picture is totally different. What mankind needs to do is drop the illusion and see the real picture of health, abundance, joy, and so forth."

"Lyra, slow down a little. This is still too complex. I've got to let it soak in for a while."

"Maybe you're right; this is too deep with all the other things we have happening. I simply wanted you to realize that *the first step to receiving good is the total release of fear.* Once you have the guardian no longer blocking, wonderful things start to happen. The next step is to…."

"Wait a minute. If we have such power, you have it too. Why isn't your group taking care of Earth's problems?"

"You people need to grow up—learn to take responsibility for your own lives. Sure, we could fix things, but cosmic law forbids it. Like when you go to school, each student has to do his or her own homework."

"Then why is your Council interested in our catastrophes if you aren't going to do more than track this Malek down? And why don't all your people let go of fear? According to this hypothesis of yours, he would then be compelled to turn himself in."

Lyra looked her companion straight in the eyes. "We're helping more than you know. However…."

"However, what?"

"Next to lying, Malek's most cunning weapon is his use of fear. And he's a master at inspiring it. Our people are just as susceptible as yours are. Trust me, miracles are realized by using the technique I just told you about. For instance, when I get out of the way and apply the law, mountains really do move. But just like everyone else, I can get caught up in the lie, which, at the time, seems to be reality, and I forget what to do."

"Like back in the cave?"

"Exactly."

"So then, why are your people really here?"

"This is part of our spiritual destiny. We have to grow too, you know? Also, our races are distant cousins, by about six hundred million years. We are one of several groups that originally populated this planet."

"Were they all from your area?"

"No. There was the blue race, then us—the gold—your white, the red, and the black. All of which were equal in…."

At that instant, a more immediate problem forced Rig's thoughts in another direction—the murders.

Speaking out loud, albeit to himself, he says, *"Uh-oh! Ahh, jeez!* When I went to see Miller, I asked the receptionist for directions. *Damn it!* I was one of the last people to see him alive. She not only knows my face but my name, too. This means I've been framed, in not one, but…Lord! Two murders! They must be scouring the whole countryside for me."

"A government manhunt will certainly make the DAKs' job of locating us a lot easier."

"Like I said about the fingerprints, we've got to ditch John's four-by-four—and fast! Let's get going. We can grab food on the way back."

"I can be ready in five minutes."

"Make it three."

CHAPTER XVII

DREAM STATES

Under the cover of darkness, Lyra followed Rig in her rental car as he sped up Mockingbird Lane. Minutes later they pulled into the Camelback Golf Club parking lot. At the foot of Mummy Mountain, in the heart of Paradise Valley, this was the Beverly Hills of Arizona—a quiet pocket of the rich and famous, replete with gated communities and manicured lawns. Little here went unnoticed—even less, unreported.

On the return, though he was mourning his friend's death, a slight smile rippled across the Phoenician's face. He knew finding John's vehicle in this exclusive neighborhood would drive the Paradise Valley police totally nuts. But more, it would surely curdle the crème de la crème—those who felt safely cocooned in this expensive sanctuary of privilege.

As they proceeded, Lyra looked out the front windshield into the night sky. Pointing, she asked, "Know what that is?"

Dazed, yet in a flippant mood, her companion reverted to the best California Valley accent he could muster. "Duh! You must think I'm sahh-oh stew-ped! Of course—it's a helicopter."

"No, that's what people are meant to think. It is supposed to look like that but it is actually one of ours."

"A spaceship? Are you serious?"

"Sure. Flying this low, they project a hypnotic illusion to convince everyone it was a helicopter. Plus, when going over a city at night, we sometimes use blinking lights similar to those on small aircraft. That way, no one pays attention."

"Get out of here."

"It's true. *Wait*! I'm getting a message. They want us to follow."

Throughout most of this adventure, Rig had been riding an adrenaline high. Now was no exception. Beside himself in anticipation of a face-to-face alien encounter, he completely forgot that a celestial creature already sat a mere two feet away.

Snaking north along with them, the spaceship waited patiently each time the adventurers were delayed by traffic lights. Within a mile of the Deer Valley Airport, at the end of a dusty, four-wheel trail, they had to park about eighty yards from where the craft had landed. The extraterrestrials had chosen their spot well; with so much local air traffic, surrounding residents paid little attention, mistaking the saucer for normal plane activity.

Exiting the chilled, air-conditioned car, the two were engulfed by searing summer heat. Lungs filled with the stifling air radiating off nearby boulders. They proceeded without talking. Neither mentioned it, but both felt a strange absence of noise blanketing the area—an eeriness quickly diminished by the crunching of their footsteps against the gravel. The nearly barren landscape made this a foreboding place. Except for a few clumps of sagebrush and an occasional palo verde tree, there was but one saguaro cactus. In the moonlight, with its arms pointing upward, the plant, to Rig's distorted way of thinking, vaguely resembled the victim of a stickup.

Small hills ringed the spacecraft, obscuring it from view in all directions. The only telltale sign of its existence was a partially visible, flashing red light just over the crest of a tall mound. Fantasizing it as a pulsating maraschino cherry on top of an ice-cream sundae, the ex-stockbroker thought, *Man, I've seen real low-budget space movies better than this. Is art imitating life, or is life imitating art?*

The Lyrian stopped, pausing out of protocol, waiting to be invited further. Her companion did likewise. The evening, although smothering, had a pleasantness—a joy brought by anticipation of the unexpected meeting.

Suddenly, a bloodcurdling guttural cry erupted from just over the slope. In total shock, the bewildered pair froze. A second howl sent shivers down their spines. Every hair on their arms stood erect. Without a word, they spun, fleeing back toward their car at breakneck speed. Thinking ahead, Rig bitterly regretted his mindless habit of always locking a vehicle; the extra seconds needed might mean their demise.

If ever the weekend warrior felt life depended on how fast he could open a door, this was the moment. Glancing back while running, he tried in vain to see their pursuer. Although the beast's form was not visible, the growling and crashing through sagebrush left no doubt of its existence. With each second, the gap between creature and prey shortened. King looked over to make sure his companion was keeping up.

And was met by a scream, *"It's getting closer!"*

Running blind, he stumbled into a small hole. Terror made the stabbing pain of his ankle and gravel-punctured palms barely noticeable. Up, limping, wild with fright, Rig resumed his race to the car, which now seemed farther away. Arriving, he feverishly jabbed his pocket for keys. On the passenger side, driven by terror, Lyra was illogically yanking at a locked door handle.

"Hurry! Rig, hurry!"

Turning in the direction of the creature, fearing to look down, the driver stabbed blindly at the keyhole. The key ring slipped, tumbling to the ground.

A primal cry of *"Shit!"* pierced the night.

Whatever the being was, it was almost upon them. Once more Rig grabbed the keys, frantically trying to open the lock. Success! They jumped in and slammed the doors, started the engine, and floored the vehicle in reverse. Tires spun and pebbles flew as the car fought for traction. A high-speed chase on such an unlit dirt road would be at best reckless and at worst suicidal. Their concentration riveted, both stared out the rear window, not daring even a split-second glimpse at their pursuer; to lose focus would surely mean crashing.

Approaching the safety of asphalt, Rig turned, asking, "*Woman, what the fu*...Oops! Sorry! What the heck was that?"

Out of breath, more from fear than running, she attempted an answer. "I…I don't know. I've never encountered anything like it before."

In anger, her partner took the offensive. "Well, White-Lighting Expert, what the hell went wrong back there? *We nearly got killed!"*

"I know, I know. Rig, white-lighting only protects you from subconscious imprinting and energy draining, not direct communication. These beings beamed in, saying they were from the Council. It's…it's like I told you earlier. Telepathy is simply directed thought. Sometimes you can distinguish between voices, but I can't be expected to be familiar with everybody's. Besides, there was nothing telling me they weren't from our side."

Seeing her point and calming down, he softened. "*Damn! Whew!* That was close!"

Still trembling, she added, "Could you please slow down with the swearing? It is really beneath you. It…it lacks class, is lazy…and…."

"And since when have aliens become class-conscious?" he snapped with unrestrained emotion. "Sounds like we'd better cancel your planet's subscription to *Miss Manners* magazine."

"*Stop it!* You know what I mean. Words have power, and I find it hard to deal with the negative energy that your swearing puts out."

"Okay, okay."

With the throbbing of his ankle intensifying, simply putting pressure on the gas pedal was excruciatingly painful. In a state of smoldering rage, the driver gripped the wheel with all his might, as if that would help relieve the needle-like stabbing. It didn't. With nothing more to say, they remained silent until stopping at A.J.'s, an upscale supermarket.

Going inside, he tried to make peace. "Oh hell—oops! Sorry, did it again. I'll back off on the swearing a little."

"Not a little—a lot," she insisted as they began to shop.

Back at the resort, holding a sack of groceries and with his other arm around his companion, the Phoenician hobbled through the lobby and around the pool area, taking the path to number thirty-three.

As a spent warrior fell on the bed, Lyra's motherly nature took over. "I need a look at that ankle. It's a really serious sprain. If we don't do something, by tomorrow you won't be able to walk on it."

"What's to do? I can't go to a hospital without money or my insurance card. That was all in my wallet."

"Let me experiment with the wand we found in the cave. In fact, I should have tried it before on your shoulder but we were going to Master Chu anyway. If I'm right, it was a healing instrument rather than a tool for spells."

Correct. The device predated even the Atlantean civilization. Brought to Earth by Aryan-SST priests, it was mainly for medical applications. Frequencies could be regulated by twisting the knob at one end, which amplified and directed rays through a crystal and into the patient. Multi-functional, the beam could be used as a red-hot cutting tool in laser surgery, or its beam broadened to eradicate such scourges as cancer cells. In Rig's case, it was adjusted to facilitate mild repairs on inflamed tissues and to realign subluxations. Miraculously, within five minutes, he was up, walking as if nothing had happened.

"*Wow*! This is incredible! Lyra, this thing's amazing! A concept like this is worth millions."

Beside himself with excitement, the out-of-work stockbroker realized he was in possession of an entrepreneur's fantasy come true. Spreading the rest of the items on the bed, he said, "*Man*! San Tropez, here we come!"

Lyra, back at the laptop and adding to her script, glances up. "We?"

Although her companion's enthusiasm is almost uncontainable, it was too late in the evening to call Master Chu's chiropractor friend in Flagstaff.

Regarding the queen-size bed, the representative from the Ra Foundation quickly made it clear that her companion was to be relegated to the hard, uncomfortable sofa at the other end of the room. Banished like a puppy sent to a corner, Rig's eyes stared longingly in the dark, toward what he imagined to be a soft, forbidden land of milk and honey.

A few minutes after settling in, he broke the silence, whispering, "Lyra? *Pssst*...Lyra?"

The reply was gentle, but firm. "*No*!"

"Okay, okay...just thought I'd ask one last time."

For the treasure hunter, this was one of those nights when dreams and reality became indistinguishable. While his physical body seemed to require rest, his soul accepted its perfection and never tired. In this period termed "sleep," King's spirit once more exited his physical shell. So many of people's souls fly to one of several destinations—most often choosing to go into the higher realms for spiritual learning. Likewise, they could simply opt to roam this planet, or explore unnamed galaxies, or even travel to other dimensions. Then there is always the possibility of going into the future.

This last dreamscape offered an explanation for the *déjà vu* experience. These were the times when, say, rounding a corner, he received a flash—a recollection of seemingly having been there before. Yet, regardless of one's destination, every trip into whatever he experienced while sleeping was every bit as real—or illusory—as the "reality" he was experiencing while supposedly awake.

Throughout his fitful night, King tossed and turned. On the dream plane, he was in a desperate struggle, using the laser wand to fight off reptilian monsters and save Princess Lyra from assassins sent by the Black Empire. Wounded in the hand by a return blast, by morning he felt completely worn out, not knowing why. Confused by the welt on his palm, his left brain rationalized its redness. "Must have whacked it on the pointed edge of the coffee table next to this damn couch."

Unaffected by her partner's dream, the Lyrian had been up for hours, excitedly deciphering the golden scroll. Pausing, she reflected on the stories passed down from Eeliopal's great spiritual teachers. Their writings often alluded to this ancient text, but she had always taken its existence as strictly allegorical. Enraptured by the clarification of her own planet's teachings, the alien was further amazed at its compatibility with various religions of Earth. She bent low over the unraveled sheet, scrutinizing each word, hoping there might somehow be a clue that unlocked the enigmatic writing on the mysterious twin discs.

Why, Lyra wondered, *would the Aryan-SST leave such an important document unprotected?* Answering herself, it was concluded, *Well, there was that one DAK; and they probably felt that it was totally secure, hidden away in such a remote and secret room. But why in Arizona, of all places? Why not the Middle East, their primary center? Unless, of course, operations will ultimately be moved here, and this will become their Holy of Holies…ahhh, that's a possibility.*

Room service arrived with breakfast. As the bellman began to set the table, Rig was ending a phone call with his potential buyer, Dr. Gillman.

Transfixed by what she was doing, Lyra was unaware of the resort employee's presence or even that her companion was still on the phone. In uncharacteristic style she blurted out, *"Rig!… Rig! Come here; you have to hear this!"*

"Hear what?" he asked, while hanging up.

"*Hear this*!" she exclaimed with unbridled excitement. "*Sit down and listen*. This explains how it all started." Speaking softly, Lyra began translating the golden scroll.

CHAPTER XVIII

PRE-GENESIS

ONE:

1:1) "In 'the Now,' before the concept of time, impenetrable blackness in every direction.

1:2) Even sound did not exist.

1:3) Encompassing all and beyond, the Infinite, or God, was, and still is to this hour, a mystery that cannot be explained.

1:4) For how can that be measured which has no reference?

1:5) That with No Name, the All-in-All, exemplifies love and the state of perfection.

1:6) Nothing can be added.

1:7) Nothing can be taken away.

1:8) Always in action, ever being.

1:9) And so It is.

TWO:

2:1) Then, in the blackness, from the Seven Sacred Directions, came a trembling, and a rumbling…building to a deafening, yet gentle roar.

2:2) And spake a voice, neither male nor female, but an embodiment of both, saying,

2:3)' Do what thou wilt, but cause harm to no one.'

2:4) And thus it was.

THREE:

3:1) Suddenly, darkness twinkled with living sparks, souls flying hither and yon.

3:2) Separate as rays of the sun, yet ye were still one within the Infinite—

3:3) Paradoxically individual but indivisible, even unto this day.

3:4) Joy, laughter…sounds poured forth from all directions.

3:5) And it was good.

FOUR:

4:1) In those ways, thy qualities mirror the totality of The Sum;

4:2) All the Creator is, ye also could, and did, express in every way.

4:3) Then as now, what was thought came into being.

4:4) As above, so below.

FIVE:

5:1) First came light to split the darkness.

5:2) This was followed by stars, whose number is more than the grains of sand upon the beaches of all the worlds.

5:3) The length between these celestial bodies gave forth distance, and with that, the advent of the belief in time.

5:4) Death too, became a concept, as well as its opposite, birth.

5:5) And although joy and laughter were first, sickness, poverty, war, and misery also manifested into belief.

5:6) And thus it went.

SIX:

6:1) Lo, it came to pass that ye assembled into groups, each according to thine own kind and thine own form.

6:2) As thy soul pretended to be separate from the All-in-All, a belief in ego was dreamed.

6:3) Ye gave him many names and a separate voice within thy mind.

6:4) In reality, however, there exists only thy higher nature, or God-self.

6:5) But according to thy play, ye endowed ego with personality, and accepted the false illusion of his power and authority.

6:6) Thus began and still exists a fictional story of a struggle between these two forces within thy being.

6:7) To perpetuate its existence, ego continuously seeks to control thy thinking by teaching greed, lust, avarice, carnality, guilt, and the fallacy of thy imperfection.
6:8) But the most deceitful lie of all is, thou art to believe in thy separation from The Oneness.
6:9) And indeed, each of these seems to manifest—brought into creation by the power of thine own thoughts.
6:10) By this ploy, thou art kept in a state of confusion—one of constant turmoil.
6:11) But all the while, ye knew it was only a game, and yet retained the power to call its end.

SEVEN:
7:1) On and on it went.
7:2) Layer upon layer, thy play grew increasingly complex.
7:3) Universe after universe ye roamed.
7:4) Thine actions became more and more intense.
7:5) If a head was lopped off, it was only done in fun or curiosity.
7:6) At the conclusion, it was placed back on again.
7:7) Around and around, up and down, thine exploits reached a frothy pitch.
7:8) Rules seemed endless, yet ever increasing.
7:9) But over time, boredom set in among the Children of One.
7:10) Ye reasoned, 'We always know the outcome of our adventures.
7:11) 'What can we do to make them unpredictable?'
7:12) And so, a gathering was called in the firmament.
7:13) It was here that Lower Self, or Ego, whispered in thine collective mind.
7:14) Then in union, together as with one voice, ye agreed to invoke 'The Final Rule.'
7:15) The veil of memory was pulled down, enabling ye to forget it was only a game.
7:16) And thus, it was done.

EIGHT:
8:1) In the present age, mankind wanders, lost in a fog of illusions—not remembering who ye really are.
8:2) Yes, the essence of thy divine core still exists, but its outward demonstration is oft obscured by false beliefs.
8:3) Thy 'game' has deteriorated;
8:4) Even the charade of death now appears real.
8:5) Having forgotten that in thy true state there is no lack or unfulfilled desire, today most beings are seemingly

forced to devour other beings just to survive.
8:6) By rules of thine own design, ye appear as outcasts from Heaven.
8:7) Still, perfection is, and always will be;
8:8) It is the only truth—the only reality or absolute.
8:9) But thine hallucination is great;
8:10) Thou hast created an all-inclusive lie, a state of personal hypnosis.

NINE:
9:1) But faint ye not;
9:2) For there is hope.
9:3) Although thy days often appear dark, not for one moment have ye ever been alone.
9:4) Regardless of thy illusion, thine spirit is always guided, forever protected.
9:5) As a gift of love, the merciful and omnipresent I-Am-That-I-Am has lain the secret of thine awakening clearly at thy feet.
9:6) Sadly, for too long, most choose to remain in blindness, each as if asleep in his or her own dream.
9:7) For them, The Final Rule yet prevails.
9:8) Still, there are those who exercise free will and dissolve this picture of imperfection.
9:9) Ultimately, they come to see neither sin, sickness, disease, nor death.
9:10) Gliding, wide awake in this and other realms, they embody a state of grace and love.
9:11) Their physical shell is but a singular point of focus;
9:12) Their existence again spans every dimension—one with All.
9:13) Awake from a dream that never was, they dwell in the Perfection that never was not.
9:14) And thus, it, too, shall be with thee.
9:15) So mote it be."

CHAPTER XIX

THE CHIP

Resting the artifact in her lap, Lyra sat in reverent silence, awaiting her companion's response.

With unblinking eyes, he stared right through her. Once more, his mind wandered. To him, while undoubtedly ancient in origin, the scroll's words paled next to the pressures of the past two days. Yesterday, his primary worry was about evading DAK assassins. Now, he was almost certainly being accused of two murders. Far worse, it was realized, most or all of mankind would be annihilated in only a few more years. Suffocating under the weight of these problems, the ex-stockbroker-now-fugitive needed time, and thought, *Thank God there's that long drive to Gillman's.* Moving toward the door, knapsack in hand, he said, "Let's go."

Heading north out of Phoenix on Highway 17, they pulled up to a tollbooth. Like mushrooms, more and more of these money-extraction-points were beginning to pop up on American highways—slipped past a sleeping public's nose under the guise of a method to help pay for the nation's deteriorating bridges and roads.

Out of habit, the Phoenician held up the back of his right hand to a scanning beam. Imbedded was a biometric chip, a device that electronically debited his bank account—

a convenient method of payment in a society that was fast becoming cashless. Practicing the sales presentation to be used on the chiropractor and lost in thought, he had forgotten his account was frozen.

A man of the twenty-first century, King was of the generation that believed in everything high-tech. Though he still used credit cards when his checking account was overdrawn, the entrepreneur saw this rice-grain-size microchip embedded in the back of his hand as the newest wave of the future. Not only was it theft-proof, it contained over fifty files—pages of vital medical, driving, and educational records, even his passport. In a traffic accident, for instance, it could provide lifesaving information—almost all facets of a person's life.

The piercing blast of an alarm shook him back to the present. Rigden King's photo and arrest warrant were visible on the tollbooth's TV monitor. The wooden arm blocking their passage remained down.

Even behind bulletproof glass, knowing the car's driver was wanted in a double murder, the state employee shrank into a corner of her mini-office. Timidly, she announced over the intercom, "Mr. King, sir, you will have to wait; the police will be arriving shortly."

These words set off an explosion in the fugitive's brain. Reflexively, he slammed the gas pedal to the floor, yelling, "*Lyra, duck!*"

Tires squealing, the car lurched forward, crashing through the wooden barrier to the open highway. Mumbling out loud, he said to himself, "*Darn*, I pictured something like this happening."

The alien's response was equally sharp. "*Are you crazy or just stupid*?"

"What? I had to! Cops'll be here any minute."

"No, not that! Why didn't you tell me you have the chip?"

Going flat-out, Rig had to decide upon another route to get up north. In this adrenaline moment, his passenger's anger wasn't as important as the logistics of flight. Even so, he made a feeble attempt at responding. "What, this? Didn't think it was important. It's so new, mostly I forget that I even have it. Isn't like I say to all the girls I meet, 'Wanna come upstairs some time and see my chip?' Half of the time, I even forget that I have it." Checking the rearview mirror and seeing they are not being followed, he added, "Besides, everyone's getting one. Trust me; this is no big deal."

"No big deal?" she half-screamed. *"You stupid idiot!"*

With a rattlesnake instinct for criticism, King recoiled. He too had reached a limit. Defenses erupted with air-bag-deploying speed. "*Stupid idiot?* Look, lady, that's twice you've called me that—in the last sixty seconds alone."

"Because you're doubly dense!"

"Hey, are all the chicks on your planet this high-strung? I mean, you can get really nasty. Give it a rest, why don't cha?"

"*Ooooh, you drive me crazy!*"

"For you," he flung back, "that would be a short trip; don't pack a lunch."

Lyra wouldn't let it rest. "You...you swollen...self-indulgent," she sputtered, "myopic mnjontin."

"What's a mnjontin?"

"Never mind. There's no English equivalent." Sulking, the Ra representative glared out the window and said under her breath, "Anyway, it was not important."

"Well, you're, ah...uh...you're a tulec."

Still furious, the alien was overcome by curiosity. "What's a tulec?"

"Eehhh...nothing—I just sorta made it up."

Her incredulity burst. "That's not even in your language? See? You really are a mnjontin. I hate you and your kind's egotistical, self-serving approach to life—everything you people stand for. Hardly a person on this planet seems to care about anything beyond their own busy, narrow-scoped lives. A perfect case-in-point—Rigden King, III's, total existence revolves around girls, cars, stocks—the...the puts, the calls, the market straddles."

"*Look, woman!* You don't know anything about me. And I can tell you this: without straddling much lately, I'm in no mood for any argument. *So get off my back!*"

Ignoring the sexual innuendo, the emissary from Washington thought, *Typical asinine Earth-male response*. Drawing a deep breath, she tried to pull a seething temper under control. "*I...am...trying to save your life*. What you don't know is, these chips are being used to kill."

"*Kill*? How?"

"Human brain cells, if you can believe this, as well as poison, are incorporated into its mechanism. You see, the living synapses of a person are far more efficient than synthetic connections. And the poison...."

"Come to think of it," he interrupted, "I vaguely remember some article on brain cells being placed into microchips. I think it was years ago, in *The Wall Street Journal*. Caught my eye 'cause I was researching the industry for an investor."

"To be exact, it was March 15, 1997, on the front page."

"How do you know the date?"

"Photographic memory. Plus, I read five international newspapers per day—at least when I'm at the Foundation."

Her partner defended his position. "Anyway, so what if they use human cells? No big deal. And what's this about poison?" Smirking, he threw in, "Like with breast implants, are people starting to go into toxic shock or something?"

"You and everyone else," Lyra blustered, "are living in some warped, Daliesque-type dream. Besides giving Big Brother a way to know everything about your life, this...this supposedly innocent little device is beyond dangerous; it holds your death sentence."

"*Death sentence*? Like *dead, deadly*? I thought you were kidding."

The alien reminded him of how a similar chip could be used to unlock a vehicle, such as seen in the OnStar TV commercials—giving others the ability to eavesdrop on you and your passengers' conversations. And if your car is stolen, simply call in the serial number. A satellite's signal beams down; the chip fries; the motor dies—end of theft."

Even more alarming, the Ra representative described how the Shadow Government was quietly beginning to use these to assassinate patriots who disrupt Baal's agenda. "Soon, they will exterminate malcontents by the tens of thousands—all with the single bounce of a satellite's ray. As the poison releases, you fall over dead, and no one in the crowd knows why. Without a chemical trace, the hospital blames it on a heart attack."

"*No way!* How are they going to explain mass deaths, like that?"

"As I told you; Malek will come promising peace. But as things worsen, martial law will take over. Then he won't have to explain anything...to anyone."

"If this is true, why didn't we see it coming?"

"You weren't supposed to. Remember imprinting? You've been indoctrinated by subliminal messages—TV, in movies, music, all sorts of ways."

"You're really serious about this chip thing. Do you honestly know, as a fact, that they're being used to kill people?"

"Absolutely—earthlings are a strong-willed lot. Without one of these in everyone's hand or forehead, you would be impossible to keep in line. This death-virus is simply one more control—a method to wipe out anyone who goes against the State as world chaos continues escalating."

"Seems like I've fallen down that rabbit hole in *Alice in Wonderland.*"

"Rig, even now, as is prophesied in the Bible, things are being set up in such a way that soon, people won't be able to buy or sell without one."

"What about money?"

"There won't be any—none. Transactions will be strictly electronic; everything will be forced to go through this miniature piece of technology. Sometime you should check out Revelation, Chapter 13, Verses 16 and 17, where it says, *'And he compelled all, both small and great, rich and poor, freemen and slaves, to receive a mark on their right hands or on their brows. So that no man might buy or sell unless he who had the mark of the name of the beast or the code number of his name.'*"

"Do the DAKs have enough manpower to put these into everyone on the planet?"

"Heavens no. Your people will do it for them—in exchange for money and titles in the new kingdom. That is, once mankind is programmed to believe it is a good idea."

More startling facts: "As I said earlier, without the public being aware, America has become a police state. For instance, you probably know there is no longer a legal court order needed for government wiretapping; or that you can be held indefinitely without being formally charged. Plus, as in Nazi Germany, there's a law going into effect that forces you to register with the local police when you simply move from one town to another. But here's a little-known fact—a real zinger: Even if a person hasn't received their implant yet, secret files already exist on every man, woman, and child in the nation. Since 1968, everything has been stored in a computer in Culpepper, Virginia. Which, I might add, is linked to the master machine in Brussels, nicknamed…*The Beast.*"

Wrapped in amazement, the ex-stockbroker continued questioning. "What do you mean, files already exist?"

"Just that. Each individual is accessed by the number 666, plus their personal identification. Although I should add that in the oldest Biblical fragments, the true mark of the Devil is really 616; but your theologians are ignoring that discovery… as usual."

"I don't care what number they use. In America, what's the identification? I mean, do we have to go through some sort of registration?"

"People already have—after 666…your Social Security number. In fact, to speed up the process, some babies are even receiving the chip at birth, right in the hospital.

"These are in a similar category as the RFID—Radio Frequency Identification Devices, or Smart Tags, now being attached to products—each with a micro battery lasting years--whose signal can be tracked from great or even small distances—across country or from one room to another. And guess what? These tags are even being put into the lining of clothes. But, as I said earlier, this chip, the one in your hand, is different—containing poison, and functioning as a library of your *personal* information."

Turning in her direction, the Phoenician was obviously becoming frantic. "In other words, if I'm a threat to the government, you're saying I can be tracked and terminated by this Silicon Valley gizmo?"

"Not tracked, like RFID tags, but yes, terminated, anywhere on the planet."

"My God! Who runs this program?"

"The New World Order."

"How are they putting this over on the public?"

"That's the genius; no one's paying attention. It is all been subtly laid out over a long period of time; each event, connected to the next, quietly setting the stage for later developments."

"Such as?"

"In America, the sales job has been so slick, the program's way below your radar. But, this soft approach won't last much longer. As I just said, in several years, having one, like having a chip in your car, will become law. Don't be so surprised; this country isn't the first. Other nations are already quietly forcing it on their citizens.

"I'll tell you how it's happening. To begin, every year for several weeks, your government instituted a national campaign complaining about its supposed counterfeiting problem with the currency. Of course, if you're looking at that as an economic glitch, it never actually existed. Even the Secret Service admitted that of the 650 billion U.S. dollars floating around the planet, bogus notes account for only about 43 million."

"That's minuscule. It almost doesn't register."

"To be precise, it's .000063 of one percent. So in reality, there is no significant counterfeiting. Those in control are simply using smoke and mirrors to make it seem like there is."

Lyra took out the golden scroll. Gingerly unwrapping it, she pondered the ancient message.

"Uhhh, what does counterfeiting have to do with this thing in our hands?"

"For the public to accept the chip concept, total eradication of physical currency is an absolute necessity. To pull it off, Malek needs something dramatic. And the United States isn't like other countries—always coming out with some new form of money at every crisis; you people don't like anyone fooling with your sacred U.S. dollar. Even this subtle switch to rainbow-colored notes is causing a stink. But frightened by this bogus counterfeiting threat, the public finally caved in.

"That's only part of it. Malek's using several ploys. The stage you are about to enter is where people will be told that by eliminating cash altogether, the drug trade problem will completely vanish. Of course, this, too, is a ruse. World governments can halt drug trafficking anytime they want. It continues not only because they use narcotics as a funding source for their secret projects, but as a way of dumbing-down a growing segment of the population."

"That's how I heard bin Laden came by most of his fortune—heroin. Say, what can be done to eradicate this terrorist problem?"

"I thought it would be obvious. The New World Order doesn't want it stopped. Like, to supposedly halt the millions of illegal immigrants coming to America, your government makes a big deal about needing billions of dollars, sophisticated border detection equipment, and more manpower. In reality, the SG2's plan has been to ship jobs overseas, ruin the U.S. wage structure, and allow others to illegally come in and so as to dilute the wage structure—paving the way for a future slave workforce. If the public would just wake up, the solution is simple; go after the employers--make hiring illegals a felony. That would cost a fraction to implement, and stop the problem *overnight*.

"The terrorism and drug trafficking problems are similar. To keep chaos going, the SG2 has the military attacking symptoms—never the cause. Going after individual terrorist cells or some drug warlord is like cutting heads off a hydra: remove one and another will grow in its place. The answers to those are also easy, but can I finish about the chip first?

"Once your higher-denomination bills were redesigned, they began to activate this current phase." A glance at Rig drew a blank look. "You know, the U.S. is now saying, 'Oh, golly! The counterfeiting and drug problems are far worse than we thought. To completely stop them, we have to take away your hundreds, fifties, and twenties.'"

"I heard something about a plan to have them removed in 2008. Say, Lyra, while I'm listening, get the map out of my knapsack and see if you can find a shorter way to Sedona."

Tracing the lines on the paper with her finger, she replied, "No, I think this is about it." Going through the tedious ritual of refolding, Rig's companion continued to address what would happen after larger denominations were discontinued.

"Phasing out paper currency is the easy part. Conning the public into accepting a foreign object in their hand or forehead will be harder…but obviously, not impossible." She shot him a smirk. "That's why some of these terrorist attacks are being fostered, and the real reason the SG2 is orchestrating the crash of the dollar—to trigger another 1930s' global depression."

"A crash?"

"Absolutely. Within the near future. You see, when American money markets sneeze, the rest of the world catches a financial cold. So as the dollar's value plummets, the whole planet comes down with economic pneumonia. That sets the stage for the Followers of Baal to argue the need for a one-world currency—to stabilize the international economy. What's more, they've already test-marketed the concept with the formation of a single European monetary unit.

"The public will then be brainwashed to believe that counterfeiters and drug traffickers won't be able to work with smaller notes; they're too bulky. World governments are going to state that electronic money transfers are the ultimate solution—easily tracked. Besides stopping counterfeiting, it's the faucet that can totally shut off the flow of terrorist finance."

"What a load of bullshit."

"Rig!"

"Okay, cow pucky. How's that?"

"Not totally acceptable, but better. Anyway, there's more. The New World Order's end goal is to have a global, interlocking, cashless society. As I said, this means that all aspects of your life will be monitored—where you travel and gas up your car, the types of movies you see, even down to which books and brand of bread you buy. Everything in your life is going on record.

"Malek, using business, under the guise of marketing, and world governments, supposedly to combat terrorism, is determined to get your every move trackable. Already, many of your major retail chains have items with RFID tags attached. One day, most of products across the globe will carry one. And when a hand or forehead is implanted with the biometric chip and there are RFID tags near, not only is that person's location known, but if he or she is traveling, the direction they are headed, as well as where and what type of transactions are being conducted. Rig, between these two devices, your whole life can be mapped—second by second…24/7."

His mouth ajar, the Phoenician mumbled, "I never suspected."

Dizzy with the implications, he asked, "But, how…how are they managing to pull all this off?"

"Overwhelmed by the magnitude of these problems, especially terrorism, the public is gladly giving up their civil liberties. Surely you can see that."

"Good grief! This boggles the mind."

"In the U.S., one of the first ploys that got the chip concept started was the big media hype concerning missing children about nineteen years ago. It was everywhere—even pictures on milk cartons. The whole thing has fueled parents' fear, persuading many to have their kids fingerprinted, tattooed, and now 'implanted.'"

"You're right; it is subtle. I never saw it coming."

"This is why those bar codes came out; they got people used to scanning. Haven't you ever noticed the perennial, fabricated news blitz about how your credit cards can be lost or stolen—that your waiter can lift information with a handheld pocket device as he or she is walking to the cash register? And guess what?"

"At this point, I have no idea."

"To get people further used to the chip concept, Big Brother has even enlisted veterinarians, telling pet lovers how important it is to register their animals this way."

"Hey, John had that done to his dog, Murphy, just before it got loose and was run over. That's how they knew to contact him. All the data was there."

"Exactly. So now can you see the baby steps? Put each of these pieces together and Baal's strategy becomes clear." The Ra representative talked on while rummaging around in her pocketbook, looking for a stick of gum. Finding two—an offer. "Want one?"

"Ahh, no thanks."

Filling in more of the puzzle, the Lyrian added, "You hear it everywhere. Their sales pitch claims: '*This can't be stolen, and you won't leave home without it.*' Another blurb says, '*Not only does it have all your vital information in case of emergency, the Smart Chip is also your passport to the future.*' The Foundation has word that their next campaign will say: '*Relax, America! Whereas terrorists can falsify identity papers, no one can duplicate your own personal chip which, for your total protection, is directly tied in to the world security grid. So be at peace! You're safer, smarter, and totally secure.*'"

The moment was somber. "Pushing the lie that the world will be safe only when all people are monitored, Malek is launching what he calls 'The Omega Plan'—something to get the chip program into really high gear. Intelligence shows that by using full-scale nuclear, chemical, and biological warfare, terrorist cells will soon be attempting to cripple two foreign capitals and three major U.S. cities. Believe me, this is far worse than the bombings, the subway poisonings, or the previous chemical attacks. Deaths could be massive. That's another facet of my mission: to find out which sites and the dates of the strikes."

Rig pushed past fear, into anger. "Then—and don't take this personally—if your people are so good, just how did the World Trade Center and Pentagon crashes slip past you guys? And what about those so-called psychics? Where have they been in all this? That's why I don't believe in this metaphysical, hocus-pocus crud. If clairvoyance is real, someone, somewhere, would have gotten the message and...*My God!...prevented those tragedies!"*

"Good point. As for the World Trade Center attack, that simply slipped by us. Don't complain! You've no idea how many attacks we've stopped—the lives we've saved, not to mention the world economy. As for your statement about warnings, the psychic ones were blocked; the others were ignored...on purpose."

"Baal?"

"Not so you would recognize him—out in the open, I mean. He's in the shadows, standing behind those who stand behind others. For example, he's got certain factions of Christianity and Islam preaching and praying to get their followers to bring World War III into manifestation.

"Whipping Christian TV audiences into a frenzy, or firing up an Islamic student to carry a bomb is but a small part of the plan. He has those groups tricked into wanting full Armageddon—a supposed validation of their teachings—the 'great eradication of Satan' by God or Allah. Rig, Baal is so convincing that some, and I'm talking major Christian authorities, have even been misled to preach that disasters such as hurricanes and tsunamis are 'heaven's wrath' against mankind for condoning gays, lesbians, the ACLU, feminists, liberals, and even those cute little Teletubbies...Can you believe that?"

"At this point, I'll believe anything. What about Muslims?"

"They've been convinced that Islam should be the world's primary religion, even if it means using mass murder.

"But to answer your question, fanatical prayers from both sides collide, creating a kind of mystic fog—a type of confusion. This stops people from getting an accurate, clairvoyant read.

"As for those who perish in a tragedy, the quick explanation is that they finished their Earth assignments and were ready to transition. All deaths, even from terrorism, sickness, plane crashes, or the sinking of the Titanic, are simply opportunities for what we see as someone's untimely exit. Trust me, if it isn't a person's moment, somehow...some way, they won't be involved. Like Chelsea Clinton—on September 11, just before those planes hit the towers, at the last minute and for no known reason, she suddenly decided not to jog around the World Trade Center. Instead, an inner guidance urged her to grab a cup of coffee with a close friend. And then you have the four thousand Jews who worked in those buildings—on that particular day they were obligated to stay longer in synagogues commemorating *Selichot,* the ritual repentance before Rosh Hashanah. Most planned to arrive at work around 10:30. So, there is no such thing as an accident. Those with life contracts not yet finished are always pulled elsewhere. Now, maybe you can see that psychics were blocked from stopping the catastrophe; it would have upset those souls' natural transitions."

"*No way!* This is where I draw the line—and why I'm an agnostic. I can't believe in a supposedly loving God who allows something like 9/11."

"Rig, like everybody, if I allow myself to get caught up in the story—and sometimes I do—the sadness rips me apart. But being spiritual doesn't mean being callous. I suggest you need to take a different perspective on these tragedies; delve further into the scroll's message. That should clarify things.

"Let's get back to the main subject. If we fail to stop this coming slaughter, the outcry will be so great, people will demand not only the passage of laws forcing everybody to carry national identification, they'll also go along with making every transaction electronic. And with the Supreme Court going to the far Right, people are about to get both, whether they want them or not."

"Whoa, Lyra. Let's back up. I'm confused. I thought you said to stop deaths would be interfering."

"Not if you know a tragedy is about to occur. Then it's your duty. What you are not supposed to do is disrupt or alter another person's spiritual path; everyone has to work those lessons out on their own.

"Look at it like this. Most situations happen for not one, but many reasons. This terrorist attack, for example, was about far more than a quick way for a number of people to leave the planet. Remember, I said it was orchestrated?"

"Yeah. And?"

"All sorts of groups were involved. One day, people will come to realize that there were those in America who actually knew about 9/11 ahead of time."

"Like who?"

"Oh, like, seven days before September 11 there was a story in a Middle Eastern newspaper telling, *in detail*, about both the New York and Washington attacks. Then…get this, just five days prior, an informant called the District of Columbia from the Cayman Islands with an even more specific warning. But those, and all the other red flags, were ignored, on purpose, as usual."

"I never realized."

"Answer me this, then. Why were—now this was within twenty-four hours of 9/11, when no planes in America were allowed to fly—dozens of Osama bin Laden's relatives secretly airlifted out of the U.S.? And what about sources who hint that NORAD, just prior to the attack, was told to, '*Stand down*?' Or who ordered that day's records of all the air controllers involved, confetti-shredded—each pile being separated and dumped at several locations? Why were several politicians warned not to travel by air to the East Coast that day? And why are your news sources terrified to ask the key question: 'Beside terrorists…who most benefited by diverting the American public's attention away from other issues?' Riggy, news is controlled. Otherwise, you would find these things out—such as who shorted the stock market because they knew ahead of time about the plot."

"Wow! The windfall profit from that would have been enormous."

"Here you have a number of groups, as well as the darling SG2, with full information—knowing the how, the day, as well as the targets. All the while, they calmly stood by and watched.

Many think some even helped things along, as in the strange collapse of Building Seven."

"I never realized."

"Because of the outcry, the public has now accepted that for security, **it i**s okay to give up many of their civil liberties. Problem is, with each new crisis, they relinquish more and more of their freedom, until nothing will be left."

Stunned, it was all King could do to mumble, "What's next?"

"The most important subsequent move will be national identification papers, then moving on to this imbedded chip."

She took a small sip of water and cleared her throat, as if preparing for the grand finale. "Oh, but wait! You ain't heard nothin' yet! After that, the U.S., along with the rest of the planet, will be divided into travel zones. Depending upon one's status within the hierarchy, ranging from a world leader to a 'Class A threat,' people will be allowed to move only within sanctioned geographical areas. That's really why these tollbooths are springing up. Now do you see how that quotation from The Book of Revelation fits in?"

Shocked by the draconian—or in this case, DAKonian—plan, Rig glanced at the back of his hand. Wincing, he threw out another question. "Do you have any more uplifting stories?"

"Loads."

"I was afraid of that. Just tell me how we get this chip thing out."

"A razor blade."

"Ouch! That'll hurt."

"Fine warrior you are." Lyra spotted a hitchhiker. "Rig, look. There's an old man standing in the hot sun trying to catch a ride. Can we pick him up? It'll only take a second."

"Damn it, woman! With cops on our tail, we don't have even a second to spare. And you call *me* stupid? They probably have me up on two murder charges, and you want us to stop for some old geezer? You're nuts. Jeez, sometimes I can't believe you."

Just then, the fugitives came upon the Union Hills exit. Turning east off the main highway, they traveled north along a lesser-known route. Its serpentine curves made the going slow. Hoping to quietly slide unobserved into Sedona, they would then take the backdoor route and head for their real objective—Flagstaff.

"I feel like we're sitting ducks in the daylight." The strain in his voice came through, despite its husky tone. "Let's pull over and travel after dark."

Bouncing down a side road, the vehicle pulled up under the shade of a small grove of trees. The decision was made to wait there for nightfall.

Lyra, mulling what she has discovered so far in the scroll's message, found it hard to contain her excitement. "This may be the missing element I mentioned earlier."

"Huh? What are you talking about?"

"Well, I need to give it more thought. But so far, what little I understand is mind-boggling. The premise seems to be that *God is all—everything, everywhere!* And this 'All-in-All' or whatever we're going to call *It, exists only in a state of perfection*. And, therefore, it is we, not the Creator, who summon all this misery. Finally, I understand what your prophet Habakkuk said in the Old Testament, 'Thine—'"

"Wait a minute. I've been meaning to ask; how come you know so much about our Bible?"

"You don't just get assigned here willy-nilly. I first had to become an Earth Specialist. Want me to quote from the Koran or the Talmud? I can do one in Arabic and the other in Hebrew. I speak seven of your major languages and six secondary dialects.

"Anyway, in Habakkuk it says, '*Thine eyes*'—he's talking about God—'*Thine eyes are too pure; they do not behold evil.*' This corroborates the message on the scroll. We are the ones who made this…this maya. We've trapped ourselves in our own illusion."

"What do you mean, trapped?"

"*We,*" she pronounced, stressing the first word, "are the ones making problems in life. People then turn around and blame God for this cesspool of misery. I guess it was like at La Brea Tar Pit in Los Angeles; we get mired in the muck of our stories. Trying to get out, we then invent even more complex tales, and in doing so, become buried under the increasing layers and layers of problems. So what we've actually done is created an hypnotic maze—our very own make-believe soap opera."

Rig's expression showed utter bewilderment.

"It's a metaphor. All I'm saying is that I need to study the lessons of the scroll as soon as possible. Now I see why the Followers of Baal are so desperate to keep this text away from both our peoples."

"I wonder why, if it was that powerful, they don't just destroy it."

"Good question. I don't know. Unless they use it ritualistically in doing a backward ceremony—one intended to cause confusion. This sort of thing is done with your Bible by Satanists all the time."

"Sacred or not, our talk's not removing this thing from my hand! Let's do it…Get it over with." He gave her his knife, sharpened to the point of almost being a razor.

With one quick slice, she deftly exposed the chip. A freshly polished thumbnail and forefinger acted as pinchers, quickly plucking the offending device from the bloodied slit. Surprisingly, her partner remained unflinchingly stoic—not one sound. This left the alien mildly amazed. She found Mr. King, III, had concealed yet another facet—courage.

Nothing to do for several hours but wait and talk. The temperature was sweltering. Having no breeze made it worse. Throughout the heat of the day, time drifted slowly. Flowing in and out of intimate eddies of conversation, everything moved with a lazy rhythm. The only point of animation came with the spark in Rig's eyes as he talked about his goals in life. Now it was Lyra who listened, captivated. She saw how their two species, while vastly different, were inextricably linked—joined by ages-old, invisible bonds.

When his companion finally spoke, for the first time Rig began relating to the opposite sex in a new way—beyond the tactile, into another's heart. He could actually feel her sadness when she talked of her loneliness on this planet. Council duties had carried her far, never staying in one place long enough to develop friendships, let alone anything romantic. And thus the sharing went, switching back and forth, each taking turns.

Lulled by the soft richness of his radio announcer's voice, Lyra's attention split into her own fantasy, or possibly a remote-viewing vision of the future. Mentally transported, she saw them walking hand in hand along a sandy, Eeliopal beach. It was sunset. Two large moons and a more distant, smaller orb hovered above the ocean's emerald waves. Both he and she were wearing the traditional garlands of brilliant flowers that abound in all but the sea's direction. Deeper in her picture and beyond the trees which stretched nearly down to the water's edge, she could hear the haunting songs of a noyona bird as it serenaded the evening.

As they talked and the hours rolled on, a delicate chemistry began to develop between the earthling and Lyrian. A fragile, budding relationship gradually opened…one petal at a time. Absorbed in each other's eyes, thoughts of the outside world all but ceased.

Around them, everywhere, the desert seemed alive in courtship. A male mourning dove bobbed his head and cooed as he tried to impress his soon-to-be mate; a pair of male quail scampered along the ground, vying for the affections of several eligible females; and a jackrabbit, oblivious to all else, quickly consummated the continuance of his lineage. For Rig and Lyra, the long shadows of evening arrived all too soon.

CHAPTER XX

PRAYERS

Reaching the outskirts of the tiny town of Strawberry, barely a blip in the road, the couple pulled up to a poorly lit Western-style restaurant set about forty yards back from the highway. Tonight, the August monsoons had layered this area of the Mongollon Rim with a black cloud covering, making visibility more difficult than usual. It was 7:00 p.m., and darkness had descended early. The only real illumination came from a flashing sign near the road and its smaller version above the restaurant door. Everything else was unlit, save for the splash of headlights from an occasional passing motorist. But even in this semi-darkness, the duo made out enough of the parking lot to see cowboy pickups outnumbered other vehicles three to one.

Rig!" Lyra cautioned. *"Look over there—a fight."*

The glare from a speeding car briefly splashed light on a gruesome scene. Four drunken ranch hands crowded around a curled-up body. A fifth held back a cursing, arm-swinging, leg-kicking, thirteen-year-old black youth. Amid laughter and taunts, Rig and his companion witnessed the fallen figure's pitiful attempts to rise, only to suffer another flurry of vicious kicks. When the victim managed to get halfway up, more headlights showed his assailants pounding him with their fists until he again collapsed.

Half-screaming, a tearful Lyra pleaded, *"You've got to do something! Rig, help him!"*

"*Stop screaming!* What do you expect me to do? There's five of them and one of me."

Tugging on his arm, she implored, *"Please, please, you have to stop it…please!"*

Going away from the encircling group, a sixth member could be seen lumbering, half-staggering, toward a solitary pickup. Lifting a six-pack out of the cab, the cowpoke turned to join the others of his pack. Over the mob's swearing, the two observers barely made out the absent man's laughing but slurred words. "Hey, guys, don't kill the son of a bitch till I git there. Save me sumpthin'!"

"Well, damn it, Dooley," came an equally beer-saturated reply, "yer gunna hafta hurry. Move yer fat ass. Otherwise, we'll take care of this ignorant lazy bastard without ya."

One of the five turned to another and said, "Hell, Roy! Killin is too much work! 'Member last time—all the trouble carryin' that body away and hidin' it?"

"Maybe yer right. And then the damn coyotes went'n dug him up." Swaying, Roy made an attempt at lighting a cigarette. The cowboy was so drunk it took four strikes to get the match lit. He then took a long drag, only to have the butt fall out of his mouth. Frustration spurred a comment. "*Shit*! Why don't we just cut off his ears and tack'em up out'n the barn?"

The one called J.D., with twin red lightning bolts tattooed on the underside of his right forearm, spoke. "Heck, yer right. We could git a showcase goin' right next to our flag. That'd make the Grand Dragon real proud. I mean, we'd nail up them ears from this here Injun, then a Jew, a beaner, and a nigger. Show them mongrels this is a goddamn, white Aryan nation!"

All but one—who was otherwise occupied, having turned away and was relieving himself on the bare ground out in the open—joined in a resounding "Yeah!"

Out of the crowd, someone asked, "What about the kid?"

"The runt? Naah, he's too small. We'll throw him back. Let'm grow 'til he's a keeper."

"Injun, yer lucky," came another drunken voice from somewhere around the circle. "If I'da know'd where yer squaw was tonight, I'd ride her…*hic*…like a bronc at the rodeo."

The least drunk antagonist threw in, "Knowin' you, Claude, ya wouldn't git no ribbon."

"*Hic* … and why…*hic*…why not?"

"Now you know, rodeo rules say ya gotta stay on at least eight seconds."

They all erupted in laughter.

"Ol' man's got spunk, though," added a short, fat one wearing a tan Stetson. "Considerable more fun than them two queers we cornered up here last week, anyways." The cowboy turned, spit, and wiped residual tobacco juice from his jaw onto his pants leg. "Them's were nothin' but pansies. Least this dog's got some fight in'im," he bragged, giving a strong kick to the fallen man's ribs.

Dooley was still staggering back across the gravel lot, hurrying to join in before he missed out on the fun.

"Quick, Lyra!" Rig ordered. "Get that second can of lighter fluid out of my backpack."

It isn't that her companion didn't feel the fallen man's pain, or that he was afraid to act. At the age of fourteen, he too had been beaten—left for dead by a gang a few blocks from his mother's apartment in South Boston. The delay? Unfortunately, inspired solutions seldom manifest on command. Finally, one had come.

Rolling slowly up to Dooley's pickup, the treasure hunter aimed a long, uninterrupted stream of lighter fluid out the driver's window. Its full contents fell onto a saddle and a bale of hay in the back. Upon his tossing a lit book of matches, there was the confirming whooshing sound, followed by a flash of light. Moving quickly, King bluffed innocence by driving around a long row of vehicles before turning back and addressing the raucous group.

With the fascination of children tearing limbs off a dying cricket, the cowboys were totally absorbed in their world of liquor and brutality. Oblivious to the blaze, savagery was nonstop as they continued inflicting pain upon their hostages.

That is, until Rig pulled up and yelled, "Hey, fellas, know whose truck's burnin' over there?"

Action froze. Several stumbled and shuffled the way a person does two beers before passing out. After a momentary pause while the alcohol finally allowed the message to reach their brains, someone screamed, “Let’s git our guns and kill the bastard!”

It was immaterial that none had a clue as to the culprit. At this moment, anyone would do. Moving, none in a straight line, all clumsily hurried over to douse Dooley’s fire. Making use of the commotion, the ex-broker jumped out and raced over to the old man and boy.

The child was bent over, cradling the head of the pummeled figure. In a whispered voice, King ordered, “Get in, kid. I’ll take care of him.”

Half-pulling, half-carrying, Rig managed to get the crumpled body into the car. As the youth piled into the back, the boy snapped his fingers and called, “Here, Toby! Here, boy.” Out of the darkness limped a small bull terrier. It was dragging a hind leg, knocked out of its socket from an earlier kick of a sharp-toed cowboy boot. With a clumsy leap, the miniature addition jumped onto his friend’s lap. Aware that there were now two and one-half more passengers, the last one probably with fleas, the driver let out a long sigh. Too late—no turning back.

Peering over the seat, Rig started issuing commands. “You had better duck down, kid. This could get wild.”

With controlled speed, the car began easing its way toward the highway as the driver looked in the rearview mirror. “By the way,” he asked, “what’s your name and why were you protecting the old guy?”

“Name’s Roger. And cuz he was gettin’ the crap beat outta him, that’s why.”

One of the cowboys looked up from his fire-fighting. Seeing their prizes being stolen, at last the sodden minds knew where to shoot. As several headed to their pickups for guns, a single runner trotted toward the escaping car. Rig was about to floor it when the Indian spoke. Words coming from such a badly beaten face were difficult to understand.

“Lyra, did you get what he’s mumbling?”

“Something about his medicine bundle. ‘Can’t leave without’...I think he said, ‘helpers,’ whatever that means.”

In the mirror, a little way back on the ground, the Phoenician spotted a rolled-up, red Pendleton blanket and a crumpled Stetson. He also saw the cowboys, climbing into their pickups. Fortunately, drunkenness bought the escapees time; the drivers found it almost impossible to insert keys into ignitions. Meanwhile, the one wrangler, continuing in his broken gait, closed in.

"Ah, jeez," Rig moaned as he saw the oncoming problem. Backing up, hopping out, and scooping up the injured man's belongings took but a few seconds. Medicine bundle and hat in hand, he was swung around by someone with a drooping mustache and wearing an old-fashioned, Tom Mix-style hat.

In fighting circles, it was an undisputed fact that "He who is sober has twice the speed of he who is drunk." A single, lightning blow and the ranch hand staggered. But there was yet another axiom: "What the sober feel, the inebriated do not." A normal man would have gone down after such an explosive punch. The wrangler simply absorbed the fist, swayed, then regained his balance.

Barely in the car, Rig floor boarded the gas. As tires squealed, the alcohol sodden cowboy grabbed hold of the bumper. Being dragged across the parking lot, anesthetized, he was unaware his leg was being ground into hamburger. Shredded pants quickly became soaked with blood. One by one, the cowpoke's unfolding fingers lost their grip. The would-be assailant dropped away, rolling several times before coming to a stop. His hat, farther back, rested upside down in the gravel.

As the car skid onto the pavement, a rifle spoke. Lead from a .30-30 ripped through the vehicle's trunk. The gun's thunderous clap could be heard for several miles in the thin mountain air—echoes upon echoes bounced through the surrounding forest. With all but one of the cowboys now in pickups, the chase was on.

Even though his pursuers were inebriated, this was their territory. With the speedometer hovering at 90 mph, Rig was uncertain of the road ahead. Flying past cars doing 65, they sped off into the night. Breathing down the escapees' necks, two pickups were close behind.

Semiconscious, the old man was slumped over in the backseat, while the boy and his dog hugged the floor. Blocked by an elderly couple and unable to pass due to oncoming traffic, the four were boxed in. Slammed from behind, the car suddenly jerked. Rig looked in his rearview mirror; one of the pickups was ramming—trying to force them into a steep ravine. A glance in the passenger-side mirror showed a form hanging out a window, wildly waving a pistol. Shaken by the pounding, and seeing the driver's panic, Lyra turned to peer out the back.

"Rig, you're going to have to trust me again."

"Now what?"

"Look, I want you to turn your lights off and let me steer."

"*In the dark?!* From the passenger side? That's insane! At this speed and in pitch-black, *you're bloody crazy*."

Hands cupped over her face, the alien frantically ordered, "*Just do it!* I can see in the dark."

"How come you can see now, and couldn't back in the cave?"

Removing her contact lenses, she turned. An oncoming car's headlights exposed two catlike eyes.

"I never told you I couldn't see in the dark," Lyra replied, as she grabbed the wheel. "I only said I didn't know if the tunnel would be a dead end or go to the surface. With the lenses in, I'm handicapped with the same night vision as humans. My eyes are the only characteristics of my former self that I brought into this female's body."

Taken aback, her companion found it hard to respond. "Well then, what was that about someone possibly stealing the Bronco and us dying down there in the cave?"

"At the time, I truly didn't know if we could get out. The signal from my tracking device won't carry that far underground; my people didn't have a clue as to where we were."

Unsure, but with no other option, he released the wheel, allowing his passenger to drive, as the space being ordered, "Now floor it! We need to get around this car ahead of us." Taking a fast corner, tires screeched. For balance, King squeezed the padded windshield visor while holding on for dear life.

Trying to take his mind off the danger, he babbled, "Say, just how old are you? I mean, you're not some five-thousand-year-old...."

Ignoring her partner's prattle, the alien abruptly directed, *"Turn the lights off—now!"*

At this speed and in the blackness, all Rig had to hold onto was faith, and there was less than a thread of that. *God, I wish*

I knew how to pray, was his only thought as he flipped off the light switch.

"In Earth time, or are you asking me how old this person's shell is?"

"No…in dog years—*of course in Earth time!"*

Just then, two shots rang out. Had the shooter been sober, with the pickup so close, something surely would have connected. Still, the cowboy should have more rounds in his clip. Those who have been pinned down by gunfire can relate to the intense fright that Rig and Lyra were experiencing. Each cringed, fearing the next bullet might be the one that splashed an eyeball and brains across the dashboard.

Feeling totally out of control caused the normally masculine King to speak in a higher register than usual. *"You know, Lyra, life with you is turning me into a religious fanatic!"*

With an IQ of 174, the alien had no trouble driving and carrying on a conversation. Her answer came with a smile. "Your planet already has too many zealots."

"I wish," he said, looking in the rearview mirror and ignoring her comment, "we could lose these guys. This is frickin' hairy."

The sound of more shots lured the boy from the floor to peer over the top of the front seat. Lights from an oncoming car briefly illuminated the scene. With eyes bulging wide, he exclaimed, "*Lord Jesus, have mercy!* Lady, you're gonna get us killed! How come you're steerin'? Why's the lights off?"

More often than not, terror trumps logic. For some inexplicable reason, the youth decided it would be safer in the front seat. Trying to climb over between Rig and Lyra, especially with her driving, only added to the commotion. As Roger began his descent, Rig lifted his arms and thrust him back.

"*Look, kid*, if you want to live, sit down and shut up. *Understand*?"

"But, Mister…I…I'm scared," replied the child, tears streaming down his face.

"It'll be okay. *Now settle down!"*

Keeping his hands off the wheel was a challenge almost greater than the ex-driver could handle. Speeding along without lights, he was far too worried to continue chatting. For the elderly couple that were passed, this would be a great story to tell the grandchildren—shots fired, a car with its lights out, and both the pursued and the pursuers racing around Gramps and Omah before disappearing into the night.

Lyra concentrated more intensely. "*Get ready.* Slow down when I tell you. There's a side road coming up."

"How do you know?"

"My guides are telling me."

"Who?"

"*Never mind!* Just get ready."

"This isn't the same group that told us to follow that helicopter, is it?"

"No…there's a difference. But don't bother me now. Just step on it. If this is going to work, we need to put some distance between them and us."

Rather than the drunken posse doubling back, Lyra was counting on them continuing on—believing their quarry had sped up, but could still be caught.

Uncertain, he asked again in a more worried tone, "Lord, how do we do this?"

"For one thing, when we make the turn, don't touch the brakes. Down-shift into a lower gear. If you hit the pedal, it'll only warn them where we are. Okay, now it's about two hundred feet, ahead around that curve."

"What curve?"

"Never mind. Okay, go slower; we're going to miss it. Take your foot off the gas."

Normally, one would speed past this semi-hidden wooded road if he didn't know of its existence. A hard right turn, down and up several dips, and around a bend, they came to a halt in a pine forest. Finally able to relax, the Phoenician let out a huge, "Whew!" Putting an arm around his partner for a congratulatory hug, both heard a stirring coming from the backseat.

Clicked on, the overhead light revealed the opposite of a male Native American stereotype. Barely able to sit up, battered and bloodied, still there was dignity to the old man. Well-dressed in a torn but expensive sports jacket, jeans, and cowboy boots, his hair was neatly parted. Two braids, both wrapped in otter skins and tied with red ribbons, were the only giveaway to an aboriginal heritage.

Wiggling one of his front teeth to test how loose it had become, the wizened Indian managed a grin. "Like up at Pine Ridge—car chases, shooting, beatings by cowboys. Feels just like home."

Rig queried, "Pine Ridge, where?"

"South Dakota, Nephew—Lakota country."

"What's Lakota country?"

"You white men call us Sioux."

"Oh."

Her contacts back in place, the Ra representative turned around and broke in, "We've got to get you cleaned up. My name is Lyra. This is Rigden Ki…."

The boy chimed in, "And my name is Roger."

Still smiling, the Lakota answered, "Yes, Grandson, but I think I will call you Cante Nitinze. Means Braveheart. You fought strong for this old Indian. Lila pilámaya. Spirits will do something good for you. You watch."

The boy was now more curious than ever. "What's lila pila something?"

"Lila pilámaya is Lakota. Means 'thank you very much.'"

Under his breath, the boy repeated the phrase several times. Being from the asphalt jungle of East Los Angeles, he'd never met a traditional Native American before.

The Pine Ridge elder continued, "Name's John George. Sure appreciate you all comin' along when you did."

Rig was eager to get things cleared up. "Say, Mr. George…."

"Call me Grandpa."

"Okay, Grandpa. Didn't we see you earlier today, thumbing a ride?"

"That was me, all right."

"Sorry we didn't pick you up then."

"Me too, but you're always in a rush."

Not one for Indian subtlety, the disbarred stockbroker was unaccustomed to the nuanced ways in which America's indigenous population often spoke.

With Roger in awe and Lyra maintaining a polite, unobtrusive presence, the Phoenician was driven by his Anglo upbringing to satisfy a burning curiosity. "What brings you down from South Dakota? And why were those guys beating on you like that?"

"Spirits brought me...for two reasons. I'm a professor of comparative religion at Sinte Gleska—a college up north. Arizona State asked me to give a lecture on the Lakota spiritual belief system." Groaning as he shifted positions, "Second reason...we can get into later."

Although Lyra knew the full explanation for Grandpa George's trip, she kept it to herself.

Rig's internal Wall Street voice analyzed the situation: *Not only am I on the run, but I'm schlepping an alien, a child, an Indian, and a dog...If there were only a clown, it'd make this stupid circus complete.*

"I heard that," whispered Lyra.

"*Oh, damn*! I wish you'd stop listening to my thoughts."

"It's hard; you're really loud. But all right, I'll try to tune you out."

Grandpa George gazed squarely into Rig's eyes, offering a remark that seemed a non sequitur. "Careful what you wish for, *Wasicu*."

"Wash what?"

"I gave you a Lakota name, Nephew—'*Wasicu.*' Fits you pretty good."

"What's it mean?"

Without answering, the Indian simply smiled.

Seeing he was being ignored, Rig turned to Roger, asking, "Kid, I can't take you back to Strawberry. How am I going to get you to your parents?"

"Don't got none. Ain't got no dad, and Momma died when I was ten. Been stayin' with my auntie. Then last week, she up and ran off with someone. Now, it's jus' me and Toby here. He's been with me ever since I was little."

"Don't you have anyone else?" Lyra asked, her concern showing.

"Yeah. That's where I'm goin' now. Gotta sister in Chicago. Her husband don't like me, though; ain't got no place else. But that's cool. I'm gunna getta see Oprah's TV show in person. Like that lady. Kind'a reminds me of Momma."

Amazed, the Ra representative questioned further. "You're hitchhiking to Chica...."

As usual, her partner butted in. "*Wait a minute*! How did you get from LA all the way over here?"

"Thumbin'."

"And you," Lyra asks, "intend to catch rides all the way to Chicago?"

"Yes, Ma'am."

"Do you have any money?" she asked.

With pride, the youth pulled out a fistful of ones and some coins. "Sixteen dollars and forty-three cents. It was fifty-three, but I lost a dime somewhere."

Rig wouldn't let it rest. "How'd you end up in Payson? It's not on the way."

"Don't know. These crazy white folks said they was headin' to Denver. But they got lost, cuz they was doin' crack all the way over. When we got turned around and started headin' to Mexico, I told 'em me and my dog wanted out."

Numbed by the growing complexity of the problem, the ex-Wall Streeter didn't know what to do about either the old man or the youth.

"Guess I just have to drop them off in Flag."

Taking a hard look at the boy for the first time, the Phoenician noticed the child seemed to tilt to the left.

"Hey, kid."

"Name's Roger."

"Yeah, right, Roger. What's the matter? You're not sitting up straight."

"They say I got scoliosis of the spine."

"How'd you get it?"

"Born with it."

Lyra broke in, "Didn't your mother take you to a doctor to try and get it fixed?"

"Did once when I was five. He took X-rays. Spine's shaped like a big letter *C*. Doc said he could fix it if we did something then but we couldn't afford to go no more. Don't bother me none. But made me sad cuz Momma would cry when the kids teased me. Always told me we'd get it fixed later. Then she died."

Like most businessmen, the former broker was one who compartmentalized problems. With nothing to help the boy's situation, he coldly pressed on to the next management decision. To avoid the highway patrol, they should follow the original plan: go through Sedona, camp, get cleaned up, and slip into Flagstaff via Oak Creek Canyon tomorrow.

"Grandpa George?" asked Rig.

"Yes?"

"Got any friends where we can drop you off once you get washed up?"

"Up near Chinle at Canyon de Chelly in the Four Corners area—wife has relatives up there."

"Too bad—that's a four-or five-hour trip from Flag. We're not going that way."

"Rig!"

"Quiet, Lyra!"

Speaking between clenched teeth, the reply was beyond serious. *"Don't you ever tell me to be quiet…or you will be walking. Understand?"*

Back turned and not paying attention, *Wasicu* addressed the old Indian. "Good. Then we can let you both out in Flagstaff. You and the boy can hitch…."

Lyra wouldn't let him finish. "We are not going to dump Roger and Mr. George off in the middle of Flagstaff."

"Well, Florence Nightingale, what do you suggest?"

"I don't know yet but I'll think of something…We will be shown…."

"Yeah, right!" he fumed. "Just like this whole trip has been one long cruise on the Love Boat."

The old Indian kept his silence. He knew they would be together farther than Flagstaff.

Driving along, Roger noticed the Lakota patting his shirt pocket.

Talking to himself, the old man said, "Darn! Left my tobacco pouch back at the fight. Musta fell…."

Speaking into the rearview mirror, Rig was quick to cut him off. "Grandpa, we're not going back for it. Don't worry; tobacco's cheap. I'll buy you some more when we get to Sedona."

The elder was silent as ten minutes went by. He then made an announcement. "Well, here it is right here in my pocket. Don't know how I could have missed it."

As he said this, the Indian looked over at the boy. Having grown up on the streets, this youth was nobody's fool. He saw the old man feeling his shirt for that tobacco a few minutes earlier. It wasn't there. And now it was. The child tilted his head, giving a quizzical expression as he attempted to fathom the situation.

Keeping his voice low so Rig and Lyra wouldn't hear, the Lakota leaned over and whispered, "You see, Grandson, spirits always take care of those who walk in a good way."

Midway to Sedona, on the other side of Camp Verde, the group stopped for gas. A recorded message was left for Dr. Gillman, telling him that due to arriving late, the meeting would have to be tomorrow. Lyra, too, got out to stretch her legs.

Upset as usual, Rig issued another ultimatum, "Hauling the old man and the kid are bad enough, but we gotta ditch the mutt; he stinks."

"You can't be serious. That's Roger's friend."

"I have a rule in my life—anything with fleas has to go."

Those words hit the extraterrestrial like an electric jolt. *"If that were the case, you would never date."*

The blast was returned. *"Oh, you're real funny."*

*"*Look, *Mr. Wall Street*, when will you learn that there is no such thing as an accident? This was meant to be, and it is my car. I say *Toby stays."*

Checkmate. With nothing more for a rebuttal, the treasure hunter turned toward the gas pump. Ignoring Lyra's presence, he moved to the front of the vehicle, keeping busy by checking the water level in the radiator. Using a thick bunch of paper towels, the unscrewing was done with utmost care. Barely cracked, the hiss of steam noisily escaped—burping, with the usual bubbling loss of liquid.

Without warning, the fugitive felt a strong tap on his shoulder. Already nervous, he jumped, slamming his head against the hood. His mind raced. Apprehended, Rigden King, III, was ready to accept his fate—the Highway Patrol—prison—the electric chair.

Turning—shock, then relief. Standing before him was a tall figure dressed in a baggy red and yellow, polka-dot jumpsuit, with orange hair, pancake makeup, and a red bulb nose—the very materialization of that casual remark he had earlier flung into the universe. Past the performer, King glimpsed a sign on the side of a Honda Civic—Jingles, King of Clowns.

"Scuse me, buddy," the clown interrupted. "I'm due up at Flag at a kids' party. Forgot my wallet and the tank's dry. Can you spare me a coupla bucks? Pay ya back if you give me your address."

"What?"

"And if you can't spare change, maybe you can give me a lift; I'm running real late."

Unsympathetic as well as broke, it was explained that not only were donations an impossibility, but they were heading west, not north.

"Hey, guy," Jingles replies. "Here's someone else pullin' up. I'm gunna go see if they can give me a hand. Catch ya later. *Ciao*."

Happy to be rid of the nuisance, the irritated ex-salesman responded without even turning in the departing clown's direction, "Yeah, right—*ciao*."

Void of shame, the king of clowns continued working the parking lot as if it was his personal one-ring circus. A keen observer, Grandpa watched this manifestation of *Wasicu's* prior, flippant prayer while the errant panhandler bummed from car to car. A mild parental smile formed across the Lakota's bruised face as he gazed down on Roger, who had dozed off.

Waiting to pay for the gas, behind Rig stood another oddity—this time a four-foot-eight-inch Santa Claus of a man—complete with hot-pink suspenders over a clashing, bright yellow shirt. Adding to this customer's curious image were deformed—or at least small—strangely pointed ears, partially hidden by long, whitish hair whose ends were yellow with age.

Having more pressing things on his mind, the Phoenician's attention refocused. He constantly scanned the parking lot, fearing any sign of law enforcement.

Emerging, as if on cue, from the darkness and into the glare of the station's lighting, a police car silently glided to a cautious stop. Two patrolmen scanned the asphalted area, checking out everyone in sight. Rig swallowed hard, accidentally biting his cheek. To bolt would be a giveaway. Like the storybook character, "Where's Waldo," the fugitive's only option was to somehow stay hidden while remaining out in the open. Hoping to seem natural, he turned to the gnome behind him. "From around these parts?"

"Me? Sure am. Me and the missus there," Santa said, motioning in the direction of a station wagon. In the front seat sat a female, with what appeared to be two animal carriers in the back. "We're…." as the customer rambled on, King tuned him out. Fascinated, he was struck by the woman's almost incandescent beauty. Clearly twenty-five years her husband's junior, with fiery red hair and chiseled features, she emitted what can best be described as a mysterious radiance.

Perceiving being scanned, the woman's head slowly turned, glaring back at the intruder. Coal-black orbs, projecting an unearthly gaze, caught Rig off guard. Terrified, he felt something alive, yet very cold, had just slithered into his brain. It seemed to be crawling…searching. Frantically, he attempted to look away, but his adversary's laser-stare was too intense.

Shaken to the core, and only by a superhuman force of will did he finally manage to blink. Then, able to change targets, he turned back, rudely jumping into the middle of his new acquaintance's ongoing monologue. "Name's…name's Rig."

"I'm Earl Buckworth. Wife there's Kassandra, but she likes to be called Kassy. You and your fam…." Seeing an Indian and black boy in the rear seat, the man seemed hard pressed for a category…."Uhhh, you and your friends passin' through?"

Fifty feet away, the door to the patrol car slowly opened. A trooper climbed out. With a deliberate stride, he headed toward the fugitive. His right hand clutched the handle of a baton hanging from a thick black belt, replete with a canister of mace and two spare clips of ammunition.

Defenseless as a newborn fawn in an open meadow while a bear approached, Rig pivoted, trying to hide his face. Trembling, he responded, "Yeah…umm, ah, we're just passing through."

The officer advanced. Tinted glasses hid his eyes. A down-turned mouth forewarned a dangerous disposition.

Nervousness mounting, the Phoenician continued chatting with his newfound buddy. Sensing a change in his acquaintance's demeanor, Earl glanced to the side, catching a view of the oncoming threat. As the trooper approached, and with the agility of an obese ballerina, Mr. Buckworth pirouetted his mammoth frame between his audience and the advancing menace. Elated at his shield's change in position, Rig's ungracious mind was thankful his buffer never became a Jenny Craig devotee.

Hawking spit, mixed with a large amount of chewing tobacco, Earl expectorated, aiming at a small rock near his feet. His listener's stomach churned as the nonchalant spitter continued. "We're headin' back to Sedoner. Brought them cats to Phoenix; gettin' these here queens bred. They...."

The man in blue stopped. His right hand carefully switched positions, now resting on the butt of his holstered gun. Nerves frayed, the fugitive further tensed. Rocking back and forth on the balls of his feet like a sprinter before the sounding shot, there was but a half-breath before Rig would bolt. Turning, the patrolman yelled, "Hey, Frank! Wanna doughnut with that coffee?" Order taken, the menace maneuvered past Santa and friend only to disappear into the mini-mart.

Unconsciously, King let out a sigh and answered, "We're up here trying to get out of the heat down in the city. I...."

At the front of the line, an argument between the clerk and a miffed credit card customer reached a crescendo. Holding a phone to his ear, the attendant took a pair of scissors and snipped the man's American Express card in half.

Shocked, the patron screamed, *"What the hell'd you do that for?"*

Blocking out the squabble, the treasure hunter's mind remained fixed solely on the policeman. Although King couldn't care less about the idiotic cats, he forced himself to continue the conversation. "What's a queen? And...just how many did you say you have?"

"Queen's what we call a female. We breed Persians. The little woman and I got about twenty in the bedroom alone. Actually, it was more. I say twenty cuz you never count kittens." Earl laughed. "You know, it's kind'a funny being married to a woman who likes so many of them felines."

"What do you mean?"

"Son, with a dog you're a rock star. With a cat, you're simply hotel staff. And you can measure how long a fella's been hitched to a feline type of gal by the way he begins toleratin' them critters goin' on the bed."

"Goin' on the bed? What do you mean?"

"Yuh know, fur balls, upchucks, pee, the like?"

Grossed out, King's fear of being caught and tried for murder was momentarily eclipsed by the idea of cats having diarrhea and/or vomiting slimy chunks all over his pillow.

Interrupting her husband's exposé of life in a cattery, the woman called out through a rolled-down window. In a

Southern but surprisingly strident accent, Rig heard, "*Earl! Earl*! Car's about to overheat. Hurry up."

Reverting to a form of communication suggesting many years of marriage, the yell was returned, "*Keep your damn shorts on, woman! Can't ya see I ain't payin' till these two get through?"*

"Earl Lawrence Buckworth, don't you tell me to shut up! I'm just sayin', the radiator's 'bout to boil over. And if my babies come even close to heat stroke, it'll be another three months…if you get my drift. That's a promise!"

"Woman, they won't get heat stroke. Leave me be!"

Continuing in her grating, yet syrupy Georgian tone, Kassandra shouted her prophecy one more time. "Then, mister, you'd better count on buying some ice when you're payin' for that gas—*tah keep ma babies cool*."

Quietly, Earl confided"Man, n*ever* buy a woman a crystal ball, even as a joke. She'll get to believin' she can see the future. Once that happens, you're stuck in Oz without them red slippers; might as well forget about gettin' back to Kansas."

At last, the irate customer stormed away, leaving Rig next in line. Breaking off his conversation with the cat breeder, the fugitive handed the attendant Lyra's credit card, who was still on the phone and didn't notice that Rig couldn't be a she.

Talking over Rig's shoulder while the clerk was running the bill, Earl said in a volume his wife couldn't hear, "But she's a good woman! Just sometimes I think her spandex's too tight."

Credit card returned, the fugitive quickly took leave with a breezy "See ya," as he disappeared around the corner to the car.

During the intense period of their conversation, the treasure hunter's normally observant eyes somehow failed to focus on the unusual pendant hanging around his friend's neck. Absentmindedly rubbing the medallion between his forefinger and thumb, the cat breeder repeated his fellow gas buyer's parting words, "See ya," inaudibly adding, "So mote it be!"

Knowing Lyra's license plate was photographed at the tollbooth, King stalled several minutes, waiting for the police to leave. As the patrolmen pulled away, he glanced into his rearview mirror. A thick plume of steam rose from the hood of the Buckworth station wagon, while the pear-shaped man quickly exited the mini-mart with a bag of ice.

Heading through rolling hills dotted with juniper, the travelers looked out on an overcast evening that obscured the normally breathtaking rust-red vistas of Sedona. Occasional breaks in the clouds allowed flashing glimpses of a haloed moon, a forecast of a pending downpour.

Passing Bell Rock, a dome-shaped geological formation, Lyra began to chuckle, trying not to awaken the three in back.

Her soft laughter piqued Rig to ask in an equally low volume, "What's so funny?"

"Those from my planet haven't been entirely successful in hiding our presence here. More and more of you have come to suspect that something is going on. Many think we have some sort of hanger inside…I mean there, in Bell Rock. People come from around the world, burning sage, making medicine wheels…performing all sorts of strange ceremonies trying to get us to land. The joke is, we're already here."

Quietly, he interjected, "Yeah, according to the newspaper, weirdoes in this area do things like that all the time. There was a ton of 'em back, I think in, ahhh…'87. Like locusts, they came en masse—the *Moronic Convergence*. Maybe you heard of it."

Lyra was not amused by her companion's lame attempt at humor. She corrected him with slow, deliberate wording. "You mean the *Harmonic Convergence*. And they weren't all *weirdoes*, as you put it."

"Whatever. Anyway, do you really have ships in Bell Rock?"

He pulled the car off the road to get a better look at this famous mini mountain.

She smiled. "I was laughing because your people are only one ring out from the bull's-eye. Actually, we do have a facility. It is the next mountain over there, that one to the east. We also…."

Something unusual caught the alien's attention. Cracking her window, the extraterrestrial took a long, deep breath, attempting to draw in a faint but distinct, almost magical feeling. She inhaled again, this time filling her lungs to capacity. Her partner glanced over, peering longingly into the cleavage between her breasts. Sensing his intent as women often do, the intrusion was ignored, leaving her companion with the delusion his sexual fantasy remained undetected.

Watching Lyra test the air, his question was anxious. "What's up?"

A faint smile crossed her lips. Slowly, the space being pointed to a mountain ahead on the right. Aiming her finger at Schnebly Hill, she responded, "Nothing. Nothing at all. Look there."

Almost invisible in the semi-darkness, her eyes sparkled as she thought back, remembering sitting in meditation up there on a large promontory, overlooking the tiny hamlet below. "The sun was setting," she said, her tone soft with reverence. "That scene…it still takes my breath away. From there I could see all the way down the valley, past Sedona's lights, off into the horizon." Her face took on an even more faraway look as she explained, "The white roofs below resembled a field of mushrooms." Sighing, and then talking in an even lower volume, her whisper nearly dropped below her partner's range of hearing. "The peace up there is incredible."

Roger, awake during the tail end of her conversation, leaned forward and said, "Sounds beautiful."

Alarmed that he may have overheard the part about the spaceships, the alien took a moment to scan the boy's thoughts. Satisfied he awoke afterward, she answered, "Yes, it was—but there's more."

Not asleep but keeping his eyes half-closed, Grandpa didn't stir as he studied their reactions.

Still thinking the old man was dozing, the driver inquired in his lowest tone, "What do you mean, 'there's more'?"

"Imagine the most beautiful sunset you've ever seen. Then, as the last rays fade, lights of the town come on—like multicolored crystals strewn across the desert floor."

"Ooooh," exclaimed Roger, whose lucid imagination was quite adept at thinking in kaleidoscopic shapes and shades.

On and on, Lyra described the many ways this Brigadoon area was thick with enchantment. Its profound mystical nature prompted her to divulge the real basis of Sedona's reputation. With a sweeping gesture, the extraterrestrial pointed across the darkened landscape as she began describing a complex mix of peoples, all blending in a cauldron of differing beliefs. Floating on top, the most visible layer was that of the Christian church, replete with its numerous yet slightly varying denominations. Barely hidden beneath this placid surface were counter-streams of witches' covens—mostly into white magic, although some working the worst forms of sorcery. Also unobtrusive, giving still more flavor, existed a small, quiet, devout aggregation of Buddhists. Further down, concealed in the murky depths, were the shadowy practitioners of Satanism. And then, almost as if by accident and spicing the whole brew, was a sprinkling of post-'60s hippies, a dash of Native Americans, and the occasional Hindu.

With obvious veneration, the alien went on to speak of Lester Levenson, an enlightened being who once lived in the surrounding hills away from the community's chaotic vibrations. She recounted his ability to teleport both himself and others; how he materialized articles out of thin air, did time travel, and, the most profound accomplishment of all—his ongoing demonstration of oneness with the Creator.

Excluding him as an aberration, she stated that many of the more flamboyant groups were really only the condiments. Their songs, sermons, chanting, and candle-burning added but a side-accent to the cauldron's two quieter, but main ingredients—a huge cadre of retirees and a group of serious artists. Thrown together, this was a spiritual concoction if ever there was one, and all garnished with that obnoxiously loud and ever visible camera-toting tourist.

The extraterrestrial went on to assert that subconsciously, nearly every resident here was seeking a personal corner of Nirvana. They were lured to the Red Rock Country for a variety of seemingly unrelated reasons. For many, it was the spectacular beauty. That was, until the hodgepodge architecture blighted this God-painted picture. But unknown to most, there was—and still is—a single common thread quietly pulling people to these hills…vortexes.

Dismissed by the uninformed, vortices were subtle, yet scientifically measurable patterns of energy—tornado-like forces that emanated from the Earth. When rotating clockwise, our physical bodies would find them exceptionally harmonic; they tended to raise our vibrations to a more celestial level, decreasing internal chaos and bestowing greater clarity to one's thinking. But spinning counterclockwise was deleterious, provoking a conscious or subconscious state of confusion. And although rarely occurring, when several of these energy beams came together in one spot, they could and often did open portals into other dimensions—as has been experienced at "The Church on the Hill," the town's airport, Boyington Canyon, and several lesser publicized locations.

As the wonderment of her explanation faded, hunger brought all four back to the present. After a vote, it was decided to take a few minutes to stop at a local grocery store. One finally came into view. Rig and Lyra went in, while Grandpa, barely able to move, sat outside on a bench and talked with Roger.

The Phoenician was left to browse, as his companion proceeded to shop. Bored, he stood listening to two silver-haired ladies, whose accents revealed they were obviously far from their distant Brooklyn isle. Their discussion revolved around a tantric sex book one of them leafed through today, as well as why so many Westerners felt the need to wear guns. Moving past and around a corner, the ex-stockbroker was struck by the sight of a familiar figure. It was the one and only Earl Buckworth, intently inspecting a Charmin toilet paper display. Strangely, only the fugitive was caught by surprise.

The gnome-like acquaintance was the first to speak. "Well, *blessed be*! Knew I'd be runnin' into ya again."

"How'd you figure?"

"Little bird told me," he answered with a wink. "Hey, stranger, you rushed off without me tellin' ya about bein' married to a cat woman. Wanna hear the rest?"

With Lyra busy picking vegetables, the ex-broker shrugged, "Why not? Seems like I have the time."

"How long you two been married?"

"We're not."

"Oh, then you wouldn't have a clue what I'm talkin' about."

"Not really."

"Okay then. Stage one's the first five years. Imagine this. You're comin' to bed at 2:00 a.m., bone tired, and the missus says to you, 'Sweetheart?…Honey?'… And announces, 'One of them cats has done somethin' on the sheets. Everything's soaked, clear through.' Well, I mean to tell ya, even a priest would go through the roof. You rant and you cuss; head out after that crafty little sucker who always seems to manage scamperin' just out of reach. Then, after cornerin' the rascal and thown'im out in the hall, you change the bed—gettin' to sleep more done-in than before. That's stage one."

"And stage two?"

"Hold yer horses; I'm comin' to that. Then there's years six through ten. The marriage's risen to a new plane of understandin'. Guess you'd call it that; honeymoon's over; you're settled in, pretty comfortable bein' together. Anyway, figure it was the same time in the morning. Worn out, you're just about to crawl under the sheets. This time, there ain't no 'Sweetheart' or 'Honey.' She just ups and says, 'It happened again!' 'Course, you're kinda used to this sorta thing by now. But you'd go to any length not to change that bedding, unless it was on the side where you sleep. Here's where you ask the stage-two-type question: 'Your side or mine?'"

Rig laughed. Earl again cut him short. "No, no, there's more—stage three. That's after the tenth year."

"So what happens then?"

"Everything's about the same. Tired and disgusted, this time you don't just want to maim, you want to kill the damn critter. Plus, you'd give almost anything not to make the bed—especially if the problem's on your wife's half. But by now, the relationship's *real equal*; she's fully liberated. You can tell, cuz her tone's totally changed. She says, '*Earl…get your butt in gear! There's a problem.*' Remember son, it has been a hard day and you're more exhausted than you can remember. To make matters worse, you find out it was on your side. Still, you'd do anything to get outa changin' them dang sheets. This is where you ask the long-married, cat-lover's-husband's question…'Is it by my head…or my feet?'"

Rig could barely control his laughter as he moved past Earl, giving him a parting slap on the shoulder. This exchange was one man's way of briefly acknowledging brotherhood with another before going on their separate paths.

Outside the store, the treasure hunter arrived just after the same two ladies who, having thoroughly examined Grandpa George, were finally moving on.

Laughing, the Indian says, "*Wasicu*, you got here too late; missed the fun."

"What do you mean?"

"Should'a seen the faces of those old women; never saw a bloodied Redskin before. Came right up and wouldn't quit starin'."

"What'd you do?"

"The usual. To get 'em to stop, I first scratched my crotch but that didn't work. Then I picked my nose. If that hadn't moved 'em, I'da used my secret weapon."

From what the elder had just said, Rig knew he was about to be privy to some form of arcane, Indian shamanism.

Almost breathlessly, *Wasicu* blurted, "What's...What's the secret?"

"Well, for an old man...I can fart pretty loud. That usually gets the white folks a-movin'," Grandpa boasted, his grin broadening.

Shopping done and now winding up Oak Creek Canyon past Slide Rock, the driver took a side road—edging the car through tall grass down to a secluded campsite next to the water's edge. After Lyra's gentle doctoring, Grandpa John George announced he was in charge of the cooking. The Pine Ridge elder suggested the three go exploring for about forty minutes. Roger, ever curious, elected to stay behind while the other two walked along a trail leading upstream. Arriving back at camp, they were met by the unbounded enthusiasm of a thirteen-year-old.

The youth's exuberance poured out. "*Come, see!* Me and Grandpa made this. Smell it? It smells great!"

Standing around the campfire, the three held their paper plates out while the Lakota got ready to serve. Moving slowly, the Indian's rhythm bespoke one who knew what he was doing. Rushing wasn't part of it.

"Say, this is really...I mean *really* good." But as hungry as King was, nearly anything would do. "I didn't know we bought this much meat. What do you call this dish?"

The South Dakota visitor masked his expression by looking away into the darkness as he answered, "Indian specialty—RK stew."

Unable to contain his exuberance, Roger exclaimed, "Grandpa put in even more groceries than you bought. You know, RK."

"What's RK?" the Phoenician asked, his curiosity piqued.

Quick to reply, the boy announced, "RK—road kill. Remember that dead raccoon we saw when we turned off?"

With geyser force, Rig's stomach erupted, spewing stew into the fire. Steam sizzled as a white cloud rose skyward. Alone at the campground, there was no other noise—except the moving brook and the sputtering, crackling campfire. Slowly, the Phoenician lowered the plate to his feet. Grandpa, Roger, and Lyra quietly continued eating. After about a minute of contemplation, and pushed by hunger, he of the delicate stomach decided to pick up the rest of his dinner. Too late. Roger hadn't had time yet to put food down for his four-legged companion. Never mind; under the law of *finders-keepers*, Toby had paid King a visit.

Hungry and frustrated, Rig flashed, "*Damn it, kid*! Keep your mutt outta my food. Just get him away." A rock was thrown at the dog with such force that one inch closer, and it would have taken out the canine's eye.

"*Hey*! Who you callin' a mutt?" the boy challenged. "And Toby's not no it, he's a boy."

Embarrassed by his actions, the treasure hunter's voice assumed a quieter tone. "Sorry, Roger. Just…just call your friend over."

After an awkward moment, dinner continued. Spellbound by Grandpa's stories of how Indians lived before the white man, the youth had yet to finish his meal. Lyra, too, listened, captivated by that period of Earth's history. Rig alone noticed Toby crawling back, commando style, on his stomach, hoping to make another score. Demonstrating both skill and intellect, this time the raider stealthily approached from the opposite direction, moving up behind the log where his previous mark still sat. Feeling remorseful over his anger, the Phoenician meekly dropped the furry beggar some scraps of stew. Glancing up, Lyra saw a stony heart melting before a thin, wagging tail.

Supper over, Grandpa announced he'd be gone for a while. So saying, the elder edged into the darkness. King too, took a short walk. His goal—to find an outhouse. Crossing the creek, the Phoenician observed the silhouette of a man standing on a rocky outcropping, facing east. In the moonlight, he recognized the figure as Grandpa. Without a sound, the watcher sat under a tree, waiting to see what would unfold.

With an abalone shell in his right hand and an eagle wing in his left, the Indian brushed a billowing, smoky column of sage, sweetgrass, and cedar into the night air. Moving clockwise, he first faced west, then north, east, and finally south. Acknowledging all the directions of the Creator, the Lakota next smudged Grandmother Earth, Wakan Tanka Himself, and Wanbli Gleska, the eagle—carrier of prayers. As the last gesture, he made a sweeping motion with the smoldering bowl—a further recognition of the spirits and all other aspects of the Creator's being.

Then the old man sat, again facing east. Pulling out his *cannupa* or medicine pipe, the Pine Ridge elder paused. He glanced at Rig, who, sitting in the shadows, felt hidden by the cover of darkness. And to normal sight, King was. But the Sinte Gleska professor wasn't seeing solely with his eyes. Unaffected by the other's presence, the old man began to pray. Loading the pipe with tobacco, he sang softly, calling in the spirits. The treasure hunter couldn't quite catch the words as they hovered, before floating upward to the stars; but he wouldn't understand them even if they were audible. A match flickered briefly in the night as the pipe was lit. Insensitive as the ex-broker normally was, this time he recognized the sanctity of the moment, and remained stone-quiet.

That's what made the onslaught of this sneeze so alarming. Welling up, its tingling, hurricane force defied containment. Against the mounting tension, the spectator was determined to keep it in check; the old Indian's moment was not to be interrupted. Uncontrollable, its power, edging Rig's needle into the red zone, was nearing critical mass. Unbeknownst to him, Grandpa George stopped, looked over, smiled, and continued. Fighting dynamics similar to those of a miniature underground explosion, King pinched his nose, forcing the sneeze to implode. Mostly absorbed, only the faintest trumpeting note managed to escape.

Ceremony finished and no outhouse yet in sight, urgent practicality took over; the white man relieved himself behind a tree. Walking back together, the Native American moved with an uncanny surefootedness, while the Anglo had trouble navigating in the dark. Ever chatty, the white man worried about sleeping outside if it should rain.

Humbly, John George assured him, "Talked with the spirits; they're takin' care of it." Finished talking, the South Dakota visitor nimbly stepped over a tree root sticking up in the path. His companion stumbled.

Back at the campfire, the aging Indian again took charge. "It's time we talk. Grandson, you come. Sit on this side of the fire, to the west. Granddaughter, be here, to the east, and Wasicu, you to the south."

Seated in the north, Grandpa made four prayer tobacco ties—black, red, yellow, and white. Traditional Lakota colors, they represented the cardinal directions or aspects of the Creator, Tunkasila. He explained they would hang in a tree so the Great Spirit and the helpers would remember these special prayers. Again holding the sacred eagle-wing fan in his left hand, the spiritual warrior stood to deliver an ancient blessing.

Finished, the elder sat quietly. For a few minutes, no one spoke. The silence was almost more than Rig could stand; like most Anglos, he felt profoundly uncomfortable in the prolonged absence of sound. Finally, the Indian spoke. His words were soft, filled with warmth—from the heart. "The second reason for my comin' to Arizona is really my first. The talk at Arizona State University was only to pay my way. Spirits came and told me to make the journey—to speak with each of you. So I had them bring us all together."

In typical Rigden King, III, fashion, the ex-Wall Street broker interjected, "Do you mean to say you actually *knew* you would be meeting us on this trip?"

"Grandson," he said to Roger, *Wasicu's* question being ignored, "although you are young, *Mateo* the bear came to me in a dream. Said he wants to give you some of his power."

Barely a teenager, the boy burst forth, unable to be silent, "What type of power you talkin' about, Grandpa? What's this bear thing mean?"

"A bear, Grandson, is a medicine spirit. It means you can be a strong healer—help people if you want."

"I would like that. How'd I do it?"

"When it is time, I will show you." Turning to Lyra, the elder said, "Granddaughter, I have a special message for you. We'll talk later."

She nodded.

Grandpa stared at Rig before speaking. Regarded for but thirty seconds, the listener began squirming. "*Wasicu*, the spirits want me to ask, 'Why do you live? Why were you born?'"

Nonplused, the Phoenician responded, "I don't know. Guess I just was. Why?"

"Nephew, close your eyes."

Rig hesitated.

The elder insisted. "Go ahead, close 'em. I won't scalp ya," he chuckled.

Ever doubtful, cautiously, the subject complied.

"Now open 'em," Grandpa directed. "What do you see?"

In analytical fashion, King attempted describing, in the most laborious detail, all the things within his field of vision. Eventually, though, he wound down—finding less and less to point out.

The Pine Ridge visitor waited patiently. Only when King became quiet did the old man speak. "*Wasicu*, everything you see around this campfire, all you see in your life, is what's inside you; I mean, *how you think*. Back home on the rez, I had a vision. It showed you tryin' to ride two horses at the same time. Spirits want me to say, 'You need to choose'—make up your mind."

"Choose what? I don't understand."

"You gotta figure out on what road you want to walk."

"Sorry, Grandpa, I still don't get it."

"In the Lakota belief system, to embody the qualities of a good person is the highest path. To do so, in all things you have to walk in the right way, down the Red Road. The wrong way is the Black Road. You, Nephew, you have one foot on each. But the helpers say you can do some real powerful things for Grandmother Earth and the two-leggeds…if…if you'd get your butt in gear. So far, you've lived a day-to-day, woman-to-woman, paycheck-to-paycheck kinda life. You don't even know why you exist! More important…you don't even ask Tunkasila.

"Nephew, listen to me—hard. Soon things gonna get real bad here on Grandmother Earth. She's about to shift on her axis. Some land will sink; banks will close, and people will be walkin' the streets in gangs with guns, lookin' for food. So the spirits are tellin' me to tell you: 'To be a help in this time, and you can be, you'd better cut out the horseshit and get on with it.'" The Lakota paused to see the young man's reaction.

A full minute passed as the Anglo remained in deep thought. Sounds of the forest seemed to fade, as if holding their breath. The only noise was that of a burnt log collapsing back into the flames, and the continuous babbling of the stream, a few yards away.

"Why am I so special?"

The Indian slapped his knee and laughed. *Special*? You're not. In fact, you're ordinary." Then he grew serious again. "Except for your passion. The world," Grandpa clarified, "is divided into two types of people: those who watch, and those who hang over cliffs, lookin' for answers. The fire in your belly makes somethin' that can move mountains. Just look at what one of your medicine men did two thousand years ago. *One person with passion can change the world*. And you, *Wasicu*, you have it. That's the important thing."

"Grandpa, you talked about asking for answers. Who… how? I mean, how do I ask?"

As for 'who', you ask Wakan Tanka, God, Tunkasila…call Him or Her anything you like. Names are not as important as we two-leggeds like to think. The Sacred Mystery cannot be described, let alone boxed by a title. Ask. Then sit back and be prepared to accept whatever the spirits bring you. But be careful. If you pray, they give an answer, and if you don't do it, your life will get worse. Know that it is better not to go to them than to ask and then turn away."

"Grandpa, I've never really done this before. How…how do I do it?"

"You mean asking?"

"Yes, asking. How?"

The elder leaned forward. Looking up to the heavens, he made a motion with his hand as if reaching beyond the sky. "By asking, I mean pray; ask the Creator for help. I'm not sayin' you should pray in the Indian way. All prayer, if done sincerely, is the same."

He paused to let his comments sink in before more words streamed out. "First, think of the situation you are in and find as many reasons to be thankful for it as possible…I mean truly thankful. See somethin' good about the problem that's starin' you in the face. Know the spirits brought you this as a lesson.

You are meant to learn from it. Then put into words exactly what you want—strong!—with that passion I was talkin' about. Keep it clear and simple. Speaking with the mouth isn't necessary. What's important is to ask with your heart. Next, put your prayer into the claws of Wanbli Gleska, a balloon…or whatever you feel is right. Then let it loose and see it fly up to the Creator.

"Now, the last step is the hardest. When you've let it go, you've gotta realize that what you asked for has *already happened*—even if you don't see it. *Know, Nephew*! Know what you have prayed for already exists; *see it done. Feel it!* See it completed—finished. The only thing stoppin' it from becoming reality is a lack of faith—your doubt. Get rid of that and there's nothing you can't accomplish.

"Oh, there's one more thing: Keep your prayers to yourself. Tell no one. Two-leggeds are strange. They don't like seein' others do better. Even if they don't know they're doin' it, their spirit will shoot out a powerful thought against what you're prayin' for. It'll hit your message like an arrow goin' through a flyin' duck. That's why we say, 'Power spoken is power lost.'"

"Grandpa," asks Rig, "how do you know that things will soon get real bad?"

"Nephew, there are a whole lot of prophecies out there, all comin' together. And I don't mean they're strictly from the Indian Nations, either."

"Such as?"

"The red heifer and the white buffalo calf are the first two that come to mind. As for the heifer, about 70 AD, when Herod's Temple, the site of King Solomon's earlier version, was destroyed, the Jews prophesied that their leader would come again, but only after it was rebuilt."

Roger jumped in, "And was it rebuilt, Grandpa?"

"Not yet, but soon. You see, the Jewish people have everything they need for the ceremony except the blood of a special heifer—a red one. Now this can't be just any red cow. It has to be free of blemishes. If it has even a single black or white hair on its body, that can't be the one. Plus, you've got a number of other things that would also disqualify it."

The old man moved forward, carefully placing two more logs on the fire, sending a plume of sparks into the night.

"This type of pure-colored, red heifer is so rare, only nine are mentioned in the Old Testament." Seeing Rig's look of incredulity, the elder added, "Remember, as a comparative religion professor, I gotta be familiar with a lot of other folks' thinkin'. Anyway, it was written in the white man's Bible that three years after this tenth red heifer is born, only then is it ready to be sacrificed. And with this last ingredient, the temple can be rebuilt. Once that's completed, your medicine man will reappear."

The elder laughed and shared his Indian perspective with a slight dig. "You know the main difference between the white man and the red man?...You kill your medicine people; we hold ours as somethin' special." Pausing to see their responses, he barely missed a beat. "But as I was sayin', no pure red heifer has been born in the last 2,000 years...that is, until this year."

Aware of most of what was said, Lyra hung back, allowing Rig to ask questions. "Then what's this about a white buffalo?"

"Ahh...that took place long, long ago, during a period when the Lakota were starving. As a last resort, Chief Standing Hollow Horn sent out two young men. It was understood that if they didn't come back soon with news about finding buffalo, everyone back at camp soon would die. Several days passed. Seeing nothin', the scouts became pretty discouraged. Until from far away, they glimpsed somethin'—a lone figure. As it came closer, the braves realized that the being wasn't walkin'. It was floatin'. At that moment, they knew that whatever it was, it was w*akan*—what you would call 'sacred.' Gettin' closer, each thought she was the most beautiful woman either had ever seen."

Looking directly at Rig, and giving a penetrating glare, Grandpa continued, "One man was impure of heart and said, 'She's alone, and we're strong. Let's go down and have her.' The second replied, 'Can't you see she is *wakan*? That would be a wrong thing to do.' But the first went anyway. Walkin' up to *Pte San Win*-in your language, White Buffalo Woman—a cloud appeared out of nowhere and engulfed them both."

Roger, beside himself, bursts in, "What happened, Grandpa? What happened then?"

"A few minutes later, when the mist lifted, there she stood—a pile of bleached bones at her feet. Comin' toward the second man, she said, *'Have no fear. You recognized me as wakan. The Creator has sent me to bring good news to your people. Assemble everyone. I will come again in four days.'* She then disappeared into the air."

More excited than ever, the boy from South Los Angeles couldn't contain himself. "Then what?"

"On the day she promised, Pte San Win reappeared. Comin' to the camp, she presented Buffalo Standing Upright with a special pipe. And from that day on, he and then his offspring have been that cannupa's hereditary keepers. All other ceremonial pipes are linked to, and get their power from it. Even now, this very pipe is watched over and guarded by the Looking Horse Family, up at Green Grass on the Cheyenne River Reservation."

"So what happen' to White Buffalo Woman?" asks Roger, excitedly.

"She instructed the Lakota in the Seven Sacred Rituals. Then, somethin' even stranger happened. After passin' on this wisdom from Tunkasila, she rolled around in the dust. As the cloud cleared, everyone saw she had turned into a buffalo. But when Pte San Win shook the dirt off, her coat became as white as snow. Then, walkin' a little farther away, she rolled once more in the dirt. This time, though, she stayed brown as they look today. And as my people watched, she simply vanished."

"How does that fit in with this thing you mentioned about a red heifer?" Rig asked.

"Pte San Win said that when the sacred white buffalo reappears, it will be the beginnin' of a great Earth purification or 'cleansing,' as many of you white folks call it. And this calf has just been born. In fact, medicine people from all over the planet have had visions of this story…thousands of years before it happened. Even the *Egyptian Book of the Dead* backs up the truth I have spoken. I think in Chapter 84 it says, *'And when she promised to return again, she made some prophecies… One of those was that the birth of a white buffalo calf would be a sign that it would be near the time when she would come again to purify the world.'*

"Like I said," the elder went on, "we Indians have a whole lot of visions comin' true right about now—such as the leaves on the trees turnin' brown and the weather changin'. Yet the white man can't seem to put two and two together."

Stopping a moment while intently listening to the heavens, the Lakota concluded, "But that's enough for tonight. Just remember—*prayer can overcome all these problems."* Grandpa George finished his talk with the words, "Ho. Hece tu yelo; mitakueye oyas'in," which loosely translates: *"I have spoken. I acknowledge the oneness in all things. Amen."*

CHAPTER XXI

THE NEW WORLD ORDER

Lyra," Rig whispered, "I've got to go for a couple of hours."

"Why? Where? It's was almost ten o'clock. What's so important you have to leave?"

King was adamant. "If all you're saying is true, and I believe it is, I have to see a friend, Father Dunois. He might be helpful."

"A priest? What can he do?"

"He's the head of the abbey over in Boyington Canyon—Abbaye de la Rose."

"I've heard of it. Besides an abbey, it's a healing retreat, where world leaders go to recharge. So what are you thinking?"

"If I can just show the artifacts we found in the cave, the father might accept this whole global, alien-takeover thing. Maybe he can convince some of these foreign heads of state about what's really happening."

"It's worth a try. I'm coming too."

Without telling Grandpa George and Roger where they were headed, Rig abruptly announced they'd be back in a few hours. Delicately, in his gentle nuanced way of communicating, the Indian advised against it. To the stubborn Anglo, the Lakota's veiled warning didn't make sense. The only problem King could foresee is that the car could be spotted by the police. Even so, with the potential salvation of Earth at stake, he saw no other option.

Driving toward Cottonwood on Highway 89A, Lyra's companion mused about his concerns. "You know, I used only to be worried about the IRS and/or angering one of my Mafia clients. Now it is saving the world, alien assassins, Earth changes, and that I'm charged with murder." Taking in a deep breath, the ex-broker sighed in disbelief."

Scribbling notes, the extraterrestrial glanced up. "Welcome to the club, earthling."

Nestled in a secluded pocket of the canyon, Abbaye de la Rose sat over a major vortex. World famous since the '50s for its healing energies and natural spa, this had been a quiet retreat for the politically powerful and ultra-wealthy seeking secluded respite from life's daily grind. "The Monk House," as it was called by locals, consisted of an imposing three-story stone structure. Its high walls wrapped around a large private courtyard within which were peaceful pathways, a bubbling fountain, a shed for animals, and a small, obviously fussed-over flower garden. Beyond the enclosure, and adding to the Abbey's financial independence, were rolling acres of well-pruned grape, olive, and citrus groves.

As it was closed to the outside world, only a chosen few were allowed to pass through these massive twelve-foot-high oaken doors. The general public was welcome only as far as the parking lot, which was open all hours of the day and night. From here, tourists hiked the trails, and communed with nature throughout the canyon. But regardless of the spiritual beauty of the surrounding hills and forest, it was inside these cloistered ramparts that deep prayer and meditation were experienced.

The good father and his worldly friend had met several years ago while flying back to Phoenix from New York. Bored, Rig happened to strike up a conversation with the person in the next seat. It was one of those chance meetings where one immediately feels a strong, resonating bond with the other. And while Father Dunois offered the young Phoenician a standing invitation to spend several days at the abbey, it was never quite the ex-stockbroker's idea of Club Med. Both exchanged correspondence for a while. But due to his busy, Wall Street-playboy lifestyle, Rig's letter-writing eventually dwindled, then stopped altogether.

As they arrived, the abbey appeared void of activity. Unknown to the two, the brothers had left their individual cells and were congregating in the chapel for the evening service. Following strict rules, guests had retired early and were requested to remain in their rooms until dawn. Thus, Rigden King's thunderous knocking, using the large metal ring on the doors, went unanswered. Seeking an alternate entrance, the pair tracked along the courtyard wall, finally coming to a door left ajar through which animals were taken to and from the groves. Moving across the square behind the main building, they entered the basement. The room was dimly lit; a solitary, dangling light bulb cast disquieting shadows.

Except for eight or ten tables, the area was empty. Oddly out of place in such a spiritual setting, on each of the tables were positioned several taxidermied animals.

"Rig, what's this?"

Rocked by the gruesome scene, he said, "Dunno. Can't understand why they're stuffed this way. It's kind of freaky, if you ask me."

Both saw, of the twenty or more animals on display, none was a duplicate—each was grotesquely mounted, mouth gaping and teeth bared, poised as if to attack. Even a small squirrel was frozen in a bizarre, crazed stance, standing on its hind legs, paws in some sort of fight or flight stance. Needle-sharp teeth looked ready to rip into any adversary. And although all had glass eyes, the twisted terror on each face was unnerving.

In a quivering tone, Lyra said, "I'm scared. This doesn't feel right."

Rig tried masking his fear. Patting a frozen wolverine on the head, he murmured, "Toto, I have a feeling we're not in Kansas anymore."

His companion looked over, shooting him one of those stares. Apprehension in her voice was evident. "I wish you'd get serious. Something is definitely wrong here. The vibration in this room is pure evil."

"Weird, yes. Evil? I don't think so. You're too paranoid."

"Rig…just because I'm paranoid doesn't mean they aren't after you. Caution's what keeps me alive."

"Okay, okay. Let's go find Father Dunois. He can answer your questions about whatever these animals are about. C'mon."

Up the stairs to the main hall, they came upon two rows of pictures detailing the abbey's hierarchy. Below each was a brass plaque bearing a name and minor information. Some showed the person had been transferred to another abbey; two carried the notation "deceased." Father Daniel Dunois was one of them. Next to him hung a photo of the current head, Abbot Helmut Groth.

The tiled corridors and stuccoed walls magnified the slightest sound as the two tiptoed past the last picture. Rig whispered, "I guess we've got to find this Groth guy. Maybe he can help us."

"Which way?" her voice quavered.

"Probably in the chapel, but I don't know where that is. Look, if we just wait, someone's bound to come along sooner or later."

Nervousness mounting, the alien insisted, "I don't like it here. I'm not standing around. Let's keep going. Maybe we'll get lucky."

Down another hall and around a bend, they heard two voices. As the intruders approached, the conversation became clearer. The rich, resonating tone of the one standing carried the sound of authority. "Helmut, you knew your responsibility when accepting this post."

"But I wasn't told it included genocide. That, I…I can't do."

More loudly, the authority barked, "*But you already have!* Remember your oath to the New World Order? Realize that any, and I do mean *any* form of disruption will not be tolerated. We must keep to our schedule."

Shocked at what they were hearing, the uninviteds crept closer. Peering through the door-crack into the abbot's office, they made out a man sitting behind a desk. A few feet away, another, wearing an identical brown cassock, paced the stone floor, his face hidden by a cowl.

The walking figure continued speaking. "And now that the ten most important European nations have been added to our crown, we are forming a similar cell in Asia. Oh, what is that most sublime quote in your Biblical chapter, *The Book of Revelation*? Ahhh, yes! *'And behold a great red dragon, having seven heads and ten horns and seven crowns upon his head.'*" He laughed. "These fools don't even pay attention to their own literature. This is the expanded European Economic Community, and no one suspects. Now we finally have global unity, especially with the marriage of North and South America, at least in an economic sense. But that's just stage one. With our one-world currency, the computer chip, and the RFID tags, we will have total contro...."

Breaking in, the seated figure became adamant. "Golan, we cannot! All this need not be accomplished through mass murder."

"*We can and...you will!*" came the reply, with booming force. "Besides, most of these people are sure to starve to death anyway. We must have total planetary rule prior to the tectonic plate movements and Earth flip in 2012. You knew that."

The abbot sighed. "Yes. I...I thought I could be a part of this, but...."

Golan's anger grew. "There is no *but!* You swore allegiance to the Empire. In return, you're being crowned 'Holy Eminence' over the SG2 upon the Master's coronation. What *more* could you possibly want?"

"True, but I had no idea I'd be personally involved in putting people to death."

Adopting a more conciliatory tone, the standing being responded, "*My dear, dear Helmut,* you are not putting them to death! You are simply a witness to their preordained demise."

The seated clergyman's voice rose as he slammed his fist down on the desk. "*Simply?!* You say, simply? I'm *simply* helping the Master and his entourage brainwash world leaders, while we prepare the people of this planet for slaughter. *Don't whitewash it*! There are going to be more floods, starvation, riots... and...and never mind terrorist attacks! I've helped you pass along a massive lie—convincing heads of state that I've received a divine revelation that the big asteroid will somehow miss." The seated man cries in anguish, "*Mein Gott in Himmel!* My...my hands, Golan. They're covered in blood!"

Skilled in diplomacy, the commanding voice now took a softer approach. "You know, Helmut, you may have a point there. Perhaps we *have* been a bit too harsh. I'm sure…yes, I am certain we can work out something more suited to your personality—something that will still enable you to be High Prefect over the Pan-American block.

"Let's move past this to a more pressing topic. Tonight's arrival—it's a day early. We just received a communiqué. Congressman Lohse's replacement essence is on its way from the Four Corners base—coming via the subterranean shuttle." Golan paused, pondering. "You know, it fascinates me. Over the last three days, this politician has been remarkably resistant to our imprinting, and that's strange. Normally, government representatives aren't so strong-willed that we're forced to perform soul-switching."

The abbot wasn't listening as he blurted, *"I can't go through with this anymore!* I just can't."

"My dear Helmut, you know the situation. A preprogrammed anima replacement is our *only* alternative. And since his physical presence needs to be in Washington as a key vote for the *In God We Trust/Intelligent Design Bill*, substitution must be now…tonight!"

"No, I won't do it!"

"*Helmut, Helmut, Helmut!* Calm yourself; you're getting all worked up. I'm only asking, regardless of how repugnant you may find these present duties, that you keep focused on your task. Think about the myriad of spiritual rewards our Master has in store for you. Here, examine these new operating directives, along with additional tunnel routes to our base under Taos. That's where we'll be relocating the Southwest headquarters."

"You know," the standing figure continued, chortling, "our joint tunneling effort with the military over there drove some of those people nearly crazy—named the noise 'the Taos hum.' Vibrations from digging even caused many overly sensitive souls to get nauseated. Surprisingly, some of those weaklings were so affected they had nosebleeds. And with this particular passage now being extended past Kokomo, Indiana, a good number of those residents are having the same problems. Odd how earthlings don't catch on; they're such a stupid lot… Excuse me—present company excluded.

"Anyway, dear brother, take a moment to look these over. I'll answer any questions," he said, while handing the monk a stack of papers for inspection and signature.

"Time is of the essence," the standing figure casually added. "We have to be quick in transferring the congressman's life-force. With neutrino instability, no delay can be countenanced while the soul is being switched into the bio-nucleonic matrix. But I suppose you know all that."

He again began to chuckle. "Strange, isn't it, Helmut? Your film *Invasion of the Body Snatchers* was actually prophetic. Only we don't need to wait for our subjects to fall asleep; mind-control and soul-switching are ever so much faster. Not to mention, we can do it in large groups."

"Golan, you never told me what you do with the captured souls."

"We give them to the Master for his pleasure. My friend, your mind is wandering. Surely you knew that."

"Yes…yes, I suppose I did," the abbot groaned.

While the authoritative being talked convivially, he nonchalantly ambled past the abbot to a window facing the semi-lit courtyard. Maintaining the conversation at a less aggressive level, Golan pivoted slowly, positioning himself directly behind the desk. Silently, an eight-inch metal spike sprang from beneath his wrist. With lightning speed, moving in an arc, it was destined to sink into its victim's temple. The result should be a swift, relatively painless death. At this exact moment, however, the monk unfortunately turned to ask one last question. Unable to stop, the shaft missed its mark, sinking deeply into, and collapsing, the man's left eye.

A muffled scream filled the thick, walnut-paneled room—unheard by the abbey's residents, whose loud Gregorian chant reverberated down long corridors. In excruciating pain, the victim staggered to his feet. Swaying, he stumbled backward. A hand covered the empty socket in his face. Outclassed by one trained in killing, the father's only hope to defend himself was with a long pearl-handled letter opener on the desk. A lamp and papers fell to the floor as the monk's clawing fingers inched toward the knife. An unfortunate move shoved it…a hairs-breadth beyond his grasp. If he could bridge this normally insignificant gap, it would determine whether he lived or died. Fingernails half ripped out, the abbot continued raking the desk's wooden surface, desperately seeking traction. Locked in combat, they rolled off the writing area. Landing with a thud on the rock hard floor, the vibrant but thin Persian carpet gave scant cushioning. The cowl of the assailant dropped, partially revealing a head identical to one Rig and Lyra saw on the cave mural.

As the wounded man, insane with fear, twisted and kicked, the DAK sank razor sharp teeth into his victim's throat. Gnawing at the windpipe, it ripped out the carotid artery. The father's mouth moved to scream, but there was no longer a path for air to channel sound. The wild expression of terror on his face showed he was still alive…barely. Pinned to the arabesque-patterned rug, his remaining eye watched helplessly as a stream of blood spurted from his neck with each beat of his heart. A thin pink line exited the corner of the dying man's quivering mouth. His legs, thrashing, ceased their movement as the human's soul departed.

In startled horror, Lyra recoiled, bumping a table and knocking a vase of flowers to the floor. The DAK looked up. Kneeling over the corpse, his blood-soaked face and flashing eyes stared as if attempting to see through the door.

From the Abbot's paneled chamber, a high-pitched primeval scream sent a wave of goose bumps down the intruders' spines.

Hysterical, white with fear, they ran for the abbey's front door. Unable to work the lock without a key, the pair fled down a side hall. Through a window, they spied a robed figure in the courtyard, hurrying toward the building.

At the top of her voice, Lyra screamed, "*He's one of them! We're no match! We have to get out!*"

"*The only way*," Rig shouted at equal volume, "*is how we came in—past the abbot's office!*"

As if something had changed in the last few seconds and again approaching the double front doors, King illogically took a moment to look for a key, uttering under his breath, "Maybe we should find the group that's singing."

Jerking at his sleeve, the Lyrian begged her companion to keep running, adding, "Even if we could get into the chapel, there must be DAKs there, too."

"You're probably right," he answered, as the flight continued.

Panting hard, she scanned the hall. "Maybe Golan hasn't come out yet. It is our only chance."

Going full tilt, sliding as they attempted rounding another corner, they were relieved to see the way was still clear. Longer-legged, the treasure hunter was first. His partner lagged two paces behind. They'd nearly passed the Abbot's chamber when—

"*Rig!*" Lyra's cry was a piercing mix of terror and desperation.

Skidding to a stop twelve feet away, King spun. Golan had one arm crooked around her throat. The reptile's other wrist, holding its needle-sharp rod, pricked his companion's temple—a drop of blood forming at its steely tip. Barely breathing, Lyra knew that with the slightest movement, the shaft would easily slide through the vulnerable soft spot on the side of her skull.

Highly trained, the Ra representative was fully prepared for self-sacrifice. In a flash of desperation, she contemplated thrusting her head sideways. One move would shove the spike deep into her brain. With her dead, there would be no reason for Rig to hand over the knapsack. Her mind concluded, "It's the only solution." A suicide would leave him free to escape. Resolved, she took one last look at the earthling's face—a mental snapshot to carry on her cosmic journey. Bending her head to the side in a cocking motion, not unlike the way a hammer is pulled back on a pistol, the captive tensed…hoping for a clean thrust. Primed to end her time upon this plane of existence, and with the image of Rig safely tucked away in her heart, she shut her eyes, thinking, *Ready…set…g—*

Golan spoke, causing her to hesitate. "*Hand me that sack, human.* If you don't, I will push this into the Lyrian's skull." His voice lowered as the demand intensified. "*Do it now!*"

The earthling was torn. For the sake of the world, he must escape; but he couldn't leave Lyra. *Regardless,* he realized, *the reptile is reading my thoughts. I have to —*

For a brief moment, the Ra representative decided to postpone death. She made a last-ditch effort to save both her companion and possibly the planet. "*Don't do it!* He'll kill me anyway. *You have to get away. Run!*"

Ignoring her, the treasure hunter advanced…slowly, ever so cautiously, toward the enemy. In doing so, he tried blanking his mind—the way Lyra showed him back at the cave. At this moment, pictures of sex were impossible to conjure. Yet without a plan, the gap was closing far more quickly than King wanted. The enemy stood a scant nine feet away.

"You are stupid, human. Do you really think you can mask your thoughts? You are not strong enough." The lizard broke into some sort of guttural clicking, a form of reptilian laughter.

Failing to hide his scheme forced Rig to take another tact. Edging slowly forward, he went back over the events of the day. Holding the knapsack out in front, he switched to the only memories strong enough to form vivid pictures. On automatic pilot, his mind adrift, he thought of the time he and Lyra stopped for nightfall before heading toward Sedona. Remembering an uncontrollable yearning to lightly brush her lips with his, the floodgates of his memory flung open. Still approaching, he imagined exploring the recesses of her mouth—excitedly probing the slippery, erotic movements of her tongue. Spurred on by recalling the delicate scent of her hair, Rig's memory leapt back—revisiting the softness of her breasts—and envisioning a passionate, wet, well-centered kiss upon a nipple. Thinking of this afternoon, he dredged up thoughts about the pounding of his heart as they sat beneath that tree when he nearly made his move…but lost nerve at that crucial moment. Completely absorbed in this other world, he pulled the knapsack to his chest, pretending it was Lyra's body—feeling her nakedness unfolding in his arms while he imagined his fingers sliding—

"*Give it to me, human*," the DAK ordered, shaking the intruder back to the moment. "*Give it now!* It is good you give this to me. It will make you happy."

"Rig, No! Don't!" Lyra implored, her voice breaking with hysteria.

To keep his thoughts focused, the treasure hunter's gaze fixed on the fullness of his companion's lips. Telepathically picking up what her partner was doing, Lyra kicked the reptile's leg, breaking his concentration and mind-reading capability. Slowly, Rig straightened the arm holding the knapsack. He leaned forward, two fingers slightly unfurling while three grasped the straps that held his fortune.

"One more move like that, Lyrian," Golan barked, *"and you're dead!"*

The reptile, still pinning his captive with one arm, removed the deadly shank from her temple. Reaching toward the earthling, the creature prepared to receive his prize...when back to the moment and with a blurring lunge, King thrust two straight fingers past Lyra's head—each sinking deeply into the lizard's eyes. Blinded, the being screamed, releasing his grip. With a second quick movement, Rig deftly snatched his companion from the clutches of the enemy.

Just then, another alien rounded a corner. Golan, sightless, staggered, claw-like hands covering both eyes. A roar of pain filled the corridor. The intruders took off running. The second adversary was close and gaining. Heading down the stairs, the two jumped several steps, navigated through the basement, out the door, and across the open courtyard. As they reached the gated wall, Lyra slipped through. Before he could follow, Rig felt a compelling urge to look back. The exact instant he spun, a laser blast grazed his shirt, burning a faint line across the cloth. It blew a four-inch hole in the thick wooden door. Had he not been guided to turn, the ray would have found its mark.

Running through the opening he halted, reversed direction, and headed back.

Sensing being alone, Lyra stopped. Alarmed, she made a softened yell. *"Are you crazy?* What are you doing?"

"Here, take these. You drive," he semi-whispered while tossing the keys. Sailing through the air as if in slow motion, they began to arc.

The treasure hunter turned his attention back to the oncoming problem, positioning himself out of sight, next to the open door. Above his own panting, he could hear the pursuing enemy. Using a ploy known to every child, he put one leg out in front of the speeding reptile. The DAK, going top speed, burst through. Caught by surprise, the alien tripped, momentarily taking flight. The creature's face raked across the graveled ground, his body came to rest in a crumpled heap. Its laser weapon, bouncing, stopped slightly beyond an outstretched, motionless hand. King surveyed the twisted form, noticing a crack in the enemy's skull that should keep him out cold for a good, long time.

Elsewhere, the keys had already made their descent. With both her hands cupped for a certain catch, a problem had arisen—or in this case, dropped. One key was angled downward, away from the others. It struck Lyra on her index finger, making the rest vault over her outstretched palms. They hit the ground, skidding, finally coming to rest halfway under the car. She fell to her stomach. Wriggling, the Ra representative frantically attempted to retrieve their only means of flight.

Horrified at their newest predicament, Rig rushed past the sprawled DAK to join in the retrieval. A clawed hand grabbed his ankle. Frozen in its grip, the victim was overcome with fright. Still dizzy, the reptile slowly got up on both knees. Fighting with an effort bordering on insanity, its captive struggled, but to no avail. Sensing that his quarry was physically inferior, the alien warrior paused to gloat. Again came that guttural clicking. With no weapon, Rig's memory flashed on a helpless fly he once saw writhing, trapped in a spider web. He related to the inaudible screams the insect must have made as it waited…waited to be eaten by the slowly advancing enemy.

Still laughing and in a horrible parody of a smile, the DAK revealed two long rows of dagger-like teeth. A flashback of the flailing abbot, then John, flooded King's mind. He imagined these same, saw-like daggers soon ripping at his own unprotected throat. In desperation, the prisoner reversed strategy. Instead of pulling away, he tilted toward his assailant, placing all his weight on the snagged leg. With a massive goal-post kick, he crashed the other boot up under the reptile's chin. Spinning backward, the creature again fell semiconscious to the ground.

Aware of none of this, the Ra representative retrieved the keys and was behind the wheel. Maneuvering around the rear of the car, the earthling glanced back, seeing the enemy kneeling, taking aim. Shaky, the reptile's shot creased the trunk—barely missing the moving target. Jumping into the front seat, Rig shouted, "*Go! Go! Go!*" anticipating a quick, second blast. There wasn't any. Puzzled, the fleeing duo saw a vanload of passengers pulling into the parking lot. This romantic "Night Owl" tour ride was a sales ploy used by many Sedona real estate agents to promote the wonders of owning a Red-Rock Country timeshare. As Rig and Lyra looked on, they observed their cowed enemy slinking into the shadows, through the gate, into the safety of the courtyard.

It took only a split-second glance. Searching each other's eyes, the trespassers reached the same unspoken conclusion. It would be ridiculous to try to convince these tourists that a murdered abbot was part of a plot to rule Earth. Worse yet, this would immediately bring the police who, for reasons of pervasive mind-control programs, could not be trusted. No, they must take this to some person or group outside the manipulation of the Followers of Baal. But who?

Speeding away, they headed to the campground. A mile down the road, tears begin streaming down Lyra's cheeks. Uncontrollable sobbing forced her to pull over.

Taking her hand, Rig tried to comfort. "*Shhhh!* It's okay. It's okay. We've made it."

She stammered, "I…I…I thought he was going to kill you."

"Me? You were the one I was worried about. Come here."

As convulsive waves reduced the young woman to gasping for air, King wrapped her in the protection of his arms. In the softest tone imaginable, he whispered, "*Shhhh, shhhhh.*" Stroking her hair, he pulled her even closer. Gently rocking to and fro, the Phoenician tenderly kissed her on the cheek several times. The crying slowly subsided…until both were jarred back to the moment. Flashing blue and red lights are coming up behind their car.

"*Bastards!* They've alerted the police."

In their taillights, an officer could be seen approaching—one hand deftly unfastening his holstered gun. Standing next to the window, the trooper's flashlight shone directly into their eyes. It swept the inside—first the front, then the back. To King, the being's scowl augured confrontation. The signs were clear; the earthling felt he must kill the DAK, before it killed them.

"Step out of the vehicle!"

"Lyra, don't go! It's a setup!" *Damn it!* he thought, *I visualized something like this happening*.

Rattled, the Ra representative slowly but dutifully got out. Trying to keep his hand movements unseen, the passenger cautiously opened the glove compartment. Taking out the pistol, he set it under some papers beside him. King's thumb released the safety as his index finger stayed wrapped around the trigger.

"Know why I pulled you over, Miss?"

"No, sir."

"Look here. You have a taillight out. Gunna hafta give you a ticket for this. Would you please give me your registration?"

"Oh, it's a rental. I have the contract in the car."

Leaning through the door, Lyra spoke in a quiet voice. "One of the bullets must have hit our taillight. Give me the rental papers."

"Here you are, officer," she said, her eyes refusing to blink.

"I see by your driver's license that you're a long way from home. Visiting?"

"Farther than you know…I mean, farther than is shown on the license. And, yes, I am."

"Hmmmm. I'm just going to give you a warning but you can't drive in the dark without a light. Get to the nearest gas station and get it fixed. By the way, what made that burn mark across your trunk?"

"Ahhh… I backed into a utility pole. One of the cables came down and scorched it."

"That explains the taillight. With that much juice, you're lucky to be alive."

"Yes, sir, I know. We're very thankful."

"Look, I'm letting you go because I don't want you to think Arizona isn't a friendly place. Take care of that light. Immediately."

"Sure thing, officer."

Paperwork completed, the patrolman started to leave. Then he turned back. "Say, Miss, you look like you've been crying. Is everything all right with you and your husband?"

Managing a smile, Lyra responded, "Yes, everything's fine. Thank you for asking, though."

Heading back to the campground, Rig had questions. "Why didn't he run the car's registration through Motor Vehicles? That's the first thing they do when you're stopped. And why didn't he mention anything about the bullet hole?"

A slight smile formed across the alien's face as she answered, "Mind-printing—goes both ways, you know?"

"I'll be darned. Maybe you'll teach me sometime."

"So you can harass every tight-bloused girl on campus? I think not," she smiled.

Turning beet red, King quickly changed the topic. "Hey, it dawns on me, I didn't see any tails on those DAKs at the abbey. Thought you said they all have them."

"They do."

"Well, these two sure didn't."

"You didn't see sunglasses either, did you?"

"Why?"

"Remember, I said if we're trying to fit in with your population and don't anticipate danger, both sides wear contact lenses? As I mentioned, our sight is superior to that of humans. Unfortunately, your light spectrum reduces our perception. We use sunglasses in case of emergencies since they can be removed in a flash. As for the tails, warriors are trained to sacrifice. I suppose those at the abbey had them amputated, so they could wear robes."

"God, if they cut their tails off for that, what else will they do?"

"The SST are the most cruel and ruthless of all the renegade groups. They do whatever's necessary—even self-immolation, if they're caught."

"For real? Why?"

"'*Remain undiscovered; leave no evidence of your existence*,' is their prime directive. To do this, a warrior simply has to press a button and…*Poof!* They go up in flames."

"If they refuse?"

"Their commander does it for them. Say, did you catch the part when Golan was talking about the subterranean shuttle?"

"Yeah, I did. What's that about?"

The alien explained more about the maze of tubes that crisscross the world. The main branches, like the one they just found, went back millions of years. She reminded him of Hopi history; how they escaped underground during the flood and where they emerged when the water receded. The extraterrestrial told that several decades ago, Baal's people gave the U.S. government not only knowledge of the maze's existence, but limited access to certain caves. This was in exchange for allowing the Aryan-SST and the Greys to have underground bases here. Moreover, the extraterrestrials agreed to provide tunneling technology if the military would use it to make additional underground passages. She reminded him that the elite in Washington had been deluded, believing they were creating subterranean cities as havens for themselves and their families when the main cataclysms come. Little did they know the enemy planned to leave them trapped on the surface, using these strictly for themselves.

"Let me get this straight," Rig said as they arrived at the outskirts of Sedona. "Our military digs the tunnels, which they and the Baal-Aryans jointly share, right?"

"The new ones, they do. Remember when you used to see a lot of military convoys and trucks with missiles going down the highway?"

"Of course. Come to think of it, I haven't seen them for an awfully long time."

"Would you believe about sixteen years? The armed forces now move these through these artificial caves to keep foreign spy satellites in the dark. If your people knew that nuclear bombs and chemicals were being transported below their cities and farms, they'd be frightened to death."

"Lyra, tell me about the shifting of the tectonic plates in 2012…oh, and the asteroids."

"I was going to earlier but we got off track." A smile formed.

"What's so funny?"

"Either event is bound to mess up the Chinese's planned nuclear attack on America in 2014."

"*My God!* For real? But we'll retaliate."

"They're counting on it. Your bombs would shrink that country's population by two-thirds. Then with most of the U.S. annihilated, they would walk in, use you as slaves, and become the world's only superpower. *And listen!* Prophecy shows it could happen. That's one reason your government's debt to them has been allowed to go so high. So, even if these other problem countries aren't neutralized, the Beijing situation shouldn't be ignored; it's part of Malek's fall-back strategy."

She continued, "But first things first. As we discussed, global warming is melting the polar ice caps. It became blatantly apparent in 1999, when Antarctica lost that twelve-thousand-square-mile chunk. And it's been getting progressively worse ever since. An even bigger one fell off a couple of days ago. In about ten years, world shorelines and whole nations like Samoa and Bangladesh will be under water, wiped out because of the change in the sea level."

"Guess this is all getting worse than I thought."

"Rig, like I've said, assuming the ice age is delayed several years, the world flooding issue is only a small part of a bigger problem."

The Lyrian predicted this planet wouldn't make it another nine years the way things were going. A rapid decrease of the Earth's magnetism, plus the change in the sea level was forcing a redistribution of weight on the Earth's mantle. That, in turn, was creating an enormous pressure shift. She again warned, if left unchecked, it would buckle the planet's crust. "You'll see a small slippage next year in the Indian Ocean, but the big ones are right behind," she sadly concluded.

"What happens when they slip?"

"Earth's mantle movements have far-reaching effects, such as–and this is forecast to happen in the near future—a massive portion of the Canary Islands will fall into the sea, producing a five-hundred-mile-an-hour tsunami that will be one hundred fifty feet high when it inundates New York and then travels inland over two hundred miles. Ignoring that, geological studies show Earth-pole realignments have produced anomalous flows of volcanic rock, spanning different time periods—some magnetically pointing in one direction, and later found and recorded flowing in the opposite. In other words, the shift of landmass was so violent that the planet's poles reversed themselves—north became south—up became down."

"*Damn*!...oops, sorry. So, the doctor's right?"

"As far as he goes. Don't worry. As your Bible says, a caldera eruption or an asteroid will come first, and within a *twinkling of an eye*. However, our people calculate that when the poles do switch, your planet's rotation will be slightly higher than Kimbrell's calculation—about twenty-seven thousand miles per hour."

"No one could possibly survive that!"

"Close, but not totally true. Depending on how much of a remnant population is left from earlier catastrophes, that lone event will wipe out something like ninety-four percent of your remaining people. As is written, '*The meek,*' meaning the spiritually awakened, '*shall inherit the earth.*'"

Rig's voice began to quiver. "Isn't there anything your people can do to stop this?"

"Why do you think we're here? We've got a whole armada out there trying to keep things stable. So far, so good, but it's becoming increasingly difficult. I don't know how much longer we can be effective."

"Why?"

"We're fighting on two fronts. The Lucifarians in big business and governments are undermining our efforts. They alone hinder us from getting a referendum to stop global warming. That's what's really causing these cataclysmic changes."

The earthling's body trembled. All this brought an immediate recalling of both Kimbrell's and his companion's portents of coming catastrophes. King's voice turned quiet as he again contemplated his own death sentence, as well as extinction for most of the planet. "Lyra…this…this can't be."

"It's happened many times before and will again—soon, if this plate shift isn't stopped. And then, of course, there's the asteroid and the Ice Age. As I said, about eight or nine more years…give or take. Incidentally, you might find it interesting that the Mayan calendar also stops at 2012. Personally, however, I don't see this means the end of civilization. Rather, those who survive will have learned the techniques for switching dimensions, as well as going back and forth in time. The past and future as you understand it will no longer be used as a unit of measure. You'll move on to our standard."

There was a long, low groan.

"Rig, think of it as going metric."

"Think of it? I think I'm going to be sick. That's what I think."

"Normal reaction, but it'd be more helpful if you'd do something proactive."

"Sure, right. Do what? Like I can somehow stop the planet from flipping. Girl, you say the weirdest things. Come on, tell me. What really can be done?"

"That's really why we're trying to ferret out their tunnel systems. Maybe, just maybe, what you found in the cave can be of value in this whole mess. First of all, if you want to help, why don't you start by praying, like Grandpa George suggested? *Ask to be guided to the highest spiritual action—to be in the right place at the proper time…and then be open to doing what's revealed."*

"All right, I'll…I'll give it a try. Lyra, the asteroid or comet everyone keeps mentioning, how does it play into this whole mess?"

"I wondered when you would want to get into that. Few know of the one in 2011, because like the planet Vulcan, it's hidden, coming from the other side of your sun. To give you a picture, I first need to explain its relationship to another cosmic body. We call Planet X—a sphere having an elliptical orbit around the star Epsilon Eridani. Anyway, X isn't your problem: the accompanying space debris is. You see, X has the mass of Jupiter, some eleven times the mass of Earth. As it passes through your asteroid belt, its gravity pulls, or rather piggybacks, mega asteroids—some the size of minor planets. When X reaches its apogee and swings back, the centrifugal force flings these chunks out of its gravitational field—several being catapulted in your direction." The alien's last two points are exceptionally chilling. "By our calculations, most should miss; but the largest…the largest is dead-on. And since it will be coming from the opposite side of the sun, your government will have only a three-month warning—although, based on past performance, I doubt they'll be telling the general public."

"My God!" he bursts. "*How large?"*

"The impact will be fifteen thousand times the force of the bomb dropped on Hiroshima. If you call that big."

"Can you deflect it?" his heart beating at the speed of a hummingbird's wings.

"Slow down. Remember, fear chokes off miracles. As I said, *'no thing'* is un-preventable or unchangeable. We already deflected two back in the '90s, one in 2001, and another last year. So yes, the coming big one may be more complicated, but *the situation can still be handled."*

"What about prayer moving mountains? This is a mountain if ever there was one."

"This time *your* people need to do it—learn to take responsibility and grow up a little…Actually, you can take one of two approaches: Use Art Bell's methodology: get others to help; have them visualize a deflective shield around your planet, as well as telekinetically pushing the asteroid off course. Then see it as done—completed. Or you could do a more complete healing, like Dawn Lambert: anyone, *even those who seem the least capable or worthy*, can refocus, and problems such as these will mysteriously vanish."

"My God! This dwarfs our dinky terrorism situation. And according to you, there isn't going to be a second chance—"

"Rig…."

"*Let me finish*! So, what you're saying is that while we bungle along, your goody-two-shoes council sits back, allowing some rock to cream our planet. That's simply wonderful!" Emotions vented, he simmered down, adding, "Maybe we could guarantee the outcome by doubling up; do both methods."

"*Don't be sarcastic!* And if a person attempts both, they cancel each other; results have to fail. Like matter and antimatter, they act against the other in, I guess you would call it, a sort of prayer-nullification."

"*Look, each method can be used*, just not by the same individual or group. Otherwise, you are working with two contrary belief systems—one asserts something's in existence, and the other claims it's not. The tack you choose all depends upon your spiritual understanding. Any person or group is free to approach the problem using one way, while at the same time a second party can be applying the other.

"However, with the first procedure, the manipulation of substance is not only spiritually lower, it's merely a quick patch; the core issue, the cause, isn't permanently healed, so the situation can and often reoccurs. That technique gives life to 'the lie' by affirming its existence—thereby endowing it with validity—and in some cases, enabling the problem to again, re-manifest in tangible form.

"The second approach, the path on which the illumined Masters walk, affirms that in the *true reality*, as opposed to the illusional world that most people see, *God's perfection is all that can exist.* But be aware: to effectively use this method requires *total humility*. Here you acknowledge not only that there is a single Creator, but that He/She/It is absolutely *omnipresent, omniscient, and dwells only in a state of perfection.* Given these absolutes, or truths, *it is therefore scientifically accurate to say that man must be included within Its indivisible, flawless being. So if God is…existing without error, both we and the I-Am Presence are inseparable—seamlessly blended in a state of perfection.* To see this reality, you simply change focus—looking through the fog of maya, until truth becomes your only picture, or result. *God doesn't get sick, die, need to eat, experience poverty, or have any of what we think of as human limitations. And according to Divine Truth, when we live 'in this world but not of it,' neither do we."*

"Well, since I'm not an 'illumined Master,' I'll go with Option A. This illusion thing seems too complicated."

"Rig, if there is only perfection, and you believe that God is perfect and everywhere, *everyone must already be a Master.* We've just forgotten that fact, me included."

"Lyra, forget the esoteric for a moment. Why aren't our scientists doing something about this asteroid?"

"Their community knows about it."

"But?"

"As I said, the Followers of Baal have gotten Washington and other governments to withhold the information."

"For God's sake, why?"

"Why give a solution? Like artificially created pandemics, this is just one more way for the Illuminati to cull the population. Anyway, you...."

"*Cull*? Sounds like we're being led to the slaughter."

"To the Empire, you are; but that's fine with them."

"Sons a bitches!"

"*Rig, stop it!* I understand your panic, but...."

"*Hell, woman! Cut me some slack!* Give me room to breathe. You've shown me that mankind is about to be annihilated and you're complaining about my language? *Sheeesh*!"

"You really have to get a handle on that anger of yours."

He swallowed hard, as if trying to get rid of that thought before jumping in another direction. "All right. All right. One other point—and I know it was trivial in light of everything else—but I keep wondering about those taxidermied animals. I don't see how they fit into this whole scenario. That was really weird."

"I'm not sure. Although in ritual magic, there's a way of animating stuffed dolls—to make them do your bidding. If I had to guess, I'd say they send them out at night for attack purposes."

"You know, this story just keeps getting weirder and weirder."

The alien asked him to drive while she again went into telepathic communication with her monitor. The answer was not what she'd hoped. Unfortunately, the director would be delayed in Europe for several more days.

"My monitor says not to worry. He will take care of the abbey, in due time."

"How?"

"Oh, within a month or so you will probably read in the papers how it was destroyed by fire during a freak lightning storm—something like that."

As Rig and Lyra continued back to the campsite; Roger and Grandpa George were deep in conversation.

"You don't feel like other boys, do you, Grandson?"

"No. They jes' make fun of me, the way I lean and all. Some of 'em call me the Leaner-Wiener, or the Leaning Weenie. I'm always gettin' into fights 'cause they keep laughin' at me."

"Wanna hear a story?"

"Sure, Grandpa. Sure."

"A long time ago, nearly before anyone can remember, there was another boy, almost like you."

"Whatta ya mean?"

"Had a bad leg and was crippled. Could barely walk. Remember now, back then there were no radios, TVs, or things like that. One of the most important events was when everyone in the camp would come together and dance."

"What were they dancin' for?"

"They were dancin' around the campfire as a way of telling their stories, or just to be happy. They all would join in, except this one boy. His leg was so bad, he couldn't do any of the steps right. Even worse, he couldn't go out huntin' or play the normal games. Every time he'd try, all the other boys and girls would laugh at him."

"Kind'a like me, huh?"

"Umm hmmm. Yep."

"So what happened to him?"

"He was real sad. Had no friends. Everyone stayed away from him. Then one night, he'd had enough. Couldn't stand it no more. So he decided to go out on a hill to fast and pray to the Grandfathers for help. No one saw...."

"Who's the Grandfathers?"

"Like you have the Father, Son, and Holy Ghost, we have Grandfathers; they are ancient beings that make up The Great Mystery, what you call God," the old man explained patiently. "As I was sayin', in the darkness no one saw him slip out of camp. High up he went, climbin' over rocks, around bushes. What would have taken an hour for others to reach the top, took this boy the entire night. Up on the peak, right before dawn, he made a ten-foot circle in the grass, stepped into the center, and vowed not to come out until the Creator gave him an answer or he died."

"Did he? Did he die, Grandpa?"

"It was pretty frightening in that *hocoka*."

"What's a *hocoka*?"

"That's what we call the circle we stand in where we go to fast and pray. So on the third day, he was gettin' dizzy from not havin' any water, let alone food. Bein' all by himself, the nights were real scary. In the dark, he'd hear these sounds comin' toward him. They were the spirits, testin' to see if he would cut and run. They wanted to know if he was worthy of their secrets. Now remember, since his father had died in a raid on the Crows, the boy only had a mother. He knew she would be alone and worried, but he couldn't go on livin' this way. He was determined to stay up there to either get a vision or die tryin'. Day and night he'd stand for hours, prayin' with everything he had in his body. With all his heart, he asked the Creator to either fix his leg or tell him how to live in a good way with nobody makin' fun of him. If neither was to be, he'd take his life. And he meant it."

"What happened?"

"On the fourth day, he was so weak, couldn't stand no more. Sittin' there prayin', he felt a wind come up. Made the grass sway back and forth. Watchin' it for a while, he finally stood up and moved his body to its rhythm. The more he tried, the more he gathered strength. By sundown, he was doin' a strange new type of dance. Satisfied he'd been given an answer, the boy went down the hill and back to camp."

"Bet his momma was happy to see him, huh?"

"Sure was. She called everyone together to celebrate. After givin' away the last of the few prized things she had—that's what Indians do when they are thankful—everyone made plans to celebrate his safe return."

"Why do you give things away?"

"We give our most valuable things away to others who don't have anything. That's one way that we show the Creator our gratitude."

"Oh."

"So after the meal, and as the drum made its sound, the young men and women got up to dance. And so did the boy."

"Wasn't he afraid they'd laugh?"

"No, he'd gained somethin' from the spirits while up on that hill. He now knew who he was and didn't care anymore about what they thought. And as he danced, everyone stopped and stared. Pretty soon, they all sat down and watched him swayin' and stompin' to the beat. There he was in the moonlight, the fire glowin' bright, the drum poundin' its rhythm. He was givin' off a power they'd never seen before. Soon everyone was up tryin' this new step. And they liked it. In fact, we still do it today—the Grass Dance. It was one of those we do to heal our spirit. So through him, the Creator gave us a great gift."

"Wow!"

"You see, Grandson, Wakan Tanka has put somethin' special in each one of us, no matter who you are or how you're made. *To bring it out, all you have to do is ask for that gift to be shown. Then be patient. The waitin'—that's the hard part. It may take years, but it'll come, sooner or later."*

As Rig and Lyra pulled into camp. Grandpa motioned them over. Erasing sacred drawings in the dirt with a stick, the old man didn't look up. In a quiet voice, but one that carried great power, he spoke. "Told ya not to go." With that, the Pine Ridge elder got up and silently gestured for Lyra to follow. They walked into the darkness, beyond the range of the firelight. Sitting on a log by the rippling water, both were silent for a long time, each listening internally as well as externally. Finally the Lakota, pointing to the heavens, asked, "Which one you from?"

Beyond recorded time, Indians had interfaced with extraterrestrials. For Grandpa John George, this was nothing new. In fact, unbeknownst to most whites, many tribes had special songs they sang when hailing UFOs to land.

As they sat, the two talked about the tremendous arrogance and corruption of many elected officials—those who ignore the very people they supposedly serve. They laughed at how these politicians got the government to poke around in outer space, while equally great secrets lay, undiscovered, right here at theirr feet. The Indian recalled when one special-interest group lobbied to send robots off to scour a ridiculously postage-stamp-sized area of Mars. Supposedly, this was to help advance the knowledge of humanity. In truth, many on Capitol Hill secretly worked for companies and use government grants to develop technologies that open new frontiers of profit for their firms, though this went mainly unexposed. With corruption seldom reported on TV or in newspapers, most of today's news media cowered, disclosing only secondary, heavily censored events—ignoring the more important stories.

The old man described a private Washington, D.C., soirée, where partyers' eyes were riveted on a giant screen showing live coverage of that first Mars landing. In a far corner, musicians, dressed in period costumes of the late 1700s, filled the room with a constant stream of classical music. Amidst all the excitement, several of the onlookers momentarily shifted their attention—dipping tiny silver spoons into rounded mounds of caviar that went with their exotic cheese and imported crackers—before returning focus back to the event at hand, and their champagne-sipping colleagues.

Not one of the attendees gave a second thought to the begging homeless person they had passed just an hour before, outside, one story below. As reveries above continued, like some insignificant leaf blown to the ground by the icy winds of winter, the vagrant slumped over in that K Street gutter… dead—an outstretched hand still grasping a half-eaten can of cat food—while snowflakes silently fell, slowly shrouding his dirt-stained corpse. Around the body, the moment contained an awkward, almost holy silence, broken only by the occasional honking of an irate beltway commuter, hurrying along to more pressing matters.

True to Grandpa's word, the spirits kept their promise. The clouds suddenly parted, leaving the moon and stars to shine down upon the sleeping four. Rig and Lyra shared an uncomfortable arrangement—he in the front seat, she in the back. The elder and Roger did better. They sprawled on the treasure hunter's blanket under the night's velvet canopy. The boy had a hard time falling asleep; his mind constantly turned over the wonder of being in the company of a real live Indian. Finally drifting off, he was secure—feeling and smelling the familiar comfort of Toby's body against his face. An arm draped over his closest friend, the little warrior and his companion floated off into Dreamtime.

The first crack of daylight showed Roger standing next to the Lakota, who was offering a prayer to the sun. Often misunderstood by non-Indians, this ceremony is not unlike that of the ancient Egyptians, who saw this celestial body as strictly symbolic—representing the light of the Creator, who erases the darkness of our own thinking. Ironically, ignorant ridicule of "sun worship" often came from those who themselves worship on Sun-Day (from the Old English *Sunnandaeg*, and the Latin *dies solis*, "day of the sun"). So there Grandpa stood, selflessly praying for humility, purity, and the spiritual awakening of all two-leggeds. Finished, the Pine Ridge elder brewed coffee as he listened to the youth talk about his dreams.

"You were right. A bear came to me in my sleep last night."

Nodding in acknowledgment, the Indian stayed silent.

"But I don't know what he said. Stood up on his hind legs and…and spoke stuff I didn't understand. This bear, he lay down in the dirt and rolled around…turning into an Indian—wrinkled, like you. Didn't say nothin' more, but he gave me a braid of grass like the one you light that sends out smoke and smells good. Gave me a feather, too. What's that sposta mean?"

"That's a special dream, Grandson—very special. It was a medicine dream."

"What's a medicine dream?"

"You will know in time, when it's right. For now, you will have to be patient."

When Rig and Lyra finally stirred, Grandpa was on his third cup of coffee, and Roger was eating a banana.

During the drive north, talk focused on helping the boy and the Indian on their way. Negotiating the winding road through Oak Creek Canyon, it was mid-morning when the group unobtrusively slipped into Flagstaff.

Within fifteen minutes of arriving, they located Dr. Gillman's office. At Lyra's urging, Rig decided to use the doctor's advance and spring for two bus tickets—one for Roger and the other for the Sinte Gleska professor.

Coming out of the clinic, the Phoenician looked downcast. Last night Gillman's mother passed away. The chiropractor had already left for California to make funeral arrangements. He wouldn't be back for five days.

Broke, exasperated, and without a plan, King vented his frustration. *"I knew it…I just knew it!* Things were just too damn good to be true. My life's always been like this; the reward is forever getting jerked away at the last minute. *Damn it all!"* Breaking again from his habitually solo decision-making process, he turned to Lyra. "What do you think we should do?"

"Well, we can credit card it a little longer. But I'm almost at my limit. The Foundation will put more into the account when my monitor gets back, but we can't spend too much until then."

Grandpa spoke up. "Told you about my wife's relatives up in the Four Corners area. You can stay there for a couple days."

With no other options, the decision was made; they were off to Canyon de Chelly.

CHAPTER XXII

SENSING

North of Flagstaff, they turned east onto the Navajo Reservation. The area's sixteen million acres straddled Arizona, Utah, Colorado, and New Mexico—home to 160,000 of those who called themselves *Diné*—The People. When scrutinizing their faces, most could easily see the resemblance to Tibetans, thought to have migrated over the Ice Age bridge between Russia and Alaska.

On Highway 264, nearly halfway through this Indian reserve, lay "Hopi Land." Curiously, this second section was an island, completely surrounded by its Navajo neighbors and totally insulated from the outside world. A reservation within a reservation, there was more to this strategic location than met the eye. Hopi elders, believing they descended from Pleiadian colonists, still carried on a sacred obligation—a promise made to the Creator concerning Mother Earth and her inhabitants.

Sharing her knowledge, Lyra explained in ancient times, this tribe made several migrations: some went to the southernmost tip of Latin America; another traveled as far north as the cold and ice would allow; one trek led east to the Atlantic; another west, to the Pacific. In prophecy, the Hopi were told by the Creator to settle where the lines of their migrations intersected—establishing Oraibi, the oldest continually inhabited town in the Western Hemisphere. From that time forward, living on small outcroppings of rocks far back in the desolate desert, these people had observed unchanging sacred traditions. If practiced without the smallest variation, as was taught by the Old Ones, those ritualistic patterns ensured the continuance of life on this planet.

In the Ra representative's opinion, theirs was one of the most difficult and selfless ways of living. Walking a spiritual tightrope, the Hopis maintained a delicate balance between a fast-paced, modern society and what could almost be seen as a monastic existence. With many parts of the world still offering cascading waters and fertile soil, these traditional people, like Atlas, struggled to uphold a covenant made long ago with the God of all beings.

The alien pointed over her shoulder to the southwest—to the sacred San Francisco Peaks, home of the mysterious and very real *kachinas*. Outsiders dismissed these deities as fanciful myths, represented by masks that villagers wore as they enacted ceremonial roles. Yet many reported actual encounters with these beings, who periodically appeared in Hopi villages and whose materializations defied the white man's rationalizations.

Immediately, a different thought about life on Earth ran through Lyra's head. Coming from a homogeneous planet where all people worshiped one way, she asked Grandpa why cultures here had totally unrelated spiritual beliefs. In the case of the Navajo, their deities were the *Yebitsai*. For the Hopi, they were the *kachinas,* overseen by Mausau'u. And like Christians, who believed in the Trinity, each group was exclusionary—ethnocentrically adamant about the singular preeminent existence of their specific god or gods.

Innocently, Roger asked the authority next to him, "Why is that so, Grandpa? I bet you know."

"Good question," responded the old man.

As the elder began his answer, the car continued its monotonous journey. On the long stretch to the Canyon de Chelly National Monument, the four would drive over desolate mesas and across a windswept, seemingly lifeless desert. In all directions, there was little variation in the landscape except for sagebrush, scattered juniper trees, and an occasional antelope. With the windows rolled up and the chilling air conditioner on high, all was quite comfortable. Little did the passengers know that even up until the 1920s, Hopis routinely ran a torturous, sixty-two miles nonstop, from Oraibi to the fertile area of Moenkopi, simply to tend their crops.

Passing time, Lyra was interested in testing the boy's sensitivity. "Say, Roger, do you want to play a game?"

"Sure. What?"

"It's a feeling game."

"How do I play it?"

As Lyra and Roger talked, the old Indian looked intently out the windows, first on his side, then across the backseat through the other. Studied by Toby but unnoticed by the other passengers, the elder steadily scanned the barren land for a presence he sensed but could not see.

"It's easy," Lyra said. "Rig, you can join in too, if you want."

Pretending to be lost in thought, the driver made no reply. He momentarily forgot that Lyra was telepathic and saw through his little sham.

"Rig?"

Less than excited, the ex-Wall Streeter responded with a stretched-out *"Whaaat?"*

"Although we are on the Navajo Reservation, in about five miles we cross into Hopi Land."

"So?"

"Roger, this will be easier for you since you can close your eyes."

With electric attention, the small passenger wanted to get the show on the road. "What am I sposta do?" he bubbled.

"Rig, you with your eyes open, and Roger, with yours shut, I want to see if either of you can feel or...."

Losing his last vestige of patience, King erupted, "Ahh, jeez! You aren't going to want me to do some touchy-feely thing again, are you?" Exasperated and mimicking Desi Arnaz, he said, "Lucy, let me 'splain somethin' to you."

Countering, as if his participation would have little value, Lyra answered, "You don't have to *'splain* anything. Roger and I will play alone."

Saying *No* seemed to be King's automatic response to all that was good in life. It was one reason he was so closed off—unable to easily access his psychic senses or recognize the gifts that Heaven had strewn in his path. But a small part of his languishing soul was beginning to reawaken, enticing him to join in. Always at war, either with others or himself, as usual, he went kicking and complaining all the way.

"Oh hell, I might as well."

In a dry, comedic delivery from the backseat, Grandpa's voice chimed in, "Sure you two aren't married?"

In stony silence, the comment went unchallenged.

"Roger," the alien continued, "try to do two things. First, describe the feelings you get here on the Navajo Reservation. Then, with your eyes closed, I want you to guess when we cross over into the Hopi area."

Full of enthusiasm, the youth had already begun. "Ahhh, what I feel is…is something heavy, maybe angry…no, I guess jus' kind'a heavy…down… sad-like."

His mentor critiqued, "That's good, and now you need to keep your eyes closed and tell me when we cross over into the Hopi Reservation." Turning to the driver, she asked, "What do you feel?"

"It's hard while I'm driving, but you might say I'm getting about the same."

"No peeking; keep those eyes closed so you won't see the welcome sign."

"Yes, ma'am." A minute or two passed as they bumped along, hitting an occasional pothole.

"Hey, Miss Lyra?"

"What?"

"Seems…seems like…like things just got lighter or clearer…No, lighter. It feels real good!"

"*Excellent!* You felt it. We crossed the line into the Hopi portion about a quarter of a mile ago. Mr. King," she jokingly addressed Rig in her most formal tone, "did you feel the difference?"

"I'm not sure."

"What's this game?" the boy wanted to know. "What's it suposta do?"

"Every person and area carries its own vibration. Recognizing them is fun, and can be quite helpful. You should practice feeling the changes."

Roger didn't get it. "Why?"

"Oh, it can keep you safe—warning of places or people where there might be trouble."

The boy further inquired, "So the Navajo place is bad?"

"Not at all. Like the four of us in the car, we all carry a signature with our energy patterns. I just wanted you to feel the difference. Here, take my hand; close your eyes and tell me what you feel."

About a minute passed while the youth attempted to tune into her specific frequency.

"It's sorta…uhh, cool. I like it."

"Right." Mischievously smiling, Lyra suggested, "Now take hold of Mr. King's hand and tell us what you sense. Rig…stick out your hand for Roger."

Not wanting to partake of this hand-holding exhibition, especially with a little kid, the response was a gruff "*What?*"

"Put your arm over the back of your seat so Roger can feel your hand."

He groaned but finally complied.

Startled, the youth dropped the hand and let out a "*Yuuck!*"

Reflexively, the offending appendage was jerked back.

"What did you feel?"

"His hand's prickly. I don't like to hold it like yours."

Grandpa George then offered his.

"Ooooh…aahhh. I like Grandpa's. It's like yours."

Seeing her partner's aura turn an angry crimson, the teacher felt a need to bring diplomacy into the picture. "Roger, Rig's vibration is fine—like nearly everyone else's. It was just that Grandpa and I have been doing spiritual work for so long, we carry a higher frequency."

"How can I get this higher frequency?"

"You can do it, although it takes practice."

"I'll practice."

"I'm sure you will."

Rig's little internal voice squeaked, *Yeech!…Next she'll be wanting me to hug some damn Tree!*

Ignoring the unspoken comment, the alien told the youth he could experiment with this technique when going into a town, a house, or simply the presence of others. She pointed out when he got good enough, he wouldn't have to take a person's hand; he'd only need to think about their name or a location. Delving further, the alien asked if he had ever seen paintings of Biblical characters, like Jesus, Mary, the Apostles, or angles.

"Yep. They're sure dressed funny."

"Did you ever wonder why they have halos around their heads?"

"Yeah! How'd they get 'em?"

The extraterrestrial explained that these were natural electromagnetic fields that surrounded all living things. "Using a little practice, you can see not only colors but fairies, elves, even animals from different dimensions—like unicorns."

"I think I used to see stuff like that when I was little. But my auntie told me I was crazy, that it was the work of the Devil. So I don't see nothin' no more."

"Roger, people are simply afraid of what they don't understand."

"You mean it was not the work of the Devil?"

"Of course not."

"Then I want to be spiritual."

"You already are."

"I am?"

"Sure. Everybody is. It's just that some people know it more than others. You see, if God made everything, then everything must be good."

"Miss Lyra, there's this gang back home. They ain't no good. They be beatin' me up all the time."

"Yes, they are good. They've just forgotten. You simply remember a little more about who you really are than they do. And if you try, you can wake up a lot more of those memories."

The ghetto had taken a harsh toll on such a delicate mind as Roger's. Shaped by pain and disappointment, it had been a long time since he believed life could hold a bigger promise than the poverty and violence he'd known thus far. As all fell silent, the quiet in the car carried an unusual, spiritual peace. Yet the noise in the boy's mind was gleefully loud as he strove to remember the memories to which Lyra was referring.

As they headed east, the asphalt ahead appeared to taper into nothingness—a narrowing black line, disappearing where Earth met sky. At last, a small dot, the famous Bitter Springs trading post, *Tódich'íínii Binaalyéhé Bá Hooghan,* began to appear in the distance. Weary, Rig suggested they stretch their legs and have a look. The others agreed a break would be good.

They pulled in to the gravel parking lot alongside two pickups. Playing outside, a ten-year-old Navajo boy stared as the four passed. Roger said, "Hi," as he walked by. Without missing a beat, the Indian shyly returned the greeting.

Being raised on a reservation, seeing another trading post held no interest for Grandpa John George. He opted to sit on a bench under a tree and continue his attunement—searching for that looming presence of evil.

As the three stepped through the door of the rock-and-mortar building, it was like crossing a portal in time—going back a hundred years in Arizona history. Of course, there were the revolving wire racks with their modern postcards, the candy display and the NCR cash register. Throughout, little was without an assigned role, except for a broken transistor radio that sat uselessly in a corner. Overlaying these haphazard appointments, the place was fogged with a stifling, rancid-meat odor—a pungency to which most visitors quickly adapted—excusing it as something spawned by antiquity.

Adding to the ominous atmosphere, several windows were partially blocked by stacks of dusty merchandise. This cast the room in semi-darkness, forcing the sun to cut zebra patterns out of shadows. When shafts of light did get through, golden beams illumined a haze of countless floating dust particles—swirling, some slowly, others quickly, depending upon the prevailing currents.

Looking around, tourists found the entire store full of curiosities. Against the far wall was a long glass display case, featuring squash-blossom and various other Native jewelry. From the ceiling dangled additional wares: three saddles, several bridles, assorted pots, a tire, and a few hand-woven baskets—more than decoration—a form of currency for many of the locals who transacted by barter.

There was still another aspect—felt by all, recognized by few—the mystical pervasiveness of subtle vibrations left by the hundreds of thousands of tourists who had stopped here over the last century. At different octaves, this mingling of Red and White cultures created an intangible confusion, one that transformed the harmony of this old-time outpost, imbuing it with but yet another unsettling discord.

Easily bored, Roger swiftly made the rounds, quickly deciding what's hot and what's not. He stopped in front of a small toy area, fascinated by a rubber tomahawk. It was a difficult decision; the youth was torn about parting with $3.95 from his meager bankroll for this awesome, once-in-a-lifetime treasure. Wrestling with the choice, the rest of the world became irrelevant until he spotted the "Made in Taiwan" stamp on the other side. Disgusted, he threw it back into the basket, thinking, *Man, everybody's the same. I'm no fool; this is a rip.*

Buying his soda with money Lyra gave him, the youth went outside to talk with the other boy. Spotting the child throwing rocks across the road, trying to hit a stick on the far side, Roger thrust his Pepsi straight out at arm's length, asking, "Wanna sip?" The response was an immediate, but shy, "Okay." Taking turns drinking, the Indian offered three stones for the visitor to try his aim. And so, a brief friendship began.

As Rig and Lyra wandered the store, the boy's parents and the Navajo shopkeeper and his morbidly obese wife were embroiled in a heated discussion. Ever observant, the Ra representative took special notice of the traditional costumes of the man and woman behind the counter. Bound with a headband, the clerk's hair was fashioned in a bun style unique to his people. His helper had on a brilliant, blood-red velvet blouse and equally colorful emerald green skirt. Both were overly adorned with turquoise jewelry. Huddled in conversation, all four ceased talking as soon as the intruders were spotted. Except for creaking wooden floorboards as the outsiders walked, the trading post turned graveyard silent. The alien sensed a growing discomfort, as eight eyes followed her and her companion's every move.

Edging over, whispering to Rig in a low tone, she said, "I don't like it here. We should go."

Entranced by old artifacts, the treasure hunter's imagination had been transported, wandering somewhere in the 1850s. Absorbed in a fantasy, her urgings sounded far away, reaching him as if through a long tube.

"Mmmmm, give me a minute," he mumbled, as if to himself. "Man, this antique bow and arrow set is really neat. Wish I had one."

"Rig, something isn't right. We need to go—*immediately*!"

"All right, all right. Just let me pay for these sodas and this jerky."

Dragging his right leg, the man behind the counter limped as he squeezed past his spouse. At the cash register, the Indian leaned forward to get a closer look into the eyes of this white man. Not wanting to leave without her companion, Lyra stood impatiently at the door. Looking up, the Phoenician was mildly shocked by the seemingly intense hatred that all four Navajos were projecting.

*Lord! You'd think they'd never seen an Anglo befor*e. The mind conversation continued with, *Hey guys, war's over. You lost—get over it!*

The shopkeeper leveled a fixed, malevolent glare at his customer. The look of evil was so forceful that King took an involuntary step backward. The Indian seemed to be staring past Rig's eyes—and similar to what Kassandra did at the gas station, somehow probed the unprotected recesses of his soul. A shiver ran down the Phoenician's spine as he thought, *This is not good!*

"Eight eighty-five," the merchant lisped, having difficulty forming his words.

Awkwardly trying to break the intensity of the daggered look, the buyer commented, "Nasty limp you got there."

The man smiled, although his anger radiated so strongly that even Rig picked it up through the façade. The shopkeeper replied, "Got shot in the hip."

"Sorry to hear that, pardner. Hunting accident?"

"Sorta," he answered, still smiling. Reaching below the counter, the Indian pulled out a box which he held out. "Want some Navajo cookies? They're special."

The almost tangible loathing coming from all four canceled any sweet tooth the city dweller might normally have. "I'm sure they are, but thank you, no."

The man's insincere smile faded, leaving a blank, unreadable expression.

Lyra came over and tugged at her companion's shirt. "*We've got to go! Now!*"

Grateful for the intrusion, her companion replied, "Okay, okay. Yeah, we've got to go. Nice meetin' ya."

Several paces behind her, he stopped to take one last quick look at the bow and arrows.

The shopkeeper called out, "Storm's a-comin'. Where ya'll headed?"

As the ex-broker pushed open the door, without thought and as a matter of civility he replied, "Canyon de Chelly."

Outside, Lyra was more than a little nervous. "Their auras!" she gasped. "They were black! Come on, we've got to get out of here; something's not right."

Coming up to their car, Rig quietly reached through Roger's rolled-down window and handed Toby a bit of jerky—a peace offering for the four-legged warrior.

Racing down the highway, they came to Intersection 191, the road to Chinle, and ultimately, Canyon de Chelly. Grandpa glanced skyward, spotting a lone red-tailed hawk. It flew counterclockwise—an ominous sign. To the Lakota, all good things in creation moved clockwise. Anything in the opposite direction was contrary to the rhythm of the universe.

CHAPTER XXIII

THE HIGHEST LAW

At Canyon de Chelly National Park, there were fifty-eight Indian families still adhering to the old ways—tilling the land, raising sheep. Because this is an undisturbed microcosm of how life used to be in this region, nonresidents were prohibited from entering unescorted and without a proper park permit. As the four pulled up to the entrance, they were met by a lone Navajo, one of John George's wife's relatives, Vincent Begaye.

"Hey, there's Vince," says Grandpa. "He's waitin' for us."

Rig couldn't fathom the synchronicity; it seemed that without a phone, for Vincent Begaye to be here at this exact moment was beyond even Las Vegas luck. In a quandary, the Phoenician asked the elder, "How'd he know we'd be here?"

"Indian telephone," answered the old man, with that slight hint of a grin.

Native Americans tended to relate to other Indians as extended family members, often calling them by names such as Nephew, Grandson, or Granddaughter. Vincent, however, greeted his Northern relative more formally with the honorific title, Tunkasila. Under normal conditions, the Navajo would have adopted the more casual Lakota custom and said, "*Hau kola....*" Hello, friend," or "Hello, Uncle." But this was no ordinary visit. Such an elevated form of protocol came as no surprise to the elder; spirits told him to expect trouble.

As introductions were being made, Begaye's face was furrowed, betraying a deep concern. With little extraneous conversation, the professor transferred vehicles and left in their host's pickup. Rig, Lyra, Roger, and Toby followed.

Passing the ranger station, the Ra representative looked up. She noticed the sky had become divided into three parts, typical for this time of year. To the west, a sinking sun dipped below a nearly transparent bank of sherbet-orange clouds. Unbound, their colors stretched outward, melting into a delicate raspberry hue before trailing off into mauve. Overhead was clear except for a few white puffs, magically suspended by the illusionary laws of physics. But from the east came a mountainous, billowing wall—an ominous embankment of cumulonimbus. To the three outsiders, all seemed in order. Only the old Lakota and his southern relative could sense distant rumblings—the forebodings of a storm brought on by the terrifying *Wakinyan,* Thunder-Beings.

Diverging from Canyon de Chelly was the lesser-known Canyon de Muerto, "Canyon of Death." Merging at one end, the two small valleys joined, forming a giant "V." Within these canyon walls lay an almost mystical stillness. One could easily feel being pulled back to the way things were a thousand years ago. In contrast, the outside world was a deafening cacophony, numbing senses by the incessant honking, pounding, and barking of daily life. But in the cradle of these two narrow gorges, a peaceful realm continued.

Taking the left fork, both the pickup and car headed into the shadows of...Canyon de Muerto.

Rising high above the floor, steep salmon-colored sandstone cliffs stood as sentinels—mute witnesses to a bloody and sometimes cannibalistic history. Splashed over the sides of these rocky rims were dark varnish-like streaks, where rivulets of rain ran down during the stormy season. In stark contrast, the dour canyon walls gazed upon peaceful patches of wildflowers, circled by groves of juniper and cottonwood, whose leaves would soon be turning gold in the coming autumn winds.

Glancing out the window, Lyra furrowed her brow. Considering her origin and many exploits, most would assume the alien warrior had cold resolve pumping through her veins. True, and not; as with Joan of Arc, fortitude and caution often co-exist. Beware of those who do not exhibit the latter. As the old saying goes, *Danger and idiots keep company with the man who knows not fear.* And at this moment, feeling antlike in size beneath the towering canyon walls, Lyra took comfort in the words of the Bible's Twenty 23rd Psalm, *Yea, though I walk through the valley of the shadow of death....*

As they proceeded, the extraterrestrial got an intuitive tingling. At one time or another, most of us have felt a similar sensation, something that irritated our solar plexus—that 'gut feeling' people talk about. The farther one goes into these canyon passes, the more one comes to realize this is trespassing over sacred ground. Warned by whispers of the Ancient Ones, visitors knew that to disturb even the smallest thing could cause grave repercussions. That's why nearly everyone who journeyed here reported an unshakable conviction: This place was guarded by invisible spirits, beings that hid just beyond one's view, darting from rock to tree to arroyo. Mysterious and occasionally malevolent, these powerful forces, while often perceived from the corner of one's eye, almost always instantly dematerialized when viewed directly. But to confirm their presence, all one had to do was break a taboo.

Vincent and Grandpa bounced along the dusty road past the Antelope House Ruin, finally arriving at the Begaye hogan.

Their hosts' dwelling was a simple, eight-sided dome, which, by tradition, its door faced east. Inside was a single dirt-floor room designed for living as well as ceremonial purposes. Two small windows shed light on a cast-iron woodstove, two beds, a table, and a pair of chairs against the wall. Cramped quarters for a family of four, there was no room for the myriad furnishings, appliances, and gewgaws that most of modern society felt as absolute necessities.

Alongside the hogan was a corral with sheep that Vincent, his wife Debbie, and their two sons, Cody and Billy, counted on as a central source of income. But they didn't measure riches in these animals or in their small farmed plot across the shallow creek. For them, true wealth was 'walking in balance'—a delicate equilibrium in which every aspect of life blended in harmony with one's spiritual path. Maintaining this focal point at the center of creation's movement was their sole objective—their divine purpose in being.

By the time Rig, Lyra, Roger, and the four-legged one arrived, Vincent Begaye was emerging from the dwelling, flanked by his wife Debbie and their eldest son Cody. Grandpa stood near the pickup as Vincent approached. Briefly exchanging words, the Lakota extended both hands to the Navajo, palms up. The elder Begaye, holding something small, started to place the object into the old man's open hands. But no, Grandpa's fingers closed, indicating rejection. Still facing each other, Vincent pulled the gift back, returning it to rest against his chest. Once more the Navajo extended his offering to the Pine Ridge elder's reopened palms. The Lakota's hands again folded inward, indicating for a second time that the gift was refused. As this is transpiring, Grandpa John George looked away. His head was cocked upward. Eyes were shut. He stood silent, as if listening to unseen voices. Only when the ritual was repeated a fourth time did the South Dakota visitor accept the precious offering—a lone cigarette.

Of itself, the gift was insignificant. It was the tobacco inside that was important. From before recorded time, this herb had been used by Indians in all forms of spiritual ceremonies. It was so venerated that, should even a shred drop when filling a medicine pipe, many would not continue the prayer for fear their sloppiness might offend the Creator. By such mental intent over thousands of years, literally billions of these ceremonies had imbued tobacco with the living essence of a sacred, powerful, spiritual helper.

What just transpired was one way a traditional Lakota medicine person accepted or rejected a formal request for assistance. In this case, it was the healing of Billy, the Begayes' younger son. He'd come down with the hantavirus, which, along with black plague, was quite prevalent in the Four Corners area. Three days ago, the younger brother and Cody were bringing the sheep back from grazing when the six-year-old collapsed. Suffering a hundred-and-five-degree temperature, shaking with violent convulsions, the boy was all but assured of meeting death within the next twenty hours. The youth's only hope was the sacred *Yuwipi* ceremony, just agreed to be performed by Vincent's South Dakota guest.

Grandpa George—as well as many other medicine men and women—often healed diseases that the mainstream medical establishment insisted were incurable. Even so, detractors never failed to point to the many unsolved illnesses currently rampaging through Indian reservations. While overlooking even greater numbers of iatrogenic deaths in city hospitals, their allegation was yet an undeniable, albeit prejudiced, fact.

In truth, however, the secret to any healing lay not in what the afflicted person superficially wants, but rather in what his or her spirit really desires. Frequently, while we consciously wish for a cure, our divine aspect or soul employs that sickness as a burden meant to teach a lesson—to awaken. For when the outward self, as well as the inward spirit, feels the healing is in that person's highest interest, *there is no picture of disease that cannot be quickly erased.*

Tobacco offering accepted, the medicine man began preparation for the ancient ceremony. Normally, most major Lakota rituals started with a mind/body purification using the sweat lodge. Due to the boy's critical state, speed was imperative; today, this traditional step must be omitted.

Like an anthill under siege, the Begaye household sprang to life—each person carrying out a specific function. In his role as a Yuwipi man, Grandpa orchestrated every facet of activity. Nothing was left to chance. Even seemingly insignificant details had to be performed with utmost exactitude. As a first order, he instructed Rig, Lyra, and Roger to carry all the furniture outside, leaving the hogan as bare as possible. Next, Vincent and Cody were sent to gather a large amount of sage. Spread over the dwelling's earthen floor, the herb both drove out, as well as prevented the reentering of any maleficent spirits.

To further ensure success, the room must be totally devoid of light—blacker than black. For this, Debbie nailed blankets over the windows and door. Consummate care was taken to prevent penetration by even a single ray. Next, she began preparing a dinner for afterwards—a traditional way of thanking the spirits as well as Grandpa.

Fortunately, Billy's mother just finished what the Lakota refer to as her moon, or period of menses. For in this religion, a menstruating woman would not only be excluded from all ceremonies, but even the casual touching of a medicine man's accouterments. This was not considered a period of uncleanliness as it was in many cultures, but rather a time in her cycle when a woman's psychic senses were uncontrollably powerful. When "in her moon," a female's presence at a ceremony, however well intended, could be unintentionally disruptive. With this unleashed force, even her slightest handling of a healer's belongings could unbalance their vibrational attunement—a spiritual level of effectiveness—that might have taken years to attain. Therefore, rather than being repugnant, the Lakota felt this was a special time—one to be honored, yet balanced with respectful caution.

Preparations were now complete. The furniture was out, sage spread, the room darkened. One by one, the group began to come inside. Before going through the door, Grandpa asked everyone to remove their shoes and boots—a gesture of humility.

"Man comes to this Earth naked and humble—without pretense," he explained. "And that's how *Wankan Tanka* should be approached."

Anticipation of hope, mixed with fear, created a strange atmosphere of nervous tension. In the blackness, pupils dilated as they adjusted to the absence of light. Standing frozen, no one made a sound except for the medicine man, who moved in the inky darkness with inexplicable ease. A faint pop, followed by a swooshing sound, preceded the blinding flame of a match that showed a lantern being lit. As people shifted positions, silhouettes started their dance around the walls.

Normally, this ceremony required males to sit on one side of the room and females on the other. A Yuwipi man, however, was allowed to mold nuances of a ritual according to instruction from the spirits. In Grandpa's case, all were told to sit as they would, backs against a wall, except for Billy, who was placed on a blanket next to his mother.

At a specific point, participants were usually allowed to ask questions of the ethereal helpers. Tonight, due to the severity of the situation and shortness of time, Grandpa George said that he alone would speak.

"Regardless of what anyone sees or hears," the elder warned, "no talking or getting up. Vincent is the only one with permission to move about."

Next, the *hocoka*, or sacred circle, had to be established. Into this were placed seven three-pound coffee cans—which the Begayes have accumulated over the years as storage containers—half-filled with dirt. Into each cylinder was inserted a willow stick, to which was tied a flag and a colored tobacco tie—all representing specific directions of the universe. Using mole dirt, eagle feathers, the tail of a black-tailed deer, and other sacred items, the old man started to create an altar.

To let the spirits know that those in attendance were believers, everyone placed a sprig of sage behind their right ear. All were sternly warned that should just one attendee harbor even the smallest doubt, the ritual would be ineffective. Grandpa went on to state these beings were powerful, and could create harm as well as good. In numerous cases, those who have disbelieved or intentionally disrupted a *Yuwipi* ceremony have literally been picked up by some invisible force and thrown out a window…or worse.

Guided by love, respect, and fear, before handling the medicine pipe, the old Indian cleansed both hands, rubbing them with sage. With everyone in the room having been smudged, a prayer was given and the *cannupa* smoked, a formal way of supplicating the spirits' help. Careful to use only traditional movements, John George gently lay the pipe down before placing both hands behind his back. Starting with the thumbs, Vincent intertwined a leather thong through the elder's fingers, binding his hands in a Gordian-style knot. Extending the thong downward, the Navajo strapped the old man's ankles together before draping a Pendleton blanket over his subject's head. A second thong was wrapped tightly around Grandpa's waist to prevent the blanket's removal. Unable to change positions and nearly suffocating, the Pine Ridge elder was finally stretched out on the floor. The lantern was extinguished while Billy's father, grasping the drum, took his place against the wall.

Across the room, finding himself sitting on the protruding end of a stick of sage, Roger made a slight rustling as he quietly squirmed, trying to move to a more comfortable position.

To the steady beat of the drum, the elder began singing a spirit-beckoning song. Minutes passed. Without warning, flapping wings indicated that something was trapped as it flew back and forth across the small room. Judging by the loud sound and stirring wind, Rig assumed it must be an owl or hawk.

Under orders not to move and yet wanting to shoo it out the door, the Phoenician thought, *Oh my God! It must have been up in the rafters. Criminy, how's it going to get out? It'll wreck the ceremony*. Not hearing anyone else move, he concluded, *Damn, I can't…Ah heck; if it doesn't bother Grandpa, what the hey?*

As the drumming continued, the eerie flying suddenly ceased and the rhythmic cadence of the medicine man's rattle began. Of the 405 sacred stones within the hollowed gourd, each represented a different Lakota spirit. The shaking sound was distinctive—*ka-chink, ka-chink, ka-chink, ka-chink*. The gourd, with its continuous tone, seemingly floated about the room, supported by some unseen power. And though the blackness was impenetrable, even Rig thought he saw sparks radiating off a powdery-blue luminance as it mysteriously moved to and fro.

Going around, the rattle gently touched Lyra on the head—a blessing. Continuing on, *ka-chink, ka-chink, ka-chink*, it brushed Roger's shoulder—again, approval. When it paused in front of Rig, everyone heard a hollow *clunk!* followed by a slight groan. The smack, an admonishment, reflecting the state of the participant's spirituality. The ex-Wall Street broker was being reminded that he could, and should, try to do better with his life.

Songs completed, and in a surprisingly clear voice, the Pine Ridge elder called out for his helper to light the lantern. To Rig's and Roger's amazement, instead of being hog-tied, there Grandpa sat, in the middle of the room. At his feet, the blanket lay neatly folded. Both thongs were next to him, wound in a perfect circle. The gourd, too, rested innocently nearby. Everything else—tobacco ties, coffee cans, and altar—were all in disarray.

The old man spoke. "Spirits say to go over near Spider Rock. They will show us the right medicine plant to pick. But if we don't hurry, Grandson will die."

Without further conversation, Grandpa and Vincent departed. As they gained distance, the sound of the pickup gradually faded, but long after its taillights became too small to see.

Their destination was a lonely spire in Canyon de Chelly, home of Spider Woman, who lived at its peak. Her lair was said to be littered with the bleached bones of those hoisted up, never to return. Even today, the phrase "Be good, or Spider Woman will come and take you," strikes terror into the hearts of Navajo and Hopi children alike.

Fearing that Grandpa's healing might come too late, the mood at the Begaye household was glum. To keep his mind occupied, Rig went down by the creek to cut new poles for the photonic resonator.

When John George finally returned, the elder wasted no time. Little was said before the healing began. Giving him space to move around, the three guests stood outside under black skies. Through the closed door they could easily hear the high-pitched sound of the gourd as it set the tone for the Lakota's chants.

Inside on the wall, the shadow of the medicine man's body again moved to the cadence of the rattle. His spirit, however, has already departed—gone to connect with the ancient healing sources on the higher planes. Frozen in a pose, his form shuddered as it accepted the powerful energy of the bear spirit. The old man dropped to the sage-covered floor and started pawing the ground. He turned and rolled his head, snorting like a bear digging for herbs. As if jolted, the Lakota halted to sniff the smoky hogan air. On his knees, the animal straightened up, growled, and clawed the blackness, seemingly attacking an unseen enemy.

He approached Billy. Pulling the blanket back, the medicine man bent over the child. The Navajo boy's eyes had rolled back, his aura almost gone. A rapid, shallow breathing indicated the youth was teetering on the edge of life. Using a medicine bone as a straw, the healer began sucking on the youth's chest, spitting black liquid into a wooden bowl on the floor. Over and over, the process was repeated until the spittle became clear.

The medicine man handed the bowl to Vincent with careful instructions. "Bury it—where no one will ever walk."

The boy's eyes slowly focused. Debbie was given a signal to come forward with a cup of the wild-herb tea. Its extreme bitterness made her son gag. The worst was over. Their child would live.

Grandpa told the boy's father the sickness was sent by another family over in Canyon de Chelly. It all started when

Vincent got into an argument during a recent powwow at Window Rock. This prompted his neighbor to seek out a sorcerer to kill the most vulnerable family member. Of volcanic temperament, the elder Begaye exploded—set on taking his gun, first to kill the witch, then his employer. With aged wisdom, the Pine Ridge elder counseled against this. He knew it would only lead to an escalation of the problem. Instead, after calming the parents, Grandpa suggested a way to make forgiveness and peace between the two families.

Opening the leather-hinged door, the old man stepped outside, went two paces, stopped, and filled his lungs with a long breath of evening. The air, while humid, was fragrant with the strong scents that pervaded before a storm. He turned to Rig and asked if the photonic resonator could be set up in the hogan after dinner. Taken slightly off guard and not sure how the South Dakota professor knew of its existence, King felt surprisingly comfortable in complying.

Maybe, Grandpa thought, *this old iyeska* (interpreter or medium*) could learn what it is.*

As Rig went to the car, he saw the medicine man being approached by Roger. The boy was holding Toby in his arms.

"Grandpa?"

"Yes, Grandson."

"Can you help him? He's still hurtin' from those cowboys in that fight. Please help him."

The answer didn't come right away. Though the weathered face clearly conveyed a deep compassion, the elder's attention momentarily shifted away from the boy and his dog. Again closing his eyes, he turned his head skyward, awaiting guidance from an unseen source.

"Grandson, you don't have tobacco, and if you want the spirits to help, you should give them somethin'—somethin' that's important to you."

Without a second thought, Roger pulled out a pocketknife. Holding Toby with one arm, the youth unceremoniously presented the old Indian his offering.

The child's voice cracked and his eyes welled with tears as words flowed from the depths of his heart. "This is the only thing I have from Momma. She gave it to me the las' Christmas before she died. But I want you to have it, so you can fix my friend."

Grandpa George was pleased, not with the gift, but with the love with which it was offered. “Wa□té Lila wa□té,” he replied, meaning, “Good, very good.”

The healer gently took Toby from Roger’s arms and walked a little way from the hogan. Pausing, he turned, and with a nod of his head, signaled for the boy to join him.

“Can Cody come too?” Roger begged.

The medicine man again smiled and silently beckoned. Twenty minutes later, the giggling of two youths could be heard coming from the other side of the sheep shed.

Returning with the photonic resonator, Rig intercepted Grandpa while no one was watching. With newfound respect for the elder’s abilities, he asked, “Say, if you can do all that, think you can fix the kid’s spine?”

“Yep.”

Unfamiliar with a healer’s ways, the Anglo probed further. “Then why don’t you?”

“Can’t.”

“I don’t understand.”

Turning slowly toward W*asicu*, the Lakota replied, “Hasn’t asked me—yet.”

“He…He’s gotta ask first?” sputtered Rig.

“Yep…but he will.”

At dinner there was an almost giddy gaiety. The gathering clouds overhead appeared to be the only threat. Taking notice of the pending storm, unobserved, the medicine man entered the Begaye dwelling. Moments later he came out, holding the feathered wing again in his left hand. Dangling from a long leather thong, an eagle-bone whistle hung from his neck. Facing west and stretching his hands skyward toward the home of the Thunder-Beings, the elder whispered a prayer, then blew the instrument four times. Without further ritual, he disappeared back into the hogan to put away his helpers. The shaman had just performed the Cloud-Splitting Ceremony. Immediately, as if pushed aside by invisible hands, the massive thunderhead began parting in the middle. For two hours, while lightning flashed and rain raged on both sides of the high-rimmed walls, moonlight shown down through the middle onto the peaceful canyon floor.

The medicine man explained, “Rain’s needed but it’ll come later. Now is time for talkin’.”

In the darkened hogan, Billy slept through his first peaceful night in several days. As the boy dreamed, a shaft of moonlight shown through one of the windows. Following the Earth's rotation, it crept with imperceptible slowness across the floor. Inching up one of the tripod legs of the photonic resonator, the ray moved toward the crystal in the disc's center. As it touched the clear stone, a soft hum began filling the room. From both ends of the pointed gem, a blue beam shot toward the ceiling and downward to the floor. Likewise, from the space between the two plates, a golden emanation expanded outward about three feet, then arced around to connect with the vertical shaft. Now complete, a perfect translucent orb had formed. A minor player in the events to follow, the moonbeam continued its journey, leaving the resonator amply charged.

The intensity of the device's sound and its light was not what pulled Billy from his sleep. It was the cry of Haashch'eełti'í—the Navajo deity, Talking God. Always announcing itself four times before appearing, it began with a quiet *Wu'hu'hu'hu.* The spirit's utterance became stronger each time it was repeated. Beyond the hogan's walls, the laughter of the party was enough to drown out the being's increasing volume.

A second visitant, Haashcheewoon, Calling God, also materialized. As with Haashch'eełti'í, these two were not only frightening in their appearance, their mystical powers transcended the limits of imagination held by most two-leggeds.

Weak, half-asleep, and still thinking he was dreaming, Billy weakly called out in Navajo, *Who are you?*

Telepathically replying, Haashch'eełti'í answered: *Your spirit summoned and we are here. My grandson, you have been chosen because of your desire to learn the Blessing Way. I have seen you early in the morning each day, asking for this—wanting to know how to help people who are in need of healings in their mind, body, heart and spirit—also because of your grandfather, who was a great healer, and it would make him proud to have his grandson carry on this knowledge.*

The boy rubbed his eyes in disbelief but managed a slight nod as they continued communicating.

Outside, with the mood growing increasingly festive, Grandpa jested and told stories. Howling with laughter and distracted, no one noticed Toby staring at the hogan—tilting his head as he attuned to ethereal voices. Going over and scratching on the door, unable to enter, the dog sat patiently. Brushing back and forth on the dusty ground, his tail didn't stop wagging. At last, over the laughter, a feeble call was heard. It was Billy's. All jumped and raced through the doorway. Debbie was the first to enter.

"They were here! They were here!"

"Who was?" Vincent demanded in a soft but firm voice.

"Talking God and Calling God. They…they were!"

Bursting with words that spilled out in incoherent streams, the boy had difficulty getting his point across. His parents were skeptical, attributing the story to hallucinatory visions brought on by the sickness. That was, until Grandpa pointed to the two sets of footprints on the floor, forms outlined in sacred corn pollen where the sage had been cleared for the tripod. Seeing that they had just been visited by celestial deities, everyone except the Lakota elder and alien stood in awe.

The Begayes were beside themselves with excitement as they questioned their son. Only after the smallest of details had been wrung out was the exhausted child mercifully allowed to slip back into sleep.

Outside, Rig felt a drop of rain, soon followed by another. Looking skyward, his cheek received a third. The gap in the clouds had closed. Time to head for cover.

While Grandpa and Cody stretched out on the floor next to the stove, Billy and his mother occupied one bed, with Vincent on the other. Knowing Toby would need another healing session before dawn, the medicine man suggested the dog stay with him. Outside, sensing that the pending downpour will be violent, Rig and Lyra chose once more to sleep in her car. Being a city boy, Roger was intrigued by the sheep and opted to bunk in the three-sided lean-to, where he could observe these gentle, unfamiliar creatures. Inside the crowded hogan, a lamp's flickering flame was finally extinguished. With everyone bedded down, the ancient canyon became quiet at last.

Droplets of rain fell with exponential frequency—bending a leaf here, hitting a fence post there, bringing an effusion of concentric patterns to the watering trough. Perceptible more to animals than most humans, a strange feeling hung in the air. Sensing an approaching danger, the sheep milled uncomfortably about.

Everyone else relaxed into the night. Not far from the hogan, a crooked shaft of lightning stabbed downward, exploding in flashbulb brilliance where it touched the Earth. The accompanying thunder was deafening, erupting like a shotgun blast next to one's ear. Echoes of its roar zigzagged across the canyon, finally subsiding to a peaceful silence. All too near and without warning, another blinding flash—instantly followed by its companion explosion. As if under siege by incoming artillery, Rig and Lyra huddled together, watching Canyon de Muerto light up time and time again.

Gradually, the storm became even more intense. Outlined by a burst of lightning, two figures slipped into the shed. From a far corner, an awakened mouse and alarmed sheep witnessed the intruders bending over a thrashing boy. The roar of driving rain and explosive claps of thunder prevented even Toby from hearing his friend's muffled cries. Fighting for his life, Roger struggled with his attackers. A smash to the child's jaw made him crumble.

The first rays of morning found Rig and Lyra still asleep, huddled together, wrapped in one of two available blankets. Grandpa George and the Begaye family, except for Billy, had risen before dawn to start the day with prayer. Called by Toby's barking, Cody made the discovery. Roger was gone! The only signs were telltale footprints leading two hundred yards away and ending where a pickup truck had been parked out of sight around a bend.

Going over to the car to inform Rig and Lyra, the Lakota elder noticed a piece of tinfoil folded beneath a windshield-wiper blade. Inside, a note:

"To get boy alive," it demanded, "you and girl bring things stolen from cave. Take to Montezuma's Castle. Come between 9 and 9:30 tonight. Old man is not to come or black one dies."

Regardless of his outward demeanor, King's callousness had its limits. Sliced open, his emotional guts were ripped out—hanging to the ground. Outwardly, he tried to conceal his panic; while his first worry was the boy, he still didn't want to give up his treasure. Head bent and needing to be alone, he walked away from the others.

The decision at the abbey to save Lyra's life came easily, almost automatically—a primitive male-female response that bypassed rational thought. This was different. Setting the problem on the impersonal scales of logic, on one side he wanted nothing bad to happen to Roger, but then, it already had. On the other, the out-of-work broker reasoned, he'd nearly paid with his life for these artifacts. That made them belong to him, and they shouldn't be handed over. Their sale would fulfill his lifelong dream of *la dolce vita*—Napoleon brandy, winters on the Riviera, and his long-held fantasy of countless women, all topless, with trickles of suntan oil dripping into the curvatures of their semi-naked, bronzed bodies.

Pacing back and forth, a dilemma ranted in the treasure hunter's mind. Angrily, he kicked a rock. As he did, a long, needlelike cactus tine pierced his boot, driving halfway through his right big toe. The intense pain elicited a loud "*Ahhhhh shit!*" immediately followed by a furious "*Damn it!*" As he pulled at the thorn, his brain never ceased its twisting and turning, feverishly sifting options, trying to figure out some way of saving Roger, yet not giving up his fortune.

Equally telepathic and on a different set of pins and needles, Grandpa and Lyra listened to the battle being waged inside the Phoenician's head. Due to the spiritual rule of noninterference with another's lessons, neither was allowed to manipulate the outcome. This was a decision that could only be made by one who owned the instruments—no one else. Abruptly, King spun. As if mortally wounded, he emitted a low moan. Unable to find another solution, the only option he saw was to turn over the items in exchange for Roger's life.

Although far from where a verbal conversation would carry, thoughts were not diluted by distance. With proper attunement, a person's thinking could be picked up anywhere—even on the other side of the world. At this very instant, the alien and Indian looked at each other. Their expressions radiated satisfaction: Rigden King, III, had decided on the highest course.

The medicine man motioned the Anglo over. A tracker in his younger days, the Lakota picked up a long stick, pointed to a footprint and asked, "Nephew, see this?"

All crowded around as Rig perplexedly responded, "Is it important?"

"There are three sets of tracks," the old man explained. "A large wolf and two men. Look here. Footprints of humans are clearer than those of the wolf. The animal came at the beginning of the rain to scout the situation. Then he doubled back. See these? The two men came later. Also, the first man is hurt—see how his right leg drags at every step?"

"Okay, I see it."

Grandpa continued, "Now, look how the wolf drags this right hind leg?"

"Yeah…the wolf and the guy both have hurt legs, so what?"

"Your friend at the trading post and the skin-walker are the same."

King's mouth dropped open. Having been attacked by a gigantic beast is one thing. Actual confirmation of a human capable of shape-shifting cracked the rigid foundations of Mr. Wall Street's left-brain world.

Everyone was shaken by Roger's kidnapping. Grandpa asked Vincent to join him as they hurriedly went off to consult with the spirits. The Phoenician paced while Lyra meditated. Cody, knowing that in the rescue attempt he will be left behind to tend to the sheep, tried to think of something to help his captured friend. Dutifully, Debbie started a fire to make coffee. An hour passed.

Coming out of meditation, Lyra said, "Rig, there's someone here who wants to talk to you."

"Who?"

The alien's human shell shuddered as her soul stepped aside, allowing another being to use her vocal chords.

"Greetings, beloved. It is an honor to once again be in thy presence."

Rig's eyes bulged in wonderment.

"Ho! I see thou art bursting with questions. Please, ask what thou wilt."

Taken aback and not knowing if Lyra was making another one of her jokes, the ex-broker wondered if what seemed to be transpiring was truly happening. Leaning away, the listener's first response was more of disbelief. "*Whoa! Are you for real?"*

"Beloved, not in the sense in which ye perceive reality. I am of a different dimension. Or should I more clearly state, from another realm? Please continue."

Rig could barely mouth the words, "What…what's your name and what do you mean, 'once again to be in thy presence'?"

"I am without a name, for at this level of vibration, names are not a necessity. As to the second half of thy inquiry, I have known thee and that which calls itself Lyra, separately and together, many times over in thy experience of consciousness."

Nervousness mounted as the listener questioned further, "Where are you? I mean, where do you live?"

The being laughed, then answered, "*Beloved, within thy present level of understanding, that would be difficult to describe. Thou hast no point of reference. Simply voiced, there are far more realms than thy scientists and mystics comprehend or welcome. I do not reside in one, but simultaneously in many.*"

"Are you God?"

Again the entity laughed. "*No. I am not that which thou callest God.*"

"Then who are you?"

"To honor thy question, Blessed One, is difficult because of thy incomplete frame of knowledge. Suffice it to say, 'We are one; I am but a reflection of thy being, as thou art of mine.'" After a slight pause, the presence spoke again. "*I see that thou still thirst, as that did not quench thy curiosity. Let me add this: Is one drop of water in thy oceans different from another? The answer is No. We are all combined into one essence. True, perhaps I have been on the path seeking understanding slightly longer than thee. However, where I am now, ye will someday be. And where I am going, ye too, as well as all others, will ultimately journey.*"

Overwhelmed, the listener didn't know what to believe. The only thing he could think of was to go back to some sort of starting point. "Uhhhh…thanks. Ahhh…Can you give me further information on this guy, Malek?"

"Indeed. The one whom thou callest Malek came into existence after the inception of thy life-form. Imagine what the darkest thoughts of every mind in the entire universe could and did bring into being. Like a poltergeist, he is the composite of those energies made animate. These vibrations manifested as the entity known as Malek-the-Black, referred to in your Bible as Baal or The Prince of Darkness. He has many other names, such as…."

Hoping for clarification, Rig excitedly butted in, "Why then is he so interested in Earth?"

"Needing a physical base for his legions, Malek chose this planet from which to coordinate his expansion of evil. Such truth is even articulated in your ancient Sumerian, Akkadian, Assyrian, and Babylonian texts. Earlier, his throne of power resided on the now missing sphere, Nibiru, also known as Marduk. Before exploding, it too orbited thy sun. Today, residual chunks comprise the asteroid belt in which this planet now finds itself.

"As Malek's strength increased, his goal was to permeate the entire time-space continuum. So strong was his attempt to control the farthest regions that he became a cancer, seeking total dominion over all Souls of Light. After much deliberation, it was then that the Grand Council moved to war. And, I am sad to report that at this very hour, the battle still wages in all directions."

"But what has all this to do with us, with Earth?"

"Patience, Divine One," the being gently admonished. "*All will be revealed.*" He paused before adding, "*Have I offended?*"

"Uhhh, no…no," the listener answers, caught off guard. "Please continue."

"Then so I shall. Using Malek's ego as a strategic weakness, the Council attempted to draw him to a single point of focus by forcing a return to protect his home nest. It was hoped that this would enable his capture and subsequent annihilation. Thus, the Souls of Light caused his prized Nibiru and its satellites to collide with the planet named Tiamat. Known in thy Sumerian writings as 'The Battle of the Planets,' this resulted in the formation of many new spheres. Among these was Ki, in modern times referred to as Earth, as well as its sister Luna, or thy moon. But unfortunately, The Prince of Darkness had foreknowledge of their plan and escaped."

The Ancient One paused for the earthling's brain to assimilate part one of the amazing story.

Beginning again, its voice continued to convey an unusual blend of cool objectivity and personal warmth. "*Knowing the Council would make another attempt on his life, Malek decided to assure the continuance of his existence by dividing himself into three parts. The first segment was sent out to roam all time and dimensions, sowing discontent and laying the foundations for another siege upon the Divine Center—or as thee would speak of it, Heaven. And while this soul can fragment and simultaneously be in many places, its core focus currently resides in the Near East, unobtrusively implanted in a human shell that his followers refer to as 'The Chosen One.' The other two-thirds, however, are secreted away in separate caves on this very planet. These parts of Malek are hidden in time-sealed chambers, to be opened and reunited with his first segment at two preordained astrological moments. Once accomplished, that will mark the beginning of The Great Onslaught. Or as ye on Earth refer to it, The Apocalypse. And the first such date is now upon us."*

"What do you mean, is now upon us? When?"

"This very evening, at 10:13, to be exact."

"Tonight?" King gasped. *"Indeed,"* the voice assured him. *"However, if either of the thirds be destroyed, the full union of the trilogy will not occur. Even so, that will simply be a temporary setback. Any remaining unit will then search for the final part, should one still exist. Given enough time, each of the three discrete portions is ultimately capable of fully regenerating back into the focus of Malek's sum of gathered energies, although that would require eons. For them to meld at this moment would simply speed up the rebirthing process. And, because of current and pending disastrous shifts in Earth's political and geological climate, the ground here is most fertile—if you will pardon the pun. Therefore, it was earlier conceived that all three segments should be rejoined at this specific period. Is this clear?"*

"I…I guess so. Why are they so bent out of shape about the photonic resonator?"

"That which thou termest the photonic resonator is one of four such devices. The other three are held by the Souls of Light. These are temple communications tools used to call forth and visually manifest spirits from this or other planes. They may be used to summon Malek's implanted essence from its human shell at the specified dates. This is necessary in that only The Prince of Darkness knows the secret intonation that will be used for the opening of each cave. Without this device, the Grand Union could not take place at this time.

"Tonight," the being continued, *"the resonator's vibration will summon their master, who, using certain planetary alignments acting as time locks, shall break the spell, making the portal enterable. Thus, the encapsulated segment will then be liberated,*

placed in a transportation vessel, and ultimately reunited with its other two parts. With these monads blending at Malek's physical location, the triadic union will be complete. Doest thou comprehend, Precious One?"

"Well, I…I guess so."

"Besides speeding up the rebirthing process, there is another reason why all three parts are to be joined into one vehicle," the entity explains. *"According to prophecy, The Dark Prince must first have secured the acquiescence, or at least non interference, of earthlings. Unlike on other planets where there is little or no passion, ye are a stubborn, arrogant, curious people who surrender slowly. Therefore, to gather followers on Earth, their master must walk among thee as a man, solving problems, before ye bow down and acknowledge him as thy savior. For only when that which is thy true God is forsaken, can Malek close the net and claim this planet as his own. Having all three soul aspects back in one unit will then give him the fullest power to most expeditiously prevail at thine present period. Is this clear?"*

"Yes…I…I think so." But Rig's curiosity leapt in a different direction. "What is the writing on top of one of the discs?"

"Beloved, the inscription to which thou referrest is the key to such immense wealth as to stagger the imagination. Its magnitude may only be grasped by Divine Grace and one's constant striving to know its meaning."

"Oh no!" he gulped. *"Wealth?"*

The entity burst forth with laughter *"I see thine eyes light up as a star going nova. Yes, indeed…wealth. Given directly by the Creator, those who plumb the depths of its secrets have access to treasures beyond their wildest imaginings."*

Excited as a little boy on Christmas morning, Rig had trouble containing himself. "What is it? What does it say?"

The Phoenician's face dropped as he remembered that by tonight, the resonator would no longer be his. A wave of anger, not at Roger, then sadness for his impending loss, swept over him.

"Simply hearing the phrase is not enough," the Ancient One instructed in a tone of deliberate seriousness. *"To decipher its code, one must dive into the words; meditate on their innermost meaning. Then and only then will the way to riches open. Think of this as a door between thee and the Creator. Knock; ask for*

understanding, and clues will be given. Thus, over time, their hidden truths shall be revealed."

Disappointed at the evasive reply, Rig fell back on his marketing instincts by taking a sales approach. "Okay, okay—then I want you to know that I'm asking or, as you said, knocking. So what's the first clue? I mean, *ya gotta* give me at least one sign. *Right*?"

There was no response. Lyra's body shuddered. She took a deep breath. Her eyelids fluttered, then opened.

Shaking her head as if to clear the cobwebs, the young woman looked at her companion's bewildered face. "So what happened?"

As he began relaying the message, Grandpa George and Vincent returned from communicating with the Lakota spirits. The elder's shirt sleeves were rolled up. Blood dripped down both arms, from elbows to wrists. To strengthen his prayers, the medicine man had made a great personal sacrifice—ninety-six offerings of his own flesh. Inserting a needle, or in this case a cactus tine, under the skin, Vincent cut away the fragment with a knife. Each piece, along with a pinch of tobacco, was placed in a one-inch cloth square; then it was tied, prayed over, and attached to a string. Hanging in the branches of a cottonwood, the length of the old man's prayers stretched more than ten feet.

"Did a pipe ceremony," Grandpa said. "This is a greater evil than I have ever felt. Spirits came in strong. They said we have to move quickly if we are to save Cante Nitinze." Adding, "Vincent, you stay behind and bring the Sundancers over."

"The who?" Rig chimed in. "Who are the Sundancers?"

The Lakota, locked in thought, ignored the question as he placed the Begayes' .30-06 rifle in the backseat of Lyra's car. The elder's mood was grim. With the spirits warning him the meeting would be a trap, he had no time for the *wasicu's* questions.

What's rolling around in the medicine man's mind was, *Why does Granddaughter Lyra have to go along? And if she does, can we make the exchange for the boy?* Even more important, *How can all four of us get out alive?*

No one noticed Toby as he jumped into the car's open rear door, and burrowed under a blanket on the floor.

Cody approached, carrying a bow and arrows used for hunting jackrabbits. Knowing the white man was unarmed for the coming fight and not realizing the ineffectiveness of these tools against such a formidable enemy, the young Indian silently handed the Anglo his most precious possession. King looked down into the child's eyes with an acceptance that spoke volumes. "Thanks," was all that needed be said.

Recognizing the honor it merited, Rig placed the sacred gift in the open trunk.

Elsewhere, deep in thought, Lyra pondered how much the odds were against them. Their enemy was cunning and well prepared. Barely armed and with the feeblest of plans, it was bad enough the three must face the highest class of warrior elite. Worse, the trio were going without the element of surprise.

Yet, there was one, far more dangerous aspect: Trained to be void of conscience, to the Followers of Baal, all lives were expendable. Having surrendered their souls in exchange for what they perceived as forthcoming glory, each lived only to serve its master. The Lyrian too had been well-schooled. This was but another situation for which the Ra representative was ready to lay down her life. Without hesitation, the decision was made; she was going.

Gripped by fear, she departed from the others to sit in the shade of a large cottonwood, praying about what lay ahead. Seeing his companion had distanced herself, and knowing what must be raging in her mind, Rig disappeared behind the shed.

Until now, King's heart had dragged a weight through life, discovering at fifteen his childhood sweetheart pregnant by a supposed close friend. Having found Lyra, all that seemed moot. This was another chapter, and the moment called for something—a gift. But what? To pen a poem with the fluidity of Keats or woo with the silver-tongue of Casanova was beyond his reach. Stuck in Canyon de Muerto, all Rig's situation could offer was, at best, some second-rate gesture. Ten minutes later he approached. Without speaking, from behind his back he produced an unusual blue flower. As it was accepted, Lyra looked into eyes that seemed to be saying something they had never before expressed.

All was quiet, except for what appeared to be the wind rustling in the leaves above their heads. In actuality, these movements were caused by playful spirits, shifting from branch to branch. With Lyra's heart captured by a tender gesture, the beings flitted about freely—totally unobserved. Unaware of their curious watchers, Rig's companion reached out with the other hand, entwining her fingers into his. After a moment, they began silently walking back.

Later, except for Billy, all gathered outside, trying to work out the best strategy for an attack. The drive to Montezuma's Castle would take over five hours. For now, nothing to do but wait…wait and plan.

CHAPTER XXIV

THE INSCRIPTION

With most journeys, the return trip seems shorter than when going. It's the thrill of the unknown that keeps the mind excited; anticipation of what's around the bend makes hours feel somehow elongated. Coming back, the road has been explored, the mystery melted, and with it, the drama. Tedium sets in. Miles blend into more miles, until long distances seem to contract. Not so today.

Everything was proceeding on schedule until…a flat tire. They worked feverishly, but the changing went slowly. With crucial minutes hanging in the balance, the three would just squeak over the finish line. Yet, had they needed to arrive more quickly, there exists a simple mystical principle by which even a child can shorten or lengthen time. Today, though, neither the elder nor the alien had need of its application.

While they traveled, all three were lost in thought. Rig couldn't let go of how to hold on to his fortune and still rescue little Roger. Sitting close to the driver, her blue flower wilting on the seat beside her, Lyra stared out the window. Outwardly, the Ra representative's expression was placid. Inwardly, her soul trembled at the thought of battling the very personification of evil. As for Grandpa, the old Indian only stared ahead, down what appeared to be an unending road, his face devoid of emotion. This Lakota, head medicine man of the great Sioux Nation, had accepted his future. Earlier, the spirits were calling, saying that on this day he would probably die. And so, the three remained silent as the miles slowly receded.

Again Lyra slipped into meditation—time to contact her monitor. Instead of being in Washington, D.C., as expected, he had been diverted home to the Grand Council to report on his European trip. It was recognized that because of the magnitude of her situation, their light unarmed craft now circling the planet would be ineffective. With great urgency, five *Ton-gé*, behemoth-class warships, were immediately being dispatched. But Lyra knew that even if they traveled at hyper-light through a wormhole, the saucers couldn't possibly arrive until midnight.

"At all costs, stall until we come," the message urged.

Communiqué terminated, the Ra representative was left with but one thought: *How...How do I stall?*

The countryside was awash in the moon's reflected rays. Fifty miles south of Flagstaff, they turned off at the sign announcing an Indian gambling establishment, the Cliff Castle Casino. Coming up to the building, they saw a neon sign blinking its message: "Freddie Fender and his Tex-Mex style featured throughout this week." Adhering to the ancient wisdom of not going into battle with a full bladder, the trio made a brief restroom stop.

A typical casino, the Cliff Castle bustled with activity: Rhonda, the dyed red headed waitress in a miniskirt, distracted winners and losers alike with her free booze and fishnet-covered legs. On the opposite side of the room, Milard was vacuuming the new carpet and emptying ashtrays, as he did throughout most of his shift. Across the noisy floor, the air was choked with cigarette smoke and obnoxious mechanical gambling music, the type that synchronized every time a slot machine won.

Finishing first, Rig waited nervously playing video poker. An old man and a young woman on either side of him pushed buttons in glassy-eyed robotic rhythm. Their luck prompted an occasional tinkling of quarters, followed by the machine's ten-second symphony. Rig's slot remained silent. As Grandpa and Lyra walked over, King's losing streak continued.

Down a side road no more than several miles away, lay Montezuma's ruin. Built in the early twelfth century by the Sinagua tribe (meaning "Those Without Water"), Spanish Conquistadors erroneously assumed that these dwellings must surely be part of the far-flung Aztec Empire. Not so. The structures had actually been abandoned nearly a century before Montezuma's birth.

Thinking ahead, Grandpa reasoned their only chance was to pretend to comply with the DAK's demands—making it seem that he had not come along. This meant the elder must exit the car just prior to arriving, then proceed on foot. The old warrior's childhood games, and the Purple Heart won in combat during World War II, gave him an edge in sneaking up on an enemy. His strategy was simple. Go to the top of a small hill overlooking the ruins; using the rifle, pick off as many DAK as possible. The three agreed, shooting would start when Rig made a head-scratching sign.

Almost there. With the archeological site down the hill and around two more curves, Grandpa sensed it was time to disembark. Tapping *Wasicu* on the shoulder, he signaled for Rig to pull over. Front pant pockets bulging with extra shells, the medicine man nodded good-bye, taking the .30-06, and quietly closing the door behind him.

Crossing the ditch, he started his climb. To a young man, this would simply be a knoll. For an eighty-four-year-old, its slopes were steep, almost mountainous—an ascent few his age would attempt, although this Indian would…for Roger.

Courage was in Grandpa John George's blood, carried by an unbroken chain of warriors stretching back to the dawn of his people. But since the spirits had told him that this was very likely to be his last night to walk Grandmother Earth, the elder paused to look at the stars. Moving again, in time-honored tradition he uttered the ancient Lakota battle cry, "*Hoka hey*" (It is a good day to die).

Heart racing, panting, sweat streaming down his face, he cautiously proceeded— placing each step with premeditated care. Seeking strength, the medicine man broke into a song under his breath, repeating it again and again: "Tunkasila, hoiciciyeloÁ Un□imala yoÁ Omakia yo*!*" (Grandfather, hear my prayer. I humble myself, help me.)

To Indians, all things are alive—individual expressions of The Great Mystery. As the elder carefully picked his way between boulders and cacti, like an actor on stage, a thousand eyes were sensed, watching.

Rig's and Lyra's hearts were also pounding—out of fear rather than exertion. To maximize their hearing ability as the car crept down the incline, they lowered their windows and shut off the roaring air conditioner. Turning a corner, a metal gate blocked the road. The sign read, "Park closes at 7:00 p.m." With the way obstructed, there was no other option but to proceed on foot. Glancing at his watch, Rig was alarmed to see it was already 9:35.

Quickly walking down the winding asphalt, they cautiously approached the national monument. Scanning the parking lot, except for a paint-peeling 1998 pickup, the place seemed abandoned.

Tucked into the recesses of this concave limestone cliff, the shadowed form of the ruin was difficult to make out. Nearly five stories high, it stood as an engineering marvel, a testament to indigenous ingenuity. The original path leading to its doors had been long forgotten. To reach its base today, visitors must follow a gravel track, one that conveniently passed through the park ranger building, where admission fees were unceremoniously siphoned.

Cautiously crossing the blacktop area, Rig and Lyra listened with an intensity that made the drawing of every breath a noticed labor. She abruptly turned and tugged at his sleeve. Nerves on edge, he flinched.

"They're over near the ruins," she whispered. "We're being telepathed; they want us to come up the trail."

Looking back while leaning closer, he shot back, "Wonder where Grandpa is because...."

"Shhh! Shut up, you ninny! They're trying to listen to our thoughts. I've been blocking your patterns the way I did when you went to see Dr. Miller. So far they haven't been able to probe your mind, but you have to be disciplined."

Unaccustomed to being called a ninny, let alone by a female, King's expression pulsed with anger. Almost immediately, he corrected: this was neither the time nor the place for another of their arguments. Biting his lip, he moved toward the ranger station, knapsack full of treasure.

"At the university?" he whispered.

"Yes…now *shhh*!"

Back up the hill, Toby jumped out a car window and began to follow.

Unable to open the locked glass door of the park building, the two peered inside. In the shadows a few feet away, they were shocked to see a semi-comatose female ranger sitting in a chair—frozen like an Egyptian statue, eyes wide open. Their path again impeded, the only alternative was to climb over the fence.

From the higher vantage point, through the moonlight—a grayish, saucer-shaped craft. Rig's heart, already pounding, went into overdrive. There, nestled among the cacti, resting on what he assumed were retractable legs, sat an actual spaceship. Without windows and missing the flashing red light on top, it was similar to the one they encountered near the Deer Valley Airport. As they approached, and as if alive, it began to give off a faint glow and emit an oscillating hum. Otherwise, to visible perception the craft's surface was seamless. That turned out to be untrue; a door opened, and extended to the ground.

Two DAKs descended. Rig immediately noticed one of the reptile's armor included modifications for breasts—an attribute he'd always assumed was strictly a mammalian trait. Further observation showed the light bouncing off their scaly skin to refract a shifting aureole, a rainbow of colors similar to gasoline on water. What amazed him even more were their eyes—flashing red, with vertical, yellow, lizard-like iris slits. They differed from Lyra's, which gave off an inviting hue. Scowling and obviously dangerous, each pointed an electromagnetic pulse laser on top of its right forearm at the approaching pair.

The charged silence was broken. Lyra demanded, "*Where's the boy?*"

The female DAK noticed the aura of an interlocking triangle set in the center of the Ra representative's forehead. Golden dots on either side of the symbol denoted her Grand Council rank. In a sardonic tone, the observing lizard said, "*Sar-Doth* (Lieutenant), how good of you to come! Considering our great honor, we will endeavor to make your visit eventful."

Not one for games, the Lyrian's voice was full of fire. "I asked, *Where's the boy?*"

The male DAK pushed a button on his left forearm. Almost immediately, a third crew member appeared in the ship's portal. Carrying the unconscious youth in his arms, the reptile edged down the gangplank.

Alarmed, Rig spoke. "What have you done to the kid? If you've hurt him...."

Both the breasted enemy and the one placing Roger on the ground responded with their signature click-like laugh.

The first DAK, distinguished by a dimly glowing insignia adorning his uniform and whom Rig took to be the leader, mockingly scoffed, "Or you'll *what*, Earthling?"

The pause for an answer was devoid of response, made loud by its absence.

"You are slow to reply," the alien said, amused. "Perhaps I should introduce myself. My name is Moroth; I am the captain of this glorious expedition. And you...."

Reformulating their plan, choosing safety over fortune, King changed the earlier strategy of waiting for Grandpa. He cut short the commander's gloating. "Here's the damn stuff. Now, give us the kid, and we're outta here."

"Wait, Earthling. You seem to be in a rush to avoid our hospitality. Why?"

The enemy couldn't care less about the boy. To them, he was a pile of meat—mere protein. Towering over the youth, the male guard salivated as he looked longingly at the captive's veal-like flesh. Lost in thought, the crewman was oblivious to the protracting viscous thread of drool, dangling directly over the child's partially open mouth...before the slime suddenly severed, and dropped in. Aware of his comrade's cannibalistic nature, Moroth barked an order, bringing the crewman back from his daydream.

"Earthling, you still haven't answered my question."

Rig glanced at Lyra. Trying to appear nonchalant, he scratched the right side of his head. Upon the first shot, the plan was to pull out the pistol tucked in the small of his back and join the firing. Tensed, the treasure hunter waited for the rifle's crack. Like a sprinter at a track meet, his spring-coiled muscles were set to explode into motion at the sounding shot. Seconds passed—nothing. Perplexed, he again made the scratching signal.

If this is all of those lizard bastards, Rig thought, *hopefully Grandpa and I will be able to drop at least two, maybe the whole lot. If not, in the confusion, I'll grab the kid; Lyra can snap up the backpack, and we'll run like hell.*

A few more seconds elapsed while the commander impatiently awaited an answer. For Rig, who was stalling for time, the silence all but shattered his nerves. As the leader again started up the conversation, King's mind scrambled to find a reason for the Lakota's delay. Dangerously nearing the point of snapping, tenseness mounted—with beads of sweat popped up on the earthling's forehead. Worse, his left eye began twitching. In the background, the two Aryan-SST crew members chatted among themselves.

Age had slowed the Pine Ridge elder. He was late in getting into position. At the moment of Rig's second head scratching, the medicine man was just arriving at the top of the hill. Stepping silently, he squeezed between several large boulders, looking for the best sniper position. From out of the darkness, someone called his name. Perched atop a cactus—an owl, a Lakota harbinger of death. Having delivered its fateful message, the bird took flight. Once more, all was relatively silent.

Grandpa didn't hear or feel the impact of the two-by-four stud as it smashed into his skull. Falling forward, he lay facedown, motionless in the dirt and rocks. The sharp edge of the timber had sliced through the back of his head, exposing the white of the bone moments before the gap filled with blood. Above the prostrate body, his soul hovered, deciding whether or not to sever the silver cord and permanently leave. Other spirits floated nearby—ready to escort this being over the sacred river on its journey home, should that be the elder's decision.

Standing over him, the skinwalker's black form stood out against the rising moon. Shifting weight from his injured leg to the other, the assailant sneered, "Think you're the only one with power, Old Man? My helpers were stronger than yours. They told me where you'd be." Gloating, he continued, "Now I'm sendin' you south," a reference to the direction a Lakota soul goes when dying. With both hands, the Navajo raised the club high into the night. Aiming it again at the back of

Grandpa's head, one more whack and the eggshell skull would cave in completely.

"Stop!" cried a second Indian, grabbing the skinwalker's arm. "We're to take him down to the brothers."

Below, while the ship's captain talked on, Rig scratched a third time.

Bemused, the leader looked him in the eye and said, "You seem to have a nervous tic, Earthling. Anything wrong?"

Feigning deep thought, the Phoenician replied, "Huh? Wha'd you say?"

The leader continued, "There is something I wish to discuss. But first tell me why your vermin companion is trying so hard to block your mental patterns." Toying with him like a cat with an injured mouse, the DAK probed further. "Is there something you don't want us to know?"

As the enemy spoke, Rig's mind drifted. *Grandpa hasn't fired!* Beginning to tremble, he reminded himself, *Hafta keep talking, till he shoots*. Glancing at Roger, but addressing the enemy, the treasure hunter said in a tone of annoyance, "Let's get on with it. Here's your stuff." Although, not all of it. When leaving the car, King took off the ring, cramming it into his pocket, mumbling, "Damned if I'll return this, too." Back to real time, he demanded, *"Now give us the kid."*

"Slow down, Earthling. Slow down. You rush too much. We have things to discuss. *Come*! You are about to witness the most glorious event of all time."

Rubbing his neck, pretending it was sore, King glanced back over his shoulder, hoping to spot where the medicine man might be positioned.

The captain commanded, *"Human, look me in the eyes*. What I have to announce is sacred—not to be profaned by your split attention." The DAK's voice became almost hushed as he continued in a rhythmic cadence, "With the emergence and uniting of Malek, our master, a new era is about to begin. In fact, you will be—"

"Rig, don't listen to him," Lyra broke in. *"He's hypnotizing you!"*

"Silence, Lyrian!" Regaining composure, Moroth continued, "Mr. King, as I was saying, you will be rewarded far, far beyond the value of these simple trinkets."

"Kid's reward enough. *Here, take the crap! We're goin'!*" The knapsack and photonic resonator were thrust at the third reptile as the rescuer headed toward Roger.

Hurriedly, the female warrior inspected the sack's contents. Holding the discs up, she gently rubbed her clawed fingers over the enigmatic inscription, mouthing its words under her breath.

Alarmed, the third crewman whispers, "*Be quiet! Do you want to get us killed? Don't you know how disastrous it would be for their species to learn this phrase?*"

Petulant, the female replied in a low growl, "*I don't see what can be so harmful in the saying, 'I am one…You are one…* W*e are one.' This is stupid; it has no meaning whatsoever.*"

Worried their leader might overhear, her comrade became even more agitated. Under his breath he barked, "*Fool! Simply speaking those words can mean both our deaths.*"

Exclusively trained in warfare, the female had never been told of the discs' importance. Only officers and selected crew members were given nonmilitary information, and then only when conditions made it absolutely necessary. Ignorant about the reasons for such secrecy, she asked, "*Why*? it was *just a valueless saying.*"

Turning his back so the leader wouldn't hear their conversation, her crewmate whispered, "*According to Moroth, these words are the foundation code to the Ji'nea's—* (nonbelievers') *entire spiritual system. As with this scroll, those nitwits try to give credibility to their religion by claiming that this cluster of words is the key to enlightenment. They even delude themselves into believing it was received directly from their mythological creator.*"

"*And what do you think?*"

The male alien's attempt to quiet his shipmate appeared fruitless. "*What we think is irrelevant. It's dangerous propaganda. The Ji'nea see this as the most powerful phrase in existence. In fact, Moroth says our ancestors thought they had erased all record of it. Then it turned up again on this. It is said, if the meaning is truly understood, they can rise up and conquer us.*"

Furrowing her scaly brow, the female flatly inquired, "*If it was really that deadly, why not just grind the letters off?*"

"I asked that, too. Regrettably, its removal would change the molecular balance of the device, rendering it ineffective. And we can't risk that—especially now."

That compelled the female DAK to ask another question. *"One more thing I don't understand. Why is this specific instrument so important?"*

"To open the time-locks of the two caves. Although there are overlapping cycles, the captain said the original dates for reunification were set for Earth years 2006 and 2008. *But this planet's quickening spirituality and imminent climatological disasters force us to act now."*

"Okay. So we need the device. Then what's so important about the scroll? What's that about?"

"Dolt! I swear, you're determined to have us both disintegrated!"

The smugness of the female came through in her tone. *"That's okay; I didn't think you knew."*

"Of course I know! But that's just as deadly to talk about as the resonator. Our priests use the scroll in a backwards ritual, hoping it will cause the Ji'nea to doubt their deity. Now don't ask any more."

"We use it to make them confused, huh?"

"I told you...don't ask any more questions!"

Still embroiled in his talk with Rig, the commander had no idea of his crew-members' conversation. "Before you draw any conclusion, Earthling," the captain said, "first let me show you something. Time is short. If you are not amenable, I must know now in order to use my alternative."

The leader approached, while the reptilian female kept a close eye on Lyra. "I suggest you tell your Lyrian friend to stay here. Or...we will kill her, without a second thought."

"Amenable...to what? What do you want?"

"Only for you and me to take a little walk. There is something I want you to observe."

Lyra pled frantically, "*Rig, don't go; it's a trap!*"

"Nonsense," the leader said with a certain tone of gentility, trying to allay any fears. "If it were, we could have easily killed you both as you approached the ship."

In a bold attempt to stop her companion as he began following the reptile, Lyra rushed forward. With a fluid move, the female soldier swung her arm. The laser blast hit the Grand Council member between the shoulder blades.

Struck by its full force, she spun, and fell—collapsing to the gravel.

Turning to see what was happening, Rig screamed, "*You've killed her, you sons a bitches!*" Stroking her hair, he cradled Lyra's head in his arms while rocking back and forth. Swallowing hard, the human was overcome with fury. As tears began to swell, a blurry move was made for the pistol.

Without his partner's telepathic blocking, the captain was aware of his captive's intentions long before the Phoenician's muscles could even begin to respond. *"Try it, Mr. King,"* he barked, "and I will blow your head off, followed by that of your vermin friend here. Calm yourself; she's only stunned. Don't worry. This worthless creature will come to in a few minutes. I am giving you but one second to make your decision. If you don't want us to kill you both, drop your gun and follow me... *now!"*

Slowly, the ex-broker's fingers opened, allowing the pistol to fall. Rising unsteadily to his feet, he was startled by a sound from the direction of the parking lot. The two Navajo were lowering a body over the fence. It was Grandpa's. Unceremoniously, the old man was dropped to the rocks five feet below. Landing with a soft thud and rolling into the three-inch-long tines of a barrel cactus, the Lakota's limp form became impaled on the needlelike spikes.

"No, he's not dead either," Moroth said, "but close to it. I sensed he would be coming. In fact, he and the boy will make good witnesses—once they're revived, that is."

Starting the short walk toward the ruins, the commander ordered his soldiers to follow in twelve minutes, bringing Lyra and the youth. The Diné were to carry Grandpa.

Breaking in, curious and angry, Rig shouted, "*Witnesses to what?*"

"My Little Humanoid, you weren't paying attention, were you? As I explained, you and your friends are to witness the glorious emergence and uniting of our most Exalted Master. In fact, soon all of Earth will bow down and...Pardon me, in the excitement, I digress. The most important thing is for you to watch what is about to happen. A mere nineteen minutes, forty-two seconds remain until the appointed time."

"And then what?" The DAK leader simply smiled and motioned his captive to follow.

Picking their brief way along the foot of the apartment-stacked ruins, the commander chattered on, all but delirious with anticipation about the impending event. "Think, Mr. King; think of yourselves as the latter-day Three Magi! Of course, none of you really qualifies. You see, the term 'magus' really means witch or sorcerer." Guttural clicks indicated a slight laugh before he continued. "Your masses of misled Christians would roll over in their graves if they knew their beloved...." The DAK leader grimaced as he mouthed the name, "*Jesus*, was first honored by witches back at that manger. You people purposefully avert your eyes from that and other uniquely important historical facts...Rather titillating, don't you think?"

A momentary break occurred in the conversation as the earthling's mind raced. Depression set in. He now not only feared for Roger but also for Lyra and Grandpa. Trying to guard his thoughts, King reasoned that if anything was to be done, it would be up to him. But knowing he was helpless, the conclusion was crushing. Fortunately, this mental conversation went unnoticed due to the alien's state of euphoria. As they proceeded, each became mute. Only the sound of their walking disturbed the silence.

"It's okay, though," the captain picked up. "I'm talking about your apocryphal messiah; we took care of Him once before and we'll do it again. I mean, yes, He's still working interdimensionally. But that, too, will soon be fixed. Anyway, I'm getting off the subject. You see, even though you, the boy, and your Indian accomplice aren't true magi, you can still be witnesses. In fact, *you personally* can be something far more special!"

Perplexed that the commander didn't include his companion, Rig asked, "What about Lyra? You didn't mention her."

Enjoying the repartee, the alien played with his captive's emotions. "It goes by the name Lyra? How quaint. You would think a Lyrian would have more imagination. But that's why we are winning and their side is losing." The reptile again made the grating chortle.

"What about her?" the earthling demanded, a panicky quiver rattling in his voice. "Why don't you include her as one of the magi?"

"So many questions, Mr. King—so many questions. Relax."

Having arrived at the ruins, they stopped. Giddy with joy, the DAK babbled on as he started setting up the photonic resonator, saying, "Anyway, Malek, Emperor of All That Is, has secreted away a part of himself in this very mountain. This device will call forth his free segment, which will then enable our master to dematerialize the cave's entrance. That's how we'll…."

"What does all of this have to do with me?"

"With you?… Possibly nothing, but then again, maybe quite a bit."

"And that's supposed to mean?"

Busy continuing to set things up, the commander responded, "You are a little slow on the uptake, Earthling, a little slow. If I were you, I'd give up my membership in that MENSA society; it doesn't seem to be doing your mental acuity any good." Again, more DAKonian laughter. "Seriously…I'll attempt to answer your question. One-third of our Savior's essence is in this cave, waiting to be rejoined with its other two parts. It needs, shall we say, a living vehicle in which to be transported."

"So, why us? How are we involved?"

"Not us, but rather…you. You see, the crystalline container in which he is housed could possibly break in transit. I know; I know…you are about to ask, being so delicate, how it has survived in a cave all these eons."

"Yeah, I was."

"The ceiling has been reinforced to withstand any natural calamity, even a direct hit by a meteor. But this special receptacle is different; once taken outside, it becomes vulnerable. We know the possibility of it fracturing during the trip is quite remote, although…mathematically possible. And, we choose not to take even that slightest chance.

"You see, the reference to our Most Holy One in your Bible is, so to speak, the watered-down version; it represents only a third of his sacred being; you might say, we were fighting with one hand tied behind our back." He gave his trademark chortle, before continuing. "So, when the triad is brought together, our Ruler's sum will be far more powerful than your little churches can possibly conceive." An arrogant gloating, visible even on a reptilian face, began to form. "This time, your kind will lose." The captain's continuing laugh sandpapered Rig's already raw nerves. "And after being asleep for such a length of time, when these segments receive the spark of life from an unsullied, vibrant soul…." Moroth spun, looking his captive straight in the eyes…"from a soul such as yours, it will speed our Master's full awakening."

"*Whoa!* Wait a minute. What do you mean, 'a soul such as yours?'"

"Quite simply, the Creator has been dormant, in a state of suspended animation. It will be expedient, although not totally mandatory, for The Great One to be jump-started with the life-force of a spirit…as I said, one like yours."

"*Holy shi*…." his prisoner responded, more stunned than ever—not even being able to finish his sentence. Taking a full breath, Rig asked, "Are you telling me, you want my soul? Why me, and not one of your soldiers or…or those Indians?"

"A reasonable inquiry, I suppose," the DAK sighed. "First, it is imperative that the infusion comes from a nonspiritual, yet unsullied, being such as you—a *tabula rasa*, so to speak. You fit that requirement to a T. Also the body must be in excellent physical condition, able to withstand the pressures of Master's essence during his time of residence in the surrogate, prior to transference into his primary, corporeal vehicle."

"I still don't see. Why me? Like I said, why not use those damn lizard friends of yours?"

"Tsk, tsk! Such language! So pedestrian." The leader continued arranging the altar while he spoke. "Forget my crew; I personally would give *anything* if I could accept this honor. You see, I and my lizard friends, as you so disrespectfully call them, do not have your completeness of being. Oh…we all know you aren't a Puritan, but you're still reasonably… how shall I say—spiritually vibrant? Add to that, you happen to have an athletic physique."

"I still don't understand why one of your crew can't do it."

"Quite simply, neither I nor my warriors have your spark of life. Unfortunately, that aspect of our selves has become, to put it bluntly, slightly dimmed. And I should add, the promised remuneration for your participation will be worth a trillion times over what your paltry treasure would bring."

"Moroth, there's something else I don't get."

The commander paused. "Just one thing?" came the answer, followed by more irritating clicking and a deepening smirk.

"*Don't be funny!* If your souls are dimmed due to serving Baal, where does cosmic light come from?"

The response took on a confrontational air. "I take it," the alien challenged, "that you are alluding to the myth that all luminance originates in your supposed deity. Am I not correct?"

Putting the enemy on the defensive, Rig pressed, hoping to find a chink in the commander's armor. "Well, let me put it this way—if luminance doesn't come from your master, it certainly must originate somewhere."

Angered, Moroth attacked. *"Fool! You are incorrect!* At least on an ethereal level, light is throughout all of time and space. Living things are merely points of its concentration. Surely, Mr. King, you know that luminosity is the foundational state of all matter." Continuing to place articles on the altar, the enemy added, "It's simply one of those mysteries that defies understanding."

"Then, you're telling me this master can't explain where light comes from. Right?"

"I did not say that! *Nothing* is beyond our Supreme One."

"Well, it looks like something is." Rig quickly sought more traction, scrambling for any advantage. "Okay then, why not use the Indians?"

"Ahh, these Navajos—trust me. They are going to be used. In fact, I will share something with you I find rather interesting. The older one, Jake—his real name is Hastiin Be'ena'í 'Adah 'Ayídziił Taałii. It means, Man Who Kicks His Enemies Off The Cliff." Thinking aloud, Moroth added, "I like that." Then, looking at his prisoner, he absentmindedly linked another thought, "It has, I think you people would say, a certain *je ne sais quoi*, don't you agree?…Excuse me, I'm getting ahead of myself. We have…."

Building in hatred and with nothing more to lose, the captive let go of the last fragment of his fear. "*So why in the hell do you think you can have my body? Stupid ass! I'm not givin' it to you...or anybody else, for that matter!"*

"Tut tut! I suspected you might take that stance. Try not to be so impulsive! Before you say No, allow me to suggest what would be required...I mean, what your reward will be." Seeing the human's disgusted expression, Moroth feigned avuncular familiarity. "Truly, Rig... May I call you Rig?" Without waiting for an answer, the commander continued, "I sincerely appreciate your quandary; you or anyone else couldn't possibly cherish the wonder of this opportunity until it was properly explained. Let me just say, hundreds of millions...No, *anyone* in our entire army would instantly...joyfully, take your place, if only they could.

"Therefore," he continued, while laying out a pattern of rocks that form an upside-down pentagram, "I shall elucidate. After all, clarity will help you make up your mind. To begin, you do not lose your soul. As a gift, it ultimately becomes merged with that of the Master. Once this portion of the Divine One enters your body, you merely accompany us to the ruins at Palanque in Central America. There you will absorb another soul-unit from a cave similar to this one. Then we move on to Syria, where you will wait. That is, until the entity containing the first third meets its death in the streets of Jerusalem—thus fulfilling Earth's Biblical prophecy. You see? It's all really quite simple."

Shaken by the entire concept, Rig exploded, "*No way!*"

Ignoring the recalcitrant outburst, the alien went on, "As I said, to start the process, you must merely renounce the—I hate to even mouth the words—*Holy...Spirit*—three times after you place your hands upon the cylinder. And, oh yes," the captain concluded with an afterthought, "I forgot to mention, *sincerity* is the key. The renunciation must be made with *absolute* earnestness."

"Forget it! I'm not doing it!" the prisoner softly responded, while trying to unobtrusively edge away from the commander, who was absorbed in preparation.

Glancing up, furious, the extraterrestrial again became more formal. Raising his laser arm, he ordered, "*Not another step, Mr. King!*"

Rig froze.

"Shame on you," clicked the DAK. "You haven't heard the most sublime part. When Malek's vehicle is killed, and this is even stated in your Bible, the body will lie in the streets of that city for three days and three nights. Just like—and again, it was one of those names I truly hate to say—your *Jesus*, our Master too will rise from the dead. That's where you come in. On the third day, as the shadows of the buildings are creeping over his shell, you will lie down on top of him as a person in mourning. This is when the transfer takes place. His other two segments within you, as well as your own soul, will then enter his dormant form." In his ebullience, the DAK began to stutter. "Y…You…you, Rigden King, III, will become part of the glorious Holy Triad. You…."

"*Hey, moron!* Or whatever your name is. What part of *No* don't you understand?"

"I thought you might be obstinate. Tsk, tsk! And you've not even heard the best part."

"There is no best part. *Kill me! I'm not doing it. Got that… Jack?"*

"Trust me," crooned the alien, replacing his low growl with diplomatic smoothness. "I…."

The captain's voice faded into background static as the stitches of King's sanity were popping apart at the seams. Hysterical, in terror, he recognized Moroth's conciliatory tone to be the same as the one used by Golan just moments before ramming that pick through the abbot's eye.

The commander approached, barking, "*Do not move!*" Beyond his will to refuse, Rig slowly froze in a statue's pose. Stretching out his hand, the alien touched his prisoner's third eye with a ring similar to the one the earthling had in his pocket. Done, the creature whispered enticingly, "See, Mr. King? See what glory our Master will give for this service?"

Although the Phoenician's eyes were closed, he was overwhelmed, seduced by a phantasmagoria of indescribable images. The reptile's voice rolled on. "Behold the power to rule! Not just this planet or galaxy, but *all that is!*"

Lascivious swirling pictures intoxicated Rig's mind and senses, while the extraterrestrial presented the ultimate fantasy. "*Imagine having anything you want! Create anything…anything your thinking can possibly conceive!*" Moroth's mouth was so near, the smell of his acidic breath overwhelmed. "You, Mr.

King, shall possess all that exists. No soul will equal yours. And since I've scanned your belief system and you don't feel there is an afterlife, *this is your one and only chance for immortality.* This is the ultimate freedom to do whatever you wish. Think of it—unending life, plus wealth, power, and *sex... Yes, sex*—far beyond any dream one could imagine. *You...you will be in the holy center of the Lord of All."*

Unmoving, hypnotically transfixed, Rig stood rigid as the creature slowly circled— talking, goading from every angle. "What has your nonexistent god ever done for you? Plucked you from your mother's arms and given both your parents agonizing deaths? Your memory banks show that life has been the enduring of sickness, poverty, and broken dreams, all while you wait for that grand day when worms begin to eat your flesh. As for this mankind you want to protect, where have they been through your tears and pain? And the Lyrian, you will have ten thousand...No, a million just like her.

"*Rig...Rig*! You've been lied to by your religions; they want to maintain their control; Earth is your real Hell. What is being offered, this...this, my friend, is Heaven.

"Ask yourself: What kind of loving deity would allow its children to go through such suffering and sorrow as you humans experience? The only answer is: Your world places candles at the feet of a false god of stone, adorned with feathers and paint, while you dance around it like primitive savages. *Wake up!* Cease your obsequious deifications. What lies ahead for you is a kingly existence of ease, joy and *exalted adoration!*

"Kingly? I said 'kingly.' Fascinating! Inasmuch as there is no such thing as an accident, I find even your having such a last name, to be the ultimate touch of irony—as if this were all predestined. Wouldn't you agree? "

At first glance, for most, choosing or rejecting such an offer should be simple. Actuality, it was quite complex. Balanced on the scale of decision, both of the earthling's trays were piled high: on one side, all he could ever want—unimaginable delights, plus the sweetness of briefly saving his true love as well as humanity. Unfortunately, this sugar coating hid a bitter core—the sentence of eternal damnation. On the opposite tray—a most heavy option—to refuse meant the loss of all, except his priceless soul. But this was not one of King's management decisions. Confused, his mind reeled—the way the body did when it nearly fell into the other Grand Canyon.

Time was running out; the creature would force a choice in the next several seconds. Internally, mental chaos and pressure had all of Rig's voices screaming, trying to out shout the other. Struggling to find the right answer, the earthling dove into the deepest aspects of self. Verging on insanity, he was pushed with an intensity of a swimmer whose lungs were about to burst, and yet, was forced to go farther—beyond comprehendible limits. Somewhere, at the bottom of his consciousness, Rigden King, III, retrieved an aspect long assumed lost. Surfacing, he shouted: "*Damn it! I* won't; I just wo…. "

Irritation mounting, the reptile grew impatient. "I suspected you might possess a noble streak. But then again, we always have the Lyrian."

The word Lyrian jostled the captive back to present time. Eyes opened slowly. "What do you mean?"

Just then, the alien crew arrived with Roger and Lyra. Lagging farther back down the trail, the two Navajos struggled to carry the unconscious medicine man and his gun.

"It's really quite simple, Mr. King," the DAK said, his words bloated with arrogance. "What I'm offering is both a carrot and the stick. Do what I ask, and all of creation lies at your feet. Refuse…and your situation becomes progressively regrettable."

The Phoenician's expression was etched with lines.

"Ahh!" Moroth injected another thought. "I can see curiosity in your eyes. Let me explain. First, refuse and you will helplessly watch as I erotically explore this female in ways your marshland of a planet still labels 'perverse.' And, if that doesn't motivate you, I will methodically begin amputating each of her limbs."

"Uhh…." Rig stuttered. "Am…amputate?"

"Observe." The alien stretched out his arm. With a casual sweeping motion, the laser's low-pitched, humming ray instantly sliced through a ten-inch-thick, nearby cottonwood.

As the tree fell, the prisoner, lost to the pressure of the moment, looked once more for the quickest route of flight. He hesitated; without Lyra, he couldn't go.

Angered, Moroth barked, "*Mr. King,* again you're not paying attention! Time is growing *extremely* short. So much so,

I'm afraid we will have to dispense with the sexual torture. *Pity!* Anyway, watch closely. Using this, I will commence by cutting off her right hand."

"Noooo! She'll bleed to death!"

"You earthlings fret so," the DAK clicks in amusement. "A quick kill would spoil our fun. And we couldn't have that, now could we? You see, this laser instantly cauterizes any blood flow. Trust me; your pretty little rodent will simply be left with a stub at her wrist."

"A stub?"

"Don't worry; we'll use sufficient anesthetic…precisely enough to enable her to suffer the maximum without passing out. The object is to keep your girlfriend at her pain threshold—the hairline of consciousness that can be endured without going totally insane. So if the vermin drools a bit, don't get alarmed. We've been doing this sort of thing for ever so long, you know? We're actually very good at it—virtuosi, in fact."

Flinching in horror, Rig took a step back.

"I mean," the DAK gleefully clicked as he talked on, "if our Lyrian slipped into a numbed senselessness, she wouldn't enjoy the full experience. Don't you agree?"

"You wouldn't!"

"Come now, Mr. King. I've only just begun."

"And if I don't do it?"

"*Earthling*," he said in a booming voice that left no doubt, "if you continue refusing our offer, I will be forced to cut off her other hand, and so on." Pausing, the captain peered past the earthling's eyes into his soul, before continuing, "Until you agree, that is. We have but a few minutes. Therefore, I suggest we begin."

Lyra, still groggy, spoke up. "Begin what?"

"I was just explaining to your friend here that if he fails to comply, I will cut off all of your limbs—beginning with your hands. And if that proves insufficient motivation, we will move on to your arms, feet, calves and the thighs."

Conjuring up images of bloody pieces of Lyra's body strewn about the desert, Rig's shock intensified.

Seeing his captive's thoughts, Moroth enflamed the scenario of surgical savagery. "You see, Mr. King, we have the ability to sever every one of her limbs and still keep your companion alive. Use your imagination. The scene isn't hard to envision: the acrid smell of her cauterized flesh; a stump of a body, with only its moving head attached; nothing else. And then...."

"*Shut up, you cretinous son of a bitch!*"

"Calm down, Mr. King...calm down. Your vulgarities... this backwoods patois does become tiresome," he sighed. "As I was about to say, I will prop her up. Then she and you can watch as we devour her soft, juicy thighs. They are the most succulent portion, but I wouldn't expect you to know that."

Unable to contain his anguish, Rig put both hands to his head and cried out in a voice that didn't seem human. With a frozen look, the human stared blankly at the ground. The only idea that surfaced was, *If I rush him, he'll kill me. No! That'll leave Lyra, Roger, and Grandpa alone. I can't—*

Hearing the mental statement, the captain agreed, "Correct, Mr. King—you can't."

Few in their right minds would want to switch places with this prisoner. Until recently, at least from the world's perspective, Rigden King, III, was your common man—an undistinguished tree, blending in with the vast forest of humanity. Knowledge now separated, setting him apart. Terrified, he had just witnessed prophecy of the indescribable evil...evil that *he* would be a party to unleashing. Adrift in an emotional storm, desperation had him grabbing onto any solution, even the most tenuous of lifelines. One by one, as the practicality of each severed, it was dropped.

If I refuse, I'm dead anyway. His mind raced, Rig knew time was running out. *Naah, that won't help. Think! Damn! Gotta think fast. What if...no! That won't work. With or without me, Malek's going to get his power. It's simply a matter of when.*

Bemused by his prisoner's inventiveness, the DAK leader crossed his arms, watching without interfering. To achieve the level of sincerity needed for rejecting the Holy Spirit, the decision must be reached of the subject's own accord.

Cut off from hope's oxygen, Moroth's captive ceased to struggle, conceding, *There's no chance for me. At least I might buy freedom for the other three by being absorbed in Malek's consciousness. Then Lyra's people will....*

Tears streamed down the face of a being that knew it was about to be forever damned; there would be no chance of reprieve...an eternal resident of hell. The earthling's expression appeared frozen, like one wearing a mask—as if all vital life force had been sucked from his being. Slowly, he pulled together enough energy to speak. "If I give up my soul, will you…will you let the three go?" The words were groaned at an almost inaudible level.

Affecting a tone of sympathy, the DAK agreed, "Of course…of course. On that, you can trust me. I give you my word. Simply renounce your deity three times while touching the capsule, and allow Malek's essence to enter your body. Do this and we will have no further use for your friends. Even the Lyrian will be set free to go tell others of this glory."

With decreasing volume that faded into a whisper, the captive replied, "O…kay… Ok…."

"What? I didn't hear you."

"*Okay! Okay!* I said I'll do it!" came the reply with surging obstinacy. "Let's get it over with."

"*Excellent!* In a few more minutes, the moon alignment will be perfect. It was quite wise of you to accept our magnificent gift. Now using Dilbert, the skin-walker's apprentice, will be unnecessary." More guttural clicking.

Ever curious, even under these circumstances, Rig asked, "Why not use him? You never did make that clear."

"It never really was my intention. That simpleton was no more than a spare tire, so to speak. He and his mentor were made promises to get them to do my bidding. Although, by dabbling in the black arts, the Indian sullied the purity of his vessel. He is, as I think you would put it, 'a second-stringer'—to be allowed into the game only as a last resort. Then you showed up."

The two Diné, now arriving, were unaware of the conversation.

Keeping his voice from carrying far, Rig asked, "What are you going to tell him?"

"My benighted duo? Oh, they will be served, all right; and I mean, in the literal sense!" Again came that frenetic clicking. "At our blood feast, a…celebration, if you will."

Repulsed at the idea of witnessing cannibalism, the prisoner's stomach began to churn.

Perceiving his revulsion, the lizard taunted all the more. "And you, or might I say the Master within, shall enjoy the first cup of blood before dining on the most delectable parts." He clicked happily, as his captive turned further ashen.

Absorbed by Moroth's gruesome promise, Rig was only vaguely aware of the female soldier quietly injecting Grandpa and Roger with an adrenal stimulant. Considering their physical conditions, the old man and the youth awakened with startling clarity. Lyra was left to gradually come to on her own.

Everyone gathered, waiting. Strategically placed in such a way to coincide with the exact instant of the moon's correct tangent, the photonic resonator began its high-pitched emanations.

Turning to Rig, Moroth said, "Watch, Earthling. See the power of a seemingly innocently spoken word!"

Again, the blue shaft of light shot from the top and bottom of the orb. The golden beam shown outward from the discs, arcing around, once again forming the sphere. A few feet away, a semi-humanoid shape began to materialize. Devoid of light, the concentration of evil was such that its black form was visible, even under these clouded heavens. And though the ambient temperature was still ninety-two degrees, a cold wave moved outward from the form, rapidly spreading across the ruins.

The three DAK warriors made a deep and reverent bow. In unison, they chanted, *"Hail to Thee, Most Exalted Master*."

As the humming from the resonator reached its peak, turning toward the cliff, the figure intoned a powerful mantra. Just as a crystal can be shattered by a musical note, so too the vibration of these sounds were to disintegrate the entrance camouflaged by Malek's ancient spell. Its voice, starting low, grew unbearably loud as it intoned, *Juharot-ishkem-hewhay-tsidektah.* An ocean of force built to the point of becoming semi-visible. The fullness of its energy focused on the cave's hidden opening. Once more the shadow rumbled the arcane invocation. Then a third time, and a fourth.

The vibratory level increased—fast approaching the threshold beyond which humans could physically withstand it. A few stronger oscillations and the membrane of every cell in their bodies would rupture—creating a torturously painful death. Futilely, Roger instinctively placed both palms over his ears.

The cliff shuddered. Its broad face began to roll and heave. Several boulders dislodged at the top—one whizzing past the boy's head. As the sound reached a crescendo, the most beautiful section of the ruins cracked, collapsing into a cloud of dust and rubble. Back down the trail, the park building's glass doors had shattered into a thousand pieces. At the same time, above the ranger's head, along the ceiling, overhead lights noisily exploded before the glass crashed to the floor. Oblivious, locked in her trance, the employee's induced sleep continued. All the while, wavy, vertical lines began to appear on the cliff's surface. Following the last intonation, a rippling occurred as a ten-foot-wide opening appeared.

The cave was a symbolic 616 feet in depth. Mysterious balls of light imbedded in its walls illuminated the passage with daylight brilliance. At the far end, an oblong crystalline cylinder rested on an altar. Roiling out of the entrance, a translucent, although visible fogbank of indescribable evil. For the humans, the sensation caused every square inch of their skin to itch, even the most delicate of locations.

Mission completed, the black figure dissolved before all eyes. In reverence, the commander and his two crew members again bowed low, while this, the first and the only free segment of the triad, headed back to its human Syrian host.

As the beast left, the DAK leader turned and ordered sharply, "*Mr. King, come! The moment is at hand!*"

Thinking he was about to be honored as the sacred vessel as promised, Dilbert stood patiently, along with Jake, ready to enter the cavern. Tension grew among the remaining members of the party; no one dared to speak. Walking briskly, the captain and his prisoner arrived at the altar. Still muddled, Lyra stared blankly into the cave, not quite able to comprehend what was happening. None outside could hear the exact words but, by the commander's hand gestures, all understood that he was the one talking. A jolt of power hit Rig as he put his hands on the cylinder. His body stiffened, assuming a wooden rigidity. Unable to release his grip and knowing he was eternally lost, the Phoenician gazed longingly into Moroth's insanely burning eyes. All hope abandoned, the human was a picture of unspeakable despair.

The DAK commanded, “Use the exact wording I gave you as we entered. And remember, do it with conviction, or your friends die. If not, I use the Indian.”

“Holy Spir….” Sadly, Malek’s cat’s-paw began his denial of the one true God. Overwhelmed by what he was about to do, King struggled to form the words.

Incensed by his balking, the leader barked, “*Do it* or I’ll drag the Lyrian in here and begin the amputation.” The being’s eyes flashed with such intensity, the yellow iris-slits gave off a glowing purple beam. “Next, I’ll torture the boy and the old man.”

Pushed to the edge, the living container had nowhere to go. With incomprehensible difficulty, he mouthed the words, “Holy Spirit, depart from me…*now!*”

Coming alive, the object began to pulse, the swirling cloud inside turning from gray to blood red. “*Again!*” Moroth shouted. “*This time with more conviction!*”

Once more, Rig steeled what was left of his courage. Aware that with each repetition he was edging closer to the abyss, he again forced out the sacred phrase, “Holy Spirit…*depart from me, now!*”

Livid with anger, Dilbert saw it was the Anglo and not he who was being used as the sacred vessel. Speaking in a low tone, he said to Hastiin Be’ena’í ’Adah ’Ayídziił Taałii, “Uncle, the lizard people have broken their word.”

At the back of the cave, Rig began the final recitation. “Holy Spirit, *depart fr—*”

Before he could get the words out, the young Navajo had snapped the .30-06 to his shoulder. Normally, the alien crew would have perceived his thoughts and swung into action, but this was the most riveting moment of their existence. Finally sensing the Indian’s intent, they fired just as Dilbert squeezed the trigger. The space warriors were a split-second late; a bullet flew toward the altar.

Oblivious to all else, the ship’s captain had been concentrating on carrying out his master’s orders. As he craned to get a better view of the beloved cylinder before the final words were mouthed, lead smashed into his chest, coming to rest in the right lung. It threw him into the surrogate, interrupting the sentence needed to complete the process.

The sound of the shot echoed back and forth, magnified by the cave's acoustics.

With attention divided between the various segments of the unfolding drama, no one noticed more rocks had broken free, falling from the top of the cliff. Guided, as if by unseen hands, the ritual done by Jake earlier that day against the Lakota was still in effect. A baseball-size piece hit Grandpa on the head, knocking him semiconscious. (But such is the life of Indian medicine men and women—often being forced into deadly duels, seldom witnessed by those outside their circle.)

Literally blown apart by both laser hits, Dilbert fell to the ground. Jake grabbed for the rifle. Before the barrel could be raised, the DAK crew fired a second time. He, too, dropped. Not knowing both were dead, the captain didn't want to take any chances; the container might be shattered by more violence. He pulled Rig's hands off the cylinder, shoving his captive aside. Dazed by the force of the voltage, the human stood stunned while the commander grabbed the vessel and staggered toward the entrance. As one of Moroth's claws clutched the cylinder, the other covered the oozing orange hole in his chest. With equilibrium only partially regained and swaying, the earthling too began a zigzag course back toward the opening.

Coming to, Lyra saw what was happening. Intent on delaying the commander by any means possible, she stumbled into the cave. Grandpa too had regained consciousness and looked for any advantage. Even if it resulted in her death, the Ra representative hoped the DAKs firing on her would enable the medicine man to grab the rifle—killing the two crew members, then their leader. Attention diverted from the old man, the two warriors took deadly aim.

Walking quickly, Moroth called out, "*Don't shoot at King or the Lyrian! You might hit the Master!*"

As the ship's leader rushed past, he reached out with a bloody claw, seizing Lyra's arm. Dragging his prisoner kicking and screaming out of the cave he sneered, "*Sar-Doth, you were always meant as a bargaining tool to be used against your father on the Grand Council. That's why we only stunned you.*"

Passing the resonator, the commander momentarily released his hostage to grab the discs. Woozy, Lyra's reflexes were too slow to escape. With the device tucked under his arm, and still grasping the cylinder, the creature re-snatched his captive. Weak, she was no match as they headed down the trail toward the ship's ramp. Turning, he shouted, *"And don't shoot the other two. They will be excellent witnesses to this blessed evening!"*

Chaos reigned.

"Rig, help me! Help me!"

Bleeding profusely, the captain also shouted an order to his warriors, *"Come!"*

Everyone except Roger was moving. Paralyzed with terror, the boy simply squatted, trembling, palms still over his ears, a pee stain visible in his crotch. The female DAK grabbed the knapsack as the two enemy aliens turned to sprint for their saucer. Lyra's cry had pierced Rig's muddled mind; he staggered more quickly.

Using the confusion, Grandpa seized Vincent's .30-06. He fired, blowing out half the brains of the male soldier. The female spun, swinging her laser arm. The situation overrode the captain's non-kill directive. Dizzy and still hurting from the beating and rock to the head, the old warrior fumbled. The gun jammed. Seeing her prey's predicament, the DAK smiled, spewing that guttural laugh as she slowly took aim at the center of the Indian's wizened face. Looking directly into the reptile's glowing eyes, the medicine man straightened up, making no attempt to shield himself. His winter count was over. The Pine Ridge elder knew this was where he would meet his end—with dignity—in the way of the Lakota. Beginning to sing his death song, already the old man could hear drumming. In the distance he saw teepees, cooking fires, and a pantheon of great Sioux warriors who had gone before.

Suddenly...Roger lunged, crashing into the DAK's arm, sending the laser blast high and wide. Livid, the alien turned, now drawing her bead on the youth. From out of the shadows, Toby flew through the air, sinking his teeth deeply into the lizard's wrist. Flailing, her shot went awry. Shaking the dog loose, and more furious than before, the crew member took new aim. A chartreuse-colored ray shot out. Its energy sliced the little canine nearly in half...a partial whimper, then silence.

Once more the .30-06 exploded, this time catching the female in the chest. Knapsack in hand she stumbled as the laser fired. This disorientation was the apparent reason her blast went off course—only grazing Grandpa's shoulder. But as with Jake's Navajo forces, unseen Lakota spirits were also at work. A slight instant prior to being hit, the old man pulled the trigger, putting a second bullet into the alien's forehead.

Down the path at the spacecraft, Lyra fought a loosing battle; Moroth almost had her to the top of the ship's ramp. Exiting the cave, King saw the bodies of two dead enemies. Thrown to the ground by the grazing blast to his shoulder, the Pine Ridge elder struggled, without success, to again aim the rifle. Running past, Rig swooped it up as he hurried toward the saucer.

"Rig!" Lyra called. *"Take the gun and hit the cylinder!"*

Frantically twisting and turning as the commander edged near the top of the incline, his captive was losing the battle. In just a few more seconds, they'd be inside; the door would close.

"*You must do it*, even if you kill me. *You must destroy Malek*!"

It went against every fiber of Rig's being to take a chance of hitting Lyra. But he'd seen the future—what evil would do. With cold resolve, he snapped the .30-06 to his shoulder. For the smallest of moments, there yet existed a rapidly closing opportunity—a clear shot. He started squeezing the trigger. As the gun's internal mechanism began its micro-movements… tragedy! Lyra's frenzied struggle put her directly in front of the cylinder. Now, the only conceivable way to destroy the crystalline vase was for King to let the bullet pass through her body. His finger let up.

With clenched teeth and tears welling in his eyes, the earthling decided. The rifle exploded. . .He missed! Writhing, the lead passed under Lyra's armpit, hitting the captain's wrist—the one holding her captive. Forced to release his prisoner, the commander focused on his primary objectives—keeping the cylinder and resonator safe. Falling backwards off the ramp, she was finally out of the way, giving King one last fleeting, although, excellent chance. Instantly, he chambered a final round. As the reptile scrambled through the portal, the bullet whizzed past its scaly head—again failure. The ramp folded shut.

Weak from exhaustion and terror, Lyra cried, "*We have to move!* If we don't get clear, the ship's blast will scorch us on takeoff! And don't look up when it starts; it can blind you!"

Reflexively, they dashed for to safety. Seconds later, with a heavy pulsating wave, the saucer silently rose. For a moment, it hovered. Below, the bodies of its two dead crew members burned with such phosphorescent brightness that the observers were forced to shield their eyes. The female lay draped over the melting glob of, among other things, a sacred message—a key that would have shown the way to enlightenment. Quickly incinerated, they left only a slight powder—insubstantial evidence of an alien visitation. In all directions, there was no sound other than the rustle of leaves from the vacuum the UFO made as it streaked into the blackness. Unfortunately, not having gotten totally out of range, Rig and Lyra would carry a mild burn for a few days.

The Ra representative was devastated. Not only did she fail to destroy a third of Malek, but the photonic resonator remained in the hands of the enemy. Either would have bought precious time in delaying Baal's regeneration.

Grandpa, limping, took the rifle. With the barrel of the gun, he lightly touched each of the remaining piles of DAK ashes—his way of counting coup. For by tomorrow, mounting winds would blow away the evidence. The old man then put his arm around Roger, who, in shock, began crying inconsolably. The boy stared down at his best friend. Toby was severed in half, dead, his spirit gone. Yet one of the back legs still twitched.

Thinking his friend was still alive, Roger implored the shaman, "*Please, Grandpa…please help him.*" Sobbing, he managed to say, "*I…I'll do anything. You can make him better. I know you can. Here! Take all my money! Please!*"

As with any spiritual leader, there were moments when they must comfort those with a wounded heart. In a low gentle tone, the old Indian said, "It is good to cry for our friends. Lets them know how much we love them."

Whimpering uncontrollably, the youth wouldn't stop hoping as he implored, *"Please, Grandpa, do something. Please!"*

"Grandson, in each being's life there comes a time when we finish what we came here to do and we must go on to begin other things."

Rig and Lyra joined the old man and the boy. Roger finally accepted the hard lesson and agreed to let the medicine man conduct a ceremony freeing Toby to go on his journey. Afterward, they buried his friend away from the trail, under rocks where no tourist would ever walk.

In true Indian fashion, the elder suggested they erase any sign of their presence wherever possible. This would encourage the white man's world to arrive at its normally faulty conclusions. Jake and Dilbert were left where they fell. The police, the adults agreed, would be stymied by the laser wounds. But then, where can the investigation go? A dead end—another unsolved mystery—a double homicide soon forgotten, probably put down to nothing more than a fight between two drunken Redskins.

Grandpa turned his attention inward, to the stabbing pain from the fracture to his skull and shoulder wound. Using a technique unknown to modern science, he used its application to dull the intense throbbing. Moving, however slowly, he led his troop back down the path.

Pausing to rest, the elder chuckled, explaining how anthropologists would likely explain the newly discovered cave and altar, postulating that they belonged to the Sinagua tribe—uncovered during a freak earthquake. He continued laughing at their theories, especially the myth that all Indians came across a land bridge from Siberia when, in fact, it was but one of several gateways of entrance.

Stepping through the broken glass door of the ranger station, the Lakota looked at the stupefied park official. "She'll be okay. Maybe a headache. Falling asleep like that, she's gonna have some explaining to do." He laughed some more. "Wonder what she'll say about the ruins and the windows?"

Outside the building, Vincent and Cody were just arriving in a pickup with four Sundancers. Apparently, they were able to jump the shallow ditch, driving their vehicle around the gate.

Time together concluded, at least for now, Grandpa took Lyra aside for a private message to the Grand Counsel and to say his personal farewell to the star-visitor.

Walking back together, the elder turned, looked Rig in the eyes, smiled, and said, "Nephew… be careful what you wish for."

Then the old Indian gazed at Roger. "Grandson, our boy and his family died last year in a car accident outside of Rapid City. My wife and I are lonely. I know she would like to have you live with us. How would you like to come stay with this old Indian? You'll learn to see more with your heart than most people do with their eyes."

Without a pause, the boy answered, "*Wow! Sure.* I'd like that fine!"

The old man's response couldn't be contained, "*A ho—wasté; lila wastéÁ*"

Rig and Lyra decided to catch a ride up the hill to her car by riding in the back of Vincent's pickup. Heading toward the truck, everyone left the gravel path and crossed a brief expanse of dirt worn into fine powder by the heavy traffic of tourists.

Unseen behind them, in the dust, a paw print appeared, then another and another. Even such severe wounds had not lessened the Pine Ridge elder's extraordinary perceptivity. Sensing something, Grandpa turned to see what was following. Then he smiled and put his arm over Roger's shoulder as they continued.

CHAPTER XXV

PLAN "B"

His fortune lost, Lyra's mission failed, the gloomy duo drove south. On the run with no money or job, the ex-broker reluctantly figured that returning to the familiar environment of Phoenix was his only hope. Hiding out among friends, he should be able to borrow enough cash until he could get a grip on the situation. Possibly, he reasoned, there may even be some way of proving his innocence in both murders.

But what about Lyra? an inner voice pleaded. Although he couldn't let her go, the alien's situation appeared intractable. The Grand Council had ordered her to return to personally report on the fiasco. Most likely, while they would view the loss of Malek's segment and the harmonic resonator as tragic, it would be accepted—the unforeseeable outcome of a valiant effort on their representative's part. The agent's emotional involvement with an earthling, however, was in a different category—an inexcusable error in judgment that would force her immediate transfer to another section of the star system.

In the throes of depression, the Ra representative went into meditation to communicate with her monitor. Orders were unequivocal, "Head to Dr. Chu's; abandon the car and, take the tunnel to your departure point in the Estrella Mountains."

Beyond weary, Rig began to see double. Needing a break, he pulled into the truck stop at Cordes Junction. Always a coffee junkie, as many stockbrokers were, the Phoenician yearned for a caffeine fix to ease the strain of driving. Remembering his constant use of artificial sweeteners, Lyra again suggested he either drink it black or, better yet, switch to a noncaffeinated soda.

Overwhelmed by her impending departure, the loss of his treasure, and being on the run, this hounding about artificial sweeteners had him ready to explode. Then the thought was reversed. Counting remaining time with her in precious, jewel-like minutes, he quietly acquiesced with an order of caffeine-free Coca-Cola.

Not realizing that before melting, the photonic resonator carried the most sacred of messages, the alien focused on the points in the ancient scroll, weaving those ideas into the last part of her script. She reasoned that the only hope of helping Earth was to complete the tale and share these mystical truths. Even without her, perhaps Rig could still get a movie produced. *After all,* she hoped, *the people of Earth may yet be able to save the planet, even if I'm not here to see it.*

Getting to the end of his drink, King saw more liquid at the bottom. Watching the road while tipping the sixteen-ounce cup, he played with a delicate balance—between draining the container fast enough, then lowering it back down, before the frozen block cascaded into his face. Cup up, soda emptying, all was flowing perfectly until…he was cut off by a car full of students.

"Damn those kids!" Pointing to the Northern Arizona University bumper sticker. . *.Did you see that?"*

As he spoke, the cup-holding hand jerked. The icy drink lurched forward, some rolling into the open collar of his shirt, the rest landing in his lap.

Vehicles ahead were slowing to a stop, momentarily detained by road construction. Infuriated, King flung the empty container out the window while frantically brushing the sticky slop from his crotch before it melted further. Hearing a howl of laughter and a few whistles, he looked out and up, only to be greeted by the busload of N.A.U. cheerleaders and students, mistaking the reason for his groping.

Facial color quickly brightened to scarlet as he hurriedly raised the windows, clicked on the air conditioning, and turned to Lyra. Challenging her pretense of not having noticed the debacle, he mumbled, "What are you smiling at?"

"Smooth move. Real smooth. I especially admire the lightning reflexes."

"Then what's so *damn funny*?"

"I was simply wondering what a person with so much elegance could possibly do for an encore. *And stop swearing!* Remember the negativity it puts out?"

Huffing in disgust, and with no gas station nearby, the Phoenician's anger overrode wisdom; he decided to use the cell phone and chance being located. *If the call was fast enough*, he reasoned, *they probably wouldn't be able to pinpoint our location.* After putting the battery in, he reached a relative, who, despite their differences, Rig hoped might help him out.

His uncle was working into the a.m., preparing for an early-morning, pre-trial hearing. A successful lawyer and workaholic, the elder King had always been critical of his nephew's Wall Street choice. Over the years, the attorney pushed relentlessly for his brother's son to pursue a legal career. After many heated arguments, sadly, the strained relationship between the two had grown cold.

On Central Avenue, the two moved through the imposing ceiling-high doors of the powerful Cohen, King, and Cox law offices. Making their way through the marble foyer, past several oil paintings and potted palms, they headed down walnut-paneled corridors to an office overlooking Camelback Mountain and its 160-degree view of the twinkling, Phoenix skyline.

Naturally, the treasure hunter offered a radically abbreviated version of their adventure. Any references to aliens and photonic resonators would be far too much for the staunchly conservative Brandon King. The portrait of events they did paint, while seeming strange, came across as credible—enough to convince the jaded uncle that his nephew had accidentally become entangled in a serious mix-up. The lawyer felt that with a bit of luck and his political connections, he could clear him of all charges. After a discussion of money, the barrister drew the wished-for ten thousand dollars from his safe.

Cautiously, Rig introduced Lyra only as his close friend. No eyebrows were raised. Versed in the ways of the courtroom, the lawyer was astute in analyzing people. After only a few minutes, the young woman had made a favorable impression. With her out in the hall, back turned while printing out a hard copy of her script, the uncle quietly advised, "*That* girl's one you should pursue!"

Leaving them to finish her manuscript, the tired barrister headed home. With Lyra busy, her partner took a few minutes to look over the movie synopsis. Once more, a heated argument broke out. He insisted that without absolute proof, no one would ever believe that aliens live among us, let alone were poised to take over the world. Jaw clenched, knowing the story was true, the Ra representative held her ground.

His comments were less than kind. "If this ever gets made into a movie, reviewers will probably hail it as '*A truly remarkable tour de* farce,'" adding, "Lyra, these critics dip their pens in acid; someone like Rex Reed would consider it kind just saying something like 'Your story should be hermetically sealed.' And God only knows what Ebert and Roper will do with those thumbs of theirs." Frustrated, King switched to a softer approach. "It's a good story, but look; people don't want to hear stuff this far-out. You've said so yourself."

Crushed and realizing he's right, the alien hesitatingly threw the summary treatment, along with the full script, into the wastepaper basket. Earthlings would have to figure it out for themselves, but by then, it would be too late. Leaving, Rig turned off the lights as he and his companion headed toward the elevator.

Except for the glow of the streetlamps coming through the windows, the law office became dark. A minute passed. A handle turned. The door slowly opened. The silhouette of a formidable-looking, helmeted being, holding what looked like a spear, reached inside. The creature groped the wall for a light switch. In the glare of the lighted room, Maria, the bandanna-wearing cleaning lady, armed with a hefty mop, started her nightly work. Emptying the garbage, she noticed the stack of discarded papers. Curious, the charwoman began to read Lyra's summary.

In the corridor, the two adventurers waited for the lone elevator running at this hour of night—still arguing about earthlings not being ready to accept a tale such as hers.

On the twelfth floor, the maid slumped into Brandon King's overstuffed chair. In shock, the woman lapsed into Spanish, whimpering, *"Oh, Dios mio!"* Spellbound, she started reading the full manuscript.

Working at an office across the hall, two of her friends stopped by to say hello. Breathlessly, pointing to the synopsis, Maria gave an overview of the coming world events. After translating the three-page treatment, all exchanged worried looks, each making the Sign of the Cross.

As the elevator door opened onto the main floor, Rig and Lyra stepped out…as usual, still fighting. Only the topic had shifted; he wanted her to remain on Earth, while she lay out reasons mandating her to leave.

Exiting the building, they pushed through the revolving glass doors with the alien nervously inquiring, "What are you going to do now?"

Heartbroken, words had a difficult time coming. "I… I…."

In stark contrast to the chilling air of the office building, the two were engulfed by a blast of stifling heat still held in the downtown's rivers of asphalt. On the way to the sidewalk, Rig tried to put up a bold front. His reply was coated with a W.C. Fields impression: "I'm off to Palanque, my little tulip—going to Palanqueee. Would that I could do prestidigitation and have you with me…Ahh, yes, indeed!"

Perplexed, Lyra didn't know if he was still after the photonic resonator or trying to stop Malek. "Why Palanque?"

Lifting a line from the film *Casablanca*, he explained, in a weak Bogart impersonation, "Sweetheart, I'm simply rounding up the usual suspects."

Worried, the alien's voice trembled as she objected. *"Are… are you nuts?* You don't have the foggiest idea where to go or what to do when you get there. You'll be walking into a death trap."

Flipping back to his W.C. Fields voice, he replied, "Never you mind, my little dove. I have a plan—ahh, yes…a plan! One of Biblical proportions!"

Shaking her head in disbelief, Lyra squinted directly into her companion's eyes while countering, "No, you don't."

A wry look came across the Phoenician's face. "Yes, I do."

"Riggy, I'm reading your thoughts, and no, you don't."

Smug as ever, he replied, "That's where you've gone amiss, my love. It's so good, even you can't figure it out."

"You're bluffing. You don't have a plan."

"Do so!"

"Do not!"

"Do so!"

Giving up, the extraterrestrial took him by the arm. As they walked, she was submerged in thought, trying to work out a way to stay on Earth yet not defy the Grand Counsel…a way to stay—with Rig.

King's bravado evaporated. A sadness overlay his voice. "Hard part is, I need to figure a way of keeping you here." Sliding his arm around her shoulders, he flipped into his mock Bogart act, and with forced self-assuredness, said, "Anyway, kid, I think this is the beginning of a beautiful relationship."

For Lyra, everything had its season. From the vibration of her companion's body, she sensed a quickening in the pace of their intimacy. Never having been romantically involved, her feminine instincts desired to dance the waltz of courtship, if only a little longer. Rig, however, was telepathically projecting images more in keeping with the erotic Latin dance, the lambada.

Not one to be rushed, she replied sweetly but with concrete firmness, "*Friendship!*"

Playfully insistent, he threw it back, "*Relationship!*"

"*Friendshp!*"

Frustrated, the Phoenician demanded, "What's so bad about our having a relationship?"

And so, lightheartedly arguing, the earthling and alien walked off into the Phoenix night.

CHAPTER XXVI

DÉJÀ VU

As the pair disappeared, slowly…irrationally, so too, every object in view began to blur, then dissolve. Within moments, a blank nothingness; above, below, in front, behind—all had vanished. As if orphaned in the midst of a starless void, there stretched a vacuum of seemingly infinite proportion—a desolate, frozen place without light, sound, movement, or form. Where but a few seconds before were comforting landmarks and unfolding drama—now a non-reality—possibly extending to the edge of time. Lost in this illusion of Eternity's womb, and without points of reference, the gentle reassurance of sight, touch, smell, and hearing, no longer existed.

Senses strained, approaching overload. For many, within moments that line into insanity would have been crossed. Whether upside-down, moving at one hundred thousand miles per second, or tilting at a forty-five-degree angle and stationary, it was impossible to ascertain. Confused, wanting continuance of the mayan chronicle, there was a yearning for any, even the most minute response indicating other life. That was until . . .Ring . . . ring. . .ring.

Light returned, illuminating what appeared to be an apartment. A TV flickered while CNN's 24/7 newscast blared. In front of a couch was a coffee table strewn with the

Thursday, August 5, 2004, *Wall Street Journal*, a magazine called *Millionaire,* and a stack of unpaid bills—one threatening to cut off the electricity. Next to an open Pizza Hut box on the floor, beer cans surrounded a compact disc of Cajun singing sensation Queen Ida and her Bayou Band. Adjacent was a magic marker lying on a topographical map. To the untrained eye, the chart revealed nothing but a single meandering line, leading to an extremely remote region of the Grand Canyon. It abruptly ended at an 'X' surrounded by a circle. Carelessly thrown alongside was a photocopy of an April 5, 1909, newspaper article.

On the couch snored a male. Age: somewhere in his late thirties. The sleeper wore blue jeans with a T-shirt pulled up, exposing a belly exhibiting thirty pounds of excess baggage. Hand dangling in the marinara sauce of last night's dinner, he dreamed. Flying deep in the etheric realms, three dark beings approached, saying, "We, Mr. King, have been sent by the Overlord of Time and Space. On these planes, you informed us of your intended trip. *Don't go!* We won't kill you where you live because of the questions it might raise. However, if you are still foolish enough to come, rest assured, we will be waiting. With our warning, we bring a gift—this ring. Wear it as a reminder."

The phone continued ringing. Half awake, Rig made an attempt to ignore its intrusion. As he turned over, a ring fell from his pants pocket and into a crack between the cushions. *Ring…ring…ring…* Fighting back to consciousness, he groped for the receiver.

Seizing it with tomato-stained fingers, the words had trouble forming. "Hel…." Before success, he cleared his throat several times.

"Hey, Rig, this is John," blurted the voice at the other end. "You asleep?"

"Asleep? Ahh, no—just watching TV. What time is it?" Clearing his throat again, the listener blinked while trying to focus. "Had this strange dream…about these three guys. Wish I could remember what they said. Oh well. Say, you sound excited. What's up?"

"It's 11:30 already—time to get up. And damn, I've got some good news and some bad…you ready?"

Swallowing to remove the taste of garlic from his mouth, the half-asleep man replied, "I guess; let me have it—the bad first."

"Okay, here it is. Last night I was having a drink over at the Ragin' Cajun—sitting next to that little chunk of vomit. Ya know, Charley, the boss's nephew?"

Rig jolted awake. "What's Dog Puke up to now? I don't trust that toad-headed little bastard."

"Yeah, well, you know he's been after you for the past six months, ever since…."

"And if I ever catch Little Lord Fauntleroy trying to rape another secretary, I'll cream him again. So, what's the bugger up to?"

"He's gotten his uncle to look into your sales sheets. You're not churning the clients enough. Remember Farley's last warning?"

"*Whoa*! Stop, Johnny-boy. We've been over this a dozen times. I don't care what he wants. I won't flip my clients, at least not too much. It wasn't in their best interest. Plus, I need to sleep nights. Jeez, this is like I'm working for Dewy, Cheatham, and Howe."

"*Rig, listen!* You know brokerage houses wanna make money regardless of whether the investor is winning or losing. Anyway, the little pimple's gone and gotten you fired."

"*Fired*? No way. How? My sales numbers are too good."

"I'm telling you; he got you canned! Come Monday, he says his uncle's cleaning out your desk."

Slouching back onto the couch, John's friend groaned. "*Damn!* I don't need this! I've got bills up the whazoo; they're about to shut off the utilities, and I'm two months behind on my rent."

"That's the bad stuff. Wanna hear the good?"

Trying to recover from the shock, Rig held the phone to his ear by raising his shoulder. With both hands free, he ripped off a drooping slice of cold pizza and picked up an open can of beer gone flat.

"Hey…you there?" John asked, afraid his friend may have fallen back asleep.

Stuffing the limp wedge into his mouth, King, mumbled, "So what the hell's the good news? Gotta be a pony somewhere in this damn box."

"Pony nothing—it's a Clydesdale, baby. You remember two weeks ago when you were wishing some day we could have a little excitement, like a trip to one of those resorts in Belize?"

"Yeah, so?"

"You'll never believe this. Driving to work this morning, I was listening to Pat McMahon at KTAR, and he had a...."

"A contest."

"How'd you know?"

"Heard it the other day. So what happened?"

"*I won!* Can you believe that?"

"Well, I'm happy for you but...."

"Be happy for both of us, amigo. It was two tickets to Cancun...*Hello*?! Did you hear me? *I said Cancun!* You can be my date. . .Can you handle it?"

"Two tickets? Well, I have been wanting a little adventure in my life."

"Me too. It was us, swimming with tons of those topless chicks. I hear some even go bottomless. Tell me—am I good or what?"

"John, what part of the word 'pervert' don't you understand?"

"Thanks a lot. So do you wanna come or not?"

"Are you crazy? Of course I'd go, if I weren't so broke."

More jubilant than ever, King's friend fires back, "Dude, that's the best part! Thing's free...six days, seven nights, airfare, meals...the whole enchilada. Like, you don't need any money. *Comprende?*"

"*John-John, stop!* Slow down and take a breath. Listen, I don't want to rain on your parade, but this all sounds too good."

"No, no, it was real. I checked it out with the station's receptionist."

"How long did you say those tickets are good for?"

"Dunno. Why?"

"I found this article at the library about a lost cave that may have treasure in it. Anyway, it was worth a shot. I'm takin' a trip to the Grand Canyon tomorrow to find out. How 'bout coming?"

"Can't. And neither can you."

"Why? What's up?"

"I promised this girl, Holly, and her friend I met last night that we would go over the border and show 'em Nogales. Tell you what: I'll convince'em to skip that trip and I'll go, if we bring 'em along."

"Are you kidding? Women? C'mon, that's stupid."

"Rig, I'm serious. You gotta hear what I fell into."

"How Freudian can you get? So tell me, Casanova, just what crevasse did you slip into this time?"

"O ye of little faith—some pal you are!"

"I don't know…You find more dogs than they have at the pound. I think the animal control shelter needs to give you a price break."

"No—you gotta hear this. These foxes are to die for."

"That's what you said about the pair you found at that coffee shop last month, who were posing as coeds; or those two, cloven-hoofed…."

"*Ehhh*! How was I to know those bunnies were underage runaways? As for the other two, we were at a Halloween party. *Give me a break!* Anyway, I'm telling you these are different. Yours is out from D.C. for a week on some sort of…I don't know, business, I guess. I got too drunk to remember; puked all over the parking lot."

"Real class, Johnny—bet that impressed 'em."

"They'd already left. Anyway, *shut up and listen*. Yours is the type of fantasy girl you were describing the other day—you know, sorta golden-skinned, Egyptian eyes…and legs…Ooooh Lord, you gotta see those legs! Like a fashion model, I tell ya. And damn is she smart; speaks a whole bunch of languages, I…."

Only partially paying attention, Rig stuffed in another bite of pizza while managing to murmur, "What's this Cleopatra's name?"

"It's…uhh…on the tip of my tongue. Kind of strange sounding, like one of those stringed instruments. Can't think of it at the moment but it'll come to me."

The listener stopped chewing.

"Besides, you'll find out soon enough! We're all going out tonight."

Coming back to the conversation, King injected, "All right. But stop with the women for a minute. We can talk about them when you come over, say about six. Okay?"

"Isn't that a little early?"

"Look, I'm serious about this cave. Tell you what; if I come along tonight, you'll go up to the canyon, right? Oh, and we'll need your SUV."

"Only if we take the babes."

"I'll think about it but that's no promise. Of course, knowing you, that's assuming they're still talking to us."

"Buddy, I'm telling you, once you see them, you'll change your mind. And hey—sorry about you getting sacked."

"That's okay. I have a weird feeling this is the beginning of some sorta strange adventure. Anyway, see you at six."

"All right, six it is. Later."

"Yeah, later. *Ciao*."

As he hung up and clicked off the TV, the apartment finally took on a peaceful silence. Easing down on the floor, Rig began to reexamine the map. Pausing, he was haunted by a nagging feeling—the similarity between this Washington, D.C., girl and the one in his dream.

Even so, he took it simply as just some freaky coincidence."

Not wanting to make his assault over a treacherous cliff, he was trying to determine where the cave might have a topside entrance. Slowly, the trail on the map was retraced with an index finger. Enmeshed in planning, the adventurer was oblivious to an almost undetectable wisp of an unusual, yet somehow familiar, sweet-smelling smoke. Bending backwards for the last stale slice of pizza, he flinched—startled by a voice over his shoulder: *"Remember, Nephew,"* came the chilling warning, *"every thought is a prayer. Be careful what you wish for."*

Epilogue

Pilgrim, as you ponder the foregoing, somewhere the sun's light creeps across our spinning sphere. Yet, irrespective of the hour, most of humanity will sleepily spend this life in spiritual Darkness—their divine eye still closed. You, however, have knocked at the door and entered into the realization that this mortal, materialistic existence is simply a holographic dream—an illusion.

Beware, however, the lure of the story. True, the foregoing adventure, while seemingly unbelievable, is actually based on far more facts and bona fide events than I care to divulge. But to give it undue significance would be a trap. Focus, rather, neither on the postman nor the letter's tale. Look instead upon the Real Author and the beautiful discovery that you are infinitely greater than you presently know.

Additionally, it would be well to contemplate, that while Humankind seems both made of many and full of woe, the truth declares, "All is One" and "God is Perfect." In obvious contradiction, the answer to this enigma but lies in simply holding a picture of reality, instead of the illusion, as the focus of one's thoughts. Over time it will be realized that there never was a dream; you are, and always have been…free.

Nevertheless, this does not mean you are God, any more than a drop of water in the ocean is the ocean. Even so, that particle is seamlessly inseparable—imbued with the identity and properties of the entire sea. The difference is, unlike faceless water, you never lose your sense of individuality; it is simply that the personified uniqueness of singular self expands—to an ever increasing realization of its oneness within The All.

Consequently, as a being grows in awareness of its indivisible unity with the infinite I-Am-That-I-Am, the more the Cosmic demonstrates divinely occurring natural acts (erroneously called "miracles") through that human portal—a gateway also referred to as "point of reflection."

With this greater allowing and expression of truth, you increasingly dissolve the illusion of your separation from God. Then again, this is the Grand Paradox: There is no separation to erase. To think there exists two or more is simply the blind belief in maya.

And you…you, Blessed Pilgrim, have boldly just taken an important step. Your newly gained level of understanding cannot help but demonstrate significant luminance—thereby rousing from slumber the part of the Great Collective Unconscious that mistakenly feels a gulf between itself and the I-Am-That-I-Am. Can you imagine any greater mission—any higher calling?

FIAT LUX

ACKNOWLEDGMENTS

The first acknowledgment goes to the Creator, the All-in-All—the *only* Source and that from which good alone emanates. And then thanks to those individual portals through whom God's light shone in demonstration to bring forth this message. Their inspiration and support was a priceless blessing. They are: Charlie; Dick; Terrance; Eldon; Kay and Stephen Cox; Jason Czaplicki, D.C.; John Dahlberg; Delmary Dennis—Cover Artist; Angela Farley—Cover Design; Fred T. Ferguson; Don Feldheim, A.P.R.; Terry Ferra; Shari Gackstatter; Lisa Hanes; Gunter Hansen; Holly Hollan; Jo-Ann Langseth—Editing; Kate Mohler; Robert Morningstar Shirley Salgy; Eric Von Schleicher; Marcia Schutte; Bob Spear—Editing and Interior Design; Laurel Steinhice; Dr. Richard Allan White; Amisa Osihahtu Yellowbird; and to you—for this has appeared in answer to your wish. *Ho; hece tu yelo; mitakueye oyas'in.*

ABOUT THE AUTHOR

President and CEO of an international investment business for over twenty-four years, Dane Alexander has often been called to be a lecturer on economic trends and investments. This has further led to serving as a financial columnist for Millionaire magazine, as well as for radio and television appearances. With his wife, Arrianna, he is also co-owner of a patented facelift device based upon ancient Atlantean principles, quantum physics, and the discoveries of Nikola Tesla. This and associated products will soon be available worldwide. Explorer, adventurer, mystic—Dane has been trained by the mystery schools of Egypt, by traditional Native American medicine people, and is further guided by an ancient modality that awakens one to the Divine Infinite.

Though he never intended to be a writer, numerous mystical experiences compelled the author to write this book. At the heart of its sacred message is a chain of catastrophic, global events, while already started, can yet be reversed. MAYA's principles, ancient in origin, show that while humanity is headed to the brink of annihilation, the scales of Earth's future are yet to be tipped by but a handful of those willing to apply these timeless concepts. Are you one of them?